GW00322756

BEST OF
BEST
WOMEN'S
EROTICA

BEST OF
BEST
WOMEN'S
EROTICA

Edited by

MARCY SHEINER

Published in the United States by Cleis Press Inc.,
P.O. Box 14697, San Francisco, California 94114.
Printed in the United States.
Cover design: Scott Idleman
Cover photo: Celesta Danger
Text design: Frank Wiedemann
Logo art: Juana Alicia
First Edition.
10 9 8 7 6 5 4 3 2 1

The following stories are reprinted from *Best Women's Erotica 2000*: "Lita" by Cara Bruce; "Ratatouille," by Susannah Indigo; "Kali" by Maryanne Mohanraj; and "Cal's Party" by Lisa Prosimo. The following stories are reprinted from *Best Women's Erotica 2001*: "Tara's Stew" by Michelle Bouché; "Contented Clients" by Kate Dominic, which was also published in *Leather, Lace & Lust*, edited by M. Christian and Sage Vivant (Venus Book Club, 2003); "Tic Sex" by Debra Hyde; "Infidelities" by G. L. Morrison; and "The Heart in My Garden" by Carol Queen. The following stories are reprinted from *Best Women's Erotica 2002*: "Emergency Room" by Kim Addonizio; "Shadow Child" by Cheyenne Blue; "Learning to Play Chess" by Isabelle Carruthers; "Riding the Rails" by Sacchi Green, which was also published in *Electric 2* (Alyson Press, 2003) and appears by permission of the author; "The Amy Special" by Susie Hara; "Twisted Beauty" by Elspeth Potter; and "Greek Fever" by Anne Tourney, which was also published in *The Mammoth Book of Best New Erotica* (Carroll & Graf, 2001) and appears by permission of the author. The following stories are reprinted from *Best Women's Erotica 2003*: excerpt from *Portrait in Sepia* by Isabel Allende; "Betty" by Ann Dulaney; "Mail-Order Bride" by Saira Ramasastry; "Thought So" by Cecilia Tan; "Bad Girl" by Alison Tyler; and "What You're In For" by Zonna. The following stories are reprinted from *Best Women's Erotica 2004*: "Grit" by Kathleen Bradean; "Doing the Dishes" by Rachel Kramer Bussel, which was also published in *The Mammoth Book of Best New Erotica, Volume 4* edited by Maxim Jakubowski (Carroll & Graf, 2004) and appears by permission of the author; "A Love Drive-By" by Susan St. Aubin, which was reprinted in the "Sex and Politics" issue of *Clean Sheets* in October 2004, and appears by permission of the author; "Cutting Loose" by María Elena de la Selva; and "Danke Schoen" by Helena Settimana. The following story is reprinted from *Best Women's Erotica 2005*: "Nine Seven Zero" by Marianna Cherry.

CONTENTS

LEARNING TO PLAY CHESS

Isabelle Carruthers

THE WET HISS OF TIRES ON THE STREET
reminds us that the window was left open.
We've plunged into the Ice Age. I burrow deeper under the blanket, pretending to be asleep.
I know that Adam will eventually brave the
cold. He groans and rolls against me, his erection announcing a triumphant return against
my hip. Our breath rises and floats above us in
a small cloud.

"Close the window, wench," he grumbles. I
snore lightly in response but Adam isn't fooled.
His tongue slides into my ear and then oppor-
tunistically into my mouth when I open it to
protest. This becomes a kiss that turns into
another, deeper than the one before. I fondle
him beneath the blanket and he pushes his cock
against my palm with a sigh.

I

"You cold?"

"Mmm-hmm," is all I can manage. He tugs at the tuft of fur between my legs. I push him away, mumbling about the window.

Adam bounces from the bed. His feet pad across the bare wood floor and end in a grinding scrape as the window is forced into submission. The footsteps continue in a circuit around the room as he stops to throw more wood on the fire, cursing and prodding the reluctant flames with a pyromaniac's zeal. The iron curtain rod we've been using as a fireplace poker clatters back into the corner.

He climbs back in bed, pushing the blankets and sheets to the floor, and from this I know that he wants to make love again. Adam likes to sleep under stifling layers of blankets, but he can only fuck in open space, with nothing to cover him or impede his movements. Frigid air envelops us in shocking contrast to the warm tangle of arms and legs as we come together. He settles on top of me, his weight pushing my legs wide.

"Thighs aren't meant to be apart this long," I complain, only half kidding. I'm sore from hours of bending and stretching around him, unprepared for this marathon of sex. Except for a nap and a shower, we've done nothing else since I arrived home ten hours earlier.

Adam laughs, undeterred, knowing that I won't resist for long. He maneuvers me onto my stomach and begins to rub, kneading the abused muscles of my calves and thighs. Soon this remedy becomes foreplay and his hands embark on another mission. He strokes between my legs, teasing, waiting for me to open. I do. Two fingers slip inside and continue the massage.

Adam turns me to face him and we make love, another

reunion after our long separation. He enters slowly but holds back, presses deeper and then pulls away. He watches my face and wants my reaction. This is the way Adam does everything, with this deliberate intensity. Nothing escapes his notice.

I close my eyes to avoid his. I'm afraid he'll see that I'm in love. I'm afraid I'll see that he isn't.

"Tell me," he coaxes, his lips grazing my ear and cheek, moving toward my mouth. Adam knows what I want but he waits for me to say it. I wrap my legs around him and strain upward, craving more. By now my brain is unable to form words, only syllables that mean nothing until his name escapes in a whisper. It sounds like a plea but it feels like a prayer. He touches the center of me and begins to move.

"Come for me." He is relentless, whispering this refrain again and again between kisses that leave me breathless. And this is my journey into Adam, the moment when I let go and fall into a place where there is only the sound of his voice and the rhythm I move for him, when the words that he wants to hear spill from me without restraint. Later, we surround each other with sweaty limbs, motionless for long minutes, the pulse slowing inside and out. I lie still and try not to breathe, hoping he'll fall asleep inside me, the way he used to.

Adam kisses me and rolls away to light a cigarette. Our bodies no longer touch, not like before when he always kept me close against him after making love. He's staring at the ceiling, absently rubbing his chest. I think he's forgotten I'm here. This is his bed now and I'm the stranger, this apartment suddenly a place I'm only visiting.

I wonder if he's remembering some other woman who shared this space with him in my absence. I wonder if he has a guilty conscience.

I don't ask about the nights when I called him and he should have been home but wasn't. I don't ask about the woman who answered the phone once when the machine didn't pick up. There's a feeling of something unsaid between us, and it only disappears when we make love.

It occurs to me that maybe he's been screwing me just to avoid talking, to delay an inevitable confrontation. Now I feel angry. I lean down to the floor and grab the blanket, dragging it over me. This gives me an excuse to turn away from Adam, wrapping myself against the chill. I hug the far edge of the bed, punishing him for these transgressions I imagine and the awkward silence he's caused.

Meeting Adam was a weird twist of fate, one of those things that defies destiny. Just three weeks away from leaving for a teaching assignment in Germany, I was desperately looking for someone to sublet my apartment during my four-month absence. Adam, the brother of a friend's friend, was looking for a short-term lease. By coincidence, our situations somehow became a topic of conversation between these friends, and we each ended up with a phone number to call. We arranged to meet at a bar to discuss details.

Perhaps because we both knew I would soon be gone, there was no need for the flowers-and-candy seduction that most people tolerate in order to satisfy their lust. We were on an accelerated schedule. At the pub that night we spent hours talking, and arranged a date for the coming weekend, dinner at my place and then a movie.

We never made it to the movie.

The bottles of wine that I served with dinner, much of which I consumed on an empty stomach, left me with a raging libido but hopelessly numbed senses. I managed to seduce Adam despite his insistence that he would rather wait until I was sober. Finally, unable to put me off, he took me to bed where he pumped me ferociously for an hour, to no avail. Our first sexual encounter is a disaster.

But the next morning when I wake up, Adam is still here.

I'm surprised, after the fiasco of the previous night, which I recall in gory detail. He shakes me gently awake to a breakfast of aspirin and water and then tells me to go back to sleep. I wake up two hours later and find Adam dressed and reading by the window. He's already made a trip to the coffee shop for croissants and juice. I feel wonderful but disheveled, and excuse myself to take a shower. When I return, Adam is undressed and back in my bed. He looks like he's decided to stay. He asks if I'm free for the rest of the day.

"Yeah, I guess," I say. "What do you want to do?"

"You." Adam hands me a glass of orange juice as I stand there, dumbly pondering his response.

"Oh." I wonder if I should say more—say yes, say no, say fuck-me-then-and-be-on-your-way. For once, I say nothing.

"You have a chessboard under your bed," he observes, strategically changing the subject. "Do you play?" I had forgotten it was there. I don't think to ask why he's been exploring under my bed.

"Only badly," I confess.

"Good. I'll teach you." Adam rummages around underneath the bed and reappears with a large slab of black and white marble and a box containing the chess pieces, each wrapped carefully in white tissue. He sets up the game at the foot of the bed and we reverse positions.

"You can go first," I offer graciously.

"Okay." Adam grabs the belt of my robe and yanks, and it

falls open. He arranges the fabric so that my breasts and hips are exposed. I might as well be naked.

"Better," he says, moving a pawn forward. My game goes immediately to hell. I try to avoid looking at his face because I know where his eyes will be. The sheet that barely covers him does nothing to conceal his arousal.

"There's something else interesting under your bed." His tone is casual, like he's about to tell me that I have dust on my floor. A smile plays around the corners of his mouth.

"Oh?" I feign disinterest, but I'm thinking *Uh-oh*. I know what he's found. "What would that be?"

"A vibrator."

"Oh, yeah. That." I force a careless laugh as heat stains my cheeks. "Well...that was just a gag gift that I got a couple of months ago for my birthday," I say. This is true. "I've never even used it." This isn't.

"Uh-huh." He's grinning now, and I know he's imagining me and the vibrator. I wish I could crawl under the bed. I lose all composure and make a stupid mistake not even an amateur would commit. Adam takes my queen.

"Ouch. Damn. You took my queen?" I frown, knowing I'm in big trouble without her. "I can't believe I let you do that."

"I'm sorry." He reaches out and fondles my breast with the smooth marble tip of the captured piece. My reaction is immediate and physical. Adam drags the queen down and across my stomach while he edges closer. His mouth covers my nipples, one and then the other, tugging gently with his teeth. The chess game is forgotten.

Adam touches me everywhere. His fingers slide over and inside, searching out the sensitive spots that distinguish me from the women of his past. The soft stubble of his morning beard rubs between my legs as his tongue begins a heated exploration. I become aware of an unfamiliar pressure against my thigh as the marble chess piece begins an unhurried ascent to the place where his mouth nibbles and sucks.

The two halves of my brain do not agree on what will happen next. One half thinks this is a pretty novel approach, definitely a man who can improvise. My inner-sinner is intrigued and curious.

The other half warns that this scene is about to become kinky. My inner-saint, who strongly resembles my mother, reminds me that I'm supposed to act like a lady and should not engage in such debauchery. I reluctantly agree.

My hand moves strategically between my legs, fingers splayed to shield my virtue from further encroachment. This is a wasted effort. Adam licks my hand, his tongue moving between my fingers, wordlessly urging me to give in. I do. All inhibition disappears, and I want what Adam wants.

The warmth of his mouth recedes, replaced by the shock of a cool surface that strokes and then presses between my thighs. Adam gently works the marble figurine inside me with shallow thrusts, so slowly that I involuntarily lift against his hand and the pressure of his tongue. He brings me to the edge of climax only to pull away. And then he does it again. He makes me wait until I can't wait anymore, and the queen falls to the floor, forgotten. Adam slides into me and I slide into bliss, unaware that the sound and fury of our lovemaking travels far beyond the confines of my bedroom to entertain the neighbors as they weed their garden.

By nightfall I was hopelessly infatuated with this total stranger who, in the course of a single day, had eradicated all memory of other men, proof that the best moves we make can't always be planned in advance. We were inseparable for the few days we had left. Many mornings we would linger late in bed and play chess. Our games always ended unfinished, with the chessmen tumbling to the floor while we explored new ways to move each other. He never managed to take my queen again.

But the days passed too quickly and we never made time to talk about us, or what would happen while I was away or when I came home again. And I never told him I was in love.

Adam's weight shifts in the bed as he moves closer. His fingertips draw through my hair, starting at the temple and combing slowly to the ends, pulling the length against his chest. This is what he did once when I went to bed with a headache. I assume he's about to give me one. The silence between us is heavy with the innuendo of our stilted conversations.

"There's something I need to tell you...." His fingers stop stroking my hair and slide down the bare flesh of my arm. This is it and I'm not ready.

"It doesn't matter," I hear myself say. "You don't owe me anything." I already know what he wants to confess. I already know I can't bear to listen. He's met someone else. She's slept in our bed. Maybe he's fallen in love with her. I decide on a preemptive move to save him the trouble of destroying me.

On the pretense of stoking the fire, I leave the bed, dragging the sheet around me. I grab the iron curtain rod and beat ineffectually at the flames.

"I don't need to hear this, Adam," I say. "It's not like we're involved in some deep, committed thing. You can see who you want, do what you want. It's not like we're together—not lovers, not anything."

I've never known when to shut up, and I still don't.

"I mean, I called here a couple of weeks ago and a woman answered the phone. So I know about her. I don't care. It doesn't matter."

My diatribe complete, I turn to face him. His expression is one of stunned disbelief. He gets out of bed and begins to put on his clothes. He doesn't look at me.

"No. That's not it. That's not what I was talking about." My heart falls to my feet. "I had this card game here while you were gone. Me and some of the guys, my friends. We played poker here a few times."

I don't understand what this has to do with me. I stand there staring at the back of his head, uncomprehending. My mind stumbles over all the things I've said, trying to recall. What I remember is very bad.

"I lost your guitar."

"My guitar?" My voice rises a couple of octaves, the way it does when I've had too much to drink. "My guitar? How'd you lose my guitar?" It dawns on me that this is what he wanted to tell me.

Not a woman. Just a guitar.

"I bet it and I lost. He had a straight flush. It was stupid and I'm sorry. I really am. I'm trying to get it back."

Adam is dressed now, and walks past me to the door. He still won't look at me and he stands in the doorway, with his back to me and his hands braced against the doorframe.

"I wasn't with any other women while you were gone. My sister stayed a couple of days, that's all. She must have answered the phone when you called." His voice is thick and I can barely hear him. "I wasn't with anyone else because I didn't want to be. It mattered to me."

And he leaves, his boots beating a steady rhythm down the stairs, not pausing, not waiting for me to run after him. He's gone. I hear the door open and close and I know he won't be back. In some long-dormant area of my brain, the words to an old song begin to play and trigger an epiphany. *Love has no pride.*

I run to the window and try to open it. Hopelessly stuck. I wipe away the frost and see him getting into his car. Heedless of the sheet tangling dangerously around my legs, I dash down the stairs. He's left the apartment key on the table by the front door. I retrieve it, and my only thought is getting this key back into his hand.

Adam's car is backing out of the driveway, already swiveling into the street. Snow is falling heavily now and his headlights aren't on. I'm not sure he can even see me in the blizzard of white, draped in a sheet the same color that makes me only part of the landscape. I run into the yard and stand there, buried in snow to my knees and waving the key at him. He finally sees me and the engine dies.

I yell at him. "You forgot your key!" After endless seconds, he starts the car again and pulls back into the driveway. He opens the door and gets halfway out, one foot in the car and one foot on the concrete. He looks at me like he thinks I've gone insane. Finally he closes the door and begins to walk toward me, his boots crunching on the snow. I'm shivering and crying and turning blue. I no longer feel my toes.

"I lied, it *does* matter," I begin, blurting out all the things I should have said earlier. "I was hurt and I didn't want you to know."

He comes closer.

"I don't care about the guitar. I can't even play it. I want you.

I want chess, naked in bed with you, and whole days making love." I say more that runs together in a stream of nonsense about guitars and chess and things that lurk under my bed, but at least he's listening.

He's heard everything. It's still my move.

"I love you." I hold out my hand, offering him the small silver key. Snow falls into my palm and he stares at the key as if visualizing his life with and without the key. Life, with and without me.

Finally Adam takes the key and stuffs it into his pocket before lifting me up out of the snow. My arms wrap around his neck as he stomps across the porch and into the house. His lips are warm on my frozen cheek, tasting the tears that haven't stopped yet.

"Don't cry." His voice is soft and sympathetic. He brushes the snow from my hair. "It's okay," he says.

It will be. I climb the stairs with Adam close behind until he veers suddenly away, heading back toward the door.

"I forgot something. Be right back." I stand at the door and watch as he shuffles through the snow to the trunk of his car. He returns with a large box.

"What's that?"

"Chess," he says, trudging up the stairs.

"A new chess set?"

"Yeah."

"Oh. Did we need one?"

"We needed this one." He drops the box to the bedroom floor and unlaces his boots, tossing them in front of the fireplace to dry out.

"What's so special about it?" I move toward the edge of the bed where Adam sits, unbuttoning his shirt. The box is a bothersome obstacle on the floor between us, and I step over it to get to him.

"You'll see." He flashes that wicked grin that I love.

I straddle Adam's lap and rock against him, communicating my desire. I unbutton his jeans and stroke him through the parted fabric. "Love me," I whisper against his ear.

"I do." Adam pulls the sheet away. It hangs in loose folds to the floor and his hands cover me.

"Fuck me." I bite gently at his bottom lip, no longer shy about saying what I want.

Adam eases me from his lap and onto the bed, pulling me beneath him. I watch his eyes, knowing what I'll see reflected there.

"I will," he answers, his mouth descending to mine. "But first, I'll teach you how to play chess."

A LOVE DRIVE-BY

Susan St. Aubin

MONICA'S LATEST BOYFRIEND THINKS SHE LIVES alone. He has no idea there's someone living in her closet, not a roommate, really, but a woman Monica thinks of as a fellow sufferer on the road of life. "Chandra," Monica whispers, feeling the syllables slide off her tongue. Surely nobody's parents could come up with such a name, but Chandra says hers did.

"It's Sanskrit, for *daughter higher than the moon and stars,*" she says in the bored tones of someone who has been repeating this information all her life—but Monica is still impressed.

"I love the way it sounds like Sandra, but not so ordinary," she says.

The first time Monica saw Chandra was through the peephole on her front door, a view that pushed Chandra's beautiful face forward, her curls framing her head like a dark halo. Monica had no idea who this bell-ringer was, so she opened the door cautiously, leaving the chain hooked. It was like looking into a mirror that reflected an image of what she wanted to be—a slender girl wearing nothing but a silky tank top and matching jogging shorts, her hair pulled on top of her head in a scrunchy, bouncing on her toes to cool down from her run.

"Hi," she said breathlessly. "You're Monica, right? You don't know me, but a mutual friend told me where you live. We have a lot of the same connections in D.C. I'm Chandra."

Monica took the chain off and opened the door a bit wider. Of course she knew that name from the newspapers, from television, from radio, and knew the hell of having everyone know all about what you once thought was your private life.

Chandra stopped moving and pulled the scrunchy off her head, shaking her curls.

"I read you'd been missing for three weeks, but you don't look like you spent all that time running from Washington to New York," Monica said.

"Of course not. I've been traveling, staying with people I meet along the way. I'm no long-distance marathon runner, but since I'm running away, I thought I'd actually run the last couple of blocks."

"I'm starting a new life here, too," said Monica, pushing on the door. "I'm letting D.C. go. That's something I've learned in therapy. I'm sure I don't know whoever it is who told you where I am."

Chandra put out her hand to hold the door open. "I met your guy Bill once," she said. "We've got more in common than you think."

Caught off guard, Monica relaxed her hold on the door enough to let Chandra into her living room, where all the windows were open to the sun.

"You didn't..." she began, but Chandra immediately laughed and shook her head.

"I have my own man, I don't need yours." Chandra blinked, as though used to dark rooms.

In the bright light, Monica could see that her well-made-up eyes were slightly red around the rims, with white cover-up no doubt hiding dark circles underneath. Monica knew the signs.

"So, Gary told you to take a hike?" she asked.

"No, I just took off. Obviously. I'd had about enough." She sank to the couch and held her head in her hands while she sobbed. Monica didn't need to hear the story, which she knew by heart from her own life.

"So where's your luggage?" asked Monica.

With a dismissive wave of her hand, Chandra answered, "I left everything behind me, except these keys." She threw her key ring onto the coffee table with a clank. "The last thing I wanted to keep," she said. "I'm not going back. I don't need any of that old stuff."

But Chandra did need a place to hide, some place where even her best friends wouldn't find her, so Monica gave up her closet, the one the size of a small room that was in fact being used as a baby's bedroom when she'd first looked at the apartment. There was a smaller closet in her bedroom across the hall so it was no trouble to make room for Chandra by removing coats, and boxes of stuff she hadn't unpacked yet. She even bought a futon, something she'd been meaning to get for guests, and curtains for the small window. She took out the clothes bars, except for one so Chandra could hang a few things, and put in a four-drawer dresser and an extra bedside table she had. Until the room was ready, Chandra slept on Monica's couch; Monica let no one in, telling even her boyfriend that she'd gone to Miami for a couple of weeks.

Lying on the futon in her new room, Chandra begins to spill her secrets, most of which are common knowledge by now, but Monica notices how Chandra avoids watching the news or reading the papers, and knows how rude it would be to tell her that everyone's already heard what she's telling. Monica lies beside her, like girls do at a slumber party.

"He shaved his whole body," says Chandra, clutching a pink flowered pillow she carried in from Monica's couch. "We had this ritual before sex—we'd have a bath together and shave each other all over. He even shaved my crotch, and I shaved his. He had a thing about hair, hated it anywhere but on his head. He'd had hair transplants and I used to tease him that he should use his pubic hair there, and his underarm hair, but he really didn't think that was funny. Actually, he didn't think much of anything was funny.

"You know, all that smooth skin, it was like making love to a snake." Chandra shudders. "I should have known. Especially after he talked me into getting a Brazilian bikini wax where they even do your pubes and your butt, yanking every last hair so it won't grow back for months. The only really nasty thing he ever said to me was that Jews are just too hairy down there. But even then he was apologetic, like it was his fault."

Monica sighs. "Yeah, both of us should have known, especially when they pretended to be so nice. Excessive politeness is always a bad sign."

"Right. That's why I came to you. Who else would understand? I mean, everyone knows what you went through with..."

"Yeah, but I'm so over him now." Monica takes a deep, meditative breath. "There was a time I thought—well, you know what I thought—that the big creep would leave his wife, quit his job, abdicate just for love of me. Me!" She laughs, but Chandra, who isn't ready to laugh yet, can only manage a weak smile when she whispers, "My guy still might, if I tell him."

"Tell him what?" Monica is caught short.

"That I'm pregnant with his child," Chandra whispers.

"No!" says Monica. "Now you're really trapped."

"Don't *say* that!" shouts Chandra.

Monica shushes her because someone might hear and call the police since she's still supposed to be on vacation in Miami.

"I'm happy," Chandra says with a shiver as she cradles Monica's pillow in her arms. "I'm so happy, but you're the only one I can tell. I was going to tell my aunt, but she can't keep her mouth shut. I mean, I love her, she's like my best friend, but I couldn't let her tell my parents. They might want me to have an abortion, so I have to wait until it's born. I can't kill his child. If I can't have him, I want his baby!"

"Don't be stupid," says Monica. "What are you going to do with it?"

Chandra sits up, shaking her silky curls. "I always told him I wanted a child, I wanted us to be together as a family, but he said he already had a family and wasn't interested in starting another one."

Monica puts an arm around Chandra's slender shoulders. "I guess both our guys already had what we wanted—real lives, with homes and kids. We were just love drive-bys for them. They shot us through the heart, and sped off. The big creep and the little creep, that's what they are."

"What's left for us, then?" Chandra pounds the pillow with balled fists, raising a cloud of dust. Because of the hours she spent decorating the closet, Monica hasn't kept up with the housework.

Life in Monica's closet isn't as cramped as you'd think. It's very spacious, with a window that frames a view of the city lights—but Chandra only opens the curtains at night, so she doesn't know what it looks like during the day. There's an overhead light, which is too bright, so Monica has had a wall lamp installed, with a soft pink bulb. The bathroom is next to the closet. Chandra is free to roam the apartment on weekdays when Monica is out working. Chandra isn't sure what she does, but Monica says she's self-supporting, which she encourages Chandra to become when this is over. Monica's involved with fashion, designing and selling purses or something—but Chandra doesn't pay much attention because she's focused now on what grows inside her.

On nights when Monica sleeps alone, Chandra doesn't have to hide, so she wanders around the apartment thinking of her man. He hasn't lived with his wife for years because his work keeps him in Washington, where she was until she lost her internship and couldn't find another job, and what did such a powerful member of congress do about that? She doesn't want to go there. It was different with Monica and Bill—he lived with his wife and he always worked behind the scenes to find jobs for Monica, even if they were jobs she didn't want. Chandra looks behind her own scene and finds nothing but dangling, empty strings. She's been cut free. The play is over. Time to move on. She moves around the apartment, running her hands over her still-flat belly. She wonders what's inside—a real baby, or something as horribly smooth as a snake, ready to devour her from within.

"I don't see how you do it," says Monica over a breakfast of low-fat yogurt with strawberry jam on cornflakes. "I could eat nothing and never be as skinny as you. I'd kill for your body."

Chandra thinks she'd kill for Monica's breasts—that cleavage, that sensual mouth chewing the cornflakes. Every move she makes is sexy. She's glad *her* man never met Monica. She runs a hand through her curls, feeling their spring and bounce. Her hair, at least, is better than Monica's, which looks frizzy and bushy in the morning before she washes it, taming it with half a bottle of cream rinse until it's slick and smooth.

"What are you?" asks Monica. "Three months? Is there really room for a baby in there?"

Chandra helps herself to a bowl of cornflakes.

"You should see a doctor," says Monica.

"I did," Chandra replies, "and everything's okay."

"You need regular visits," Monica tells her. "My dad's a physician, so I know these things."

"So's my father," says Chandra, a catch in her voice. "I know how to take care of myself."

"Is he an ob-gyn?"

"No, an oncologist."

"No kidding—mine too. Doctors of death. What do they know about birth? To them, everything's cancer."

"That's not true!" exclaims Chandra. "My dad cures people. Cancer doesn't have to be fatal."

"Life doesn't have to be fatal," Monica answers, "but it usually is. Listen, my boyfriend knows this guy who's an ob-gyn, an older guy, very discreet. He used to do abortions back when they were totally illegal. I mean, even if you don't want an abortion, you can trust this guy not to say a word, whatever you decide to do."

"No, no one must know about this," says Chandra.

"So, what about the doctor you already saw? He knows, doesn't he?"

Chandra looks down at her cornflakes.

"Ha! You never even saw one, did you? Look, I'll ask Mike for this guy's number. I won't say you're here, I won't tell him anything—except that it's not for me, of course."

Mike is just one of Monica's boyfriends, the one she calls the current one. She's trying to diversify, as well as train herself away from older, married men. She recommends her program to Chandra, but Chandra, peeking out of a crack in the closet door into Monica's open bedroom door, is not impressed.

Mike, an obsessive tennis player with a preference for night games in the heat of summer, usually arrives at Monica's apartment around eleven, dripping with sweat, his thick blond hair held off his forehead by a blue bandana. When Monica opens the front door, she shrieks and giggles for reasons Chandra can't see, then wrestles him down the hall and into the shower, where things become strangely quiet, except for the sound of running water. Once Chandra went into the bathroom and saw through the glass shower door that Monica was on her knees while Mike stood, his raised arms gripping the shower head.

Mike doesn't notice much—not the extra glass on Monica's sink, not the extra bottles of shampoo and cream rinse on the bathroom windowsill or the second razor on the side of the tub, a green one next to Monica's pink. Chandra wonders if they ever shave each other in there. She misses the shaving ritual she once thought was so weird, and thinks about it whenever she shaves her legs. She had Monica buy her a green razor because Gary's was black, and she wants to be similar, yet different. She's letting her pubic hair grow back, and is surprised at how smooth it is after the wax job.

With her closet door open a crack, she has a clear view of Monica's bed, but mostly what she sees is Monica's ass as she bends over the supine Mike, who just lies there groaning. That seems to be all they do. No wonder Monica is so dismissive of him in the morning, as she thoughtfully spoons cornflakes past her swollen lips.

"I think guys aren't worth the trouble," she says. "I'd rather just earn my own money, and take care of myself for sex."

Taking care of herself in any sense is a strange concept for Chandra, who wants above all to be wanted. What good are your own fingers if they don't love you? What good is the vibrator you buy, like buying time with a prostitute? What good, for that matter, is peddling purses for a living? Chandra is ambitious, not so much for money as for pride. She wants to be more than someone's wife. Her internship in D. C. was supposed to be the beginning of her career as a lawyer, then a judge, perhaps all the way to the Supreme Court, with her man supporting her goals along with his own.

Monica has plans, too. One hot Saturday afternoon in August, while they lie on Monica's bed to catch a breeze from her open window, she says, "I have a design concept—a vibrating purse. Listen, it's obvious: you hold your purse on your lap, right? In restaurants, on buses and planes. You have everything you need inside this bag—but also, you have satisfaction whenever you want."

"What kind of satisfaction is that?" Chandra giggles uneasily. "A purse instead of a man?"

"Listen," says Monica. "A vibrator may break down, but it'll never break your heart. It won't make comments about your body, or refuse to leave its wife for you, or make you have an abortion, or even make you *need* an abortion. It'll never get you in the news, and you won't have to fix it breakfast. Let me introduce you to one of my favorites."

She reaches under her bed and pulls out a long rod with a soft rubber ball stuck to one end.

"What do you do with that thing?" Chandra squeals.

Monica laughs. "No, it doesn't go inside. God, you're so *penile*." She places the end with the soft ball between Chandra's thighs and presses the switch on the shaft.

Chandra sucks in her breath. "Oh," she says. "Oh! Turn it off."

But Monica follows her as she tries to twist away. "Oh, please," says Chandra, pushing the vibrator away with her hands while her hips and belly still thrust against it. "I can't take it!" She's breathing like she was the day she ran up to Monica's door. "I don't think I want to do this now," she says, glaring at Monica.

"That's okay," Monica answers. "But you can borrow this any time you want. I keep it under my bed. You can try the other ones I have there, too."

Bob the fireman is another one of Monica's boyfriends, but he's married so he's not part of the program. Chandra watches through the cracked closet door while Bob carries Monica into the bedroom. Sometimes he even wears his red fireman's hat, while Monica cries, "Ooooh—save me!" Bob carries her like she weighs nothing at all. Chandra is impressed by the muscles rippling under his thin white cotton T-shirt. He always closes the bedroom door, but Chandra can hear the buzz of the vibrator, and Monica's low-pitched growls of pleasure.

"Politicians suck," Monica says the next morning, her eyes half closed. "Actually, they don't suck, which is more often the problem. Except for…" Her eyes seem focused on something beyond the apartment walls. "They're basically all afraid of losing—their wives, their families, their jobs, the next election. I only date real people now. Single, if possible." She sighs, as she always does after a night with Bob. "Of course, the best are already married."

Chandra nods. "I was tired of little boys by the time I was fifteen. That's when I started smoking. I'd light up a cigarette, and all the little boys would go away. Then I started meeting men."

"Yeah, I used to smoke, but I never inhaled. It was just for show. Do you think our mothers did any better than us, marrying doctors like they were supposed to? Mine ended up divorcing him."

"My dad's a saint," Chandra answers, her eyes filling with tears.

"But marriage to a saint—what's that like? Saints can drive you crazy. My mother accused my father of verbal assault, which wasn't exactly true, but still—saints have their ways."

"I wish I could go home," Chandra whispers.

"But Daddy's a saint, so you can't. A saint would never understand what happened to you. At least our guys weren't angels. Politics teaches you to be a realist. All your illusions about helping anyone get stripped away pretty fast, until nothing's possible but your own pleasure." Monica chews her cornflakes.

"No, our moms did well for themselves, marrying respected professional men like oncologists," says Chandra. "Where'd we go wrong, getting mixed up in politics? What are we, the world's only Jewish *shiksas*? Marrying the *President*? A *congressman*? What kind of ambition is that? And you, with the tennis players, and firemen. Is that any better?"

"It's a start," answers Monica.

At night they often lie on Chandra's futon in the closet, talking. Chandra feels more comfortable here than she does on Monica's bed with the vibrator lurking underneath, but suddenly one evening Monica drops something furry and pulsating just below her rising belly.

"Oh!" says Chandra in surprise as she struggles to sit up, but Monica pushes her shoulders down.

"Relax," she croons. "I want to try this out."

Chandra puts her hands down and strokes a fur even slicker than her own.

"It's fake mink," Monica explains. "No cute little animals were snuffed to make this baby."

Chandra opens the flap of the fur purse, feels inside, finds the pouch for the batteries, finds the switch, and turns it off and on again, up and down. When she starts to feel a glow in her cunt she gets nervous and turns it off.

Monica strokes the purse, then slowly slips her fingers under Chandra's shirt and up the slope of her belly, which rises like a mountain growing out of her. Monica is amazed to think that a child floats in there. She runs her fingers up the fine line of fuzz rising from Chandra's pubic hair to her belly button, following the curve of the dark line that has formed in the skin beneath. Chandra is letting that hair grow back, though she still shaves her legs and underarms.

"Your creep doesn't know what he's missing," Monica murmurs. "You are beautiful." Monica's fingers edge up over Chandra's belly button, which is starting to stick out now like a cork in a wine bottle; tenderly she fingers it, then slides down the smooth slope of her side and back to her pubic mound.

"I'm not into this," says Chandra.

"Neither am I," says Monica, working her fingers into Chandra's moist cunt, then sliding them across her clit. More than anything else, she feels curious.

"Why does everything feel fuller now?" Chandra murmurs, as though this were some sort of medical examination. "My whole crotch feels swollen all the time, like I'm always turned on, even when I'm not. And I'm *really* not right now."

Monica notices she sounds a bit breathless. She sits up and spreads Chandra's legs, to have a better look at her cunt. Beneath its furry covering are lips so purple they almost seem dark brown, and what she can see of the interior looks richer and heavier than her own light pink. She stares, half expecting to see a tiny baby slide out. With her hands on Chandra's swollen sides, she feels a fluttering, as though doves were trapped in there.

"It's moving," Chandra explains. "It seems to like this."

Monica puts her tongue to the tip of Chandra's purple clit, experimentally, because she's really not into this, either, and is surprised to feel an almost electric jolt shoot through her, down to her own little clit, which throbs even though no one is touching it. Chandra lies still, not breathing, which worries Monica.

"Keep breathing for the baby!" Monica orders, running her fingers up and down Chandra's inner thighs while circling her clit with her tongue until Chandra shivers and inhales deeply, her belly surging.

Earthquake, thinks Monica as her own insides tremble. *We're just two California girls sharing a good old earthquake.* Her hand massages Chandra's stomach until all is quiet in there.

Monica wants to turn around, thinking, *Why not? Her mouth is as good as any of those guys I fool around with*—but Chandra's belly is in the way, and Chandra definitely isn't going to be into sucking her anyway, so she puts her fingers to her own cunt, sliding its moisture over her clit, and breathes in unison with Chandra. Monica thinks of the big creep, as she always does at such moments, and knows that Chandra, her eyes closed tight, is thinking of her little creep, who would only suck her after every hair was waxed off. Monica licks Chandra's soft hair just to prove she's better than him, and feels Chandra's belly contract at that moment, feels the flickering throbs of Chandra's clit with her tongue as she comes.

Monica lies with her ear to Chandra's belly, to see if she can hear splashing inside as the baby swims, but all is quiet. Her fingers keep sliding around her own clit until she comes, too, but Chandra, snoring lightly now, doesn't notice. After a while Monica sleeps, dreaming that she hears the baby hum inside Chandra like a small whale.

Chandra takes the vitamins Monica brings her, on the advice of her father, who is at least a doctor even if he's not an obstetrician, and watches her diet. When Monica flies out to California to visit her father, to prove she's not the one who's pregnant, Chandra stays alone in the apartment. She's developed the habits of a person in hiding during a war—sleeping all day and walking at night. Some nights she even goes outside and walks the streets around the apartment building, relieved that the few people she passes don't notice her, even though her face is sometimes on the front page of all the newspapers. *Where is she?* the headlines ask. Even Chandra isn't sure she knows anymore. The air in the city at night is clear and moist, as though the weight of darkness has pushed all the oil and dust down into the pavement.

Inside, she stands in Monica's closet looking out the tiny window at New York's skyline glittering and flickering through the dark. She's not afraid because she doesn't think she'll need Mike's doctor friend, whom Monica keeps pushing her to see. Everything seems simple: the baby will just come out and be there, unlike its father.

Monica brings old textbooks back from her father's library, books on obstetrics and labor and delivery from a course he took in medical school, and she studies them intently. Even if Chandra isn't interested, Monica wants to be prepared. Mike's doctor friend knows a midwife whom Monica consults, a woman named Starbright.

"Call me anytime," she says. "I'll just come over to talk, to check her over, or deliver the baby. Whatever she wants. Birth is a natural process."

"Thanks," says Monica, but she can't stop worrying.

For Chandra and Monica there is no future because their future is already in the past. Who could do better than having the President lick her twat? Unless it was a congressman doing it. All they have to look forward to is one anticlimax after another.

"I'm *really* not into this," groans Chandra when Monica crawls onto her futon her first night back from California. Still, she doesn't move as Monica licks her belly, from popped navel in a circle down to her cunt, which smells and even tastes like a fresh oatmeal cookie.

Besides Mike and Bob, Monica has other boyfriends whose names Chandra doesn't even know. One is a skinny guy with a guitar who seems to be giving Monica music lessons in exchange for sex. Monica plucks away like a good student, and sings a song she wrote:

> *Caught in a love drive-by*
> *Spray of bullets in my heart—*
> *Should have been red roses*
> *Oh why did we ever part?*
>
> *How long can I bleed like this?*
> *Forever and a day.*
> *Try and make me stop—*
> *I'll blow your head away.*

The boy applauds. "I love it," he says. "You've got that country sound down, but it's so urban!"

"That's me, city eastern via L.A., " says Monica.

Chandra longs for a cigarette, though she doesn't smoke, especially now—just one cigarette to make the little boy go away. But Monica takes him into her bedroom, shutting the door so Chandra can't watch.

One night when Chandra looks out her window, things have changed: there's a hole in the lights of the city. Something's missing from the skyline, but she can't remember what. She feels cold, as though something more than summer is coming to an end. When Monica finally comes back, it's noon the next day. Her eyes are swollen and her nose is red.

"Well," she says, her voice husky. "Neither one of us is ever going to be on the news again. We're free. Look." She turns on the television, but Chandra doesn't want to watch. Instead she stays in her closet and looks out her window as smoke rises from the gap in the skyline.

The next morning it's still gray and smoky on the horizon where buildings once stood. Monica leaves early. She does volunteer work now, to help the victims, she says. Bob the fireman is missing and presumed dead. "His poor family," she says, her voice at the edge of a sob.

The skinny guitar boy hasn't been heard from, either, though possibly, like Chandra, he just decided it was time to disappear. Mike drops by every evening but doesn't stay, and when he leaves, Monica crawls into bed in Chandra's closet, where they lie together, curled around the baby.

"Everything's changed," Monica whispers to Chandra. "We're what's left over. We're safe now, safe," she sings like a lullaby, her lips pressed to Chandra's belly.

Chandra doesn't believe in change, which is why she stays home when Monica goes out to do what she can. Still, Chandra stays up all day now, turning on the television often enough to know that she and Monica and their guys no longer matter.

She cooks dinner for Monica and whomever she might bring home, usually Mike, but often a fireman or two, firemen who aren't Bob, though they knew him and still hope to find him as they search for bodies in the ruins of the collapsed buildings.

"He was there when it happened," says one of them, a guy

with dark, curly hair whom Monica watches with eyes that seem to possess as they caress, letting Chandra know that he'll be next in her bed.

Chandra calls herself Sandy now, and no one questions that, or her presence in Monica's apartment. The city is full of refugees. She's cut her hair short and her face is as round as her belly. She's becoming someone else.

Fascinated by the talk of searching for bodies, she bursts into the conversation: "Someday they'll find a body and say it's mine."

Everyone at the table looks at her.

"I am officially missing," she explains. "I might have been in one of those buildings. Or anywhere, in another city. But when they find me, it won't be me they've found, because I'm here."

She puts a protective arm around her belly. She hasn't thought much about the baby for the past few weeks, except when it occasionally kicks her ribs. It's her only family now. She feels removed from her old family in California, the people to whom she'll never return, and distant, too, from the baby's father, whom she thinks of now as its non-father. When she notices the curly-haired fireman looking at her while Monica watches him, she blushes and looks down at the lasagna she's made for their dinner.

Monica is offended. "There are people who really *are* dead," she says. "You aren't missing, you're right here. You could go home anytime."

"Not anymore. I'm not who I was," Chandra/Sandy murmurs to her plate, feeling herself dissolve, feeling she's invisible, even to those beside her, eating the food she's put on Monica's table.

"Hey," says her new fireman friend, running a hand through

his thick dark hair. "We all have our reasons for wanting change."

Monica looks away from him, stuffing a chunk of sausage into her mouth.

What will happen? For this evening, Sandy will take the curly-haired fireman into her closet. He's married, he has three kids, he makes love to her rising belly with a sort of worshipful admiration that almost makes her giggle. He says he loves pregnant women. His tongue massages her belly button, then finds its way down the slope to her cunt, which he licks as clean as he licked the dinner off his plate. She puts her hands over his furry back while he rubs his hairy legs against her smooth ones.

He worries she won't be able to get up off the futon on the floor, but she shows him how easily it's done, rolling onto her hands and knees, then standing up, panting only a little.

"It's excellent exercise," she tells him. "Pregnant women go to the gym to learn to do this. I've seen them." She lies down again, snuggling her face into the fur of his chest.

Monica, in her bedroom with Mike, has become the voyeur now, paying more attention to the sounds from the closet than to her own. What will become of this new person, Sandy, and her baby? She still worries about them, but senses they won't need her. Like everyone else, she wonders what became of Chandra.

Monica will work as she always has. Volunteer work can turn into a career—she wouldn't be the first to use the Red Cross as a stepping stone to teaching or law or even politics. She'll be in the news again because she needs to explain herself to protect her future, to show people she's just like them before she disappears for a time. She might be seen occasionally, perhaps on the street with a boyfriend, laughing, licking an ice cream, her tongue circling around it to catch melted drops of chocolate.

Sandy, on the other hand, will be someone you see out of the corner of your eye, the girl with the baby, the woman playing football with her ten-year-old or driving to work, a woman so much like you that you'll never notice her. The group that sat around the table, complete in itself before dividing into separate bedrooms, or leaving to continue rescuing whoever can still be saved, will be gone by morning. Only Sandy, about to be born, to change into someone she would never have planned to be, will stay a few more days before she leaves to become the woman no one will ever find because she is everywhere.

TARA'S STEW

Michelle Bouché

TARA ENJOYED MAKING HER DISPLEASURE
known to the entire household. How dare they
hire someone else to cook in her kitchen! She
banged the shiny pots as she put them away,
slammed the smooth metal of the icebox door,
and glared fiercely at anyone who paused at the
doorway. For the last five years she had owned
this kitchen, loved it back to radiant life after
the old cook had allowed grime and decay to
build up around the edges. She'd nourished the
family, too, brought them back to vibrancy
after years of bland heavy food had caused
their taste buds to surrender.

She remembered the day back in 1952 when
she'd decided she would rule the Beaumonts'
kitchen. Serving dinner in her crisp black-
and-white maid's uniform, she overheard the

Missus announcing her decision to pension off the old cook. Tara spoke up right at the table, surprising everyone—including herself. The Missus agreed hesitantly. Some vague reference was made to a trial period. Tara just smiled and squared her solid shoulders, confident she could engage them in her passion for sumptuous food and flavors. Later, walking home in the light of a full moon, she thanked the spirit that had prompted her to ask for her heart's delight.

She threw away the hated black-and-white maid's uniforms and spent two weeks' pay on three new, sparkling-white chef outfits with matching linen aprons. Then she proudly marched into the kitchen and conquered it. At first it was reluctant to yield to her fierce and loving care, but within a month the place glowed with new life. Pungent herbs grew in the window boxes; warm fresh bread cooled on the racks, and mysterious concoctions bubbled on the stove. These aromas contrasted sharply with the clean tang of bleach and lemon. The family, never before inclined to linger in this realm of the servants, took to finding excuses to dawdle there, to breathe deeply the now-magnificent air, rich with basil and cilantro, orange zest and seared meat, and sumptuous coffee laden with milk and cinnamon. But her stew was their favorite dish. They always took seconds, not caring if they suffered for their gluttony. Hearty yet tender, the stew was exquisitely delicious. Many a night the women complained that they would have to let out the waists of their dresses.

Despite their grumblings, they couldn't help but indulge themselves at her table. Keeping Tara happy became important. They humored her by painting the kitchen a dazzling white and even put in a fan that twirled from the ceiling, diffusing the luscious smells throughout the house. When Mr. Beaumont rewarded Tara with her own little cabin behind the big house, she smiled and waltzed her rounded figure gracefully through the kitchen, dancing the dinner into a pirouette of tastes to excite their palates.

That night she'd stood outside the door of her new house, reveling in the light of the full moon. Tara opened her nightgown up so moonbeams could caress her breasts as she whispered words of thanks to the beautiful orb shining down on her. It filled her soul. The waves of light beat in time with her heart. She wept as she seldom allowed herself to, magnificent tears of joy, grateful to the family for fulfilling her secret desire.

Since then she'd continued daily, weekly, monthly to tease out the tangiest of flavors, the juiciest of fruits, the most succulent recipes to feed her family, as she thought of them.

And now, for the young Miss's big party, they had betrayed her, cast her aside.

The Missus, obviously flustered, had called her into the parlor to talk about the menu. This surprised Tara, since the Missus usually liked to sit at the little table in the kitchen, sipping her sweet dark coffee and reviewing Tara's plans for special occasions.

Tara refused to sit in the unfamiliar territory and instead leaned against the doorframe, her arms tight over her ample bosom.

The Missus fidgeted. "Now, Tara, Cherry's coming-out party is going to be bigger than anything we've done since you've come to us. We know what a burden it will be for you, so we are going to get you some help. Clara Sue, we've had her before. She has family members who will come special for that night."

Tara shrugged and nodded. Clara Sue would do. But that

wasn't what the Missus had called her in for. She fluttered her hands in the air under Tara's silent gaze. "Cherry's daddy wants this to be the biggest, best coming-out party ever. He's hired a band and even a real bartender, though of course the children won't be drinking anything hard. Mr. Beaumont went so far as to hire a man to come in for you. He's a chef all the way from New Orleans."

Tara stiffened. She couldn't be hearing this right.

The rest of her employer's words came out in a rush. "Mr. Beaumont says it's good business to bring someone in from the outside, and Cherry wants something really fancy. And all the best families are fighting over this man. Studied in one of those fancy schools down in New Orleans. It will be really good for Cherry's social standing to have him coming in to help you. I know it will be an adjustment, but it might be fun. Of course, we'll be depending on you to make your best desserts. Mr. Beaumont says no one can touch Tara's desserts." Hearing the Missus say they had hired this *man* to come cook for the party hit Tara like a slap in the face. She had been working on the menu for Miss Cherry's party for weeks—and all for nothing. After all she had given them! She stood up to her full height and glared down at the quivering woman.

The Missus, apparently seeing the impact of her words, tried to take the sting out. "This way you don't have to work so hard. He can bear the brunt of the work. See, he already sent a menu for you to look over. I think you'll love it."

Tara didn't speak. She simply took the menu and left to prepare lunch.

In the weeks that followed, the family didn't linger much in the depths of her kitchen, nor did they complain about the bland food they had to leave uneaten on their plates. Young

Miss Cherry came in once to apologize. Tara just turned her bottomless eyes on the girl and waited until she ran crying from the room. They must have told that chef man about it too, because with each menu change he sent, a little token was included. Once, tissue-wrapped ginger candy, another time, dried rose hips. Finally, a jasmine-scented hankie edged with lace, and a written thank-you for allowing him to assist in her kitchen. She sniffed at each gift, tossed them on the windowsill, and refused to release the anger burning in her chest. That he'd chosen jasmine, her own scent, tormented her. How could he have known?

She ordered and stored the food he requested, things she seldom used. She took care to shine her kitchen to its highest polish. Late at night she reviewed cookbooks for the parts of the menu she would carry, determined to prove that she didn't need him.

The week before the party, she got on her knees in the damp, dewy grass and prayed to the moon. "Help me, Grandmother. Someone is invading my life. I'm sure you have a purpose for this, but I don't know what it could be. I've worked hard, Grandmother. Don't let me lose it all."

Would the moon forsake her? No, not when Tara needed her support so much. The Beaumonts' house had become her home in these last five years. She would hate to leave. Surely the moon would respond. It always had, ever since her grandmother had initiated her into the old rites. But she had been lax. It had been a long time since she had come to the moon like this.

She got her answer when the moonlight filled her as her grandmother taught her it could, its power throbbing deep inside her. As always, she felt it pounding in her bones, in her heart, and in that sweet place deep between her sturdy legs.

Confident that the big house was quiet, she stepped behind the jasmine bushes, stripped off her gown, and lay in the grass. The moon made love to her, kissed her breasts, stroked the wetness between her thighs, cradled her in its warmth. Moaning and writhing, grasping the moonlight as her lover, she climaxed, peaking once, then again.

The prayer and the lovemaking completed, she lay in the lush velvet grass, confident for the first time in weeks that she would hold her own. Exhausted, she crawled to bed. She looked forward to a good night's sleep—the first since she'd gotten the news about the invading chef.

She waited for him, fear pounding in her chest. Trying to control it, she wiped furiously at the squeaky-clean counter. The maids assigned to help her ducked their heads and made up excuses to avoid her. Remembering last week's foray into the moonlight, she shook her head, frightened by the power of what she had felt and done. The moon had never touched her so deeply. Would it show her the way to defeat this man?

Then the Missus came in to introduce him. "Tara," she said, her hands fluttering. "This is Mr. Charles."

Tara stared at the small, compact black man. He winked at her. His brash laugh filled the kitchen, filled her ears. She reminded herself that she couldn't afford to like him. When his gaze traveled up and down her body and he gave her a brilliant appreciative smile, heat rose in her cheeks. She was appalled; the heat threatened to spill over into her heart. Something loosened inside her.

He swept his eyes across her kitchen and whistled through his teeth. "I don't see many kitchens this well kept," he said to the Missus. "I don't know why you hired me. You've got your own chef right here." He turned back to Tara, again giving her that brazen appraising look. "I'll learn a lot from you, Miss Tara. I've heard of you clean down to New Orleans. They say your stew is the sweetest-tasting thing you could ever get your mouth around. It'll be like getting paid to train under one of the greats."

She tried to push away his flattery, the look, the little emphasis he had put on the word *under,* but her heart thumped, and her mouth puckered from sudden dryness. Licking her lips, she chose not to respond. Instead she watched him closely, relieved when he shifted his attention back to the Missus. He obviously knew how to handle women. Teasing the Missus gently, he soon had her blushing like a youngster and giggling behind her hand. Finally, she allowed herself to be ushered out of the kitchen.

Mr. Charles turned back to Tara. He wore a crisp white jacket and black pants that hugged his narrow waist and caressed the roundness of his backside. His shoulders were broad on his small frame. She guessed at a well-muscled chest and arms under the jacket. His hair was cut sleekly against his head, a good choice for hot kitchens. He had oiled it shiny. She licked her lips again then shook her head, trying to rekindle her anger at this invader.

He watched her watching him. She saw a gentle hunger in his laughing eyes. Not a predatory all-consuming hunger, but the hunger when your appetite has just been whetted, when the saliva flows watery in your mouth and you can barely wait to be satiated. A lazy smile spread from his eyes to his mouth, exposing gleaming teeth, dazzling in the dark planes that made up his face. She squinted at him, trying to block out the glare of his smile. He beamed up at her like the rays of the hot sun searing the jasmine bushes.

For a minute he simply radiated heat and desire. Then he eased back and began talking, soft and gentle, as if to a skittish colt. "Now I know I'm interfering here in your territory, but you know these rich folks, even when they got the best already, they find it hard to appreciate what they got." His gaze fondled her body again. "And I can see they got a lot here to appreciate." He took a step closer. "If I thought I would be a threat to you in any way, I would walk out that door. But Missus Beaumont there has got her heart set on that menu she had me send. And it would be a shame to waste all that food."

Casting his eyes to the floor, he stroked the gleaming countertop, making small circles on the tile with his thumb. "I sure would like to work *with* you, Miss Tara," he said softly. "Nothing makes me happier than cooking with a beautiful woman who's an artist in the kitchen." He kept his head down but moved his eyes up to watch her. "And from what I hear, you're known all over these parts as an artist. Mmmhhhmmm, what I hear you can do with food." He raised his head and looked at her full on. "And when I think about what we could do together, why it just makes my mouth water. Nothing like dancing the food to life with another artist, Miss Tara." He bowed genteelly from the waist and reached for her hand. "Will you dance with me?"

She tried to put him off with a scowl. But he just smiled. Reaching into his pocket, he fished out a small box tied with a lavender ribbon. He presented it to her, holding out his hand flat and steady, waiting patiently, giving her time to come to him. Glowering, she hesitated before reaching out to take the present. Did he really think he could buy her off so easily? Resolving to give it back, whatever it was, she pulled on the bow and removed the lid. A beautiful little stone winked up at her. She reached out a finger and stroked it, the fire of a cat's eye dancing in the light.

"It's a moonstone, Miss Tara. Now I know it's a bit on the extravagant side, but my last big party was for a jeweler and he let me have a choice of a few things as a bonus. This one was small, but when I saw it, well, I don't know why, but I just thought of you, Miss Tara. Let me help you put it on."

Stunned, she allowed him to pick up the necklace and step behind her, draping it around her throat. Tara could feel his breath on the back of her neck and smell the sweetness of his cologne. Her heart began to pound.

"Come on, Miss Tara. Let's step out into the light and see it. 'Sides, I think you promised me a dance." Charles whispered the words into her ear, and Tara felt the heat of his presence behind her. Sweat broke out on her forehead. She stepped toward the door, more to cool off in the breeze than to accede to his endearments. Dizzily she tried to make sense of it all. He'd brought her a gift from the moon! How could he have known? Could the Missus have told him? But the Missus didn't know about that part of her life. No, this must be the answer to what she had prayed for. But was it what she wanted? Reluctantly she allowed him to pull her into a twirl. He held her close, his feet swift and sure. Then he was waltzing her around the kitchen and out the door. They danced in the sweet clover grass where just days ago she had lain with her legs spread, an offering to the moon. She closed her eyes and let him lead, faster and faster.

She floated in his arms, becoming weightless and small, her body molding to his rhythm. The sun beat down on her, radiating from him as intensely as it did from the sky. And then somehow he was behind her. Holding her close with his arms around her, hugging her, he hummed a tune as he rocked her back and forth in the morning breeze. A trickle of sweat rolled down her neck toward her cleavage, caressing the pendant. He smelled spicy and musky, a little peppery. She inhaled deeply. His body fit behind her solidly even though she stood inches taller than he and forty pounds heavier. She leaned into his swaying, allowing herself to relax a bit, to surrender to the sun, and the heat, and the man. Sighing, she relinquished her anger and chose to follow the path the moon had offered her.

"You sure are a great dancer, Miss Tara," he murmured. "We're a team now, and if you'll let me join you, together we'll create a feast like nobody's ever seen."

She settled more deeply into him, not worrying that her bulk would overpower him. A soft moan escaped her. For a small man he had great strength and agility. She felt his balance shifting slightly with her, letting her know he was in control, that he was confident in his ability to lead this dance.

"Miss Tara," he whispered again, his spicy breath tickling her neck. "The Missus thinks I came here to cook for her party, and I can do that. But I would rather make this dance with you, this whole night a joy to behold, like it must have been for the good Lord when He was creating the world. Only there'll be two of us, so we'll get more gladness out of it. Why, I expect He'll see us and be downright jealous at the way we'll dance together." He ran the tip of his tongue lightly along the edge of her ear and the last of her resistance drifted away with a shiver. He planted a kiss in the hollow where her neck and shoulder met. "Let's make this food a part of our dance, Miss Tara."

I'll pay for this, she thought. But the moon glowed high in the sky and she could feel it tickling the jewel. Earlier she had noticed how the moon and the sun were both shining on her through the window. Together they had raised her temperature even before Mr. Charles had danced his way into her kitchen. The heat had forced her to open the top button on her uniform this morning. And now it encouraged sweat to run down the crevice between her breasts.

The dual light of moon and sun joined the female and male together. It caressed her face as his hands began to caress her body. She drank in the light. She closed her eyes as his hands stroked her arms, her waist, and then her breasts. She made up her mind to let the moon guide her. They said that the moon was the force behind the tides down at Toledo beach. She could let it be her force. He would be her sun. The gleam of his smile and the heat of his personality mingling with her dark yellow glow, all this would warm the night.

Finally, when she thought she could stand this ecstasy no longer, she pulled away. But she turned back quickly to take his hand. "We got work to do," she said. Once she'd made up her mind, it was easy. The power of the moon remained with her, pulsing in the stone, making her movements liquid as she scrubbed and peeled vegetables. He seared the meat and broiled the canapés. She liked watching his quick, efficient movements. His hands deftly turned radishes into beautiful little roses to decorate the plates. The carrots became swirls of orange cascading around trays of succulent pineapple, honeydew, and mango. His strokes with the paring knife as he slit the fruit open were sure and sweet. She admired how each dish got its due—a pat here, a caress there. He kept up a running banter throughout, not seeming to care whether she responded.

She found herself smiling at the way it all seemed to be choreographed. Each of them twirled around the other, working, moving closer and then farther apart. Brushing past the other casually, raising the heat each time. The friction created a spark so hot the kitchen seemed to swell in an effort to contain it. He watched her knead the bread dough, swirling it around in her fingers, working it to the peak of perfection. She allowed it to rise, and rise again. It was the only time that he was quiet. The moon surged within her and she knew they were equals; each had gifts to bring to the other.

She listened while he explained the exotic foods as he worked, turning each lecture into a love song. When he talked about the artichokes he stuffed, he warned her about the outside bristles, how they could prick the skin. "But if you're patient, you get to savor the sweet meat on each leaf and deep in the core." He showed her how to gently scrape off the flesh with her teeth.

She was dripping by the time the meal was served by the silent maids in their black-and-white uniforms. Every pore of her body was open to him, ached for him. It was late. Now the moon poured in through the darkness that had settled over the landscape outside, shining on her dark skin and singing through the stone on her breast. He had faded a bit too. His once-clean white jacket was mussed and stained. The top button lay open and his skin glistened with sweat.

He pulled the dessert from the oven and motioned for her to bring over the chocolate sauce. Islands of meringue swam in the depths of black cherry richness, bubbling temptingly around the edges. Carefully he placed a serving in each dish. Then she drizzled the chocolate in lazy, seductive swirls. Each pass with the spoon was an invitation, each turn of the dish an answer. When the last one was done they stood silently, poised on the edge of the moment, swaying slightly with exhaustion, the soaring heat of the kitchen, and their desire.

She took charge now, dispatching orders to the maids about

serving the drinks and cleaning up. Then she reached for him. She took him to her cabin through the moonlight that graced the stone path. The moon encouraged her, pushed her, pulsed in time with her heart.

She left the door open and drew back the curtains. She wanted to see him in all his glory. And glorious he was. She sat on the bed and watched as he slowly unbuttoned his jacket, undid his shoes, and took off his socks, tucking them neatly inside the splattered black footwear. Then he removed and folded his pants, hanging them over the foot of her bed. She liked how neat he was, his body as tidy as his actions. His underwear and his smile gleamed white in the reflected moonlight and then only his smile remained. He spun in the light of the moon, humming that same tune he'd sung when he'd asked her to dance.

She stood to remove her clothing, but he stopped her. Kissing her slowly, his mouth moist with sweat and desire, he took over. He blew on her neck; it was cool and hot at the same time. He stepped behind her, unzipping her damp uniform and pushing the dress down over her shoulders. He nuzzled each shoulder before dropping the dress to the floor. It had been too hot to wear a slip and she was conscious of being exposed. She worried suddenly about her size as his hands roamed over the front of her while his mouth and tongue roamed her back. His thumbs circled her nipples through the cloth of her bra and she arched abruptly, caught by the depth of her arousal. He unhooked the cloth and allowed her breasts to swing free. He moaned a little, kneading her breasts as she had kneaded the bread dough.

Stepping back, he broke the connection to unpin her hair. With his skilled hands he began brushing it, using long gentle strokes with her grandmother's brush. Then he brought a cool cloth and ran it across her body, rinsing away the sweat. She shuddered slightly. No one had tended her like this in a long time. Finishing, he washed his own body. Then he took her hand and turned her around, appraising her in that way he had. Then, in the same singsong voice he'd used to tell her about the artichokes, he described her body, comparing her breasts to the sweetest honeydew melons he could imagine, dark, heavy, rich. He inhaled the smell of them and his tongue traced her nipples. Finally, he popped one into his mouth and sucked, his tongue searching and probing.

"Just like our cherry dessert," he said, and switched to the other dark mound. His hands were on her panties; he slid them down her thighs and allowed them to pool around her feet. "Come, Miss Tara. Dance with me." He pulled her out the open door into the moonlight, and in the shadow of the blooming jasmine they swayed on their feet for a while, drinking in the light of the moon and the kiss of the gentle breeze. The gleam of his smile and the jewel on her breast sparkled. Then, as if planned, they danced into the bedroom. His lips met hers again. She returned his passion, sucking on his tongue, biting his lips. They hungered. They wanted to devour each other.

She couldn't say how or when she ended up on the bed, only felt herself falling onto the feather mattress as she had fallen into his eyes. Tara looked up at him. He stood, caressing her body with a look. She reveled in his admiration.

"We just need one more thing," he said, and, grabbing her old robe, he sprinted across to the kitchen. He returned with the last of the chocolate and triumphantly drizzled it across her body, murmuring that she deserved to be garnished. She squirmed and squealed with pleasure as he licked off the sticky sauce. He compared each part of her body to an exotic food and told her how he would lovingly prepare it. She was flowering, changing beneath his hands, his tongue, and his words, rising like sweet dough. Finally she could stand it no longer and brought him into her, wrapping around him, kneading him with her strong muscles. They climaxed together, fiercely. The moonlight caressed them as they lay in the dying heat.

Tara wriggled her toes in pleasure, stretching like a contented kitten. She loved the way her orgasm passed through her body, traveling down her legs and settling in her feet. His weight descended on her slowly; she felt the slackening in his muscles, the looseness as he gently slid out. She inhaled his peppery, musky smell. The fragrance of his sex, tinged with the scents from their work in the sultry kitchen, was delicious.

He slept, snoring lightly. But she couldn't. She spent hours going over each step; the food birthed together under their joint parentage, the sensuous smells, the ability to anticipate the other's movements. She hugged all these memories to her heart as she wanted to hug him. Instead, she stroked his back lightly so as not to disturb him. She wanted this moment to go on just a bit longer before she had to face the kitchen alone.

The new day was coming on fast. Their loving had lasted most of the night. The sun's morning rays nibbled on the edge of the horizon. The moon hadn't yet gone down—nor had the pounding in her veins ceased. Suddenly she hated the sun, cursing it for bringing her this sweet morsel and now coming to take him away from her.

He responded to her caress and snuggled his head down on her chest. She smiled at him. He was so small yet so perfectly formed, like a miniature god nestled in her arms. She liked the image of holding God. Overlooking the blasphemy, she thought about what a good lover he was. She yearned to have him tease her again with his tongue, taste her ears and neck, nuzzle her breasts, and feast at the sweetness between her legs. She heard again the sweet phrases he had spoken, how he planned to work his magic and skill on the banquet that was Tara. Beneath his touch and fingers, words and tongue, she felt beautiful. He appreciated her size and muscles, her meatiness and strength, her artistry both in the kitchen and in bed.

A small tear rolled down her cheek. It had been too sweet, like the pain in your head on a blistering summer day when you sucked in that first huge mouthful of ice cream. You wanted it so badly that the shock and pleasure reverberated throughout your body and focused on one nerve in your head. The anticipation had been like that. She had known somehow that the sweetness of the night would turn into the painful cold of the morning. But she couldn't have stopped herself. Nothing else would do but to drink in as much of him as she could. She clutched this ache to her too, allowing the tears to roll down her cheeks and neck, to wet the pendant, now cool on her chest. Silently she sobbed, not wanting to disturb him, not wanting this moment to end.

He shifted slightly and his face moved closer to her neck and found the small pool of her tears. Instantly he was awake. He assessed her with hooded eyes. Would he get up, begin the going-away process?

He smiled his big brash smile and propped up his head with one hand. With the other he traced the tracks of her tears. "Miss Tara, no need to be crying now. We made us the sweetest dance last night."

She smiled, trying to hide the fear creeping through her stomach. He moved down, closing his mouth over her tears. He kissed and licked them away. When he rose again a seriousness rested behind the light in his eyes. "Seems to me there is some bitterness in those tears. Is this going to happen every time we dance?"

She searched his face, checking for any falseness in his words. What did he mean, "every time we dance?" She couldn't reply—just looked at him, frozen, wondering.

He laughed, yawned, stretched his arms over his head and rolled away from her. "You aren't much of a talker, Miss Tara," he said. Stretching some more, he rolled back to her. His fingers traced a pattern on her stomach. "But I like that. You're like a wonderful stew—pretending to be simple, just hearty and filling, yet really subtle and deep. Well, it's okay, Miss Tara, I'll talk enough for the both of us." He blew all over her body, chasing away the sweat. "Making a good stew takes time, you know. You've got to tend it well, stir it up. Add a little spice now and then. And you want to make sure never to burn it." He stopped and looked deeply into her eyes. "I never ruined a stew in my life, Miss Tara. And I won't leave this one unattended. I already told Mr. Beaumont that we would need to come to an understanding about my staying on here." He hesitated. "Of course, that is if you'll have me. What do you say, can I add a new ingredient to your stew?"

She let out her breath and smiled up at him contentedly. He grinned at the change in her. He cocked his head to one side for a moment then reached down to kiss her, a slow velvety kiss that tasted of salt and sweat and chocolate and lovemaking. Tears welled up again in her eyes and he kissed those too.

"I can see I won't have to worry about this ever being bland," he laughed. "Plenty of spice here." His lips found hers again, his tongue probing deeply inside, lingering as he mixed their juices together. He finally pulled away and they both gulped for breath.

A ray of sunshine broke through the window and splashed across them. It lit him up from behind like the god she had imagined him to be. She caressed his cheek, the moon's promise beating securely in her heart and in the gem on her breast. Finally she spoke.

"What would you like for breakfast, Mr. Charles?"

THOUGHT SO

Cecilia Tan

I HAVE NEWS FOR YOU, BOYS: THERE ARE HORNY women out there. There are women walking the streets and bookstore aisles, or riding trains, who are practically crying inside because they want it so bad. Either that, or I'm the only one. But I would put money on the fact that I am not the only one. Especially given what Jason has told me.

It's because of Jason that I don't have to prowl those aisles, those trains, anymore.

I first noticed him in Walpenny's, in the cookbook section. I was thumbing through a spiral-bound volume on Thai cookery when I caught him looking at me. Or maybe it was he who caught me. By that point, I was frustrated. It was a summer evening, cool and breezy, and though I wore a brief, swishy dress, and had arranged my hair suggestively, I had not had good luck. The only mild interest I'd gotten was from people I had no interest in. And while I was starting to think I'd hump an aardvark if I had to, I knew better.

I was biting my lip and trying to decide if I should give up and go home, the book open in my hands but my eyes unfocused, when Jason stepped out from behind a tall bookcase. My eyes flickered up and then back down to the book. He was tall, a little underfed, with blue eyes and light brown hair...and was he looking at me?

He was. I gave him a longer look, and a smile. He returned the smile in a knowing way. *Thank goodness.* The hook was baited. I put the book down on the table, and let my head fall back, some of my curls brushing my bare shoulders. I saw him gulp—hook swallowed. He came toward me and said, "Hi."

"Hi," I said, lowering my eyes with a shyness that wasn't entirely unreal. I was accustomed to being the cute one, the desirable one—but Jason would have turned my head even if I hadn't been having one of my horniest nights. Suddenly I wasn't sure what to say to him.

He saved me by speaking first. "I've been following you for a while."

"How long is a while?"

He blushed. "Since Alton Station." He reached his hand toward mine, and brushed his fingertips against my arm. I had to stifle an audible intake of breath. "Would you like to go somewhere?" he asked.

I nodded. "My place, if that would be all right with you."

There was that smile again. "Lead the way." He orbited me with a crooked arm as I turned toward the door, but he did not touch me until we were sitting on a bench at the station. I was almost shivering by then, fantasizing about his arm around me, waiting for it to happen—and then he slid close, his blue-jeaned leg touching mine, and his arm slid across my shoulders. His breath was warm in my hair, against my ear, in the air-conditioned coolness of the station. If I had an engine, it would have revved.

I didn't want to wait until we got home. It would be twenty minutes on the train, and then a five-minute walk, and I was so hot and ready that I was afraid I'd slip off the peak and lose my edge. The frustration and need of the long evening made my jaw stiffen, the ache in my belly only intensified by the proximity of our bodies.

His lips nibbled at my ear and tears almost sprang to my eyes. He smoothed my dress down over my legs. I wished I could just lie down on the concrete bench, put up my legs and let him root around to his heart's content (and mine). Another pass with his hand.

I hadn't felt so hungrily frustrated since junior high, when I used to sit backstage during drama club rehearsal, on Daniel Pera's lap. We were too young for sex and knew it, I guess, because we never took any of our clothes off. But he used to trace every line or design on the fabric of my shirt with his fingertip, roaming featherlight over my chest and up and down my neck. Sometimes he would trace the seams of my jeans. We'd sit like that for hours, while rehearsals were going on, in the darkness of the wings, until we were needed onstage. Sometimes I went on flushed and dizzy, unsure of where my feet were, unsure even of who I was, which character I was to play, or the words I was supposed to say. I went home every night dying to masturbate the minute I got to my room.

Now Jason's fingertip began to trace the flowery vines on my dress. I shuddered a breath, in and out. I wanted to murmur sweet nothings in his ear, to give him a taste of the painful anticipation I was riding—but I could not speak. His finger slid along the center seam of my dress and came to rest at the crook of my hip. Then he turned my chin toward him, and before I could say anything, he smothered my unspoken words with a kiss.

His fingers were drumming now, like a piano arpeggio, closer and closer to where my clit throbbed under layers of clothing. Yes, I wore panties, even when out on the prowl. His gentle tapping intensified my longing. I didn't dare open my eyes, afraid that people were staring at us. He kept his rhythm even, his touch light, as if there were no urgency in him at all. The urgency was all inside me, making my shoulders tighten under his arm, my breath grow shallow, my jaw clench.

And then came the train. He held my hand and pulled me into the car. There were only four or five people within earshot, none of whom paid us any attention. Jason pulled me down into a seat and right onto his lap.

That finger of his was busy again, this time underneath my dress, pushing aside my cotton panties, then nosing back and forth through my wetness. More liquid was forthcoming, and I licked my mouth as if to match it.

When his finger slid into me, I started to cry. *You ninny,* I was thinking, *you're going to ruin it, he's going to freak and run away on you.* But I couldn't help it. His slow, gentle touch was going somewhere deep inside of me, somewhere I needed to be touched so much that the relief triggered tears. I clung to his neck and sobbed softly, my face hidden by drifts of my own hair, while his finger went in and out, soon joined by a second one. He could barely move his hand, jammed between my legs like that, but it was enough, just rocking. Then his thumb perked up and rubbed against my lubricated clit, and I sobbed harder.

"It's okay," he said into my ear. "I know."

Feeling as I had during those confused moments of stumbling from the curtains in the wings, unsure where to stand or where to go, I now found myself being carried from the train. He had me in his arms and whispered in my ear and nibbled my neck, and the next thing I knew we were at my door and he was asking for my keys. He set me down on my feet and I opened the apartment door and we climbed the dark stairs.

At the time I didn't think it odd that he knew where to go; I was too grateful to be there, mere steps from the bedroom, where we soon were, me kneeling on the bed, him standing while I unbuttoned his white cotton shirt, unbuttoned his jeans, and revealed him. His silky red erection came free and I sighed. I cupped his balls with my hand and let my lips fall around him. *Ahh. Mmm.*

He sensed that I didn't want to waste time, and let me swallow him deep a few times before he pushed forward onto the bed, flattening me in the process. We shed the rest of our clothes and I pulled a condom out of the side table drawer. I kicked off my socks while he put it on. I wrapped my legs around his back and pulled him into me.

With every thrust I felt like sparks flew down to my toes and shot out the tips of my fingers. I thought again of junior high, of a trip to the beach—baking in the sun for an hour and then running headlong down the sand and plunging into the cool water. An intensely pleasurable shock. A shockingly intense pleasure. Jason gave me that again and again.

I thrust my hips up to meet him, trying to match rhythms so as to achieve an almost violent crash of bodies. It's hard to admit this, but I wanted him to fuck me hard enough to hurt. It was one of the reasons I liked picking up strangers—they were unlikely to worry much about whether I was in pain or not. People in anonymous encounters tend to fuck with abandon. Of course, that sometimes meant that *I* would end up abandoned, if he came before me, or if he couldn't keep it up. But Jason was hanging in there, giving it to me and giving it to me.

When I'm that wet and I've wanted it for that long, I can fuck for a long, long time. I started to worry that he wouldn't last, but I didn't say anything. Just when my worrying began to distract from the pleasure, he whispered, "It's okay. I can do it." And he began to fuck even harder, and I lost myself.

The orgasm was coming—but if I followed my usual pattern, I would need a tad more clitoral stimulation. I tried to slide my hand along my stomach, but bumped into his hand, as he beat me to it. He had turned his long arm partway over and slid his thumb down over the very slippery, sensitive bump at just the right moment. Instantly, I felt the ripples build and break loose. My legs shook and my heels drummed on his back as I quaked with the power of coming. I wondered if this would make him go off, too, but when I settled back into the bed, he was still lodged deep inside me, fucking me slowly and contentedly.

Wash, rinse, repeat. After a while, he sped up, my muscles started to contract, he rubbed my clit, and—insert sound effects like Fourth of July fireworks. And again. And maybe again...I can't do math when I'm like that. I kept thinking, *Oh, this time he'll go off, too.* But he didn't. And then I started to feel like I'd had enough and I feared that he hadn't, and I was going to end up having to go through the ordeal of letting him fuck me when I didn't want to anymore. It would not be fair, after all, to get what I wanted and leave him unsatisfied.

Suddenly he pulled out, lay back next to me, and smiled.

"You didn't come," I said.

"Are you sure?" he asked.

"Yes." I put my hand on his chest and felt his heart beating hard. "I'm sure of it."

"You're right."

"Do you want me to go down on you?" I could not move at that point, as I lay there, thoroughly screwed, but I figured I'd be able to sit up in a few minutes.

"No, that's okay," he said, sounding sleepy, or maybe I was projecting. "You just rest."

We lay there in the semidarkness of the streetlight, and after a short nap, my brain began to perk up. That's when I realized that I had never told him where I lived, nor how to get there. He had been following me all evening, by his own admission. I didn't think I would feel so comfortable snuggling up to a psycho. Did I have a stalker?

"No," he said, stroking my hair. "I can read your mind."

"What do you mean, you can read my mind?" I guess I thought it was some mushy romantic thing he was trying to say. But I was wrong. He meant it in the most literal sense.

"In the bookstore, you picked up that cookbook because you thought the cover image looked phallic."

"Spring rolls and bananas."

"Then you watched that clerk, the one with the nose ring, walk by, and decided you really didn't like the way he smelled." His voice was soothing. "That's the smell of patchouli, by the way."

"And what was I thinking about when we were in the train station?"

"*The Man Who Came To Dinner.*"

"Holy shit." That was the play we'd done in drama club. He really could read my mind. "So you were following me around all night, and knew how horny I was the whole time?"

"Yes."

I propped myself up on an elbow and slapped him on the shoulder. "That's for making me wait so long." Then I kissed him, long and deep, until we were both breathless.

He started to get up and I thought, *Aha, now he'll want to come*. But he made a quick trip to the bathroom, and when he returned, began to get dressed.

I asked him if he wanted to come and he smiled that sweet smile at me. "Yes, very much. But I'm going to wait."

I wasn't sure what to think about that. "Why?"

"You wanted me to experience the exquisite pain you had gone through. I figured I'd try it." He leaned over and kissed me on the lips, then again on the forehead. It struck me then that I couldn't just let him walk away, like any other anonymous encounter. "Will you come back tomorrow?"

"If you want me to."

"You have to." I told him I wouldn't feel complete until he came, too.

And he said: "I know."

NINE SEVEN ZERO

Marianna Cherry

You get too much from sex for it to be truly casual: Beauty. Self-esteem. Pain. Great email material. But I think Marvin Gaye got closest to it.

I was standing at the window of my Victorian room in Cole Valley. Outside, the neighbors were at it with their little shovels and knee pads, weeding between cactus and bright clusters of medicinal plants. Usually it cheered me to look down at the crush of flowers, but not today. Behind me, Trevor lay on the bed. He'd just ended it—giving me an earful about his "need for independence," his "need for focus." He had a new job and debts to clear, and he was, at thirty-three, having the revelation that he couldn't work and make love to a woman at the same time. "I won't have time to go to the movies for six months," he declared. "I have to clear myself, you know?"

But whatever—it was a fling; I just thought it'd be nice to stretch it out another week.

He lounged naked on my bed after what is cynically dubbed "breakup sex," as if you can taxonomize these things. Bass-player arms, junkie-lean chest, unshaven around the mouth and jaw, darkening the pale. God, he was fine—sort of anonymously fine, like a snapshot of someone's lowrider dad found lying on the sidewalk. Meanwhile, I was in a state, so pent up with words that when I opened my mouth to speak I wound up sucking air.

"You can't freak me out," Trev said. His voice drifted around my back like a shawl. "And I won't bolt. I don't know why you feel the need to tell *me,* but I'll listen."

What a voice he had. Like paper—scratchy, strong, a tear in it. Higher than most men's, and with more noise to it than melody, like wind stirring up alley trash, or the slap of an oar on water. I'd stop myself from coming just to hear him talk more, hear him beg me on.

It was over lunch a few hours earlier that he'd ended it, and we kissed in parting intimacy, but soon we were kissing for real, and then feeding each other leftover chicken koorma and orange slices by hand, our fingers rammed in each other's mouths.

"Are you sure?" he asked with chutney on his breath, "because I really mean this," and I said I *was* sure, and let him take me down, my skirt inching up, just my delicate nothing shoving up against his moist jeans, and then my red T-shirt off.

"Ow!"

"Sorry."

Readjustments.

Teeth.

Chests pressed against each other in heat, his mouth chewing up my neck like a summer corncob, and I clenched my eyes against the infliction, then opened them to behold the refreshed beauty of my ceiling as viewed from the perspective of ravishment: the cracks, the light fixtures, a single thread of cobweb catching the sun in pinks.

"Let it down for me, girl," he whispered—the great melting, the great expansion inside a woman like another mind taking over—and when I started to come he made a face of *Oh, no you don't* mixed with *I told you so,* and just like that he stopped, and pushed himself inside, and then it hit me that I would never feel this beautiful giant hard warm smooth intuitive penis ever again, the way he filled me, the way his hair smelled when it dragged over my mouth, the way he bored his eyes into mine—almost never let me close my eyes. "Hey, you," he'd say, "don't you fall away from me." My fingers to his chest, the white scar.

Afterward, his full weight on me, his sweaty collarbone against my nose, he spoke my name three times, and murmured disbelief at how good it could be, about the greatness of my "pussy," as was his preferred nomenclature (I'm a "cunt" girl, myself), and I thought about how this would never happen again, which was fine, but I'd become accustomed to thrice-daily scenes like this on Sundays and Wednesdays (as our schedules worked out) and it seemed a pity, it seemed unfair, it seemed a loss not only to ourselves but to the United States of America that this should stop.

I'd met Trevor during a weird chapter in my life when I went almost three years without sex. When I was twenty-seven, I decided to wait. I wanted *Eros,* not noncommittal fixer-uppers insulting me with lines like, "I tried to call you...." (How do you *try* to call? You aim for the keypad and miss? You can't, in this telecommunicative country, find a fucking phone?) No more wasting time on boring guys who kissed nicely, or interesting men with whom sex was a hopeless fumble. No more flings that ultimately left me feeling more alienated from my body than the emptiness of unwanted celibacy.

When I dropped to some friends that I was waiting for someone real, they looked at me like I was crazy—worse, like I was naïve. Before I knew it I was waist-deep in rants on sexual politics, on the "myth of gender difference," on sexual openness—as if casual sex were a sign of maturity, on all kinds of topics that I didn't think belonged on the menu. Meanwhile I was left to defend what I thought was a time-honored notion: that sex is related to, like, super-special intimate feelings. "Of course," Cate agreed, "but there's nothing wrong with a little sport-fucking. It's how I met my husband."

"Great. But I can't do that anymore. I'm *different.*"

"What do you mean you can't do that? What's to do? Just go have fun!"

But random sex was the opposite of fun for me. Why have sex with someone only once if it's so fun?

"I'm *different* than you," I repeated, emphasizing the word *different* to try and trip her P.C. valve. San Francisco is all about tolerating difference—unless of course your difference is that you want something vaguely normal. Then it's a tough town. I told Cate about a man I made out with on a second date but didn't sleep with. "Why not?" she asked in a tone bordering on reprimand. "Because I wasn't ready to," I said.

"Huh. If I'm ready to kiss a guy, I'm ready to sleep with him. You're not sixteen."

Truth was, I enjoyed not sleeping with Jeremy, my last boyfriend. It prolonged the good ache.

It can be a drag living in a place where your private life is so relentlessly politicized. We're full of revolutionaries fighting to smash the repressive normalcy of missionary sex—which is fine, until the fight becomes an alternative repression, until "normal" becomes the straw man people flagellate to prove how open-minded they are. Read the *Bay Guardian* sex polls: I bet far fewer people are masturbating their pets and having *ménages à trois* in the office restroom than the ads would indicate. I think people just don't want to be caught with their pants up. Fringe, shock, wild nights with weirdos—it's like truffle oil: one drop is good but you don't want to make the whole sauce with it. The new imperative here is either to fashionably distress your heart with jaded cynicism or to shatter your sexual boundaries until you're left with a vagina full of broken dishes. Well, suck my backlash: I am tired of the word *fuck*. After a while, the clamor for exotic-erotic, academically groundbreaking, retrospectively funny, it-seemed-like-a-good-idea-at-the-time sex becomes a white noise distracting people from the most pioneering act of all: namely, erotic *intimacy*, in whatever freaky or romantic or counter-cultural way you want to define that.

So, I decided to wait until a man pinned me to my bed with two determined hands and a hard dick and said to my face, "You make me want to give up red meat and cigarettes, the more days on earth to be with you."

Off I went on my waiting spree. And waited. The joy of looking is in the finding, and there was no finding to be found. Bars, parties, openings, the Internet—looking became a second job. People should get paid for dating. It's hard work, sifting through the rubble.

Then I met Trevor, at a party. I quickly decided he was self-absorbed and arrogant, a garage-band purist whose tastes were beneath his talents. He was obsessed with money, with not having it, that is, and every conversation ended up a polemic against the "piggies," i.e., those robber barons who drove, like, *used BMWs,* and whose jobs paid more than his—followed by a long defense of his minimalist financial habits. Seriously, I once brought up snowboarding and within two carriage returns he'd transitioned to the impact of recreation on the environment and the "piggies who can afford lift tickets."

Once again, a dead-end guy.

Still, we clicked. He was smart, funny, and emotionally grown up in many ways. Above all, he had one quality that was clear and beautiful—acceptance—and I recognized it instantly because it was so lacking in myself. He accepted his flaws in ways I couldn't accept mine, and by the time he wrote down my phone number I sensed that Trevor was unconditionally unafraid of his own psyche. In calling him back, I wanted to get closer to that quality. I wanted to learn what it felt like not to care.

The first time we hung out, he brought me *The Catcher in the Rye* as a present, which I'd told him I'd never read. It was his high school copy. "Hope you like the pretentious notes in the margin," he said.

We walked to Ocean Beach for a picnic he'd prepared, and then he took me for pints at Beach Chalet. He won major points for these niceties, and yet I soon tired of the lefty loop-groove of a conversation that decelerates many a Green date.

Then he kissed me. Trevor was a good kisser, or maybe

we were both bad in complementary ways, but whatever, we couldn't stop. I mean, the language in there was like some Farsi-Romansch hip-hop dialect—slang double-meanings—hours of it.

And Trevor smelled like—I don't know how else to describe it—a man. Like salt air and amber and a worn T-shirt. Like wool and unwashed hair and a winter day in Death Valley. Which is all to say very good.

Over the next week, we played pool at the Elbo Room, hiked in Marin, saw a movie about the miserable labor conditions of charcoal producers in Brazil (*The Charcoal People*—rent it). Still, I couldn't do more than kiss, even in marathon stretches, even in the yearning twilight of red wine and pot. Finally, he pressed.

I was in the kitchen making tea after our video ended. He was impossible to watch a movie with because of nonstop commentary on the "bourgeois pigs in Hollywood who make this crap." It was better when he shut up and slipped his warm hands under my clothes. This was before we'd lain together naked in a dark room, and so it was a thrill when he dragged his finger along the edge of my thong, about which he asked "jokingly," was it Victoria's Secret and was I promoting prison labor.

In the kitchen, Trevor came up behind me, scooped my hair away and licked my neck.

"Sooo…" He knew about my sort-of celibacy, said it didn't bother him. I pressed against him, swooning, by which overused word I mean that I stopped thinking *Is he sane?* and *Will my heart get trashed?* and instead allowed his animal presence to fill a fractured mind. I felt like dancing, like losing myself in a cheesy club and being felt up rudely.

"I want music," I said, and bent at the waist over the Formica to grind my ass against him. He pulled himself close, pressed my bones into the counter, yanked me up by the hair.

"I'm still kinda shy," I said, and meant it.

He laughed. "This is shy? You're the one that's all bending over doggie-style. I'm as gallant as I can be, under the circumstances."

He had a point.

He embraced me as if we'd been lovers a long time, even took my face in his hands. "I have really selfish reasons for saying this—but you're due to be violated by a man who has your every best interest at heart."

I breathed in nervously. While everything I said about looking for Señor Right was true, there was another side to my withdrawal: throughout my twenties, my sex life had been complicated by one evil little factor. No matter how hard I tried to cover it up beneath a veneer of sexual confidence, I was crumbling. Every one of my fantasies focused on some kind of crime scene.

It had been the worst with Jeremy: I felt a gun to my throat, winced at the sound of it firing. With one guy after another I fell on my sword in female *hara-kiri*—the metal piercing my throat while ninjas raped me from behind. The tingle of orgasm was accompanied by the spattering of blood on the wall. I told myself it was harmless fantasy—even "Dear Abby" said fantasy was okay. For a while I was proud of it as avant-garde eroticism, like *The Story of O*. Or I reasoned that I hadn't found the right guy. But day in and day out, it isn't healthy to think of sex as a murder-suicide—killing myself while others killed me.

Though I resisted listening to F-Man, I nevertheless found it had something to do with Daddy; doesn't it always? There was guilt, there was revulsion, there were dreams. For years I lugged around my confusion like the purse that breaks your shoulder with loose change and old lipstick. I wanted to abandon the whole thing, wanted my vagina to stop aching for it and be normal, like an elbow or a toe.

Not good.

I knew the source. Certain of my memories—my father's game of touching my tongue to his when I was little, the time he gave me a bath at ten years old "for old time's sake"—anointed themselves as significant. But you know how it is with this stuff: you can know something yet not know it. Through celibacy I thought I'd sort it out. It was cheaper than therapy.

"I'm not sure," I said again, in the kitchen.

Trevor said, "I think it's time."

I lit a candle. The room was cold, and outside the fog swirled low and thick. Trevor took stock of my room, my *Wings of Desire* poster above the desk, books arranged against the wall because I wouldn't spring for bookcases. His gaze settled on the ceiling corner, where a crosshatched shadow flickered like bad German Expressionism. It was my old lacrosse net. Suddenly, I was embarrassed to have kept it all this time, as if at thirty I still lived in a dorm room. Trevor said, "Your room's way less Pottery Barn than I thought it would be."

"Gee, thanks."

From his tone, I knew he was bummed that I didn't have the Normandy end tables. His contempt for money only belied how much he wanted it; I think Trevor would happily have become Catalog Boy, dialing 1-800 numbers all night and having UPS shovel it in.

Trevor decided the room wasn't clean enough for him, and tidied up, clearing shirts and magazines off my bed, gathering laundry tailings—a bandana, three socks, a kitchen towel. He turned on the space heater, straightened the comforter with a few tugs. At first it irritated me, like the time he was carrying my groceries and gave *my* five-dollar pineapple to a homeless man—but then it was also sweet how he niced up the place.

He sat on my bed and removed his socks without taking his hazel eyes off me.

"I could give you the vacuum cleaner and wait outside," I said.

"Messy room bad. You gotta have a clean bedroom. Where are your condoms."

"They expired."

He unbuckled his belt, pulled the leather free, tossed it on the floor.

"There's a man on my bed," I said.

"Yes'm."

Trevor, his dark eyes sparkling even brighter in the candlelight, a man, here, a man in bare feet, rumpled jeans, T-shirt and button-down, this man slid his hands around my thighs and pulled me to him. He grasped my ribs, my shoulder blades, my spine, and he kissed me in the candlelight of my room. How many nights had I stared at the walls—nine hundred and seventy, to be exact—and wondered and hoped? And now—*a man in my bed!* An arrogant man with a deep contempt for the upper-middle class I was raised in (he spent a few years of his childhood on welfare), a man who'd expressed a not-so-subtle scorn for my current economic deal: "for editorializing about dog food and bird toys for Pets.com you're paid money taken from strangers who'd invested in a VC company stupid enough to bankroll MBAs intent on eradicating the need to go shopping." I was going to have sex with this man and I was not going to tell him about the thing having to do with Daddy.

And then Trevor kissed me the way a man kisses you when he is not on the couch but is in your bed. I unbuttoned his thin blue shirt, but when I lifted his T-shirt he seized my wrist. "You know that thing you've been feeling on my chest?"

I nodded. I was curious but had never asked about the long ridge along his sternum. Trevor pulled his T-shirt off, placed my hand on the hairless scar between his ribs. "I had open-heart surgery when I was ten. I had a leaky valve."

"Wow."

"I was too young to be scared," he said. "I was mostly mad I couldn't play at recess. Mom was freaked out, though."

He let me touch the scar, answered questions. I sensed it was a routine with him, introducing the new lover to this medical event; I also sensed that it was fresh, that this exchange was unique to us.

"I'm okay now. Don't worry—I won't die on top of you."

There is nothing like a man taking your clothes off when you haven't had sex in three years. There is no feeling like nudity. There is nothing more precious than an erection against your thigh, the exquisite waiting. There is nothing like a man's tongue tilling the field of skin below your navel, his hands moving to spread your thighs apart. He spreads you with abandon, reverence, curiosity, destruction, like a boy running through mustard flower, arms flung, forging a trail for himself in something wild and weedy and tall. There is nothing like a man's tongue moving down and toward, as his hands pry at the opening to what you can't see. His eyes are on you now, and you try to imagine what he sees, but it's not like the books, you know. And a man has a point of view you'll never have, not even with a mirror, his cheek to your mattress, looking up and into your weird oyster complexity—this strange, gilded lily-thing. I propped myself up on my elbows, stopped thinking, and submitted to the greater wisdom of his tongue and fingers. Sexual Maoists, listen up: this man had knowledge to lord over this woman and I yielded to it and it felt *good.*

"You are so wet," he said, and licked me, and wedged his fingers inside and, pressing my G-spot with two strong fingers, fairly lifted my pelvis off the bed to meet his mouth. For a while Trevor seemed to be eating persimmon with both hands tied behind his back, interrogating the ineffable borders between fruit and wall, and my fingers reached out for his, but it didn't last long before he stopped and knelt upright. He stroked his penis even more erect than it was already, and I looked at this marvelous thing, *a big hard dick! And a man's hands on it!* And he was stroking it as if to say, "Behold this, girl," as if he didn't need a woman, so content was he to hold his own hard cock. And I beheld: the dark bush of hair at his groin, his cock upright, the tip of it pink and smooth with a drop of moisture at his urethra, and then his smooth hard stomach—a physique groomed on brown rice and bubbly water—and his bottom rib, and then the violent white scar between his nipples ("cracked open" is the slang cardiologists use to describe sawing through sternum and butterflying the rib cage apart). His collarbone. His neck. The tilt of his chin, the usual smirk, his eyes checking me out sideways as he stroked himself for me, and when I shifted in reeking wet lust, my walls glazed against each other slickly.

By now I was open and pliant, hot with syrupy martyr agony—that suffering when it's four in the morning and there's no one, not ever anyone, and flat alone on your bed, you clench your legs against it—only now I had Trevor there, doing something about it.

"You're gorgeous," he said—not to my face. And as much as Trevor's gaze made me feel exposed and unfairly known, I saw in his eyes how badly he was hooked. Yes, behold *this,* boy, because I know that every political ideology and armed revolution, every campaign speech, every manifesto written about theater or art or music, the gunning down of JFK, the erection of the Berlin Wall, the Intifada, the Taliban, your disgust for wealth, when you boil it all down, is somehow about the creepy loveliness of this, my Great Wet Equivocator.

When he moved for me, his smell, the airborne ineffable presence of sex, swirled around me like hot water, when eddies of volcanic water elicit cold goose bumps of pain, and it was like that as Trevor came near me, crawling toward me in the candlelight, him and his raging hard-on, the bearing down on a woman by a man, the lowering of his torso on mine, the clouds of his scent that cleared away as the distance between us diminished, the great big *Yes you are going to get it now, it is going to happen and there's nothing you can do to stop it now, I am going to enter you and I am going to fuck you, Ma'am and don't look at me like you don't want it, like you're not sure. Like all men are potential rapists—that insulting trash— because we are, and we aren't, and that's what makes us burn so splendidly in your lonely bullshit fantasies every night. Isn't that right, Ma'am?* and I said aloud, "Yes."

"Far out," Trevor replied.

He braced his legs and positioned himself, and I tilted to accept him, and he pushed pretty hard but it didn't go in.

"Damn," he said with a big smile. "It *has* been a while." It took real effort to get in there, which only made him sigh, "You are so tight," and it was worth those many moons as finally Trevor pushed past the forbidding muscle, the moat of the castle, the drawbridge, the mah-daddy's-gonna-kill-yew muscle, ramming his way past that and inside, and for a second both of us were stunned by the fullness, and hardness, and wetness, the utter totality, and we looked in each other's eyes not like strangers anymore, and he kissed me tenderly, the smoothness of his chin against me (nothing more flattering than a close shave, the ritual preparation for me—and take note I was a lover now, not just a woman-flesh-thing who bought tampons once a month and inserted them, but a *lover*) and with six zillion nerve endings rejoicing I said, "Why did I do that to myself?" and he said, "I can't imagine."

I rocked beneath him the better to feel him against my furthest reaches, though I had no idea where that was. It's the coolest part about being a woman: you have no idea what's really going on in there. Then Trevor kissed me as if he were trying to talk me off the ledge of a building ("For the love of God, please…"), and heat spread out from me and I had to turn my face, but he tracked me, kissed me while I made noise, eased in and out slower than I could take it. It felt like dragging a wet string in honey, and all my thoughts converged in meditation with Trevor's tongue, my brain sinking against the floorboards, blank now, zeroing out. The bed creaked and rocked (would anyone hear?) and I hadn't come like this in years.

He breathed in my ear, "You like it when I open you like this?"

"Yes."

"You like my cock all the way inside you?"

"Yes."

"Come for me."

"Uh-huh."

"I want to see you come. I don't want one of those shy

orgasms either, I want you to come *hard,* come like we're all going to get blown up tomorrow."

And then the images of the ninjas crept into my head, the default fantasies so hardwired in me by now. The coldness at my throat; on a ritual floor mat, the sword puncturing my neck as Trevor assaulted me from behind; the sight of myself as a bloody corpse. As usual, next came a wave of low-grade fear and asthmatic shutting down, the part where I floated away from my body like a rusty, abandoned screen door flapping in a wind, and I felt nothing anymore, just a man on top of me doing his thing. So I turned my head to the side and made sound.

But Trev noticed. "Get back here," he said, and cranked my chin toward his face.

"I'm here," I said.

"No you're not. You're spacing out."

I met his eyes, then looked at his shoulders. They reminded me of my father's. Like at the beach when I was little and he played with me, resting me on his chest. "I can't believe you're my daughter," he'd coo. He tickled me and snatched off my baby bikini. Which maybe was fine: I was six, and some of the other girls weren't wearing tops either.

So lost was I in this memory that I didn't notice Trevor touching me, still hard inside me, waiting for me to speak, kissing my cheek and temple with something like tenderness, but I thought, *I can't come and I can't deal and I want to crawl under the covers and start over as another person.*

"You need to let go," Trevor said, and stopped moving. "I don't know what's up with you, or why you had to go celibate for five years or whatever, but you're in bed with me now, so..." He rested on his elbows and twisted a strand of my hair, softening inside me. "We all have our shit," he said.

I wanted to shout, "Some more than others!" To deflate the conversation, I tried to think of a line to feed him, but his expression was too generous and unafraid for me to steal from him like that.

"Whatever issues you got, I don't know—you seem pretty open to me, legs all over the place—you seem a lot less burdened than you think you are."

Which was not anything I expected to hear.

"Really?"

"You're a fine lay," he joked, and I would've been pissed if it hadn't been the perfect thing to say.

He stretched out his arm for me to rest my head upon. "I'm only guessing, but you act like you're really damaged, and maybe you are, but everyone's messed up about sex." As he spoke, he brushed his fingers across my chest. "Like they are with money, family, religion—all the bigs. People are even more demented about money than sex because we think our psycho spending habits are actually reasonable, like I criticize *everyone* and then blow it on bike gear, and then I'm all, You *have* to have this gear to ride!"

I laughed. "You are definitely weird about money."

"I'm impossible. I think with sex, it's the opposite: most fall within a happy bell curve of malfunction, but we're all convinced we're more damaged than everyone else."

I curled around a pillow and shut my eyes. "I think I've got that in spades, Trevor." With a sense of defeat, I said: "I'm sorry. This was supposed to be light."

He touched my back. "Sex is never light."

And through this intermezzo, he kept touching me, kept vibing me, and soon we were kissing, and soon Trevor was rock hard again, and it was true that I was craving a bigger O than the puny ones I usually settled for, the kind where I tamped it down so as not to scare the guy off with what I saw as the sexual and emotional gigantism of women. Now, with Trevor, I gave myself a break, and it was *fun*.

And that's how a quasi-Marxist blowhard led me back to my womanhood after nine hundred seventy nights, and after the heavy conversation we were laughing again, and he couldn't help but pound at me, saying, "I can't hold out much longer," but I promised him that if he did I'd come for him like Midwestern hail. He worked his ass on me until the sheets were wet, until I was in pain and then he slowed, and made sure I felt every nerve as written by himself inside me, made sure I didn't drift off, and after nine hundred seventy nights and two hours, this woman's halves dissolved like the ripe fruit of audacity in a young man's mouth, which is to say that at long last, I came better than I ever had before.

Three weeks later Trevor was ending it over Indian food.

"Work," he said. "Getting some direction in my life."

As I stood at the window, I assumed Trevor would dress and split, but instead he waited, picked up the *Adbusters* on the nightstand and flipped through. Childhood memory smarted in me. Though it was a moot point to tell Trevor what all the fuss had been about—his jeans lay in the corner, ready to be put on and walked out in—I knew that there's no substitute for words, for voicing in plain English the shames that gnaw at us. In bed that first night, I'd never actually told him what was wrong. And why did I need to tell Trevor of all people? Not Jeremy, not girlfriends, but this guy. I figured it was part of the intensity of that period—one of those times in life when perspective fritzes out and you become a disembodied, photonic light-storm of emotion, when you'll say anything to anybody. But I think I'd actually handpicked Trevor. Like I said, he had acceptance going for him.

"It's not a big deal," I started. "So many other girls have had worse."

"So?"

He put the magazine away and stared at the wall, which at first I took as a sign of ignoring me. He said, "I'm listening." I addressed the rug at my feet.

"I was around thirteen, and I was...there was a guy I liked in school who I wouldn't shut up about, and he lived a few streets away but he was over at the neighbor's one day, so I went outside to hang around and be noticed. I had on shorts and a white T-shirt with satin trim on the sleeves which was simply the shirt to have at the time, and my dad was watering the front yard, but he kept staring at my chest. Staring at it. When he turned to the bushes, I looked down thinking I had spaghetti sauce on my shirt, which, in front of this tall eighth-grade boy would have been the end of civilization, right? And I realized what Dad had been staring at—I had those itty-bitty tits that girls get. Mosquito bites. It dawned on me that that's why other girls wore tanks under their shirts, and that's when the boy came outside on the driveway, him and this other guy, and I waved at them and said something I thought was very sassy. And my dad turned to me with the hose and nailed me, and was laughing, and he shouted, "Wet T-shirt contest!" And the guys busted up. I stood there topless, basically, with a see-through shirt clinging to my dark skin."

I stopped and looked up. "That's it," I said, embarrassed. "I ran inside. It sounds stupid," and then I started laugh-crying.

"That's so fucked up."

"I know. Three years and a lot of melodrama over a small thing."

"No, what he did. That's mean. That's strategically cruel."

"Millions of women have had much worse. I shouldn't have let it get to me."

"Your father humiliated you at the first sign of sexuality. It's terrible."

"Yes," I admitted. This was my father we were talking about, the man I called every week not out of duty but because I liked talking to him. Except for recently, as I was in such a rage that the sound of his voice made me ill.

"Yes. And it's more than that, Trevor," I said to the rug again. "So often he treated me like his property to be admired, like my coming-of-age was happening for his entertainment. Or was an aberration. When he hugged me or kissed me goodnight, he always made a little groan."

"Come here." Trevor waved me over, and I sat down. Taking my hand, he said, "You're stronger than you think," and, "I'm sorry that happened to you," and, "I usually mean this as an insult, but you're totally normal."

I lay down next to him, cuddled up against his legs while preparing to let him go.

"Thank you," I said, as much to the world as to him, because my search for Mr. Right had for now brought me three-week Trevor, who showed me that a great fling is as precious as a great love.

TIC SEX

Debra Hyde

THE FIRST TIME I HID RICHIE'S HALPERIDOL
he went apeshit on me right there in the kitch-
en.

"Where are they?—Bitch cunt! Cunt face!—
Where?"

Naked, I sidled up to him, caressed his chest,
and ground my groin against him. An instant
erection rose in his pajama pants. Richie was
right about one thing: I was a bitch cunt.
Especially when I wanted it.

"Come on, Richie," I urged, "I'll give it
back. Just make love to me first."

He glanced up to the ceiling, rolled his eyes
upwards, then back and forth four times. As
he lowered his head to meet my gaze, Richie
nodded violently four times. He was working
in fours today.

"Come on," I continued, "you know I like it."

Richie sighed. "And you know I hate my verbal tics. They ruin things for me."

"Not all things," I countered. I took his hands and placed them on my tits. "I like having sex with you and your tics. I'm the freak here, not you."

His hands, callused and rough, covered my little breasts, and my soft flesh encouraged him to squeeze. Four times, of course. His fingers found my nipples. He toyed with them, pinching them lightly, alternating from left to right, one, two, three, four.

Richie ate eggs the same way, in fours.

"Tit shit, tit shit," he muttered. Already he was aroused enough that he spoke instead of barked. Focus does that; it dulls his tics. I reached into his pajamas and brought out his thick meat. I slipped to my knees and took it into my mouth. I sucked and tongued him and broke his focus.

"Dick licks! Oh God! Dick licks!" He groaned, then sputtered four more "dick licks." I tasted precum.

"Yeah, baby, I'm licking your dick. Like it?"

"Bitch mouth!"

He liked it.

I kept at it, sucking and nibbling and tonguing him until "dick licks" degraded first into rhythmic grunts, then into normal moaning. By the time he reached that point I was wet and ready. I pulled away from his dick and looked up at him. Richie looked down at me, plaintively, and asked, "Why?"

"Because I like how you talk dirty to me."

"You are sick," he decided.

"Yeah but the sex is great, isn't it?" To prove my point, I lay down on the kitchen floor and spread my legs. "Come fuck me," I invited. Richie stood there, wondering whether to scowl and stamp out of the room or fall to his knees and take me. So I helped him decide. "Right here, on the floor, Richie. Everybody does it on the kitchen floor at least once."

Everybody does it. That did it. That normalized my request and normal appealed to Richie. He lowered himself to his knees and then onto me.

"Fuck floor." Jesus! "Fuck floor!"

I took him by the dick and guided him to me. I parted the lips between my legs as I brought my other lips to his cheek. I kissed him lightly as the tip of his cock nudged at my threshold.

Richie pushed into me hard, but it would take three pushes for him to access me. Three, not four. Richie compensated with four massive, full-body jerks, which righted things enough for him to start fucking me.

"Squish, squish," he muttered as he screwed me.

"Yeah, I'm wet for you," I agreed.

Richie quieted then. The rhythm and focus of fucking made the tics recede.

But I didn't care by that point. Richie's verbal dirt had worked its magic on me, and I grunted and went at it like the sex pig that I am. I clutched Richie's ass and pulled him into me, encouraging him to pump me hard and fast. I bucked, giving better than I got. Richie grabbed my breast and pinched the nipple hard enough to make me thrash and squeal and come. That was all he needed. Richie slammed into me and came, snorting like a wild animal.

Soon after, his cock limp enough to slip from me, me wet enough with juice and jism to slick the floor, we rested in a tight embrace. The stillness of lying close made Richie's tics reemerge and he shuddered and jerked several times in my arms. As he yelled "Cunt fuck!" explosively, I realized that the tics were mimicking his orgasm.

Yeah, cunt fuck for sure.

Cunt fuck, cunt fuck, cunt fuck, cunt fuck!

GRIT

Kathleen Bradean

I WAS WALKING ACROSS CAMPUS WHEN I HEARD my roommate, Janine, yoo-hoo me. Mortified to hear her rebel yell attached to my name, I turned just in time to see her pulling into the parking lot in front of the women's dorm in a ratty old used-to-be-blue Trans-Am.

Janine's boyfriend slithered out of the car through the window; I suppose he fancied himself a race car driver. I could just picture him working languidly on the wreck he drove, wearing an old R.E.M concert T-shirt, sucking down beer, pissing away a hellish eternity of duplicate days in a town so shell-shocked by time that it didn't realize it was already dead. I immediately christened him Grit.

I admit I saw the attraction. Long and lean, Grit had a beautifully sculpted face, Michael

Stipe lips, and thick eyelashes that shyly hid cornflower blue eyes. Fringes of dark hair lay just beneath his nipples. A stripe of hair below his belly button disappeared into the waistband of his tight jeans. My imagination followed that line down to a delicious end.

He leaned back through the window of the Trans-Am to grab his Marlboros, giving me a chance to stare at the way his denim second skin defined his ass. That body promised sex. Not lie-in-the-bed-for-hours-exploring-your-lover's-body sex, oh no. Just straight out animal fucking: hard and fast, dirty and low.

I wanted a piece of that.

Heat welled up and slid down between my legs until I tingled. He turned and fixed a look on me as if he could smell my musk over the sooty oil the Trans-Am's engine was pissing on the asphalt. Keeping his eyes locked on mine, he jostled a cigarette out of the pack, insinuated his lips around it, and yanked it out. His long fingers slid into the front pocket of his pants. A lighter followed his hand out, pressed between two fingers; he cupped his hand protectively over the tip of the cigarette, touched flame to tobacco, pulled in a full drag, looked me up and down, exhaled, and grunted something like a greeting. We walked into the dorm together and left Janine to manage suitcases on her own.

First thing Grit did when he got inside my room was roll and light a fat doobie. Janine staggered in, dropped the bags, pulled a chair up next to him, and started cooing. Here was irony I understood but didn't appreciate. I had specifically chosen this college for the wealth and connections of the other students. Yet here I was, stuck with a roommate from the same social class (low) that I was determined to escape. College was supposed to have been a clean break for me, a chance to reinvent myself.

Now I leaned against the wall, arms folded. I radiated disapproval. The dorm probably reeked of pot, and I could picture our resident narc down the hall, dialing campus security as fast as her little fingers could tap out the number. I didn't need that kind of trouble. I had a scholarship to protect.

Janine finished off the joint. She handed the last of the paper, impaled on an opened safety pin, back to Grit. He took a final toke, then rubbed the last bit between his fingers until it fell molecule by molecule onto the floor. At least he knew how to hide the evidence.

Normally Janine suffered under the delusion that we had some sort of friendship, and she took great pains to keep me around. This time she dropped hints that I should leave. I ignored her, pretty much the way I always did.

Grit grabbed her hand and mashed it into his crotch. Janine protested, trying to pull away. He smiled his devil's grin at me and held on to her. Janine caught the direction of his smile and looked at me, her eyes full of venom. She flicked her lit cigarette into my closet with her free hand.

Bitch burned a hole into my only jacket.

I ground the cigarette under my heel. Grit unzipped his pants and pushed Janine facedown into his lap. She was flinging her arms around and screaming at me, as if it was my fault. I winked at him, grabbed my laundry basket and my calculus book and headed out the door, leaving the two lovebirds alone.

Three loads of laundry and a chapter review later, I parked my hamper with a study partner and we went dancing. Well, *she* went dancing. I went hunting. During my first semester, I'd kept my head down in the books, focused like a laser beam burning a hole through a block of solid steel. I didn't even allow myself to *think* about committing the sweetest sin. But that night, four months of denied need came crashing through my loins. Naked desire radiated from my body. Stupid college boys drew near, lured by the siren song of my pheromones, and got sucked into the jet engine of my hunger, to mix a metaphor or two. I left a chewed-up bunch of mama's boys in my wake. My skin crawled for something beyond their bland flavors—something with a bit more *grit*.

By the time the bars closed I was vibrating with frustration. There was nowhere to go but home.

The lights were off in my room. Carefully I picked my way across the floor. Some little sound or false motion betrayed them; suddenly I realized that Janine and Grit were still awake. They were on the top bunk, tense and still, pretending to be asleep.

I made a big production of undressing. In the utter silence that descended, I was sure they could hear the progression of the zipper on my tight little skirt. I turned my back so they could follow the movement of my pale hand, glowing in the moonlight streaming through the window, as I teased the zipper past the small of my back, up the rise of my buttocks, down and around my curves.

They were still holding their breath when I turned toward the bunk and moved my hands from button to button on my blouse. I flexed my shoulders, revealed my bra, and wriggled the skirt down to the floor. Still in high heels, I moved across the room, walking the slow rolling walk of the very drunk. (I was, of course, stone cold sober.) I imagined their greedy eyes glinting when my bra came off. One of them sighed when I removed my panties. Nude, I strolled boldly across the room.

I lay down on the bottom bunk, turned on my side, and propped myself up on an elbow. The mirror over our small sink gave me a full view of the upper bunk and there, in the mirror, Grit's eyes met mine. He wanted me to watch.

I pulled back into the shadows just in case Janine turned her head in the same direction. Then I made sounds like I was falling asleep. Controlled deep breathing was difficult. My heart pounded, and amped-up adrenaline surged to every muscle in my body.

Janine protested when Grit rolled on top of her, but he put his mouth over hers in a consuming kiss and insinuated himself between her legs. His hand slipped below the covers. Before long she was moaning, and the smell of her sex wafted through the room.

He pushed the covers down. She clung. He tore. She frantically whispered. He pushed her knees to her chest and mounted her. She turned her face to the wall.

I watched.

He searched for me in the mirror. I emerged from shadow for a moment, then receded back into darkness. Only then, after seeing me, did he pump. The movement of the sculpted muscles on his thighs and buttocks was a fascinating, beautiful dance of balance and counterbalance. Every plunge required the work of his long, lean thighs and hips. His pelvis tilted up with each delicious thrust. I wanted to place my hands on him and feel the muscles moving under his skin as he took her. I wanted to press his back to my naked breasts, tease his nipples between my fingers, nibble the nape of his neck, and cushion his thrust with my mound.

But all I did was wrap the bottom of the bed sheet around my ankle. Gathering and pulling tight, I brought the wad of cloth between my needy thighs and rubbed my clit into the starched linens.

His eyes demanded mine, so I moved closer to the edge of the bed. My hands slid over my engorged labia. He wanted to see; slowly I shook my head. He pouted and turned back to Janine.

Oh, to bite Grit's bottom lip, to hold it in between my front teeth and draw it to my tongue! I wondered why Janine didn't press her lips to his. I would've sucked his soul right out through his mouth.

I pinched my clit between my thumb and forefinger, then drew it away from my body and tickled the stretched skin with dancing fingers. Swirling circles dipped into my growing dampness, spread across my inflamed skin. I fueled the fire as I willed myself to feel him inside me. Suspended above me, he was inside her—but our eyes joined again in the mirror and I realized that she was just a proxy. He was making love to me through her.

"Harder," I mouthed. My body rose from the mattress, my neck angled and exposed like a virgin in a vampire movie. I pinched my nipples. Shivers shot between my legs. "Harder," I silently demanded.

He pulled her ankles to his neck. Recklessly, I braced a leg against the wall and openly humped my fingers. My ring finger pressed against my anus while the index finger skated through my brine and stroked my clit. My scent rose and mingled with theirs. The combined aroma hung heavy as night jasmine in the air.

Grit lifted his head and pulled in my perfume, he looked like he was tasting it on the back of his tongue like a wine connoisseur testing for hints of raspberry or oak in a cabernet. He pounded into her; I pounded into myself. Our eyes locked; Janine's eyes stayed closed. She started making little noises that sounded phony, noises she didn't really mean, like a telephone actress. I bit the inside of my cheek to stop growls from escaping my throat. Grit threw his head back. My muscles clenched. Wave after wave rolled through my pussy. I gushed hot release onto my fingers. He moaned and spurted into her.

We all collapsed. Two of us exhaled contentment. After a minute, she climbed off the bed and went to the shower. We waited in silence for a few minutes. My pussy throbbed lush joy, thankful that I'd brought her pleasure again.

I swung my legs over the side of the bed. My head was swimming. Blood refused to return to my brain—it pumped around my legs and clit, looking for one last tremor of orgasm to surf.

I could see him in the mirror, lying on his side, his cock slowly shrinking. He caught me admiring the package and flashed a smile. Then he went through his cigarette lighting ritual again, complete with the eye-lock on me.

I stood carefully and rested my elbows on the frame of the bed. Our heads were at the same height. My lips could've easily reached out and caressed his. I yanked the cigarette from his mouth and took a long toke on it. "Do her doggie next time." I said. "I want to see her tits shake while your balls slap her clit."

"Damn, you've got a dirty mouth for a girl." He shook his head in admiration.

"Not dirty," I told him. "Just a little gritty."

EMERGENCY ROOM

Kim Addonizio

HE ASKS IF I'VE BEEN TIED UP BEFORE. I TELL
him yes, and he wants to know for how long.
Tell me about it, he says. I feel shy; I don't want
to go into details. We're sitting in Vesuvio's at
four in the afternoon, drinking gin and tonics.
He has his hand on my thigh. I'm madly in
love with him—we've known each other three
weeks. I'm not ambivalent like I usually am,
everything about him seems perfect: his close-
cut black hair, the way he puts his tongue down
my throat when he kisses me, his blunt, square
hands. He's the sexiest man I've ever been with.
It scares me that I can feel so happy. None of
our friends think it will last.

I want to tie you up, he says. I want to do
things with you that you've never done with
anyone.

A man at the bar is doing card tricks. He holds up the queen of diamonds and shows it to a pale, pretty girl in a black leather minidress, black fishnet tights, and heavy black combat boots. The girl looks bored. She glances over at us and sees me watching her. She takes a card from the magician's deck, looks at it, and sticks it back in.

We get drunk sitting in Vesuvio's. At seven o'clock we're still there, kissing passionately, his hand under my T-shirt squeezing my breast. No one pays any attention to us. The magician is still there, too, talking to another woman. He holds up the queen of hearts. Finally we get hungry and walk around the corner to Brandy Ho's and eat Kung Pao chicken and Szechuan shrimp, sitting next to each other in the red leather booth. I feel like I'm in an alternate universe. Everything looks familiar but it's different than before. The sexual intoxication is overwhelming, I can't function in the real world: I haven't called my friends, paid my bills, read a newspaper since all this started. I don't want it ever to end. I feel vulnerable and it's terrifying; I can't help being in love with him, even if he leaves me or treats me like shit I can't hold back the way I usually do, I have to give him everything. Then I won't know who I am anymore.

With his glasses on he looks like a different person: shy, slightly studious, younger. It's as if he's in disguise; I don't recognize him as the same person I fuck. I like him in his glasses, like the idea that there are things about him no one could ever guess from the way he looks. He takes his glasses off, sets them on my kitchen table.

Take off your clothes and stand against the wall, he says.

I peel off my T-shirt, drop my skirt and underwear, and lean against the wall, facing him. He tells me to put my arms above my head. We've just finished dinner. He pours himself more wine and tips his chair back, drinking the wine, watching me.

Don't move, he says. He leaves the kitchen. I hear him pissing in the bathroom. I'm excited, scared, I don't know what's going to happen next. I close my eyes, listen to the stream of piss hitting the water in the bowl. My neighbor in the next apartment starts playing the clarinet. She's just learning so it's all honks and squeaks. The walls are thin, I'm worried someone will hear us, I don't want anyone to hear us. I don't want anyone to know what we do together, what he does to me.

He comes back to the kitchen, zipping his pants. He takes an apple from the bowl of fruit on the table.

Open your mouth.

He shoves the apple against my mouth; my teeth sink into it. I'm gagged. He's not gagging me. I can drop the apple any time. I want him to dominate me, use me; I want to be his slave. I have to understand submission, why it's so erotic for me; I can't reconcile it with the rest of my life. I've never let myself physically explore how I feel because intellectually I can't accept it. Women are shit, they're only here for men's pleasure, men control everything.

My beautiful slut, he says. Look how wet you are. He puts his middle finger inside me, then in his mouth. He unbuckles his belt and takes it off in one smooth motion.

One Saturday night when we're fucking the condom breaks. I know I'm ovulating, I don't want to get pregnant. He calls a sex information hotline and asks what we can do, and they tell him there's an abortion pill I can take; I should call a doctor to prescribe it.

I call the advice line at Kaiser and get put on hold. I wait forty-five minutes, then a voice comes on the line and says there's one more call ahead of me. I wait ten more minutes. The woman on the other end tells me she can't help me, I need to talk to Doctor X. I ask her to connect me. She connects me to the wrong extension; the people there tell me to call a different number. I hang up, dial the main hospital, and ask for Doctor X.

He's not on tonight.

I explain what's happening. The woman on the other end insists that Doctor X isn't there, and no one else can prescribe the pill. Finally someone else gets on the phone and tells me that Doctor X is being paged. I'm put on hold again. A Muzak version of "We've Only Just Begun" by the Carpenters plays, followed by the Beatles' "Here, There, and Everywhere." Twenty minutes later another person gets on the line.

Can I help you?

I think I'm being helped. I don't know. I've been on the phone for an hour and a half, I'm trying to reach Doctor X.

I want to scream at the person on the phone but she is very nice, it's not her fault, there's nobody to blame, I don't want to scream at her. I don't want to have a baby. I'm thirty years old, I work at a café and never have enough money for art materials. My mother was a painter, she stopped after she had me. I can't be a painter if I have a baby. He doesn't want a baby either. Not this way, he says. Not by accident.

Please hold, the nice person says. I listen to a few bars of "My Cherie Amour." A minute later Doctor X gets on the line.

You have to come to the Emergency Room to pick it up, he says.

Can't you just call it in to a drugstore?

We have to see you, he says. There are certain risks involved.

He says that if the pills don't work and the fetus is female it could be turned into a boy by the hormones. Masculinized, he says. The fetus might be masculinized and if you decide to have the baby there could be problems.

I don't want to have the baby, I say. I want the pills. If they don't work I'll have an abortion, but I've had three abortions already and that's why I want the pills. Please, I say. Can't you call it in?

You have to come to the Emergency Room, he repeats, sounding annoyed. We have to have a record that we've seen you.

I hang up. It's ten P.M., we haven't had any dinner. He puts his arms around me.

He says, I hate to see you go through this.

I hate doctors, I say. I hate Western medicine. I hate Kaiser, you never see the same doctor twice. Nobody knows you or gives a shit about you, you're a name on a chart. Why can't they just give me the pills?

Let's go eat first, he says. I'll take you some place nice, we'll forget about this bullshit. The Emergency Room will be open all night.

He takes me to North Beach. We drink a lot of wine. I start to feel better, now it's an adventure we're having together instead of a lousy experience. We joke about it, he puts his hand over mine on the red-and-white checkered tablecloth. I've never been so in love with anyone. I tell him I don't think I want any children.

I'll get sterilized, I say. I'm no good at birth control, I always blow it one time and get pregnant from that one time. I'll make an appointment and get my tube tied. I only have one tube and ovary because I had an infection once and had to have an operation. A gynecologist told me once that if I ever got sterilized it might be major surgery, because of the scar tissue from the other operation.

I'll get a vasectomy, he says. It's easier, it's just an office procedure.

What if we break up and you want to have a baby with someone else? As I say this the thought of it makes me jealous and depressed and I'm sure it will happen.

I can go to a sperm bank, then. Besides we're not going to break up. And you might change your mind. Five years from now we might want a baby and we could have one.

We get to the Emergency Room a little before midnight. We sit in the waiting room, and after half an hour a nurse leads me through a curtain and takes my blood pressure.

I'm only here to pick up a prescription, I tell her.

She ignores me, fastens a yellow plastic ID bracelet with my name and policy number around my wrist. She leads me to an examining room where there's a metal table with stirrups, and puts a blue plastic gown on the table.

Wait here, she says.

I sit down on the only chair. After forty-five minutes a Chinese medical student comes in.

I need to examine you, he says.

No, you don't. I'm not sick, I just need a prescription.

I'm supposed to examine you.

I think of him looking at me, my legs spread apart, my heels in the cold stirrups; I don't want him to look at me. I start crying and saying I just want the pills, there's nothing wrong with me I don't want a baby you don't need to examine me, please just give me the pills so I can go home.

He writes something down on his chart, then walks out, muttering something I can't hear. A minute later the nurse says I can go back to the waiting room.

A man with long blond hair is passed out in one of the chairs.

Three well-dressed black people are sitting together. The man is doubled over, holding his side, and the two women are on either side of him talking to him and rubbing his shoulders. There's a Toyota commercial on the TV, then an episode of *Miami Vice*. The nurse comes out after twenty minutes and tells me that Kaiser's pharmacy doesn't have any more of the pills; there might be some at Mount Zion, she has to call and then send someone there to pick them up.

I lean my head on his shoulder; he strokes my hair. The blond man wakes up and looks around the room. Fuck this shit, he says. He gets up and walks out.

At three A.M. the nurse calls me in behind the curtain and hands me a paper cup of water and another paper cup with three tiny white pills in it. She gives me three more to take in twelve hours.

When we leave, the black people are still sitting there.

I have an almost pathological need for other people's approval. If someone criticizes me I fall apart, I feel useless, stupid, insignificant. When I confess this to him he says I need to learn not to internalize other people's negativity. I experience this as subtle criticism and move to the edge of the bed, away from him.

I used to sleep with men so that they would like me. I always had a lot of lovers. Now I only fuck him; he excites me more than anyone. When I masturbate I don't think about strangers fucking me, the way I used to; I think about him looping a rope through a ring screwed into the top of the doorframe, slapping my breasts and cunt. I think about the way he growls low in his throat, the violence of his orgasms. I masturbate imagining he is watching me, and come saying his name over and over. My life before I knew him seems impoverished, a desert. I'm afraid of losing him; he has to keep reassuring me that he loves me and wants me. At parties I'm jealous if he talks with other women. I'm convinced they're more attractive, more desirable than I am.

We're in someone's loft studio, it's too crowded. I feel like I'm suffocating. Everyone is talking to everyone else, huge paintings hang on the walls, the paint laid on layer after layer—thick dark colors, blues and blacks. I can't find him. No one is talking to me. Someone gave me some mushrooms earlier and now I'm starting to come on to them, I feel jumpy and want to find something to drink to calm me down. I bump into a woman, she stares at me in dislike, turns away. I get through the crowd and pour myself some wine, drink it quickly, and pour another one, asking people if they've seen him. No one has. I'm panicked, sure he's met another woman and left with her.

I go into the bathroom and lock the door. I feel sick so I crouch at the toilet but I can't throw up. Sitting down on the floor, my back against the wall, I stare at the postcards tacked above the toilet. I know I'm seeing images but I can't tell my brain what they are, specifically; they're like abstract paintings, they have no meaning. I feel violated by images, I can't help seeing them on billboards, on TV, in ads and movies, they get into me through osmosis and change my thought patterns: what I'm supposed to look like, feel like, be. I close my eyes and see blue snowflakes.

He's pounding on the door, his voice sounds far away. I get up and open it. He takes me in his arms.

Please fuck me, I say. Fuck me here, on the floor.

He locks the door and undresses me. I lie down on the floor; it's cold, I'm shivering. He takes off his shirt and tucks it under me. He's standing over me, unzipping his black leather pants.

I start hallucinating that he's a demon, his eyes are frightening—dark brown, he's wearing his contacts so there's a yellowish ring around his irises. I realize I don't trust him, I'm afraid he'll hurt me. I want him to hurt me.

Slap me.

He slaps me across the face. I feel myself clench, get wet. My head lolls to the side; he looks in my eyes, I'm naked, I'm begging him to do it again. He takes a condom from his pants pocket and puts it on, then slaps me again and enters me. I start to come almost immediately.

Not yet, he says, and stops moving inside me.

Please, I say, thrusting up at him; I'll go crazy if I don't finish coming. He stays still while I writhe underneath him; the orgasm goes on and on, I can't seem to stop. After a while he starts fucking me again, faster and faster, he comes with a loud moan and falls all the way on top of me.

I feel secure again feeling his weight, listening to his heart slowing down.

I talk to my friend Simone on the phone; we haven't spoken for weeks. She tells me about her lover, whom she's just broken up with.

At first it was great, she says. We did things sexually we'd never done with anyone else. But then he confessed that he likes to cross-dress. I mean, I just couldn't handle it. He wanted me to pretend he had a cunt; it was too weird.

I don't talk about my sex life to Simone; at least, not the really intimate details. My girlfriends and I discuss the size of our lovers' cocks, tell each other if they're any good in bed; I told Simone about the time I met two guys in North Beach and went to the Holiday Inn with them. Simone likes being tied up, but I don't want to talk about it with her. He and I have our own private world, we spend hours together absorbed in each other, seeing how far we can go. We close the curtains, nothing gets in. I tell Simone I want to marry him.

You're kidding, Simone says. How long have you known this guy?

Ten weeks.

Forget it, Simone says.

No, I mean it. I've been with enough men. I don't want to do that anymore.

The Virtuous Woman, Simone says.

Something like that.

You can't do it. You know how you are—if you like some-body and he wants you, you let him fuck you.

But I never felt like this about anybody else. And he's the best lover I ever had, I know I couldn't find anybody else who does what he does for me.

It's not about better, Simone says. Sooner or later you'll want something different, something he can't give you, and you'll go out looking for it. And anyway, you're confusing sex with love. You're hot for this man so you think you love him.

I wonder why Simone does this to me; she can't be happy for me, she always finds flaws. She says she's just being my friend, trying to protect me. I don't call Simone for weeks because I'm afraid she'll convince me that she's right.

The more I fuck him, the more I want him; I've never had this much sex with anyone before. It's all we do—sex, work, eat, sleep. Sometimes we don't get around to cooking dinner until midnight, and sometimes we end up at two A.M. eating cheese and olives and pita bread in bed. Simone tells my other friends I'm obsessed. He's late for work all the time, his boss blames it on me. No one understands us. There's a conspiracy against us, to separate us. Romantic love is always tragic; the lovers can't stay together, death or lies or fate separates them. It's dangerous to be erotic, then you aren't so trapped; if you do it in public they look at you and their minds are filthy so they see filth, then they try to put you in jail.

After a few more weeks we quit our jobs and move to a hotel in the Tenderloin where we can be together all the time; between us we have enough money for about four months. I don't know what's going to happen after that and I don't care. I set up my tubes of paints, my chalks and charcoals and brushes, on a table in the corner of the room, and he models for me. We have a small refrigerator with a freezer that keeps tiny ice cubes frozen in plastic trays, a hot plate, an indoor barbecue, a stack of books we've bought over the years meaning to read but that we never got around to; we have a portable cassette player, tapes, potted violets, and an aloe plant. We never go farther than the corner grocery half a block away. We cook or eat takeout Vietnamese food from next door. Whatever we need from the outside world, the son of the woman two doors down picks up for us. We fight sometimes. We fall more deeply in love. Underneath everything we're blissfully happy. We know how to live. All we want is for you to go away and leave us the fuck alone.

BAD GIRL

Alison Tyler

MY EX-BOYFRIEND AND I USED TO PLAY A GAME
that seemed so naughty to me, I still blush at the
thought. I'm sure other people have done worse,
and I'm sure some folks will think it was nothing
to feel guilty about. But to me, it was as if we'd
crossed a line, some line of decency. After we
played this game I would look at Paul with an
expression of stunned satisfaction, pleased that
we'd escaped a thunderbolt once again.

It's not that we were normally tame. From
the beginning, Paul and I had a fairly wild sex
life. He was a teacher at a high school in town,
and we made love on his desk after the kids had
left for the day. He spanked me. He tied me up.
We fucked in public. I sucked him off while he
drove. I fucked him at his mother's house. At a
Christmas party, he took my cup of coffee into

the bathroom, came into it, and brought it back to me. While I drank, he stood across the room, staring, excited to the point where he could no longer make idle conversation with those around him.

These activities paled in comparison to our brand-new game. It started while we were on vacation in the northern part of California. He'd rented a stone cabin in one of those old-fashioned vacation parks. There were twelve other cabins in the resort, all carefully spread out beneath a scattering of redwoods so that you felt as if you had the whole forest to yourself. Our little bungalow contained two beds, a small living area, and a kitchen. For some reason, and I still don't know why, I climbed into one bed and Paul climbed into the other. Maybe it's because it had been such a long day of driving. Maybe we were just playing around, as if we weren't going to fuck that night—unlikely for us. I rolled over, facing the wall, and stared at the pattern of the stones. Several minutes went by before Paul stood up and lifted the covers on my bed. As he climbed in next to me, he said, "Shhh, angel, we don't want Mommy to hear."

I froze. This wasn't our normal type of game. When we did S/M, he would talk dirty to me. He might say, "Lisa, you've been a bad girl, haven't you? Bad girls get spanked. Hold on to your ankles, and don't you stand up. Don't you flinch." He was the dominant, but he was always just Paul, my handsome boyfriend. If I played the role of a younger me, I was still me.

Now he said, "You be a good girl. You be nice for Daddy." I stayed totally still. His hands wandered between my legs, touching me through my panties, tracing the outer lips of my vagina. It felt good and bad and confusing, and I drenched my underwear.

"Uh oh," he said, "my little girl's all wet for me. Did you get yourself all wet for Daddy? Is that what you did?"

I couldn't answer. I just let him keep touching and stroking and playing. When he pressed up against my leg and I felt his hard cock, I thought that alone was going to make me come, that insistence of his cock brushing against my thigh.

"We have to be really quiet, Lisa," he said softly. "Mommy's asleep in the other bed, and we don't want to wake her. Then she'd know what I know. She'd know just what a bad girl you are. What a sinful little girl you are. I'd have to punish you severely if she ever found that out. Do you understand me?"

I nodded.

"Good girl," he said, "That's my good girl."

He spooned against me, lifting my nightgown, lowering my panties, and entering me from behind. His hands wandered over the front of my nightgown, cupping my breasts. He pressed his lips to my ear, whispering, "My girl is getting so big now, isn't she? Look at the way your breasts fill my hands." He rubbed my nipples against the flat of his palms and they stood at attention, poking against the flannel fabric of my nightgown. "Yes, she is. Nice and big for me. And look at how hard your little nips get. I only have to brush them lightly."

His voice was a husky whisper, as if he were honestly trying to keep quiet. His cock throbbed inside me, and he brought one hand to the front of my body, raising my nightgown and placing his fingers against my pussy. He pressed against me, finding the wetness, then locating my clit and sliding his fingers over and around it. I moaned at the sensation, and instantly he hissed, "Didn't I say to be quiet? We're going to have to go outside behind the house for a little punishment session if you can't control yourself. Look over on that chair, Lisa." I turned my head slightly. "See Daddy's belt?" I murmured an assent. "I'm going to have to tan your bottom with that belt if you can't keep yourself under control. You know what that feels like, don't you, girl? Don't you know what it feels like to have your bottom thrashed by my belt?"

His fingers played me. They stroked up and down, and I tried so hard to do what he said, to be quiet and behave. I'd never been that turned on before. Not when he used masking tape to bind me over one of the little desks in his classroom, slapping the wooden ruler on my naked haunches. Not when we snuck off at his sister's wedding and fucked during the reception. This was it. My pinnacle. The dirtiest thing I could think of, and it made me weak. I didn't moan again, but my breathing came hard and fast.

"You need to be quiet," he said in that hushed, menacing tone. "Daddy gets so tired of having to punish you. Why can't you be a good girl, Lisa? Why can't you be good for me, like your sister?"

That did it. That made me come. Sick and twisted and over the top, I leaned back against him and let the riptide of orgasm slam through me. He gripped his arms around me, bucking faster and faster until he reached it, too, pulling out to come all over my backside, holding me tight so I couldn't turn around to face him, to see whatever expression of horror would reflect my own. What had we done? What had we just done? What line did we cross? Where would we go from here?

"Bad girl," was all he said, lips against my ear. "I always knew you were a really bad girl, Lisa. And bad girls get punished. Why don't you go over there and get my belt so we can deal with this? Go on and get it for me. You know you deserve it, Lisa." He shook his head. "Such a bad little girl."

Bad girl, I thought as I stood and walked to the chair. That's what I am. That's what I was the whole time, I just hadn't known it for sure.

TWISTED BEAUTY

Elspeth Potter

ONE TUESDAY, ALEX TOOK SYLVIA TO HONG'S Special Famous in San Francisco, his favorite restaurant because of its commodious and solid wheelchair ramp. He liked being able to enter a place beside his date, briskly propelling himself, instead of bumping clumsily over doorsills and fending off metal handles that tried to smack him in the face. He had always hated appearing a buffoon; and since the accident that had crushed his legs, he needed all the confidence he could get.

Having a beautiful woman beside him, if no longer on his arm, helped considerably. Constanza, his first girlfriend after he'd returned to his life, was a busty blonde paralegal from the contracts department of his firm. She always wore snug power suits that showed most of her shiny nylons; not his type, ordinarily, but entering a room with her sent a clear message to other men, a message in which Alex took savage delight: *Yes, cripples have sex, and they're having hotter sex than you.* Except he hadn't been. With Constanza, he'd been too nervous in private to get it up, much less suggest any more exotic activities.

Good-hearted Mary had been next; she'd done extensive research on spinal injuries on the Web, and arrived at his apartment prepared to help him with all sorts of private bodily functions that he could manage perfectly well on his own. His spine wasn't damaged: only his legs had been splintered like sugarcane, scarred and bent out of all recognition. He and Mary had managed a little fucking, because by then he'd been in dire straits and not about to turn down sex if it was offered. But being Mary's charity case, however much she denied it, quickly palled, and he'd been relieved when she'd left him for Topher the waterskiing instructor.

Sylvia was different.

Sylvia was comfortable enough with him that she made fun, as he had learned to, of his struggle with everyday tasks like reaching the top buttons in an elevator. Her teasing put him at ease, as if his twisted legs were merely a delightful, kinky sex toy. She kept him so involved in sensation that he had no opportunity to obsess about his appearance, his awkwardness in certain positions, or the uncontrollable spasms of pain and cramping that sometimes interrupted them in the heat of the moment. He could hardly comprehend the sheer relief of regular sex without pity.

Even considered objectively, their sex had been fantastic, as good as any he remembered from before, perhaps better. Sylvia demanded, and he rose to her challenge.

Tonight's trip to Hong's was part of a pattern they were establishing together. They ordered, and Alex deftly stripped the paper from his chopsticks, snapped them apart, and used them to place deep-fried noodles dipped in duck sauce between Sylvia's full lips. Then, between one breath and the next, he found himself fixated on her neatly manicured fingers enfolding the round, handle-less teacup, his gut fluttering as she expounded on new albums they'd received at the radio station that week, and related anecdotes of her promotional trip to a music festival, minutiae that suddenly loomed larger to him than global warming. They'd been lovers for two months, but only now did he know he was in love with her. And Sylvia with him? How would he know?

What if she wasn't? If she didn't love him, would she leave him, like the others had? If she didn't love him, would he want her to stay?

After dinner, Sylvia drove them to her house in Suttontown, Alex talking about the ocean dumping case that had landed on his desk that day, a case he thought he had a chance of winning. She seemed interested in what he had to say, but no more than usual. Did she sense the new intensity he felt? In the twilight they swam in the pool, laughing and slipping in and out of each other's grip like sea lions playing. He was no longer able to free climb, but he felt almost as free in the water. Later, in Sylvia's living room, he sat naked on her enormous Turkish rug, wishing he could feel its softness on the backs of his thighs. A single lamp pooled bronze light on the rug's jewel tones, showing her pale skin, his darker skin, and Sylvia's damp auburn curls. She knelt in front of him and began to dry his hair with short, luxurious strokes, complaining of how thick it was. "No Rogaine in your future, Sasha," she said.

Alex needed to touch her. He needed all of her, but he sat still, waiting, knowing she liked to lead their encounters.

Sylvia tenderly combed her fingers through his hair. His scalp prickled, and warmth cascaded down his spine. She trapped him with her gray gaze, her eyes seeming to say, *You are mine.* She rubbed his ears gently between her fingers, just on the edge of roughness: first the tops, then the lobes, then up the outer rim, then her cool fingers slipped inside his ear canal, and out again, and up to the tops, and down, and...

"You're drowning me," he said dizzily.

"You don't want me to stop."

"No," he said. "Yes." The heat in his belly wasn't enough. He couldn't sense what she felt. He had to touch her or die. He swayed forward. She pulled back.

"Tell me what you want," Sylvia said, so close to his mouth he could feel her rapid breaths. "I want to hear you say it. Then I'll let you touch me."

"Kiss me," he said. "Now."

They toppled and rolled, her body pressing softly to the length of his, her warmth almost agony. Each heartbeat thrust him more tightly against her. He stroked her with hot hands and flushed face, and sucked her tongue into his mouth, hearing throaty sounds of pleasure. His.

She pulled away and grinned; her hand cupped his scrotum and his muscles clenched. He wouldn't come. He wouldn't. He hadn't figured this out yet, how she felt. His unbearable tension faded over the next few seconds, and he loosened his fingers from her waist, one at a time. The velvet of her cheek stroked near his mouth; one hand smoothed absentmindedly over his ribs; her free hand caressed his balls, feather-like, each touch distinct.

Sylvia murmured, "Let me—let me do it all." She trailed her silky-smooth knuckles along his cock, an easier sensation to tolerate than her evanescent brushes against his balls, until she swirled a finger under the edge of his foreskin, rubbing it gently between finger and thumb, sliding the skin forward and back, ignoring the dripping head. A soft groan escaped his teeth and he reached for her; Sylvia pushed his hands away, pressing them to the carpet. He contracted his belly so hard that it hurt.

Sylvia squeezed his balls lightly and Alex sucked in a breath. "You look intense," she said. "I love it that I can do this to you." She disentangled from him and sat up, not letting go, her thumb and forefinger teasing his cock deliberately, with more pressure now. His entire life spiraled down to those two fingers. "Like this...you're beautiful."

Did she really think that? His twisted legs bore no resemblance to her flawless curves. If only she knew how radiant she looked when he buried himself deep within her body. That was love, wasn't it, when the other person was the most beautiful you'd ever seen? Sylvia, nude, was that person. He trembled at the mere thought of it. He arched his neck as his muscles spasmed, but he didn't ask her to stop and wait for him. He was afraid to try to speak in this half-world between desire and culmination.

"Close your eyes," Sylvia said.

Compelled to obey, Alex closed them. Sylvia released his cock and he relaxed fractionally, as her soft hands passed over his hair, his face, down his chest. "How do you want to finish this?" she whispered into his ear.

It seemed years since he'd made a decision. He opened his eyes to see Sylvia's face above him. "Us," he said. "Together."

Sylvia bent closer. "Me on top?"

He was too far gone to laugh. "My turn."

"Beg me," she said.

He didn't want to play this time, but he would do anything. "Sylvia, please."

Sylvia stretched out with him, and he sighed and shivered as her skin contacted his. "If I don't, right now..." With this disjointed sentence nagging at him, he twisted atop and slickly into her in one motion, attempting to merge with her whole being, not just her body. He tried to catch his breath, but her inner muscles contracted and in one ignominious instant it was too late for control.

No matter what people said, coming was nothing like falling.

A few minutes later, still shaking with reaction, he laughed a little and said, "You did that on purpose."

Sylvia rolled sideways, bringing him with her, and stroked up and down his back. His muscles fell limp under her hands, even as his throat tightened with exhaustion or emotion, he couldn't tell which. He'd wanted it to last longer. He cupped her ass and pressed her against him to savor the erratic pulse of her cunt as their bodies relaxed. The rug exuded their musk, like incense.

"Tell me you liked it," she said. Her leg hooked around his; he felt it at his hip.

Alex met her eyes, a foggy gray universe in the blur of her face. "Yes," he said. He kissed her, slowly, the barest touch of his tongue to the damp gloss inside her lower lip. Truthfully, he was relieved his stamina hadn't been tested, after having been on the verge of explosion ever since that moment at Hong's.

"Ex-cellent," she purred in a fake villain accent, trailing a finger down his chest, lighthearted as always, a surface Alex longed to penetrate. Tonight, he'd bitten away only her pale lipstick.

"And you?" he asked.

"None of your business," she said, grinning.

Alex pulled her against him, suddenly exalted like dawn in the Grand Tetons, rapturous from love and from fear. Sylvia curled against him and they lay, quietly, while outside, rain spattered against the patio.

LITA

Cara Bruce

IT WAS RAINING AGAIN. I SAT IN MY THIRD-STORY room and stared out the window. If this didn't stop soon I was going to lose my mind, I was sure of it. It had been almost two months since my last lover had moved out, and it had been raining ever since.

I sighed and walked to the window to close the shades. Just as I began to draw the heavy linen curtain, I noticed my neighbors across the street. The woman was topless, with her face and chest pressed against the glass, and the man was behind her, his large hands reaching around and caressing her breast, his mouth planting kisses on the slender curve of her neck. The rain was beating in slanted sheets upon the window, almost creating a screen for the lovers. I moved the curtain so that only one eye was peeking out.

I could almost feel when the man entered her. The woman's entire body was heaved upward, hard against the glass. I could now see that she was completely naked, her legs spread. One of the man's hands was wrapped tightly around her waist, the other moving up and over her clit. Her head lolled from side to side in orgiastic pleasure. I could almost imagine the moans that were escaping her lips, and my body quivered. I slipped my hand down the front of my silk pajama bottoms, feeling the cool fabric on one side and the hot breath of my cunt on the other. My fingers grazed over my patch of curly hairs and gently parted the swelling lips of my labia. The lovers across the street were still going at it, and I let the curtain fall away, sure they wouldn't notice me in the midst of their revelry.

I drew a finger across my nipple, making it harden. Lightly I pinched it, gently pulling it outward. My pussy was beginning to drip. I stroked my clit, letting that grow as well. My legs felt weak. I rubbed myself and watched as the man thrust into the woman across the street. He lifted his hand and dragged a finger across her mouth. Her tiny hands were balled into fists that beat against the window and I could practically hear her screaming with pleasure.

Quickly I slipped off my pajamas, the cool air hardening my nipples until I thought they would pop off. I stood there completely naked, my legs spread like the woman's across the street, except that instead of him behind me I had my own hand working its magic. At this point I wanted them to see me; I was sure they wouldn't care, and I almost needed them to know how much I was enjoying their spectacle.

The rain picked up, so hard that it almost provided complete coverage. I matched my frenzied flicking with the sound of the battering drops against the glass. My legs were tightening and I was about to get myself off when the sound of breaking glass and a piercing scream shot through the air.

I squinted my eyes and the rain seemed to break for a second. The window across the street was shattered into a million pieces and the man was standing there, naked, still half-hard, his arms empty and his mouth frozen open. He looked up at me. Our eyes locked for one second before he turned and ran out of the room.

I looked down to the street at the woman. Her long hair was soaked, one arm twisted upward and the other one stuck to her side. Her neck was turned so that the right side of her face was plastered to the pavement.

Hurriedly I put on my pajamas. I glanced down once more, in time to see the man running down the street. I sprinted down the stairs of my apartment and out to her. I no longer felt myself breathing; I felt as if I had stepped out of my body.

The woman's face was frozen in orgiastic rapture. Its twisted comicalness sent shivers up my spine. Other neighbors were coming out of their houses, and in the distance of the morning I could hear the faint whir of sirens. I knelt down in the wet and blood-stained street. All I could think about was how sorry I was that everyone had to see her like this, soaking wet and broken. How incredibly beautiful she had looked just moments before, making love against the window.

I slipped back inside my building and up to my apartment. I sat in the window and watched them cover her body and take it away, the white sheet clinging to her beautiful figure in the rain. The police were in her apartment, placing shards of glass into tiny plastic bags. I just sat there until one of them looked up, right into my eyes, as I knew he would. A few minutes later he was knocking at my door.

The officer was young and good-looking. He asked the basic questions, and I told him what I had seen. I told him about the sex, the way the newly deceased woman had been pressed up against the window, how her chest had heaved, how her hair had gotten caught in her mouth, how the rain had been falling. My officer was becoming a little flustered, his face growing red and his pants beginning to bulge. Even with the thought of her on the pavement, I was getting slightly aroused myself.

"Are those all the questions?" I asked him.

"Yes, for now." He handed me his card, "If you think of anything, call me." I took the card and smiled, glad he didn't wink.

Two days passed, and I heard nothing. I spent most of those days staring out the window and watching people going through her apartment, watching the street cleaners brush up the million pieces of sparkling glass, watching the white chalk drawing slowly fade into the pavement. I even walked across the street and looked at her mailbox to try and learn her name. It said *L. Morano*, written in an almost childish scrawl. I wondered how old she was. The end of the second day, someone—it must have been her mother—came and gathered up clothing, books, and knickknacks. I sat on my couch and watched her, shoulders slumped, burdened by her grief. There was a part of me that wished to call out to her, to take her in my arms and comfort her. By this point, I was more than intrigued, I was obsessed. And through it all no one thought to close the shades. I began to suspect the dead woman had had none.

That night I lay in bed and tried to sleep. Guilt crept over me: every time I closed my eyes I could see strands of her wet hair stuck to her face on the street, and that awful, horrific image triggered a sexual response in me so great that I was compelled to put my hands between my legs and attempt to get myself off. But no matter how much I tried, I could not achieve release, and eventually I would get tired and stop. My only comforting thought was that I was not Catholic—if I was, I would surely be permanently fucked in the head and in therapy forever.

But one night when I lay in my bed after my third failed attempt at masturbation, I heard a knock at my door. I knew it was going to be him. I put on a robe and opened the door. There stood the man from across the street. His eyes were bloodshot and his hands were trembling. I stepped aside and let him in.

He stood for a second looking out my window, imagining what I must have seen, probably remembering the feel of her hair against his face, her heaving tit in his hand, her hot cunt clenching around his hard cock. His breath quickened, and he turned to face me. Silently I slipped out of my robe, letting it puddle around my feet on the floor. He took a step toward me, lifting his T-shirt off his body. His eyes traveled over me, lingering on each curve for that seductive second that makes one's blood boil.

His mouth pressed down upon mine. His lips were strong and his hand held the back of my neck. My fingers groped with the buttons of his jeans, releasing his cock so that it sprang out hard as a rod. He stepped out of his jeans and bent his neck until his mouth was on my tit, his warm tongue licking over my nipple; his fingers almost viciously grabbed a handful of flesh. He lifted me up, settling my pussy on his cock. I was tight for his entrance, his hands grabbing onto my ass as he lifted and lowered me. I wrapped my long legs around his waist and twisted my fingers through his hair. He pounded into me, thrusting and pumping, fucking me hard and fast. I tossed my head back and pretended I was the woman. I began to moan, and he entered me harder and faster. I looked over his shoulder and out the window, half expecting to see somebody there.

"Lita," he groaned. I pulled his face to the curve in my neck.

"Fuck me the way you were fucking her," I whispered.

He lowered us to the floor and held my hands over my head. His cock rammed into my quivering cunt, and I felt my body on the urge of a breakthrough.

"I'm about to die," I said.

He thrust in deeper.

"The window is going to shatter and I'm going to be lying dead on the pavement." I couldn't help myself; I knew it was twisted, but it was turning me on. He grabbed my hair and harshly tugged.

"My hair is going to be soaking wet, plastered to my face," I whispered in his ear, imagining the orgiastic grin it would be hiding.

Suddenly he picked up the pace and was fucking me hard and fast, as if his life depended on it. My hips lifted and my pussy began to spasm; my legs shook and tightened under him and I came. He thrust hard into me one more time, and then pulled out and shot his hot, white load all over my stomach.

He collapsed on top of me, in a crying, quivering heap.

I held him until the indigo sky began to melt into violet. He got up, dressed, and left. I put my robe back on and stared out the window, watching as the last of the season's rain washed away the remains of her ghostly chalk outline underneath my window.

THE AMY SPECIAL

Susie Hara

WHAT SHE REMEMBERS MOST IS THE SILKY feeling of sliding down his chocolatey body and the distinct sensation of his tightly coiled hair, wiry against her face.

"I like your pubic hair."

"Well, that's a first."

"The way it's so crinkly." Like brand-new steel wool, she thinks.

"Courtesy of Africa," Michael says.

So she's sliding down and she smells him, clean and musky and—no it's not just a cliché, the chocolate, he actually smells like chocolate, from the cocoa butter lotion he uses on his skin. And when she kisses him on the mouth, she smells the cocoa laced with the cool scent of the mints he perpetually sucks on.

"You're my long, tall chocolate mint," she

says as she slides down again, first licking, and then slowly draping her mouth over him.

The amazing thing was, ordinarily she didn't love dicks. Not *really*.

"You know," she told him once, as they were driving down the coast, "it's not like I *love* dicks. That's why it's so special that I love *your* dick—yours—it's personal. I don't *need* a dick to come—I like tongues and fingers better."

"I know," he said, raising his eyebrows, with that slow, quiet grin.

But in truth, she thinks to herself, watching him drive, his long fingers resting lightly on the wheel—she *likes* dicks. She likes them inside her, pumping away hard and deep like there's no tomorrow, or pressing against her thigh, or outlined under the fabric of blue jeans, or sliding into her delicately like a hot whisper. She just doesn't feel...worshipful—something like that. Should she? Are there women out there in the real world who say, "Please, baby, let me suck you"? Who don't get sore jaws and lips, or don't even notice, because they're so turned on? Does she in fact have a double standard, wanting a man who worships at the altar of the divine yoni, yet not worshipping his (what was it called?) lingam. She looked over at him driving, at his profile, and then down at his crotch. He caught her looking and they laughed.

So anyway, there she is, sucking away on him, and she looks up for a moment, and—this is it, this is what she remembers most about him—she sees him watching her, his eyes dark and hot and liquid, and this turns her on more than anything, him looking at her sucking and her looking at him looking at her, it goes direct to her clit and then up to her nipples and back down again. After the first time this happened, every time she sucked him she would always look at him to watch him watching her, even though it strained her neck, and she would watch for a time until she went back to her handiwork. And as she teased her tongue down the shaft and then slowly back up to the head, he would moan, and then she would put her whole mouth on him, making sure not to bite him, sucking on him just like Amy.

It was her ex-husband who told her about Amy, the toothless old Vietnamese woman who gave the best head in Da Nang. Amy was renowned among American soldiers, who came to her for, well, succor. When he first told her about Amy, she was pissed. Were our tax dollars paying for this? Sexual and racial imperialism, colonial exploitation of women, and so forth. But Amy intrigued her. Who was this woman—a victim of political exploitation, or an accomplished businesswoman? Did Amy turn the loss of her teeth into a boon, taking the secret pain and polishing it, using it, until it became something beautiful, the basis for her famous craft and art? So her ex-husband taught her how to do him just like Amy, as if she were toothless, unarmed, a gummy mistress who gives the ultimate, bite-free blow job. She learned to pull her upper lip over her top teeth and her lower lip over the bottom ones, so that as she sucked, she felt like a toothless wonder, and her lip muscles grew strong and resilient.

So she's giving Michael the Amy Special, and he's happily moaning, and then he inevitably says, "I want to eat you."

So what does she do? She doesn't argue with him, she slides up and kisses him on the mouth and falls off to the side, languorously, because languor suits her. And he starts kissing her thighs but she moves him up to her nipples and says, "Start high," and he practices his magic on her nipples with his tongue, pulling and rolling and sucking and flicking. Then he gradually moves south, stopping for nips here and there, down to her belly and her panties. He slides his tongue under the elastic and all around the edges, moving down to the apex and *flick-flick,* he teases her at the edges of the crotch of her panties. She is fairly soaked now, waiting, impatient, but enjoying the torture. She doesn't want to beg, but she wants him to get on with the show. She starts to moan, and then—this is what she remembers most about him—he traces his fingers along the edges of her panties as if he's finger-painting in slow motion, and hooks his fingers under the elastic right next to her pussy and slowly pulls them down. At this point she stops breathing. She knows breathing is a good thing but she stops anyway while she waits. Then he picks up the nipple action again, but now with his fingers, twisting and pulling and pinching, and her breath comes out in pants and plaintive sounds, mewling sounds that she would stop if she could but she can't so she waits while he licks around the edges of her hair and labia until he gets closer and closer and laps one side of her pussy, and then the other. She lets out a sigh of relief from deep in her throat, which is short-lived because then she is on the next rise of terror and pleasure, as he starts in with the slow circles. The circles trace around her clit but don't quite reach it, which is torture and of course she could take his head and move it but at this point she has given up control, hoping that he will really take her there, won't he?, that she won't be abandoned at the crest or just before it, that it really will happen and just as she is fighting this last shred of control, he moves his tongue over to her clit and she lets out a guttural sound of affirmation, and then they are on the homestretch, and he goes slower and slower, which gets her closer and closer until she is so close that if he would only go a little faster she would go over the edge but he knows and she knows that if he goes too fast she will never come at all so he keeps going slower until she wants to pound him, but she waits because she knows that he knows what he is doing and finally it does hover and break, and she is scream-ing even though she has promised herself to try not to make so much noise, it could wake the neighbors, it's too much, she's too much, she's embarrassed even, but then it doesn't matter after all, it just comes out of her like a righteous wail, and she comes like a long fountain, one of those luxurious comes that starts locally and spreads to her womb and toes and mind and she confirms this with a soft sigh of relief.

And then it is quiet. Almost. Because now he is putting on a condom and sliding himself in, wasting no time, and he is mak-ing those extended animal sounds and saying things like, "I'm going to pump you so good, do you want me to?" and she is whispering "yes, yes, yes" like Molly Bloom, and he is filling her up, it feels like coming home, they are both coming home, and this brings on a different kind of come now, a ripping, longing love sort of come, a don't-ever-leave-me kind of come, a you-belong-to-me-don't-ever-fuck-anyone-else kind of come. And she's looking into his beautiful dark eyes and she says, "I feel it—I feel it in my heart." She doesn't know why she's saying this, but it's as if her cunt and womb had moved up into her heart, no longer relegated to their functional geography, and he says, "I want you to—I want you to feel it in your heart." And then she's having another one of those bonus orgasms riding the tail end of the last one, a ripple effect, and then he comes too, thrashing and moaning, and then they are lying there, sweaty and proud of themselves, and breathing hard into the silence, and that familiar feeling comes creeping over her, she can't help it, the habit of it, and she thinks, *What will I remember most about him?*

THE HEART IN MY GARDEN

Carol Queen

THESE DAYS THERE'S A LOT OF MONEY TO BE made if you're in the right place at the right time, if you keep your shoulder to the wheel. That's how Mike and Katherine got their nice house, their cars (hers with that new-car smell still in it), an art collection, and a healthy nest egg. The house is close to San Francisco. Her car is a Mercedes. The art is mostly modern, up-and-coming painters you'll read about in *ArtWeek* any day now.

They're young enough that they don't have to worry about kids yet, so they don't—if you asked them, both would say, "Oh, kids are definitely on the agenda," though they'd sound a little vague. They're old enough that the honeymoon's over, neither of them quite remembering when it ended.

Seven years is a long time to be married. Still, aside from that, things are sweet. The rhythm of their weekdays, long-familiar now, has them clacking along toward the weekend like they're on a polished set of tracks. They fill weekends with rituals of their own.

It dawns on Katherine very, very gradually that she can't remember the last time they made love. She knows they did when they spent that weekend in Monterey—Mike's last birthday. In that romantic B&B, how could they resist the impulse to fall into each other's arms? And it's always a little exciting to be away from home. But they had to break it off in time to get in a day at the aquarium—the whole reason they went—so Mike could see the shimmery glow-in-the-dark jellyfish, delicate neon tendrils floating in the black water. He had seen a special about them on the Discovery Channel, had to see for himself. She lost her heart to them too: she and Mike stayed in the darkened room for almost an hour, silent, side by side with their hands clasped together so lightly that for minutes at a time she lost track of the sensation of his skin against her palm.

That's what she likes about being with him. It's so easy. They can drive together silently, not feeling as if a conversational black hole has swallowed them; they can spend Sunday mornings reading the paper and trading sections with a touch on the arm; they fill each other's coffee mugs without being asked and hand back the steaming, fragrant cups accompanied by a little kiss. After that they work in the garden, sometimes side by side, sometimes like her grandparents used to: Granddad in the vegetables, Gram in the flowers. She can imagine the next fifty years passing this way.

They must have had sex since Monterey—that's four months ago—but she can't remember it. Mostly now they do it late at night, right before sleep, but it's not on a schedule like practically everything else. Neither is it very predictable, tied to watching the Playboy Channel or *Real Sex* on HBO; lately they don't watch those shows much anyway. If you asked Katherine, she'd probably say she doesn't really notice, nor does she notice being turned on, wanting sex, thinking about it very often. There was a time when she lived in almost constant arousal, but that was years ago. She and Mike had just met; she was so much younger then. She's always too busy now, tired all the time, except when they get away for a few days. And they haven't had time to leave town since that weekend in Monterey. Katherine's a lawyer; Mike's software company will go public early next year. And if you asked Katherine whether her friends have more sex than she and Mike, she'd probably tell you not much—everybody's so busy now. Everyone has to concentrate on reaching for the brass ring. How else could you afford a house with a garden, two cars, the basics?

Katherine masturbates sometimes after Mike has fallen a-sleep. Lines of code lull him into light snoring, while Katherine's legal cases keep her awake. She goes over arguments, making mental checklists of every point she'll have to hit when she's in court the next day. She considers this productive time, until she has it organized in her mind—then the arguments begin to repeat themselves and she's so wound up over them she can't nod off. When she gets to this point, she pulls her vibrator out of the nightstand. It's one of those quiet vibrators, barely audible—even though Mike sleeps right next to her, once his breath has evened and slowed she won't wake him.

If you asked her, Katherine would admit that this proximity feels erotic: a little illicit but comfortable too, like the comfort of being with him while they weed or watch glowing aquarium fish in companionable silence. She sometimes slows down her breath to match the rhythm of his, a lingering synchronicity within which they are alive, alone, together—it doesn't matter that he's not conscious of her; it calms her down. Her climax, when it comes, drifts up on her gradually, and its power always surprises her.

Sometimes she gently places herself against him: pressing a-gainst his back when he's turned away from her, or reaching out with just her toes to make contact with his soft-furred calf. It's funny that she doesn't necessarily think of making love with him during these times, but in a way she *is* making love with him. If you asked her, Katherine would say that Mike knows she's doing it, knows it in his sleep. (When she first developed this habit she used to ask him if he had dreamed about anything in particular, but he could never call up sexual dreams. Or if he knew, he never said so.) Katherine respects Mike's sleep too much to thrash or buck, and really this is more about her own tension than about passion. And a tension-tamer orgasm can be quiet, an implosion that rocks her to sleep without rocking her world.

She wakes up refreshed the next morning and goes to court.

Mike has his own private time a couple of days a week, after Katherine leaves for the courthouse. He works a flex schedule, a perk of having stayed at his job for over five years, and two days a week he works at home. He's just as efficient at the home office as at the one downtown, even though this one overlooks his and Katherine's garden. In fact, he's *more* efficient at home, getting at least as much work done in less time. He takes one if not two breaks to jack off, the first in the still-rumpled bed-clothes right after Katherine leaves (she accepts without question that Mike will make the bed on the days he stays home).

The first one is his favorite, especially because the bed still smells faintly of Katherine; he buries his nose in the pillow and lets the scent keep him company as he strokes himself hard. It's his way of keeping her comfortably close, even though she's already halfway to work by the time he begins. He takes plenty of time, a slow hand-over-hand on his cock while his mind wanders; he's in no hurry. His eyes closed, usually, he drifts through a lifetime's worth of mental images until he finds the one that sends a jolt of heat through his cock, maybe makes it jump a little in his hand. That's the one he'll use, embellishing it into a fully fleshed-out fantasy. If you asked him, he'd say he doesn't feel that he guides the fantasy. He feels like he's along for the ride, almost like the folio of erotic images riffling inside his brain has a life of its own, each separate image, in fact, a separate reality that he's simply stumbled into the way Captain Kirk is thrust into a new dimension if his crew doesn't set the transporter controls just right.

For half an hour twice a week Mike drifts in and out of dreams that take him to all sorts of places, sometimes even out of himself. When his orgasm comes it almost always swells up like music at the climax of a movie, the place in the plot where you're supposed to just give yourself over to the story, cry if it tells you to, or clench your fists in fear. When he's done he almost always writes code for two or three solid hours before even thinking of making himself some lunch. When the weather permits he takes his sandwich out into the garden.

He doesn't always take a masturbation break in the afternoon. Sometimes he's on a roll and wants nothing more than to work—Katherine comes home at six or seven and finds him still at it, though on those days he falls asleep really early. But once every week or two he gives himself an hour or two to surf the Net.

THE HEART IN MY GARDEN

He has his favorite sites bookmarked. On the Net he always travels with a tour guide, the sensibility of all his favorite web-masters leading him into cul-de-sacs of sexual possibility he hadn't even known existed. Katherine uses the Net for email and shopping at Amazon.com—for her it's just a handy extension of the local mall—but Mike goes to the bad neighborhoods and stays there as long as he can.

He thinks about going in and never coming out. Only his work ethic stops him from spending all day in this perpetual peepshow. If he overindulges, he knows, he could get his telecommuting privileges yanked, so he doles out his Web visits, perks he allows himself when he's done a good afternoon's work.

In Mike's mind there's no infidelity in exploring chatrooms and cybersex sites as long as he stops before Katherine gets home, as long as she's busy doing something else. He's never told her about it but he doesn't think she'd mind, as long as he gets his work done and their marriage doesn't suffer. For all he knows, she has her own favorite bookmarks on her computer at the office. He wouldn't mind that; it's just play, nothing real. Virtual.

It isn't often that Katherine comes home early. Once in a while she can get out at midafternoon on Friday, usually because she and Mike have decided to go up to the wine country or to a spa weekend. In the eighteen months Mike's been working at home, she's never arrived home before 5:30.

He makes sure he's zipped up by then, either back at work on his code or in the kitchen starting dinner. They often cook together, and sometimes Mike has dinner waiting when she has to work late. She pages him and dials *7:30*—he knows that's when to expect her. He doesn't even call back unless he needs to ask her to swing by the store for bread or a bottle of wine. They shop on Saturdays, though, so usually everything he needs is waiting in the kitchen. Mike likes to cook. So does she, though she rarely makes dinner by herself.

Today, though, the judge continues Katherine's case because a prosecution witness didn't show up. She's out of the court-room at noon. She usually eats with the rest of her team on court days, so they go around the corner to the little Italian place. It's so close to the courthouse that Katherine almost always recognizes most of the diners—judges, other attorneys, people from the jury pool.

She's working with Marla today, the newest member of the practice. Marla's just-married, still trying to balance an intense work life with being in love. She's never late, but Katherine has seen her come to work breathy and flushed—if you asked her, Katherine would say she remembers those newlywed days when once in the morning and once at night wasn't enough, when she and Mike would sometimes skip dinner because they were on each other the minute they got home, when once Mike even got them a motel room at noon.

Marla fishes around in her purse and shows off the set of cufflinks she's gotten Bill for Valentine's Day. They're porcelain ovals with tiny pictures painted on them: one has a bottle of champagne, one a cancan girl with her ruffled skirts thrown high. "Wine, women, and song!" says Marla gaily. "And I got him a really good bottle of French champagne, and I'm taking him to see *Cabaret*. Katherine, what are you doing with Mike?"

Katherine hasn't planned anything special with Mike because she's forgotten that today is Valentine's Day. Jesus, wasn't it just Christmas?

"Ummm, just a really nice dinner and some private time."

This is the best Katherine can come up with without notice, but it satisfies Marla, who has very few brain cells to spare for thinking about Katherine and Mike. She's probably too busy imagining the way she'll tug Bill into an alley when they leave the theater, and give him a sneaky hand job right there in public, Katherine thinks, only a little sniffy about Marla's single-minded focus. You're only young once.

Still, with the afternoon suddenly free, Katherine decides to give Mike a Valentine's Day surprise. He's probably forgotten it too—he's been just as busy as she has—but thank goodness it's a holiday that lends itself to last-minute planning. Katherine detours by Real Foods on the way home, picks up a good wine, some big prawns for scampi, a couple of cuts of filet mignon. On the way to the register she passes the bakery and adds a little chocolate cake to her basket. *Strawberries too,* she thinks, *if they're any good yet.* The store has a heap of huge ruby berries that look like they were grown in the Garden of Eden. And right next to the flowers stands a card display. She picks one that looks like a handmade Martha Stewart crafts project, a slightly-out-of-focus heart against a sapphire-blue background, blank so she can customize its message. She stops at the coffee shop downstairs for a latte and writes *Dearest Michael, you are the heart in my garden. All my love, Kath.*

She thinks about using the pager—*3:30*—but decides against it, decides instead to slip in and surprise him. If she can get into the kitchen via the back door, she might be able to start dinner quietly without interrupting his work. She parks the Mercedes a couple of houses down from theirs.

Her grandparents' house and garden were in Idaho: at this time of year the garden would be cut back and mulched, maybe even buried under a drift of snow. Katherine loves living in

California because even in February the garden blooms with life. The roses are finally gone but the pink ladies, tulips, and irises are starting; in the corner calla lilies burst whitely out of a clutch of huge green leaves. When she picks them she always includes one of those big leaves in the vase; otherwise the sculptural, curved callas almost don't look like flowers.

Passing the window of the room in which Mike works, she glimpses him, so riveted to the screen that he doesn't see her. *Must be on a roll,* she thinks, but then she sees that he is moving in a way that she wouldn't expect to see from a man writing code. Though his body is partly obscured behind the desk and monitor, it almost looks as if he is masturbating.

Katherine noiselessly lets herself into the house and heaps her shopping bags onto the kitchen work island. She lays the store-bought roses carefully on top, drops her purse and briefcase beside them, slips off her shoes. She makes it to the door of Mike's office without being heard.

He's on a roll, all right: onscreen Katherine sees not lines of code but a tiny movie looping repeatedly, a naked man in a blindfold lying on his back, a woman in a shiny black catsuit—it looks like it's made of rubber—crouching over him. The suit encases her body completely, except for her crotch, which is naked, shaved bare, and she engulfs the man's hard, upstanding cock over and over with the shockingly exposed pussy—at least, Katherine finds it shocking, but not in a bad way, more like a shock to the system, cold water in the face, waking her up to feelings she barely remembers.

Clearly, Mike has not forgotten anything. His hand pumps his cock rhythmically, eyes riveted on the miniature tableau as the catsuited woman thrusts down and down and down. He times his hand strokes to the woman's down thrusts, just as

Katherine herself times her late-night strokes to Mike's slow and even breaths.

If you asked her why she isn't upset, discovering him like this, she might tell you it's like her own late-night forays, only so much hotter: she's never seen Mike jack off in the daylight; she hasn't seen his cock this hard in years; she's erotically attuned to his deep breaths from all those nights lying next to him, vibrator or no vibrator; she's fascinated by the tiny couple on the screen, smaller than Barbie and Ken; and the fact that Mike finds them so compelling makes her pussy wet. That her pussy is wet in the middle of the afternoon is such a welcome surprise that all she can do for a minute is touch herself through her fine cotton stockings, the black fabric clinging to her almost as tightly as the tiny woman's shiny catsuit. Katherine's mind spins, looking for a way to incorporate this unexpected scene into her surprise Valentine's Day celebration. Silently she begins to unbutton her gray rayon suit.

Mike's erotic reverie has advanced him so close to orgasm that when he feels a hand stroke his thigh and replace his own hand on his cock, it could easily be a part of the virtual connection he's having with the woman onscreen. For a second he doesn't even look to see who is holding him. Then he recognizes Katherine's hand, a touch he knows almost as well as his own, and sure enough, when he glances away from the screen, she is crouched beside him. She wears nothing but her black bra, which snugly cups her breasts, and her black tights.

Smoothly she stands up, pulling him by the cock, and pushes the office chair across the room. "Lie down, Michael," she whispers. "So you can see the screen."

The rug, fuzzy against the back of his neck, gives him just enough cushion. When Katherine stands over him the screen is obscured, but that doesn't matter because she is taking the crotch of her tights in both hands and sharply ripping, tearing a hole like the one in the woman's catsuit. Katherine's pussy is pink, swelling, her arousal beginning to form visible moisture like dew on the callas' broad leaves. Mike strokes her thighs, reaching for her.

Katherine crouches down over him, and as her pussy makes contact with his rigid cock the woman onscreen is visible again. Katherine's tight wet pussy sucks at him. He's aware of the rug under his back, Katherine's weight poised just above his pelvis, her thigh muscles pumping as she matches the catsuit woman's thrusts, again, again, again. Mike's hands rove her body as he climbs again toward the climax she had interrupted. Her hands rest on his chest for balance, for contact with him, and he feels their pressure through his nipples. On the screen, the blindfolded man is completely under the catsuited woman's control.

Mike thrusts up into Katherine, his eyes wide, flashing from her to the screen, from her to the screen. He slips one hand through her brown hair, pulling the clip that holds it back in its demure professional style. The thick silky hair falls through his fingers, into her face, curtaining eyes that are getting wilder and wilder. Her breasts fill his hands; he squeezes, remembering their ripeness. Now their pelvises grind together, his cock thrusts up into her as deeply as it will go, both of them climb toward climax: maybe not together, but close. She has slipped to her knees, straddling him, her weight on him now, and he lifts her like she's riding a bucking pony when he thrusts into her. Onscreen the catsuit lady and her blinkered paramour have not changed; their fuck can never escalate. But Mike and Katherine are leaving them behind.

Almost. Without warning Katherine moves her hands. She

puts them over his eyes, a moist, fleshly blindfold.

"Fuck me, Mike!" she hisses. "Hard!"

If you asked him now, Mike would groan that he has missed her, missed this, before bucking involuntarily into a come that she has taken from him, imperious and powerful in her ripped tights, that he could not hold back from her, that she demanded.

He has barely stopped shaking when she slides up his body, threads from the torn stockings tickling his nose, her hot, swollen pussy at the tip of his tongue: the catsuit woman demanding service, Katherine demanding pleasure, letting him drink from her. He laps like a cat until she yelps, convulses against his tongue, collapses on him. For a few seconds he rests under her body like it's a tent and he's a kid hiding from everything.

They walk into the kitchen naked and steamed from a long shower. It still isn't quite five—on an ordinary day she wouldn't even be home from work yet.

She'd intended to make him dinner, but he insists on helping like he usually does, and begins rinsing the prawns while she runs water into a crystal vase, slices an inch off the stems of the roses, arranges them. They're red for Valentine's Day; the store hadn't even bothered to order any other color.

"Put a little sugar in there," says Mike. "They're wilting."

By the time the filets are on the grill the roses are perking up.

"Look," Katherine says. "You were right about the sugar. Hey, what's that beneath the vase?"

He opens the card, reads the message, kisses her, and sets the blurry heart up against the vase. After dinner they put on jackets and take their wineglasses out to the garden.

GREEK FEVER

Anne Tourney

THERE WEREN'T MANY MEN IN MY BIBLE BELT
town who practiced Greek love. One of the
few was my father, Simon. Another was
Gabriel, who was posing as our live-in handy-
man. My father believed that Gabriel, with his
charmed hands and cock, could fix anything
from a sinking roof to a rusted libido. I didn't
believe anything about Gabriel except for one
promise he made to me. And that was only
because I had wrestled my lust into something
resembling faith.

Simon and I both had Greek fever that summer. We staggered around with Greece on the
brain, the light of Athens burning our bodies
from inside. But while Simon retreated into his
fever like a trance, I was planning to act on my
affliction.

My father didn't know that I was going to Greece with his lover.

Gabriel told me what to pack: only enough clothes for sun-bathing, drinking, and fucking. We could have done all those things in Oklahoma, but in Greece, Gabriel said, you could turn a life of lazy horniness into a personal philosophy. In the town of Pawsupsnatch (pop. 3,007) that kind of slutty behavior was just another reason for people to gossip about you.

The gossip would have turned into mass hysteria if the citizens of Pawsupsnatch had known what went on in our house. On my days off, Gabriel fucked me. Nights, he made love with my father. In the darkness, soft groans would drift from Simon's locked bedroom. During the day Gabriel and I would tear the house apart as we banged our way from room to room, knocking over furniture and denting the walls. Terrified of the Baptists who ran our local drugstore, I made secret trips to Tulsa to buy condoms by the trunkload. Considering Simon's social status as a widowed high school teacher, I assumed he was doing some smuggling himself. After twelve years of exile, the specter of sex had swooped back into our home, and that specter was pissed off and ravenous.

"It's your turn, Aggie," Gabriel would murmur, starting things off with moth-wing kisses on the nape of my neck. His lips would buzz my ears while his arms roped my waist from behind. I'd burrow back into the muscular cradle of his torso until I felt his cock rise against my asscheeks. I started wearing short, flimsy skirts so that he could get to my pussy with his fingers, cock, or tongue whenever the urge seized us. Betraying my father felt like stepping barefoot on a rusty tin can—agonizing and thrilling and toxic—but I couldn't help myself. When I came with Gabriel, mighty spasms cored my body, leaving me raving and senseless. I didn't have orgasms; I had seizures.

"I could fall in love with you in Greece," Gabriel once told me. Now that summer's long gone, I know he must have told my father the same thing.

At first I couldn't stand to hear Gabriel and Simon making love. My father's celibacy was a given, part of the deal we made when I put my life in deep freeze so that I could look after him and his feeble heart. I knew he fell in love now and then, and that since my mother died he'd given up the struggle to love women. I must have known that his abstract love for men could translate into sex. I just never thought it would happen in my mother's bed.

My mother and father had always been discreet in their passion. As a child I never wondered how they made love, but whether they "did it" at all. At the age of twenty-eight, I wasn't prepared for this variation on the primal scene: my father having sex—intense, audible sex—with another man. My mind reeled. I wrote down a list of words to describe what two naked men might get up to, then I repeated those words until they lost their mystery. *Fellatio, sodomy, cornholing, cocksucking.* The throaty male voices taunted me, their moans melting and swirling like butter and bittersweet chocolate. Rituals went on behind that door that I couldn't visualize. Did they kiss with open lips and tongues? Did they rub their erections together, like two scouts trying to start a fire with a pair of sticks? Did they suck each other's cock with juicy abandon as they lay coiled in bed, each lover's heart thumping against the other's belly? Did they mount each other, penetrate and thrust?

From the shouts and pleas that rang through the house at night, I imagined they did all that and then some.

After Gabriel had been with us for a week, my fascination took on a harder edge. In my sexual starvation, I hallucinated that Gabriel was moving on top of me, and that the moans echoing through the walls came from my own lips, not my father's. My body ignored all taboos and began responding to the urgent sounds. My fingers stabbed my cunt in time to the squeaking bedsprings. I imagined Gabriel's mouth on my pussy, my mouth on his prick, our hands roving over each other's sweat-slick skin. In the daylight, I was mortified by the idea of being aroused by my father's lovemaking. But as I witnessed Simon's growing joy, I realized that the man sharing a bed with Gabriel was no longer just my father. With Gabriel, Simon was transformed into the man he was meant to be.

That's when I let myself start wanting Gabriel. I not only wanted him, I deserved him.

He came to us in June. Tornado weather—the sky was swollen with its own miserable promise. The air in the house felt as dead as dough that won't rise. Simon and I were reading on the front porch.

As soon as Gabriel stopped his battered Dodge and stepped out, my father and I were lost. We gaped as he strolled around the car, his hips rolling in frayed blue jeans. The tips of his savannah-blond hair were painted with sweat. His white cotton T-shirt sucked lovingly at his damp chest. A halo of black gnats circled his face and throat. Suddenly I wanted more than anything to be one of those miniscule insects, sipping at that man's juice, stinging, biting, living a flash of a life in the warmth of his body.

"Morning," he said. "Need any odd jobs done around here?" His voice was like his looks: bronzed, sun-creased, lubed with honey. In the bilious daylight his eyes were snake green.

Odd jobs? In a household consisting of a lonely, horny librarian; her lonelier, hornier father; and about three thousand books (half of them written in dead languages), I'd say there were a few odd jobs to be done. Yes, sir.

My father rose and walked down the front steps. Gabriel extended his hand (God, to think where that hand would end up that summer), and my father clutched it for what seemed like forever.

"I think we could find you some work," Simon said.

Gabriel stayed for lunch. I prepared the food while my father and Gabriel got to know each other. As I carried the plates to the table, my father announced, "Gabriel just got back from Athens. Agatha, he lived there for a *year*. He speaks a bit of the *language*."

Around here, that just about made him Plato reincarnate.

Simon's face was a searchlight, casting its beam back and forth between me and Gabriel, but resting mostly on Gabriel. Barring death or disaster, there was no way this stranger was going to leave our house.

And he didn't. The first night, Gabriel made a nest for himself on our sofa. Early the next morning, while he was taking a shower, I went through his belongings. I found a few dirty socks and T-shirts and a wallet with nothing but seven dollars inside: no credit cards, no driver's license. I held a shirt up to my nose and inhaled his smell, as dizzying as a stag's musk.

The water stopped running. I flung Gabriel's things back into a heap. I thought he would appear any second, padding barefoot into the living room. His brown body would be sparkling with moisture, his hair slicked back, water clinging to his nipples and welling out of his navel and trickling down through the dark-gold tendrils that fanned his pubis.

From upstairs I heard voices: masculine, companionable, an intimate rumbling.

Love banter.

I buried my hand in the heap of quilts and felt no trace of warmth. Gabriel hadn't slept on this sofa; he'd slept in my father's bed. While I was trying to find out whether Gabriel was a traveling axe murderer, he and Simon had been showering together.

Over the nights that followed, as I lay in my bed listening to the ongoing seduction of my father, I developed a theory about Gabriel. I decided that Gabriel wasn't a man or a god, but a spirit who goes back and forth between the worlds, like the *daimon* of Greek myth. This spirit came over from Athens in some tourist's shopping bag, landed in the Bible Belt, and answered the cry for love that came from Simon and me. I never thought to analyze Gabriel's sexual preferences: whether he was gay, straight, or some hybrid of the two. From the first time I saw him, I knew that Gabriel could take on any shape you wanted.

Since my mother's death Simon had fallen in love a few times, but until Gabriel, his loves were always wildly suppressed and embarrassing, like the crumb that gets stuck in your throat in a fancy restaurant. Simon had a disturbing tendency to fall for his students. He taught history and driver's ed at the high school, but long ago he had earned a Ph.D. in classics, and he missed Ancient Greek with a pain that showed in his eyes. Every so often a male student would sidle up to him and confess that he wanted to read Sappho or Plato or Aristophanes in the original. Boom—Simon would be gone. He couldn't help it; Greek was the language he loved with.

This whole affair would have been easier if Gabriel had been one of my father's pupils, and my father had suffered with love for years, waiting for an illicit yearning to ripen into a legitimate romance when Gabriel came of age.

Nothing in our lives was ever that easy.

The first words Gabriel said to me outside of Simon's earshot were "I love girls your age." The way he let the word *love* shimmy down his tongue, it sounded more like he wanted to say *crave.*

It was late at night. Somehow, under the dense shelf of heat that had been building up all day, Simon had managed to fall asleep. Gabriel and I sat outside at the picnic table.

"How old do you think I am?"

"Stand up."

I stood.

Though I couldn't see Gabriel's eyes, I could feel him looking me up and down. My nipples stuck straight out and begged his eyes to linger.

"Eighteen?"

"I'm older than I look," I warned.

I wasn't about to admit that I was twenty-eight. My personal fashion profile hadn't changed much since I was sixteen, the year my mother died.

"Take off that top, and I could make a better guess."

I could sense Gabriel grinning in the darkness. He wasn't wearing a shirt himself. All day he'd worn nothing but a pair of cutoffs, so short that I could practically hear his balls chafing against the ragged hems. Spit crackled in my parched mouth.

"I'll take off my top if you answer a question," I said.

"What kind of question?"

"Does it matter?"

"Sure. If it's about the past, I won't answer it. And if it's about the future, I can't."

"Do you love Simon?"

Gabriel didn't answer. I longed to sit down again, to get back to the promising buzz that had risen between us. But I had to keep standing there, like a prosecutor waiting for testimony.

Then Gabriel asked me a question.

"Have you ever been to Greece?"

"No. I've never been anywhere."

"How come?"

I sat down again. "My father has heart trouble, so I've stayed close to home. After high school I got a job at the public library, and I've been there ever since."

When it came to life, I was a virgin in all but the old cock-in-the-hole sense. Hand me any book, and I could catalog it even in a coma. I could find answers to questions about everything from anthills to transvestitism, but I sometimes woke up in the middle of the night, my heart galloping, and realized that I might die before I ever experienced cunnilingus.

"You should go to Greece, Aggie. You'd see things differently there. Simon knows what I mean."

"My father's never been to Greece, either."

"Even so, he understands me. He knows what I am."

"Do you think you might fall in love with him?"

Gabriel laughed. "I told you I couldn't answer questions about the future."

"If you don't love him, why are you here?"

"I like the way he stares at me when I'm naked. I like the way he touches me. And because I'm dead broke and he's letting me stay here for free."

I should have hated Gabriel for admitting that, but I didn't. I could see him in Greece, sunbathing naked in the rubble of a ruined temple, recharging his body in the light of an amoral sun. I could see myself there, too, emptied of everything but a desire for life. Free of taking care of Simon. Free of being Agatha.

"I want to go to Greece," I said.

"Me too. But I can't get there without any money."

"I have money."

"Sure, Aggie."

"I do! Not a fortune, but enough."

"Then we'll go," Gabriel said.

I believed him.

"You promise?"

"I promise," Gabriel said. "We'll go."

"When?"

"Whenever you're ready."

I didn't decide that night. I did my research, throttled my conscience, and decided we'd leave in September. By the time my father started the new school year, Gabriel and I would be in Athens. From there we'd travel to the islands whose names I murmured in my bed at night like incantations.

It started on a Monday morning. Simon was teaching summer school. Gabriel was mowing the lawn. I stood at the kitchen sink, sipping a glass of iced coffee and inhaling the fragrance of cut grass. I should have known something was up when the lawnmower's drone stopped.

"Aggie?"

I hadn't heard Gabriel enter the kitchen. Coffee spilled down my chin. The glass fell from my hand and shattered on the floor.

"Shit!" I grabbed a dishcloth.

Gabriel was on his knees, picking up the shards of glass. I knelt beside him. A ruby bead welled out of the pad of his thumb. I grabbed his hand and stuck his thumb in my mouth.

His thumb tasted of gasoline, grass, and the dangerous tang of blood. I closed my eyes and sucked at the digit as if it were a straw to his soul. I sucked greedily, drinking his experiences, his memories, the mysteries of his past. I didn't consider what I was doing until I opened my eyes and found him staring at me. His eyes were a clear, steady gold that morning. I could almost believe he was sincere when he said, "I could fall in love with you in Greece."

"I don't know if I could fall in love with you," I said, "but I sure as hell need to fuck you."

We stampeded upstairs like wild horses, tripping over each other to get to my bedroom, where we undressed in a mute frenzy. Naked, we slowed down for some sensual investigation. His skin was moist from working outdoors; my fingertips clung softly wherever they made contact. He cupped my breasts and suckled my nipples until I thought I'd cry from the keen joy. His hard-on nudged my thigh, but he wasn't in any rush to enter me. Instead he moved down, spangling my belly with kisses. A prayer took shape in my mind.

Oh, Lord, let him eat my pussy.

Oh, Lord, let this be better than that time in the truck with Hank Maples.

Then Gabriel was turning my cunt inside out like the cuff of a velvet sleeve, and his tongue was wandering through grooves I didn't know I had, places that hadn't been touched by anything more exotic than a washcloth. Gabriel's mouth had more tricks than a whole herd of circus ponies, and that morning he showed me all of them. The flutter. The clit-flicker. The figure eight, the labial lunge, the lick-out-the-slipper, the toad-in-the-hole. He licked me into a state I've only heard drug addicts talk about: a mindless, floating ecstasy.

The floating got turbulent when he started to suck on my clit. He slid one finger inside me, then two, then three, then an impossible four. Deeper his hand plunged. My body felt paralyzed from the waist down, except for the red zone between my thighs. I was wetter than I'd ever known a woman could be, until I hit my peak and unleashed a flood. My body arched so high that I could swear I saw Greece. While Gabriel rode me to his own climax, I watched a delirious light dance against a blinding blue sky.

After he fell asleep I explored him, inch by inch. Gabriel's skin was a map. His tan formed continents of bronze and seas of dusky rose. It was not the kind of tan you get working in an oil field or fishing for crappie. His body bore the imprint of ancient light.

But Gabriel wasn't interested in ancient light. He was more concerned with drinking beer and scamming free plane tickets and screwing outdoors. Yet in that sense, Simon would have said, he was as ancient as they come: the living, breathing soul of unreasoning desire.

As a teenager I'd read my father's copy of Plato's *Symposium*. Simon worshipped those dialogues; he'd have given his life to go back to ancient Athens and sit in on that dinner party with

Socrates and his friends, drinking and laughing and talking about love. I didn't know what I was looking for in that book. Possibly a balm for the uneasiness I felt about my parents' marriage, or a map to the places Simon traveled in his mind when his body seemed so restless.

When I read what Diotima told Socrates about love and procreation, my heart turned into a sack of wet cement. Love is creative, she said; it strives for immortality in different forms. A person can create with his body—have children with women, in other words—or reach for a more exalted love and produce children of the soul. It's the second kind of love that takes you from the physical to the spiritual plane, and finally earns you a ticket to absolute beauty. I figured that second kind of love was what Simon secretly craved, what kept him awake at night, incapable of resting in my mother's bed.

I once asked my mother how she and Simon fell in love. She told me, for the hundredth time, the story of how they met. He was a graduate student in classics, she was an English major who wrote poetry, both believed secretly in fate. Once they realized that they not only shared a passion for Plato, but had been raised in the same stultifying town, they started to see the handprints of destiny everywhere they looked. That same destiny brought me into being before they were married, and between my mother's longing for respectability and my insistent need to be fed, they went back to Pawsupsnatch to take reliable jobs at the high school and public library.

But that wasn't the information I wanted. I wanted a bulletin from the world of adult love, some succinct secret to the mystery of passion.

My mother took a long time to think about this. "In the beginning," she finally said, "we thought we were two halves of the same whole. Later we realized that we simply loved the same books. And we loved you, of course."

"You mean that was *enough?*" I squealed.

My mother looked at me, bemused. "Books and a child turned out to be plenty for me," she said.

When I was sixteen, my mother died of ovarian cancer. In some dirty nook of his conscience, I think Simon saw her death as the ultimate sign that he'd failed at love. Twelve years later Gabriel came along. My father didn't seem to care who he was, or what he wanted; he just clung to Gabriel's body as if it were the last lifeboat on a desolate sea.

Maybe Simon thought that at some point down the road, he would see absolute beauty through a drifter with hazel eyes and a brass ass.

The last week of August I made dinner for Simon and Gabriel every night. Guilt stripped my appetite, but it made me want to cook like crazy. The china rattled in my hands as I set out the plates.

"Are you all right, Agatha?" Simon asked.

I saw something besides concern in my father's face—a plea, or a challenge: *Don't take him away from me,* or *Go ahead and try.*

"The catfish is terrific, Aggie."

Gabriel stuffed a forkful of fish into his mouth. He winked at me. I scowled and fussed with the napkin in my lap. An angry red lovebite marked the inside of my thigh. I had been coming when Gabriel gave me that bite. He had five fingers curved up inside my cunt like a funnel when he bit me in the softest part of my leg, and I went over the edge.

"Nothing like catfish fresh from the lake," my father said.

We had bought the filets at Shop 'n Save. Every time I lifted my fork I could smell Gabriel's musk on my hand.

That afternoon Gabriel had stolen a rowboat from the dock of someone's summer cabin, and we had rowed out to the middle of the water. We had told Simon we were going fishing, but the only pole that came out on that expedition was about eight inches long.

We sprawled in the boat, our legs intertwined, and rubbed suntan lotion into each other's skin. If anyone had been watching, they might have wondered why we applied lotion mainly to the parts of our bodies that were covered by clothes. The ruddy head of his erection was nosing its way up through the waistband of his shorts, and the seat of my skirt was slippery with my arousal. My cunt must have known, even if my brain didn't, that life was going to take a peculiar turn in the next week. How else can I explain why I ordered Gabriel to eat me right there in the boat, instead of dragging him over to the sheltering trees along the lake's shore?

He grinned. "You don't care if we attract an audience?"

I growled, spread my thighs, and pushed him down.

Leaning back, I closed my eyes against the sun. Under the tent of my skirt, Gabriel's head bobbed as he tongued me. The boat rocked crazily, shivering with the pounding of my pulse.

"You've never been this turned on," Gabriel said, his voice muffled. "You're soaking wet."

"Shut up. That tongue wasn't made for talking."

But he was right; I'd never felt such a primitive, unself-conscious lust. The rude midday sun blessed us, the sexy *waa-waa* of the insect chorus mocked my sense of propriety, and I felt as if the gods of desire were urging us on. I hooked a leg under Gabriel's thigh and applied a steady friction to his crotch. His cock, still trapped in denim, was a hot, dry bulge against my shin. Suddenly he groaned and pulled back. His spine arched. His body trembled. He bit down hard on my thigh as he thrust against my leg, spilling come onto the floor of the boat. I stared up into the sun as I climaxed, watching the light pulsate with my cunt's throb, knowing I could be bat-blind when it was over but not caring if I lost my sight.

Needless to say, the boat capsized. We had to slosh around the Shop 'n Save like drowned rats to find our dinner.

If I'd known that would be the last time Gabriel made me come, I would have made him eat me till his jaw locked. I would have made him lick my pussy till his tongue bled.

Two days before we were supposed to go to Greece, I decided to leave work early and go home. I don't know why. I'd never had a premonition before, and I'd rather not have one again.

I found Gabriel crouched on the floor beside my bed. The mattress had been pushed back. His fingers shuttled rapidly; for a second I thought he was saying the rosary. But it wasn't beads he was handling; it was my money. I kept a cash hoard under my mattress, in case the bank ever got hit by a tornado.

Gabriel looked up.

"What are you doing?"

"Getting ready for our trip."

"Bullshit."

Gabriel clambered to his feet. His backpack dangled from one shoulder.

"Leaving already?"

"Yep."

"Without me?"

He sighed.

"Have you really been to Greece?"

"Sure," he said.

But I knew that even if he was telling the truth, Gabriel hadn't been to the Greece he'd promised me. He'd been to a scorched, sweaty place, crowded with disappointed tourists who couldn't find the Greece they'd imagined, either.

"Get out of here," I said. "Take the money and get out."

It took every ounce of willpower I had to say that. A rabid animal was clawing at my gut, frantic with need. Then there was Simon. I didn't even want to think about my father's fragile heart.

Gabriel let his backpack slide off his shoulder. I knew what was coming. He walked up to me, standing so close that his chest grazed my nipples. Wary as an animal tamer, he circled me with his arms, then let his hands settle on my waist. Through the fabric of my skirt his thumbs hooked my panties and slid them down. They slithered to the floor like something small and valueless drifting into murky water.

"One more time, Aggie," he said. "Let me fuck you one more time."

I unbuttoned his fly and pulled out his cock. He was already fully erect, as if my pain had turned him on. I didn't want that sorcerer's wand anywhere close to my core. I knelt and took him in my mouth. No seduction, no ceremony, just a hard, angry suck, the kind of release he might get from a stranger in a public restroom. I gripped the root of his shaft with one hand and tugged with my lips, letting my teeth scrape his skin. He yelped; I dragged harder. His body tensed.

I usually didn't swallow, but today I wasn't about to stop. I gripped his ass and drew him deeper than I'd ever taken him, so deep that I almost choked. For a moment he was absolutely still, then he bucked and yelled. I let him shoot his bitter sap down my throat, knowing it wasn't safe, but needing to memorize the flavor of his particular evil.

"I'll never forget the way you taste," I said when I had caught my breath. "You taste like a lie. Now get out."

Leaving, Gabriel didn't make a sound. I felt him depart, though. The *daimon*. The spirit who comes and goes between worlds.

After Gabriel left, I took a walk. I ended up walking all the way out to the lake where Gabriel and I had made love. I conjured my father's face in the water and rehearsed what I would say.

Gabriel's gone.

No, Daddy—

He's not coming back.

My father would know we were heading for an emotional shitstorm if I called him "Daddy." He'd been "Simon" to me since my mother's funeral.

When I got home, the house was dark. Simon must have found out already. He was probably halfway to Texas by now, driving madly through the darkness, searching the highway for Gabriel's Dodge.

All night I waited. As soon as a respectable wedge of sunrise appeared, I called the high school principal at home.

"Simon's gone," I announced, too tired to be frantic anymore. "I'm going to need help finding him."

"Finding him? What for?"

"You mean you know where he is?"

"Why, Simon got on a plane to Athens yesterday! Took a leave of absence so he could travel in Greece. Big dream of his. I wasn't thrilled at the short notice, but with his heart, you know...Agatha?" The principal's voice rose to a dumfounded squeal. "Where the heck have you been?"

Agatha?

Was that me?

Where *had* I been? So fuck-drunk that the town gossip hadn't reached me. Once I landed at the bottom of my shock, I looked around and saw sense in the depths. My father and I had a hard time with love, but we were even worse at dealing with pain. Of *course* Simon hadn't told me he was leaving. I'd never planned to tell him about my escape, either. We'd both gotten passports, purchased tickets. The only difference was that Simon got away first.

I could fall in love with you in Greece.

Father or daughter—the object of lust hardly mattered to Gabriel, who could pound everything sacred to a pulp with his magic cock.

This is the way I justified my father's flight, after I'd talked things over with the Simon who occupies my head. If Simon hadn't gone to Greece with Gabriel, he would have gone alone. But his destination would have been a Greece of his own making, and you wouldn't see him in this world again. He'd be having dinner in some Athens of his mind, a world of immortal light. Every once in a while, a nurse would come by with a pleated paper cup and order him to swallow some pills.

Blood is thicker than water, yes. But you don't crave a glass of blood when you're dying of thirst.

Hell, I hope Simon earned his ticket to absolute beauty, grabbed Gabriel's cock, and took that gorgeous bastard with him. I have no idea where Gabriel is, but in my optimistic moments I imagine he's still with Simon, drinking retsina at some taverna by the sea and listening to my father weave his own theory of love.

BETTY

Ann Dulaney

BETTY'S NOT THE NAME SHE WAS BORN WITH, but it's served her well enough.

When you think of the name Betty, you think of a flour-dusted housewife wearing Avon cosmetics and bearing French's green-bean casserole to a block party potluck. You think of a beehived waitress in a diner that serves blue plate meatloaf and mashed potatoes to a clientele willing to plunk down two dollars and forty-nine cents in assorted change for it. You think of a member of a Gals'-Nite-Out bowling team, the kind that wears matching starched turquoise shirts that say *Bluebelles* in broad cursive across their backs. You think of a kind of dessert, or a cartoon character.

Betty is none of those things, yet in a manner of speaking she is all of those things too.

When you first see Betty, like Billy did that June evening, all you want is for her to love you back. As Betty knows perfectly well, that's pretty much all anyone needs, to be loved. When you're with her, you feel like you don't want to be anywhere else.

Betty washes her hair and sets it in rollers in the late afternoon when her day is getting started; she lets it dry out on her fire escape while she sips Folgers Instant from a brown mug. Her bedroom faces east, and the fire escape is done with its share of sun by the time Betty comes to stretch out her legs. Her eyes are retro blue, the color of an open '57 Chevrolet with fins the size of surfboards and a back seat wide enough for six or seven good-looking greasers plus herself. Betty's eyes are just that blue.

Betty's hair is her pride and joy. True, you could say she spends a little too much time at the sink with her head under the chugging faucet. The neighbors have been known to complain. It's a kind of escape when the Texas sun is making the broken glass in the street twinkle like the stars above, and the stars in the night sky are too dim what with the dust on the road. It helps to drown it all out with cool rust and minerals and a deprived sense of hearing. It's a transition from bed to being. Betty lets it rain down over her head, rinses out her hair real good, rinses all the aftershaves, the colognes, and the other man-smells off herself—and gets ready to start all over again. Watching the water collect where her bottle-blonde curls have stopped up the drain makes her forget who she is, and she'll stay there longer than you'd think a person should.

Ever done that yourself? Try it sometime. It's a lot like hanging your head over the side of a dock on a spring afternoon. You lie down on your back, tip your head over the side and let all the blood collect in your brain. It doesn't take but a minute before the sky becomes the lake, and the lake becomes the impenetrable sky. Turn your head to one side, and the lake becomes a wall right next to you, a churning, hazy, pleasant kind of wall, and you know that when it comes time to meet the Maker, you will have to pass through a wall that looks just like that. You will leave the air and the clouds and the distant shore, and dive on through. And it won't hurt a bit.

Betty grew up along Highway 183, just north of Mendoza. Her daddy used to tell her she'd better watch herself before her ass grew to be the size of the Texas panhandle. He used to panhandle her some too, until one day she packed a bag and just walked clean away. The cowboy in the first dusty pickup told her she looked just like Betty Grable, hips, hair, eyes, and all—and so the name stuck.

Now Betty looks herself up and down before going out, checks the width of her rear against marks she made on the wall, just to see whether her daddy was right. She plucks the rollers from her hair and teases it out, and sure enough—Betty is right on time.

Betty has never needed any particular man. She does just fine on her own, thank you. Her daddy taught her at least that much. If you asked her what her needs were, she couldn't tell you. She likes to bring a man to that point when he just gets inside her, like a hound dog that can't wait to rush to its bowl, and she's happy to let him have it. That's when she feels the love wash right out of these men, like someone wringing out a great big mop. All their love washes into her, and she feels she's done right by herself. She likes to hear them say her name: *Oh God, Betty, oh Betty, my God!* She likes hearing her name alongside the Creator's. Then she knows her bed is a sacred place.

But it's not real, and she knows that too.

Betty's a good girl, really. And she's clean, she picks up after herself, takes care of herself. She brushes and flosses her teeth twice a day. While the man gets dressed to leave, she takes the time to wash. For him it's a little extra show just for free, and sometimes she makes it interesting. She struts herself a little as she's bending over the sink, lets the water drip a bit down her legs maybe, or, if she knows he's really watching, she'll wring the washcloth out at her throat, so that the water runs over her tits just as sweet as you please. Then she'll turn to him, coquettish, innocent, and ask some simple question like, "So you going straight home from here, honey? You be careful out in this heat, now. Yesterday I seen a tin can melt like a stick of butter."

Betty wishes she could do something constructive with her life, just a little something, like learning how to sew or crochet, or even taking care of a potted plant. Sometimes she envies the women she sees on the streets in the afternoon, the gals going into banks or the grocer's in their little white gloves and pressed suits.

The ones with children she tries not to see. But once she helped a woman whose baby had torn away from her and was *this close* to getting hit by a big old taxicab. Between the mother's wailing and the tires and the horn and the obscenities hurling all around, Betty managed to grab hold of the little tiger, dressed head to toe in baby blue and looking like a cornflower caught in an auger. The well-heeled little mother was by then squirting out crazy tears and wanting to hand Betty a twenty-dollar bill. Betty didn't take the lady's money, but she patted the little one on the head and watched them walk away, a bit closer together than they had been before, and she wondered whether it was really true that she couldn't have children of her own.

Betty had learned one thing that day, though: her looks could stop traffic.

The men treated her as if they were her neighbors—and often they were. Betty felt comfortable around them. One of them liked to lay out his money on the dresser, patting it out with hands shaped by forty years of working the wells, and say things like, "Bitty grocery money for you there, darlin'," or "There you go, gal, you go get yourself that pretty blue thing they got in Jacobson's winder." Things he should have said to his wife before she went and died and it was all much too late.

Once she had gotten a job in the club next to her building, which was a little bit more steady. Sometimes she served drinks, or danced. The men would sway with her, with their big hands on her ass, and she would wiggle it for them. This is not to say that in public she was anything but a lady. Sometimes, when she saw someone who looked lonely or sad, she would just sit down and start talking to him. She'd say, "Shucks, I been dancing so much I could suck down the Gulf of Mexico if it weren't for the salt. Say, don't you look smart in that hat."

And that's all it took. He would turn to her gratefully, with a different kind of thirst in his eyes, and begin to drink her in. *Well now—* he might say, *How about could I get you something, Ma'am?* And she would reply with ease, and he'd smile and stick up his hand to make his order, and she'd cross her legs in just the right way, and then, before long, she might suggest they head on upstairs together.

It was nothing to her, a good deed of the day, to make a boy smile. Because that's what they became with her, boys again, once she paid them a little mind. A sixty-year-old widower, with full-grown kids that never called, could become a boy of eighteen, finding joy once more in something fresh, something comforting.

She could always see past their ages, past the physical distortions time had inflicted on them. She could always see who they really were, whether that was the man they used to be, or the man they still hoped to become, or the man they finally acceded to never becoming. These men would sit on the edge of her bed with their white legs and their pot bellies, and she would let them touch her under her satin shimmy, and let them put their fingers between her legs.

Oh, Betty would make you feel ten feet tall—or ten inches long, take your pick. Yeah, that Betty. She'd take you in and then take you in some more. Betty knew her stuff. She'd take you by the hand and set you down on that bed of hers, then she'd set herself on your lap and start opening up the buttons of your shirt real slow. And you'd have to crack some joke so she'd think you were just as comfortable as she was, even though your heart was in your throat and your hound dog prick was in your pants, seconds away from busting its leash.

And then she'd do this little strip, with you all comfortable on the pillow, and she and you would laugh together as she opened up her denim vest with the fringe hanging off it. Her bra would open in the front, and she'd wrestle that deal open in the blink of an eye—and that's exactly what you wouldn't want to do, blink. You don't want to miss a single slice of what she's serving.

Then you look at her, she's tickling you and arching her back, squeezing her arms, pushing those titties out where you can see them, and your hound dog is howling at the moon. And by the time she's got her sweet little pussy open for you—just you—all you want to do is give her every cent you got, and your coat and shoes too. "Oh my goodness!" she cries while she rides you. "Oh my! My, oh my!" Damn, Sam, take a moment and just picture that.

Yeah, who doesn't love Betty?

The men all had their stories: the first girl they ever made it with, that one touchdown, that one job offer, the day their first little one was born. They would tell her all their heartaches too, about how life had mistreated them and left them high and dry. She began to amalgamate all the stories and images until finally she saw all men as one. Every man was the same. Same age, same hopes and dreams, same fears. And when they gushed inside her, with that pinched expression that made them seem like they were in harm's way, they even looked the same, every last one of them.

She had no choice but to fall in love with them all. Every man was her lover, her husband. And she was as faithful as any wife could be, and then some. When that door closed in the wee hours of the night and she listened to some man's boots going on down the stairs, the footsteps speeding up as they got farther away, she told herself he would be back tomorrow evening. He would always come back to her, and he would call her by her first name, like any husband would. *Betty,* he would say, *how are you, old gal? Been treating yourself right? How I love to see that smile on you, Betty. Betty, you know you're my girl.* The nights were cooler, and after he left, she could finally get her rest.

But then the day would come around, and with the unkind sun, the hard dawning that she was every bit as alone as they were.

Let me tell you, Betty was the finest thing around. But once in a while the heat would get to her, you know? And she would stay home, stay in bed with cucumbers on her eyes and lemons on her elbows. If you walked by her door, you might hear the quiet wail of an old record player:

Fly the ocean in a silver plane.
See the jungle when it's wet with rain
Just remember, 'til you're home again, you belong
    to me.

And you could imagine Betty in bed smoking maybe, not a thought showing on her face. If there were a tear in her eye, it was probably just from lying on her side too long. Betty never cries. Try knocking, though, and just see if that clunky old tap doesn't start running. *Sorry, didn't hear you sugar, must have been washing my hair when you stopped by.* The sound of water covers up a lot, if you think about it. It shuts out the world and keeps the world from finding out you don't always have the inclination to smile.

It was the daytime that hurt her the most—the heat, the light. When everybody else seemed to have some place to go. The big-bright-big-bright bouncing in off the street like someone shouting out the hour. Made her thirsty, made her feel dry and used up. Made her feel old.

But on good days the men would say, *That's it, Betty,* as she drew her pretty lips over their sturdy pricks. *Mmm,* as if she hadn't had a man in years and years. *That's it girl. Good girl. Oh, you come on up here now, come see Daddy, girl.* And she would be happy again, and climb on up, and squeeze her nice titties right up against their hairy chests where they liked it, and imagine herself falling in love all over again.

Give it to me, Daddy. Do you love me, Daddy? Do you?

And then came Billy.

He was a sailor, so he was used to salt and swells and sea breezes and stars that twinkled clearly overhead. When he laid eyes on Betty for the first time, he knew right away not to let her out of his sight again, that he and she had something in common.

It was the night of the summer solstice, the longest day of the year. Summer was just getting stoked, and already the grass was burning. Betty was not having the best of days. She was out of cash, hadn't eaten since the day before, and just managed to hop herself up on a stool and ask for a glass of water.

"Lady needs something a little stronger than that," came a Gary Cooper voice from a dark corner.

Betty wheeled herself around and crossed her legs just so out of habit, wicked patent leather boots sticking together where they met. But her energy was sapped. "Water'll keep me fine 'til it rains," she told the darkness.

"Shot of rye for the lady," said the voice.

She acquiesced. "Much obliged." She took her two glasses and set them and herself down at the stranger's booth. The stranger watched her drink the water first. She guzzled it so fast she didn't even breathe.

They sat quietly for a few minutes, ignoring each other, gazing out at the empty bar. Betty fingered the little shot she still had before her. Then the stranger threw back his own glass, and so Betty did the same, without so much as a flinch. He seemed to smile at her. Betty seemed to smile back. And with a gentle cock of his head, the two of them were on their way.

He followed her home, yet lingered in her doorway, resting his hands on either side of the frame, letting his own interesting kind of heat seep into her room. Betty figured it was his cologne.

She waited just inside the threshold, in front of his big open arms that seemed to bar her exit.

"You holding up the building?" she asked.

"You fixing to invite me in?" he asked.

For the first time, Betty was self-conscious. She smiled then, her pretty smile, the one that made most men melt into their boots, and gave him a little wink.

Billy was in her place, in her apartment. After all the others that had followed her inside, he was the first that made the place seem small. He's a big man, if you ever met him. But it's not like he takes up room, he just seems to fill a place. His steps were careful, but strong. Each move suited his purpose. When at last he had followed her around enough that she finally just quit moving away, they were standing beside her bed. Billy put his hands on her waist, and her stomach growled.

"Should I go get us something?" he asked, but she shook her head. "You got good hips on you, woman," he told her.

"Betty," she replied.

He bent his head down to her, so that his cheek touched hers. Betty felt overcome with him just being there, so close but not kissing her or anything. He just was. And bit by bit, she was too. They just were.

"Betty's not my real name," she said, for the first time ever.

He moved his head so that his scratchy cheek grazed down around her chin and then came to rest upon her other cheek. His breath reached her ear, and Betty realized that he wore no cologne, but he still smelled good. "Hm," he murmured. "So what is?"

"I can't recall." And then she laughed, despite herself. Billy smiled.

"Well Betty, ain't you a tall drink of water on a hot day."

And that was the moment he chose to kiss her.

The kiss frightened her. It made her think of scenes in movies, where even though you know it's coming, it still knocks the wind out of you and your eyes go soft and your body goes limp. It looks just great on a big screen, but when it's happening to you, in your own room, and you feel like all your bones have turned to syrup, and you still feel the imprints of leather-fine lips and the scrub of stubble against your cheeks and chin long after the kiss has reached its graceful conclusion—you have every reason to fear for your life. Because movies are just movies. This was real.

The only thing she had ever wanted was something real.

"You know this is going to cost you," she tried reminding him.

"Damn right, sugar."

He looked like he wanted to kiss her again, but instead he just kept his eyes on her while he put his two heavy fingers in the center of her chest. He opened up her little denim vest, then her bra, and let her stand like that in front of him. Billy sat down on her bed then, and just gazed up at her. Something about the light in that room—it was the lamp behind his head—it gave him a funny glow, like he was blessed or something. He just looked at her, and she wondered how she could be warm and cool at the same time.

He took hold of her hips again, and kissed her belly, a gentle, humble kind of kiss. Betty heard the patent leather of her boots crinkle. His hands went under her skirt, seeking her out. He asked her, "What's this right here, you got a soft spot for me, Betty? This a secret you're keeping? Lord, you are something, ain't you."

His two fingers were deep inside her, deep inside her barren womb, making it feel very much alive. "How's that? You like that, Betty?" he asked.

And she did.

They stayed like that for quite a while, making what might have sounded like polite conversation were it not for the occasional syllable that didn't quite fit in a dictionary. Billy's thumb also knew what to do.

But soon he lay back across her bed, dragging her with him, tugging at her clothes. Her feet got tangled up in her panties, and Billy kicked them away. He pulled her up and she thought he wanted her to wrestle open the big silver buckle on his belt, but he kept pulling on her and said, "Come on way up here, Betty, put your knees right here, lemme get a good look at you."

This was unusual; this was uncharted territory. He was teasing her, taking his own sweet time, taking control yet letting her know this was still her place, that she could kick him out any time she chose. Betty wasn't sure what to make of it, but then she was thinking about windmills and sawmills and oil wells and other things that are relentless and hypnotic and make you dizzy and make you want to lie down and weep. Billy's mouth could make a person melt dead away.

Those patent leather boots were making quite a scene on their own. Billy was holding on to them, passing his hands along them, keeping her where she needed to be. Finally, Betty felt like she was ready to drop right through that wall of water that led to the Other Side. But she fought it back and rolled off him, found a pillow and her breath.

"Jesus H. Christ!" she hissed.

Billy was in no sort of a hurry. He calmly rolled over next to her and fell to stroking her body. Soft, easy strokes while he licked his lips. He kissed her again, and she felt as though she could never be whole again outside of that kiss. They wrapped their arms around each other like people in love, and their mouths made soft little noises.

Billy pulled his T-shirt over his head, and his jeans came off, and there was that profound moment of skin meeting skin. Betty felt good in his arms. Too good.

"Oh, you gotta get out of here," Betty told him, her voice choking over. "You gotta get going now. I don't like you."

"That so?" he asked, but he was kissing her throat, and she was raising her chin up so he could do it. Her skirt had bunched about her waist, and the heels of her boots were leaving cuts on the sheets. It bothered her a little. But Billy's hand was at her entrance, making sure the door was open.

And it was.

His body moved over hers and she lay weighted, suspended between him and the sagging mattress. The last thing Betty saw, as Billy's honest cock thrust home, was the image of a graceful tall ship, with four masts in full sail, leaning into the salt and spray—a tattoo where Billy's collarbones met one another. She felt the wind and water on her cheeks, and her eyes fell closed.

When she woke that first morning, with a slim shard of summer light invading the room, she was surprised to feel him get up and get dressed and to hear the door shut behind him. Not surprised that he had left, but surprised he had stayed as long as he had. Sad too. Sometime during that quick solstice night, as the earth's shadow made its closest path to the sun, she had actually begun to hope.

She had time to recall what had happened before they both fell asleep. She remembered the way Billy's cock had felt the first time he sank it deep inside her. It was as if he had said,

"Here, right here. This is where we both belong." Billy was a wall, a wall of hard flesh, and she clung to it, hung on for all she was worth. He had used his cock to get deep inside her, to communicate to her that she had nothing to fear, nothing to run from.

It didn't take but a minute before the two of them were connected by a thick glossy coating of perspiration. They glided together, the hardness of their bodies dissolving. Betty's limbs reached out, welcoming it all, every last drop of him—this man—and finally, she knew it was time to let go. She blinked back images of her daddy, images of the men she had known, all the aftershaves, all the colognes. She left the bright sky and the distant shore and dove on in.

And it didn't hurt a bit.

And afterward the two of them had kissed and washed at her sink. Billy hung his head upside down under the faucet and drank great mouthfuls of her rusty tap water, like a nomad who finally finds his desert oasis. And she did the same. And for once, she actually felt at peace. Refreshed. Slaked. Reborn.

They had taken turns washing each other until finally they were so cool and clean, there was nothing to do but get hot and dirty all over again. Billy hoisted her sweet bottom up into that sink, and the water spurted and bubbled and made funny sucking sounds and pooled on the tiles below. It sprayed up between them, soaking them both, beading on Billy's chest hairs, on Betty's lips and cheeks. They drank each other, drop by precious drop. And Billy's cock had told her again: *Here, right here. We belong just like this.*

But morning came all the same. The door closed behind him, and before long she was already starting in on washing her hair, getting ready to start again.

Start again.

The water was rushing past her ears. It dropped in warm salty freshets from the creases of her eyes. It drizzled over the narrow bridge of her nose. Her tongue caught it in the little furrow above her pretty lips, lips that were stretched tight with the excruciating attempt not to cry. She coughed. Then again, violently. Betty's hands curled about her empty belly and her chin sank to her chest. Start again, gal. Get going now. Get shakin'.

No.

She felt a strong hand on her spine and froze, briefly fearful, but then not. She waited. Then there were arms around her, and a scruffy chin on her shoulder, and a towel falling to her ankles. Billy had come back ("Got us some doughnuts.") and was helping her with her hair. Helping her wash out the suds, the cream rinse. He brought fistfuls of water down over her back, and it dripped down her sides and dropped from her breasts. And he was naked and dripping behind her, and his warm wet hands were on her thighs, pulling them open, and he was deep inside her.

So good. Who would've guessed life could be so profound, so charmed? Not Betty. And now there she was, and there they were. Coupled, encased, absorbed into one another. She felt strong legs behind hers, and arms around her, and she felt Billy's strength mix with hers, and the thirst for whatever it was she had longed for all her life finally was appeased. She sobbed. She moaned. She wept hard. He was the gentle draft, the welcome sip. It's like when you're as thirsty as you can possibly be, and then someone hands you a frosty pitcher, and you can have absolutely all you want. You drink and drink, you guzzle it right down. You don't care who's looking, and you don't take time to breathe.

With his mouth full of doughnuts, Billy read to her from the morning paper, and she combed his hair for him, and they were kind of happy, like when there's a national holiday, and so you sleep in and take a day off for a change. Then Betty put her hair up in rollers and stepped out onto the fire escape.

Betty saw the city looming large through the grill beneath her feet, saw the ripples in the fabric of her life, distortions caused by the heat, and she felt real fear for the second time that morning. Made her think life was nothing but a mirage. But then Billy put his big hands around her waist and his rough cheek down close to her and said, "That stuff you put in your hair smells like bug spray," and she was compelled to twist in his arms and wrap her legs about him and let him carry her back inside, hips, hair, rollers, and all.

Billy didn't seem to ever want to go away, and that was a quality she liked in him. For a while some of her neighbors still complained about the water running a little longer than it should. But that was the sound of Billy treating her just right. It wasn't long anyway before the water stopped churning altogether, and the pipes in Betty's small apartment lay quiet for a good long time.

CAL'S PARTY

Lisa Prosimo

FOUNDATION. EYELINER. MASCARA.

I didn't want to go to the party.

Blush. Lipstick.

The towel I was wearing fell to the floor.
I bent to pick it up, and my right temple
throbbed.

"Shit."

"You almost ready, Abby? It's getting late."

Steve stood in the doorway. His eyes swept
across my naked body. He smiled. "Wear that
black dress. The one that stretches and stops
here." He tapped his leg, midthigh. "And your
'fuck me' shoes. The ones with the strap at the
ankle."

"Steve...I have a headache. I really don't feel
like—"

He walked into the room, stood behind me,

and wrapped his arms across my waist. His breath tickled my ear. "Hey, no problem," he whispered. "I've got just the right medicine for that. One hit and your headache's gone." He stuck his tongue in my ear and licked lightly.

I pulled away and turned to face him. His face was flushed, his eyes bright. "I don't want any 'medicine,' Steve. Though I see you've taken some."

"One line. A skinny, tiny little line. Cal gave me some."

"What a pal."

Steve walked to the closet and pulled the black dress off its hanger. He brought it to me. "Come on, Abby. I don't want to make the grand entrance." I took the dress, slipped it over my head, and pulled it down. The fabric settled over the contours of my body. "Oh, yeah. Fabulous."

I couldn't wait to swallow a Motrin.

The house was crowded, as usual. As usual, the music was too loud, the lights too bright, the food table too perfect. Plump, pink shrimp covered two large cones in a flawless symmetrical pattern, flowers of puff pastry adorned the face of each round of Brie. Waiters in tight black T-shirts and snug white shorts carried trays of champagne. Tonight's theme: muscled blonds with chiseled features, none under six feet tall. Each wore a small diamond on his left earlobe—a gift from the host, no doubt. Cal was always generous with his waiters.

"Abby! Steve!" Cal moved toward us, his arms flung wide, his heavy rump bouncing with each step. He was blond, too. Last time I'd seen him, he had red hair. He'd called it his "Irish Queen" look. The stud in his left ear was bigger than the waiters'. "Oh, my god, don't you look gorgeous, Abby! It's been ages. I've really missed you, girl! Kiss, kiss."

"Kiss, kiss back at you," I said.

Cal turned and enveloped Steve in a crushing bear hug. "And you, you gorgeous thing." He let go of Steve and pulled a handkerchief from his breast pocket, mopped his brow, and caught the drip from his nose. He sniffed. "So, how are you two lovebirds?"

"We're great," Steve said. "Wonderful, in fact." He smiled at me. I smiled back.

"Good, good. Well...enjoy!" He bounced away, his arms outstretched to the newest arrivals.

"I'm starved," Steve said. "Let's get something to eat."

"I'm not all that hungry."

Steve shrugged. "Okay. I'll get something, and you can mingle."

One of the blond boys carrying a full tray stopped in front of me. I took two flutes of champagne from him and walked into the great room. In one corner, a quartet banged out an A.M. hit. My temple banged along. I settled onto one of the over-stuffed sofas and downed the first glass of champagne, and then sipped the second. People I'd met before nodded and smiled, but there were a lot of people I'd never seen. Still, it was Cal's typical crowd, made up of stylish men and women, all possessing a type of eclectic beauty. These parties always gave me the feeling that I was trapped on some opulent soundstage with a bunch of extras from Central Casting. Five years ago, when I'd first met Cal, I found that aspect attractive. I was a girl from Idaho who had come to Hollywood, sure my talents and good looks would land me a plum role in a blockbuster movie. After all, in Boise I had been a star. I even had a college degree. Who could resist?

Lots of people resisted.

A waiter offered me another glass of champagne. I took it.

"Abby."

I looked up. Lloyd Thomas smiled down at me.

"It's been a long time, Abby. You look wonderful."

Lloyd looked wonderful, too, but I didn't say so. He sat down, took my hand, turned it over, and kissed my palm.

"How's...Steve, is it?"

"Yes. Fine, thank you."

"He's the fellow who builds things, right?"

"Yes. He and his brother have a construction company. And you?"

He smiled. "Still selling junk bonds."

"Ah...I see. Better be careful."

"I'm always careful, Abby." He smiled.

A tall blonde walked over. "Lloyd? Did you want to get something to eat?" she asked.

Lloyd introduced us. Her name was Jenny. Jenny was happy to make my acquaintance, she said. After a few moments of meaningless chatter, Lloyd and Jenny headed for the food table in the other room.

Lloyd Thomas had been my first man, so to speak. He took me to my premier party at Cal's. I met him while working as a temp at his brokerage firm. At first, Cal's parties were fun. Sometimes they lasted a weekend, sometimes longer. One room at the back of an old house in Boyle Heights wasn't exactly my idea of home, so I often stayed at Cal's, breaking several dozen eggs to feed Cal and his boys breakfast. While I cooked, I answered an endless stream of calls that came in from his friends and various boy lovers. I could stay as long as I wanted if I promised not to get in his way, and I made sure I didn't. Why wouldn't I want to stay? There was always plenty of food and drink, plus an abundant supply of nose candy. I remember once, in a mild rush of drugs, roving hands, and tongues, being struck by the notion that I had to be one of the luckiest girls alive. That enlightenment came at the same moment I did.

The throbbing in my temple increased, helped along by the champagne. I walked out to the patio and sat in one of the chairs and watched several men and women play in the hot tub. One of the men was sitting outside the tub, his feet in the water. A head belonging to a brunette bobbed up and down between his legs. She held his penis inside her lips and slid them down over his shaft slowly, until it disappeared. She did it without the use of her hands, and I had to admire her expertise. I couldn't do it that way. She'd obviously trained the muscles in her face and neck to do all the work. The man moaned. I yawned.

When Steve had come home the night before and told me Cal had invited him to a party, I had been shocked. "So?" I had said. He had shrugged, said he thought we ought to go. I'd asked him why. No reason, he'd said. Just for the fun of it.

Cal's parties stopped being fun for me long before I stopped going. I don't know what happened, but over time, I found myself needing more and more stimulation just to be able to get into them. More booze, more coke, more bodies. It just got to be too much. One night, I extricated my limbs from a tangle of flesh and pulled myself off the king-sized playbed, much to the chagrin of the man who was doing me. "Hey," he yelled. "Where the hell are you going?" I didn't look back, not even sure the clothes I'd picked up off the floor were mine.

After I dressed and went into the living room I realized I didn't have any place to go. Unless it was back to that room in Boyle Heights. Just the thought made me shudder.

That's the night I met Steve. I saw him first through the

French doors, hunched over, throwing up all over Cal's prize-winning roses. When he came into the room, he was shaky and sweaty and had to be helped to a chair. I went into the bathroom, got a glass of water, made him drink the whole thing, and then wiped his face and neck with a towel. He thanked me over and over and called me Florence Nightingale. I laughed. He said this was his first party. I wasn't sure just how much "partying" he had done before he got sick, and I didn't ask. He didn't ask me any questions, either.

That was the start of us. I went home with Steve and hadn't been back to the room in Boyle Heights, or to another party.

It felt strange to be back. I'd changed in the last six months; I was falling in love with a guy who built room additions, and it felt good. Lately, I found myself lingering in grocery stores, pondering the superiority of Huggies over Luvs disposable diapers.

When I told Steve I didn't want to go to Cal's party, didn't want to be with those people, he got upset. "Why not?" he said. "Those people were your friends. What's the big deal if we spend a few hours with them?"

"Why do we need to?"

"Damn it, Abby. I work twelve hours a day to keep this business going. Is it a crime to want to relax?"

One of the men in the hot tub pulled himself out of the water and walked over to me. His naked body glistened in the moonlight. "I've been watching you watching them," he said. "Why don't you join us in the tub, gorgeous?"

"Thanks anyway, but I've given up meat for Lent."

He laughed. "Suit yourself. But, if you change your mind, you know where to find me."

The great room was less crowded when I went back inside, which meant that assignations had been made and people had retired to the various rooms to play out their intentions. Cal had a rule about keeping the sexual activity confined to the bedrooms and the pool area.

Steve wasn't in the bar or around the food table. I went into the library, but he wasn't there, either. The basement had been converted into a movie theater, and many of Cal's guests liked to go down to watch the latest films. Cal had them before they hit the theaters.

Steve was climbing up the stairs from the theater just as I was about to go down.

"Abby, baby! I was coming to find you." His skin was flushed and his eyes held that wild look I'd so often seen in my own. He had done a lot of coke. I smelled liquor on his breath. The couple behind him was still climbing when he stopped to talk to me, and the girl slammed into his back. Steve turned around and they both giggled. I moved out of the way, and they followed me into the hall. "Baby, I want you to meet my friends. This is…" He giggled again.

"Darla," said the girl.

"Yeah, Darla. And this is…Tom?"

"That's right," Tom said. "Nice to meet you, Abby. Steve's been telling us all about you."

Tom didn't look coked out like his girlfriend, or Steve, did. I nodded my greeting.

"Sweetheart," said Steve, "did I tell you how much I love you and how great I think you are?" He grabbed me around the waist and pulled me to him. His sloppy kiss landed on my chin. I pulled away.

"I think we'd better go home, Steve. You need to come down, sleep it off."

"Bullshit. I feel great, baby. Lots of energy."

Behind him, Darla stifled a giggle. I dropped my voice. "Please, Steve."

His eyes grew dark and his jaw tightened. He wrapped his fingers around my upper arm and pulled me further down the hall, away from his newfound friends.

"Listen, Abby. I'm having a good time. I want to continue having a good time. With them."

I didn't say anything.

"Goddammit, Abby!" His fingers tightened on my arm. "This is fun, that's all. Just a good time."

He was angry, his voice harsh, but there was also a begging quality to it. He sounded like a little kid trying to convince a parent to let him have his way. We'd never discussed Cal's house or his parties after that night we first met. I didn't know if Steve had ever done this kind of scene. I did know he wasn't used to snorting this much coke.

It wasn't as if I'd forgotten what it was like: the coke coursing through my veins making me feel invincible; the freedom inside these impeccable, tastefully decorated walls; the beauty and sensuality of the company filling up my senses; the need to exhaust my energies in every act of pleasure imaginable.

I looked into Steve's eyes. "Is it that important to you? Is it what you really want?"

He let go of my arm. "Yes, Abby. Right here and now, it's what I really want."

Steve's request didn't make me jealous. Instead, I felt empty, defeated. "Okay," I said, and walked past him to join Darla and Tom at the end of the hall.

"Why don't you all follow me? I know every room in this house."

"You have beautiful hair," Darla said as she moved it out of the way so that I could snort the lines Tom had set up for me. The coke burned my passages, but it got rid of my headache instantly. "You're very beautiful, Abby."

I leaned back and appraised Darla. "So are you."

She smiled, got up, and began to pull her dress over her head. Static electricity crackled as the fabric passed over her long blonde hair, leaving strands of it sticking up into the air. It struck me as funny and I giggled. Darla smoothed her hair down while Tom stood behind her and undid the clasp on her bra. The lace fell away, and he cupped her breasts and rubbed them lightly. She sank back into him, her eyes closed. He whispered in her ear and she smiled, opened her eyes, and walked back to me. Darla leaned over and lightly kissed me on the lips. I looked at Steve. He was taking off his clothes, but watching Darla and me intently. She kissed me again, this time parting my lips with her tongue. I closed my eyes, my mouth opened, and I took in her tongue, sucked at it, concentrating on the feeling I got from its moist softness, a feeling made sharper by the drug racing through my blood. Tom walked up and grabbed Darla's hips. He peeled her panties back and pulled them off. "Why don't we move to the bed?" Darla whispered.

"Sure." I stood up and Darla helped me remove my dress.

Steve took the pillows off the bed, stripped down the blankets, and leaned back against the headboard, his legs tucked under him. I lay flat on my back, my head not far from his lap. He caressed my breasts as Darla's tongue worked the flesh between my midriff and knees. Tiny grunts of pleasure came out of her mouth. Tom, kneeling behind, caressed her and himself as he watched, every few seconds voicing his approval, spurring her on. I looked up into Steve's droopy, lust-laden eyes, felt the excitement he got from watching us jut into the top of my head. "Does this do it for you, baby?" I asked.

"Oh, yeah, Abby. Yeah."

It's funny how the body takes over, how you can suspend your mind and communicate using only your senses. A clitoris doesn't know or care whose tongue or fingers manipulate it. When the hunger peaks and the nerve endings scream, nothing matters.

I gauged time by my thirst and the burning in my nostrils. How much water did I sip? How many lines did I snort? We were all thoroughly immersed in the scene, greedy and sweaty and playing it out, letting the desire rise and fall, rise and fall. At one point, Darla cried out, "What do you think I am, a sex machine?"

"Do you feel like a sex machine?" Tom asked.

"Not nearly enough, goddammit!" The three of them laughed, Steve loudest of all. His laughter found its way past the heat and pleasure that rippled across my body, leaving me cold. "Do you feel like a sex machine, too, Steve?"

"Yeah. And my engine's in fine form." They laughed again.

I sat up, leaned forward on my knees, and brought my face up close to his. "How about letting your vehicle cover some new ground?" I whispered, and then kissed him on the cheek.

"We pretty much covered all of it, baby."

"Not all. You two guys haven't covered all of it." I leaned back, but kept my eyes glued to Steve's. He looked puzzled, but only for a moment, and then attempted a laugh, but it didn't quite make it out of his mouth. I looked at Tom.

"You're kidding, right?" he asked.

Darla yelled, "Hey, what's going on? You guys keeping secrets from me? What are you talking about?" I slid over to Darla and whispered in her ear. Her eyes got wide, and then she threw her head back and laughed. "Yes! You bet. I'd love to see that!"

"You're crazy, Abby," Steve said.

Darla jumped up and down on her knees. "Why is it crazy? I think it's a great idea." She turned to Tom. "Don't you think it's a great idea, Tom?"

Tom glanced at Steve. "Shut up, Darla. Joke's over."

Darla's face got red. She pushed her fist into Tom's shoulder. "A joke, huh? Since when?"

"Darla, I told you to shut up."

Darla ignored him. "He enjoys it. Likes a guy to lick his pee-pee. When was the last time? Six weeks ago?" She reached between his legs and fondled him.

"Why don't we knock off this bullshit?" Steve said. "You know I'm not interested, Abby."

"Really? I don't know anything of the kind. I don't know that much about you at all, do I?"

"Abby—"

"Look at Tom. See how easily he gets hard? Just like you." I grasped Steve's penis and brought my lips up close. I licked the glans, and he hardened against my tongue. I looked up at him, still holding him in my hand. "This is for fun, Steve. It's all for fun. You wanted the experience. Have it. All of it."

"This is enough for me, baby," he said, moving against my fingers.

I let go. "It's not enough for me. I want to watch you with a guy. The way you watched me with Darla. That's what I want."

Darla slid her hand up and down Tom's penis. "Me, too, Tommy. I want to watch, too," she crooned in a baby's voice. "You know you like it."

Tom looked down at Darla's hand moving swiftly against him. He was breathing hard. "Forget it, baby. The guy's not into it. Let's you and me play." He gently pushed Darla's head down into his lap, and she opened her mouth to receive him. He groaned.

I kept my mouth busy, too, working Steve until he sighed with pleasure. I looked up, past Steve, into Darla's eyes, sending her my challenge. After a few moments, she nodded.

Soon, both men were rocking in a steady rhythm; they seemed to be in sync, at the same place, reaching for the same goal. I shot a glance in Darla's direction; she pulled her mouth off Tom and crawled over to Steve and me, ignoring Tom's complaint. I let Steve slip from my mouth and when he protested, I covered his lips with mine. Darla began kissing him on the chest and running her hands over his belly. He tried to push her hand between his legs, but she wouldn't let him. She bit his nipples and slid her fingers over his groin, deliberately missing his penis. He moaned, sucked harder on my tongue. I pulled away and looked at Tom. He was pulling on his penis, his mouth hanging open. "Come here," I said. He crawled over to us on his hands and knees. "Touch him."

Steve made an attempt to object, but I covered his mouth with mine again. He relaxed against me at the same moment that Tom's head brushed past my belly and dove between Steve's legs. For a moment, Steve's body stiffened, and then he relaxed again. Darla sustained her licking and pinching; I kept the kiss going, moved it from his lips to his neck, to the nipple free of Darla's mouth, all the way down to where Tom's lips smacked against his hardened flesh. My tongue joined Tom's, and together we licked and sucked until Steve began to pant.

I knew his body so well. Knew how much he could take,

what would speed him up or slow him down, finish him or keep him teetering on the edge. The measure of his breath, the depth of his sighs, the whimper stuck in his throat let me know when to pull back, to sustain his pleasure or increase his agony. My hands squeezed, fingers pinched, held back his flood until the blood beating in his veins calmed, and when it did, Tom came at him, his mouth an instrument of pleasant torment, forcing Steve to start the ascent again. Above us, Darla gently kissed his face, his eyes, licked his ears, sucked at his chin while her painted fingernails flicked the tip of each nipple.

Together, we teased Steve into a frenzy; his features became blurred from sweat pouring from his body. He thrashed about, seeking release, but we held him with the power of our circling tongues, the canopy of our curved torsos, the strength of our determined limbs. Pinned beneath us clutching blindly, spasmodically, he cried out, begged us to bring him off, but we answered him with lips that grazed his penis, palms that buffed his thighs, fingers that hummed against his anus.

"Enough," he shouted, "enough!" But we didn't stop, in fact, increased the tempo until his breaths became shorter, his movements faster, and I feared that he would waste himself just to be done with our exquisite torture. I signaled Darla and Tom to stop what they were doing, pressed close to Steve's steamy body, and licked the sweat from his brow.

He turned his head to look at me. "God, Abby, you're driving me crazy!"

"Tell me again how much you love me, Steve," I whispered into his ear.

"I do...Fuck me, Abby..."

"I want you to feel as much pleasure as you can, baby. I want you to climb the highest mountain before I push you off."

"Push me off now, Abby...I'm so ready to be pushed off the goddamned mountain!"

"All right, baby. My way?"

"Any way, Abby.... Please."

I nodded and slipped off the bed, tiptoed to the closet, and reached inside. One could always count on Cal to keep a plentiful supply of restraints for anyone interested in such devices. These particular ropes were made of strong, yet soft, leather.

I trailed the leather over Steve's chest and engorged penis. He shuddered. "I want to go for a ride," I said. "You, in the dark. All right, baby?" I didn't wait for his answer, but leaned over and tongued him deeply. He attempted to reach up to wrap his arms around me, but his body shook, weakened by desire. "A long, hard ride into an exploding sunset."

He sighed.

Darla and Tom had been quietly watching our exchange. I tossed one of the leather ties to Tom, and he secured Steve's left arm to the headboard while Darla helped me with his other arm. Then I put the blindfold on him. "In the dark," I repeated. "You love it in the dark, don't you?"

He murmured his answer as I straddled him, rubbing my wet sex slowly over his chest, inching up in increments until I reached his mouth. His tongue entered me and I moved my hips upward, letting it slide out. Then, as if in slow motion, I came back down until only the tip of his tongue was inside. I hovered there for a moment, while he strained his neck, trying to gain access to more of me. I let him in, but only a fraction of an inch, and then backed off. He cried out, yelled my name in protest, and I promised that soon he would experience the most astounding orgasm of his life.

Steve pulled against his restraints, his fingers curling, clawing the air, and he raised his legs in an attempt to grab me. There was no way he could. I kept my sex dancing over his mouth, but never close enough to satisfy his hunger. As I moved, I fondled my breasts and held Tom's eyes. He watched me, tugged at his penis until it was long and hard, and then murmured for Darla to get on her knees.

"No!" I scrambled off Steve, grabbed Darla's panties from the floor, and stuffed them into his mouth. Then I tossed the remaining ties to Tom and told him to turn Steve over. He hesitated. I looked at Darla. She had taken hold of my excitement. Her eyes wide, her breath labored, she stepped up to Tom, picked up the ties, and slapped them across his face. "Yes!" she shouted. "Yes!" A signal passed between them. Tom reached across her and grabbed Steve's leg, pulled it tight, and tugged. There was sufficient slack in his wrist ties to twist them so that they gave enough to let us turn his body over.

Behind the gag, he screamed. He kicked at us, making it difficult to keep hold of his legs, but after a while we managed to secure both legs to the footboard.

Exhausted, I stood back and surveyed the X Steve's body made across the bed, his muscles pulled taut and shiny with sweat. Seeing him spread-eagled, unable to move, stirred a desire within me I didn't know I possessed. I climbed onto his back, pressed myself to his body, my arms spread over his, my legs splayed like his. "I dreamed a different dream, but it didn't come true."

On my knees between his legs, I bent to kiss the cheeks of his ass, to gently bite and lick them. My hand caressed his scrotum lightly. Steve still fought, thrashing against the sweat-soaked sheet, but I kept up my kisses, kept petting his heavy sack lightly with my fingers until his hips rolled into the mattress and his penis was shiny with his juice. His cries behind the gag had quieted to soft moans. I spread his cheeks and wet my finger, pressed lightly on the folds of puckered skin, and stroked his opening, gently escalating the rhythm until his body opened to the pleasure.

I looked back to see Darla and Tom on the floor, her mouth closed over him, drawing at him heartily. He grabbed her head and pulled until all I could see were his balls touching her chin. "Darla!" At the harsh tone of my voice, she drew her mouth away. Darla looked up at Tom. "Fuck him," she said. He didn't answer. "Go on...fuck him in his gorgeous virgin ass, Tom. His tight, beautiful ass."

Tom licked his lips, pulled himself off the floor, and walked over to the bed. He lifted his penis, slick with Darla's saliva, and motioned for me to move out of the way. I slipped off the bed and Tom took my place.

Steve lay very still—in terror or anticipation, I couldn't tell. Tom rubbed himself along the crack of Steve's ass, and I yanked the panties out of his mouth. "Don't do this, Abby," he said. His eyes pleaded with me, the fear in them unmistakable. Still, his ass quivered each time Tom rimmed his opening. Yes, I thought, it's funny how the body takes over. His own balls and cock were full. I knew what it was he feared.

"Ram it into him!"

Tom burrowed into Steve's body with several powerful thrusts. He gritted his teeth and cried out as he worked himself deeper and deeper inside Steve's ass. "Ah...so sweet, so sweet," he mumbled, lost in the sensation of this brand of fucking.

"God! He's something, isn't he? I love when he gets going like this!" said Darla.

Steve howled, bucked backward into Tom, his cries a mixture of pain and pleasure. I spread my legs and slipped my fingers over my swollen clit.

Tom pulled back, slid his penis nearly all the way out, and then rammed into Steve with such force that his eyes rolled back in his head. He grasped Steve's hips and fucked him with increasing fervor.

The man who had earlier said he loved me, told me how great he thought I was, screamed my name, flung filthy epithets at me as the evidence of his gratification splattered against the sheet. At the same time, the confirmation of mine gushed against my fingers. When it was over, Tom slipped to the floor and lay panting on the rug. Steve pressed his face into the mattress. His shoulders shook as he wept.

Soft breath against my ear broke my concentration. Darla held me around the waist and fondled my breasts. I pulled my gaze off Steve and pushed her away.

"Hey—"

"Get out," I screamed. "Both of you. Get the hell out!"

"Fucking maniac," Darla said, but she scurried around gathering their fallen garments. I kicked Tom in his side, told him to get up and get out. He rolled over and pulled himself up. He didn't say a word.

Kneeling at the head of the bed, I ran my fingers through Steve's hair, massaged the muscles in his neck, and crooned soothing words to him. Inside the bathroom, Tom and Darla hurried into their clothes. I stopped paying attention and didn't hear them leave.

Steve continued to whimper, and I cried, too, my face pressed up against his, our tears mingling together. I kept smoothing his hair, murmuring softly into his ear until his body relaxed and he fell asleep. He lay like a rock, snoring soundly, oblivious as

I removed the straps and rubbed his ankles and wrists. Light filtered around the edges of the heavy drapes at the windows, announcing a new day.

Later, I stood at the foot of the bed, watching Steve sleep. In another part of the house, Cal and his boys would be waking up, waiting to be served breakfast. I wondered who would be doing the cooking. I'd ask Cal if he'd let me crack the eggs, and then I'd ask him if he really, really missed me.

RIDING THE RAILS

Sacchi Green

"HEY, JO! JOSIE BENOIT!" A VOICE FROM MY past, fitting all too well with the setting: the Springfield train station, visible through foggy windows and blowing snow. I'd gone to college not far from here, and so had that voice's owner.

"If it isn't Miss Theresa," I grunted, and kept on tugging at the sheepskin jacket caught behind a suitcase on the overhead rack.

"I never forget an ass," Terry said pointedly, casing mine as I reached upward.

"Sure as hell wouldn't have known yours." My jacket finally yielded. I tossed it over the voluptuous décolletage of my seated companion. A few minutes earlier Yasmin had been whining about being cold. Now, of course, for a new audience, she shrugged off the covering with an enthusiasm that threatened to shrug off her low-cut silk blouse as well. Not that it had been doing much to veil her pouting nipples.

Terry, brushing snow off her shoulders and shaking it from her hair, rightly accepted my remark as a compliment. Fourteen years ago she'd been on the lumpy side; now she was buff, and all style. Sandy hair lightened, cropped, waxed just right; multiple piercings on the left ear and eyebrow, giving her face a rakish slant; studded black leather cut to make the best of the work she'd done on her body. I'd have felt mundane, with my straight black hair twisted up into a utilitarian knot and my brown uniform, not ironed all that well since Katzi had taken off—if I ever gave a damn about appearances. Which might have had something to do with why Katzi took off. Which had a whole lot to do with why I hadn't gotten laid in two months and wasn't finding it easy to resist Yasmin's efforts.

"You just get on?" Terry asked. "Didn't see you in the station. No way I could have overlooked your little friend." Her eyes raked Yasmin, who practically squirmed with delight.

"Been on since White River Junction," I said shortly. It was more than clear that Terry expected an introduction. "Yasmin, Terry O'Brian. We were in college together. Terry, Princess Yasmin, fourth wife of the Sultan of Isbani." It was some satisfaction to see Terry's jaw drop for an instant before her suave butch facade resurfaced.

"Ooh, Terry!" Yasmin warbled, jiggling provocatively. "I didn't know Sergeant Jo had such nice friends!"

"The princess somehow...missed...leaving New Hampshire with her husband's entourage," I said. "They'd been visiting her stepson at Dartmouth. I'm escorting her to D.C. to meet them." As far as I could tell, it had been a combination of

Yasmin's laziness and the head wife's hatred that had culminated in her missing the limo caravan, and her absence going unnoticed until too late. I was developing a good deal of sympathy for the head wife.

"The weather's too risky for flying or driving," I added, "but the train should make it through. Not supposed to be much snow south of Connecticut."

"Well, now," Terry said, sliding into the seat facing Yasmin. "I'll be happy to share security duty as far as New York."

"Don't get too happy." I sat down beside my charge. There were suddenly more limbs between the seats than would comfortably fit; I tried to let my long legs stretch into the aisle, but that tilted my ass too close to Yasmin, who wriggled appreciatively against my holster. I straightened up. "This is official business. The last thing I need is an international incident."

I wondered why the hell I hadn't told Terry to fuck off in the first place. Did I hope she'd distract Yasmin enough to take off some of the pressure? The tension had been building all morning. Even the rhythm of the train had been driving me toward the edge, with its subtle, insistent vibration. Or maybe it was just that the little bitch was too damned good at the game and too clearly driven by spite. I don't have to like a tease to call her on it; if I hadn't been on the job I'd have given Yasmin more than she knew she was asking for, and if it left my conscience a bit scuffed, what the hell—other parts of me would have earned a fine, lingering glow.

But I was on duty, and she was doubly untouchable, and knew it. Seven more hours of this was going to be a particularly interesting version of Hell.

"Keep it professional, Jo," Lieutenant Willey had said. "This one's a real handful."

"I noticed," I'd told her. Several handfuls, in fact, in all the right places, with all the right moves. "Don't worry. I know better than to fuck the sheep I'm herding." She should have slapped me down for that, but instead she rolled her eyes toward the door, and I saw, too late, that the troublesome sheep had just come in. No chance she hadn't heard me. Anger sparked with interest sharpened her kittenish face, segueing into challenge as she looked me up and down.

"You're off to a great start," the lieutenant said dryly. "Just bear in mind that the Sultan wants her back 'untouched,' and I'd just as soon not have to argue the semantics of that with the State Department." Something in her usually impassive expression made me wonder whether our charge had come on to her. If so, I was sure sorry I'd missed it.

By the time the train crossed from Vermont into Massachusetts, I realized Yasmin would come on to any available pair of trousers, with no discrimination as to what filled them. Even the professionally affable conductor got flustered when she rubbed up against him in passing, and she had a threesome of college boys so interested that I'd made the mistake of putting a proprietary arm around her shoulders and shooting them my best dyke-cop look as I yanked her back to our seats. The look worked fine, but it encouraged Yasmin to renew her attack on me.

"Ow!" she yelped when I tightened my grip on a hand that kept going where it had no business. "Why you are so mean to Yasmin?" Her coquettish pout left me cold, but a definite heat was building where her hand had trailed over my ass and nudged between my thighs. She knew I wasn't impervious.

"Let's just stick to the business of getting you back to your husband," I said neutrally, aware of the continuing interest of the college kids three seats back. The less drama here the better.

"Why do you worry? He can't order them to cut off your balls, the way they did to Haroun just for looking."

"Right, and you can't yank me around by them, either," I muttered. The glitter of pleasurable recollection in her eyes was nauseating. What little I'd read about female genital mutilation flashed through my mind, and for a few minutes I really *was* impervious to her charms.

Terry's company, whatever the complications, might be better than being alone with Yasmin—unless my competitive instincts reared up and made it all exponentially worse.

Terry could have been reading my mind. "Gee, Jo," she said, "remember the last time you introduced me to one of your little friends?" Her grin was demonic.

"How could I forget? You healed up pretty well, though." I stared pointedly at the scar running under her pierced eyebrow.

"Nothing like a dueling scar to intrigue the ladies," Terry said cheerfully. "You seem to have found a good dentist."

"You bet." I flashed what Katzi used to call my alpha bitch grin.

Yasmin was practically frothing with excitement, jiggling her assets and leaning toward Terry to offer an in-depth view of her cleavage and a whiff of her sensuous perfume. When she balanced herself with a far-from-accidental hand high on my thigh, I realized that all I'd done was set her up to play us off against each other.

"So, Terry," I said, firmly removing the fingers trying to make their way toward my treacherously responsive crotch, "What are you up to these days? Still living in the area?"

"I'm a paralegal in Northampton," she said. "Going to

law school nights." Her gaze lingered on my badge, and for a rare instant I was hyperconscious of the breast underneath it. "Funny how we both got onto the straight side of the law."

"No kidding," I said. "I heard that anything goes in Hamp these days, but can you go to court rigged out like that?"

"I could, but I don't." I was pleasantly surprised to see a bit of a flush rise from her neck to her jawline. "I'm on my way to New York to do a reading at a bookstore in the East Village."

"You're a writer?" My surprise was hardly flattering, and her jaw tightened, as the flush extended all the way to her hairline.

"On the side, yeah," she said brusquely. "Doesn't pay much, but the fringe benefits can be outstanding."

"Hey, I'll just bet they are, if the stories match the getup! Erotica groupies, huh?"

Terry caught the new respect in my voice and relaxed. She let her legs splay apart. I'd already noticed she was packing; now Yasmin stared at the huge bulge stretching the black leather pants along the right thigh, and her kewpie-doll mouth formed an awe-struck O.

"Loaded for bear, aren't we," I said. "Ah, the literary life. I'll have to check out some of your stuff—maybe get you to autograph a book." I was more than half serious. She started to grin, and then an odd, startled look swept over her face. I glanced down and saw Yasmin's stockinged foot nudging against the straining black leather.

It wasn't a big enough deal to account for my first raging impulse to break Yasmin's leg. I managed to suppress it, but by then everything seemed to be happening in slow motion. Terry's presence was definitely making things worse. Much worse.

Yasmin pulled her silk skirt up so that we could get the

full benefit of the shapely leg extended between the seats and the toes caressing the leather-sheathed cock. Then she applied enough force so that Terry caught her breath and automatically shifted her hips to get the most benefit; I felt the pressure as if she were prodding my own clit. But all I was packing was a gun, and that was on my hip.

I know from experience that you don't get the optimum angle the way Yasmin was working. But you can get damned close. Katzi used to tease me like that in restaurants, her leg up under the table, her foot in my lap, her eyes gleaming wickedly as she watched me struggle not to make the kind of sounds you can't make in public. She knew I wouldn't let myself come, because I just can't manage it without making a lot of noise.

The train wasn't crowded, but it was public. Terry's head was thrown back, her eyes glazing over, her hands gripping the seat. I was afraid my breathing was even louder than hers, and damned sure my cunt was just as hot. I had to stop the little bitch, but I was afraid if I touched her I'd do serious damage.

Then Yasmin, with a sly sidelong glance at me, unbuttoned her blouse and spread it open. As she fondled her breasts, her rosy nipples, which had thrust against the silky fabric all morning as though permanently engorged, grew even fuller and harder. Her torso undulated as her butt squirmed against the seat. Her foot was still working Terry's equipment, but her focus had shifted.

"God *damn!*" whispered Terry. Or maybe it was me. Yasmin turned slightly and leaned toward me, still working her flesh, offering it to me, watching my reaction with half-closed eyes, her little pink tongue moving over her full upper lip. The tantalizing effect of her perfume was magnified by the musk of three aroused bodies.

"We're coming into Hartford." Terry's strangled words sounded far away. "We'll be at the station any minute!"

Yasmin's voice, soft, taunting, so close that I felt her breath on my throat, echoed through my head. "Sergeant Jo doesn't have the balls to fuck a sheep!"

I snapped.

I lunged.

With my right hand I clamped her wrists together above her head. With my left arm across her windpipe I pinned her to the seat back. I leaned over her, one knee between her thighs. Then I dropped my hands to her shoulders and shook her so hard that her head bobbled and her tits jiggled against my shirt front and the hard edges of my badge.

A strong hand grabbed my shoulder and yanked me back. When I resisted, something whacked me fairly hard across the back of my head. Then a soft, bulky object—my sheepskin jacket—was shoved down between us.

"Dammit, Jo, cool it!" Terry hissed. "And you," she said to Yasmin in a tone slightly less harsh, "you little slut—and I mean that, of course, in the best possible sense of the word—cover up or I'll let the sergeant toss you out onto the train platform."

I nearly turned on her, but people were moving down the aisles to get off the train, and more people would be getting on. By the time the train was rolling again, I'd begun to get a grip, although I was still breathing hard, and my heart, along with several other body parts, was still pounding.

"Thanks," I muttered. "I guess I needed that."

"What you need," Terry said deliberately, "is a good fucking. Jesus, Jo, if you don't get it off pretty soon, you'll have not only your international incident, but the mother of all lawsuits!"

She was right. I glanced at Yasmin. She had stopped whim-

SACCHI GREEN

pering and sat clutching my jacket around herself, watching us with great interest.

I pushed myself up into the aisle. "Can I trust you to keep her out of trouble for a couple of minutes while I at least take a leak?"

"You can count on me," Terry said, and I had to go with it.

There was a handicapped-accessible restroom just across from us, long and roomy by Amtrak standards. I pissed, tied my long straggling hair back up as well as I could with a mirror too low to show anything above my chin, and leaned my pelvis against the rounded edge of the sink. It was cold, but not enough to do me any good. Then I shoved off and unlocked the door, knowing that nothing I could do for myself would give me enough relief to be worth the hassle.

As the door slid open, a black-clad arm came through, then a shoulder, and suddenly Terry and Yasmin were in there with me and the door was shut and locked again.

"Sudden attack of patriotism," Terry announced with a lupine grin. "Have to prevent that international incident. It's a tough job, but somebody's gotta do it."

"You and who else?"

"Just me. Our little princess is going to keep real quiet, now and forever, in return for letting her watch. No accusations, false or otherwise."

I looked at Yasmin. Her eyes were avid. "I swear on my mother's grave," she said, and then, as I still looked skeptical, added, "on my sister's grave!" Somehow, that was convincing. Just the same, I unhooked the cuffs from my belt and snapped them around her wrists with paper towels for padding, then pinned her to the door handle. When I turned back to Terry, the quirk of her brow told me I'd tacitly agreed.

To what, I wasn't sure. We sized each other up for a minute like wrestlers considering grips. Then Terry made her move, trying to press me against the wall with her body, and I reflexively raised a knee to fend her off. Her cock against my kneecap made me feel naked. I'm used to being the hard body in these encounters. I know the steps to this dance, but I've never had to do them backward.

She retreated a few inches. "Gonna stay in uniform?" she asked, eyeing my badge. I unpinned it, slipped it into my holster, unfastened my belt, and hung the whole deal on a coat hook.

"Civilian enough for you?"

"Hell, no! The least you could do is show me your tits."

I stared her in the eyes for a second—somehow I'd never noticed how green they could get—and started to unbutton my shirt. I wasn't sure yet just where I might draw the line. I hung my shirt and sports bra over the gun and holster, even yanked my hair loose from its knot and let it flow over my shoulders. It would have come down anyway.

"So how about you?" She had left her jacket behind but wore a tight-cut leather vest over a black silk shirt.

She was observing me with such interest that she might not have heard. "Breasts like pomegranates," she said softly. "Round and high and tight. Jeez, don't they have gravity in New Hampshire?"

I looked down at myself. My nipples were hardening under an independent impulse. I grabbed Terry's vest and pulled her close to mash the studded leather hard against me, then eased up to rub languorously against it. The leather felt intriguing enough that I didn't push the issue of her staying dressed. And Katzi had accused me of never trying anything different!

Terry pressed closer. I leaned my mouth against her ear.

"Pomegranates? Christ, Terry, is that the kind of tripe you write?"

"Yeah, sometimes, when the inspiration's right. But I usually edit it out later." She eased back and looked me over. "I don't suppose," she said, somewhat wistfully, "you could jiggle a little for me?"

"In your dreams!" We were both a bit short of breath now, both struggling with the question of who'd get to do what to whom. Much as my flesh wanted to be touched, my instinct was to lash out if she tried.

"In my dreams?" There was such an odd look in her eyes that I didn't notice that she'd raised her hands until they almost brushed the outer curve of my breasts. "In my dreams," she murmured, just barely stroking me, "you're wearing red velvet."

I hadn't thought of that dress in years. Maybe the last one I ever wore. She'd worn black satin. A college mixer, some clumsy groping in a broom closet, a few weeks of feverish euphoria—then the realization that instead of striking sparks we were more apt to knock chips off each other. Eventually, in fact, we had. I ran my tongue over my reconstructed teeth.

Terry telegraphed an attempt at a kiss, but I wasn't quite ready for that. I let her cup my breasts and rub her thumbs over my appreciative nipples. "One-time only offer," I said, "for old times' sake," and pulled her head downward. She nuzzled the hollow of my throat while I ran my fingers through her crisp brush-cut. Then she went lower, her open mouth wet and hot on my skin, and by the time she was biting where it really mattered her knee was working between my thighs and I was rubbing against it like a cat in heat.

"Come on," I muttered, "show me what you've got!" I groped the bulge in her crotch, and then, while she unbuckled and unbuttoned and rearranged her gear for action, I kicked off my boots and pants.

She tried to clinch too fast. I let her grab my ass for a few seconds, then grabbed hers and shoved her leather pants back far enough that I could get a good look at what had been pressing between my legs.

"State of the art, huh?" Ten thick inches of glistening black high-tech cock, slippery even when not wet. At another time I'd have been envious. Hell, I *was* envious.

"This one's mostly for show," she muttered. "Are you sure..." But it was too late not to be sure.

"I can handle it," I said. And I did handle it, working it with my hand, making her pant and squirm. I manipulated it so that the tip just licked at me, then leaned into it, and for long seconds we were linked in co-ownership of the black cock, clits zinged by a current keen as electricity but far sweeter. Then the slick material skidded in my natural lube and slid along my wet folds, and I spread for it and took it in just an inch or two.

Can't hurt to see how the other half lives, I thought, and then, as Terry pressed harder, I remembered the size of what I was dealing with and realized that yeah, it might hurt, and yeah, I might just like it that way.

She pulled back a little and thrust again, and I opened up more, and she plunged harder, building into a compelling rhythm. I gripped the safety railing behind me and tilted my hips to take her deeper inside, aching for even more pounding.

But I had to go after it myself. "Let me move!" I growled.

Terry, uncomprehending, resisted my efforts to swing her around. The black cock, glistening for real now, slipped out as we grappled together.

We were pretty evenly matched in strength. She was a bit

beefier; I was taller. She'd been working out with weights and machines; I'd been working over smart-ass punks and pot-bellied drunks. The tie-breaker was that I needed it more.

"You get to wear it; just shut up and let me work it!" I had her back against the railing now. I grabbed the slippery cock and held it steady just long enough to get it where I needed it. Then I swung into serious action.

She flashed a grin and muttered, "Fair enough!" Then it was all she could do to hang on to the railing and meet my lunges. The train swayed and rattled, but I rode it, my legs automatically absorbing the shifts, as I rode her black cock, train to my tunnel, bound for glory. The surging hunger got me so slippery that, in spite of its bulk and hardness, what filled me might not have been enough, except that my clit seemed to swell inward as well as outward, and my whole cunt clenched fiercely around the maddening pressure.

Yasmin was emitting little squeals and whimpers; I glanced at her just long enough to notice that one hand, pulled free of the too-hastily fastened cuffs, was busy between her legs.

Terry's grunts turned into moans; she grabbed my hips and dug her fingers into my naked flesh. "Steady...damn it... steady..." she said between clenched teeth, and before I knew what was happening, she forced me back against the hard edge of the sink.

"Hang on," I said, and swung us both around, not losing an inch this time, until my back was to the wall. I couldn't stop moving but managed to slow enough to match her rhythm and grab her leather-covered ass. Her muscles bunched as her hips bucked. I mashed my mouth into hers to catch the eruption of harsh groans, but she had to breathe, and anyway, it didn't matter how much noise she made. I felt my eruption coming and knew there was no way in hell I could muffle it. And didn't give a damn.

I held on until Terry's breathing subsided from wrenching to merely hard. She didn't resist as I turned her again and accelerated into my own demanding beat. I saw her face through a haze, and there may have been pain on it, but she didn't flinch, just kept her hips tilted at the optimum angle for me to ram myself down onto what she offered. My clit clenched like a fist, harder and harder each time I drove toward her. A sound like a distant train whistle seemed to come closer and closer, the reverberations penetrating into places deeper than I had even known existed.

Then it hit. My clit went off like a brass gong, and waves smashed up against the explosion raging outward from my center. A storm of sound engulfed me.

Terry held me for the hours it seemed to take for me to suck in enough breath to see straight. Finally I slouched back against the edge of the sink, letting the slippery cock emerge inch by inch. She reached past me to grab a handful of paper towels; I took them away from her and slowly wiped my juices from the glistening black surface. When I aimed the used towels toward the trash container, she stopped me, folded them inside a clean one, and tucked them into her pocket, avoiding my eyes. I didn't ask.

Then she looked toward the door. As I'd been vaguely aware, Yasmin had been rubbing herself into a frenzy, apparently with some success. "So, Princess," Terry said with the old jaunty quirk of her brow, "didn't I tell you it'd be worth it just to listen to her come? I could tape that song and make a bundle."

"You, Terry, are a prick," I said lazily, "and I mean that, of course, in the best possible sense of the word."

"I still get the shivers now and then," Terry went on, nominally speaking to Yasmin, "thinking of that alto sax wailing. The final trumpet fanfare this time, though, was better than anything I remember."

"Jeez, I hope you edit out that kind of crap!" I said, and turned to the sink to clean up. The mirror was so steamed I couldn't see a thing. Then I dressed, feeling more secure with my gun belt around my hips. Not that security is everything.

The rest of the trip wasn't bad. The whispers and surreptitious looks from the college kids and a few others who must have heard us were kind of a kick. Yasmin watched sleepily as Terry and I chatted about old times, old acquaintances, and the intervening years. Terry got off at Penn Station, offering me a book at the last minute with her card tucked into it. I took out the card and slipped it into my breast pocket, behind the badge.

"Moving a little stiffly, aren't we?" I said as I helped get her duffel down from the rack.

"Mmm, but the show must go on."

"I'm sure you won't disappoint your audience." I aimed an encouraging slap at her fine, muscular ass. "Go get 'em."

Yasmin made a few tentative advances between New York and D.C., but I wasn't that vulnerable anymore, and she gave up and slept for most of the trip. The welcoming party at Union Station was headed by a tall, mature woman in a well-cut dark suit.

"The Princess traveled well?" she asked, with a keen, hard look at me.

"Just fine," I said, meeting her eyes frankly, "with no harm done, if you don't count a few slaps to make her keep her hands to herself."

"Excellent," she said, with the ghost of a smile. "The Sultan would be happy to offer hospitality for the night, before your return trip."

"I appreciate the offer," I said truthfully, "but I have other plans. I'm getting on the next train to New York. There's a literary event I don't want to miss."

Terry's schedule of readings was scrawled on the back of her card. There's a special one at midnight. I have a notion there'll be enough erotica groupies to go around. Beyond that, I wouldn't mind meeting an editor, finding out more about the writing game. I know damned well that Terry will want to use some of today's action in her fiction. I might just beat her to it.

I've gotta edit out that "train to my tunnel, bound for glory" line, though. Too bad. That's sure as hell exactly how it felt.

CUTTING LOOSE

María Elena de la Selva

I STARE AT MYSELF IN THE MIRROR WEARING nothing, holding scissors. I like their sharp gleam. I keep them in my hand while I search for something old to wear tonight. Something from before Jack.

At the back of the bottom drawer of the long built-in set of thirteen narrow drawers Jack labeled, without asking, with his well-oiled and efficient label gun, I find them. For some reason there is no label on the last drawer, and in the back of this dark unlabeled place I find my leotards and tights and rehearsal skirts from dancing, from ballet, from before Jack who never dances. I put the scissors down but I keep them close.

Ten years old and it still fits me, black Lycra leotard, loose but no dry rot. I pull it over sheer black Christian Dior tights that I found in drawer number seven, lucky seven, labeled "hosiery," and unwrapped from tissue paper. I tie the sleek, smooth folds of the crimson rehearsal skirt around my waist. The effect is nearly perfect for tonight.

But not quite. I pick up the scissors from the dresser and I cut the past into now, less is more in the now, and I snip, snap, cut off the cone of material I have pulled out to a point just above my right shoulder; one naked globe of shoulder white looks great against black Lycra. Quick symmetric cutting snips the left shoulder open, and I shake both shoulders and untie the red skirt, then bisect it at an angle, jagged bi-level hem, so the longest point ends just above my knee. I retie the silky folds around my narrow dancer's waist.

Almost there—only one thing more for tonight. I lean into the mirror, lean into a stranger, take the pointed tips of my shiny steel scissors and cut a tiny heart in the black Lycra pulled taut between the swell of my breasts, equidistant between the uncovered shoulders of the stranger in the mirror. And the stranger in the mirror screams *I want* for tonight: I want to break into age thirty, skin to skin with a stranger, with another broken stranger, tonight.

As I drive into town the rain stops sheeting into my windshield. I can't say when that happened; I was driving on instruments only, and my radar led me here, to Belltown, to this bar. I park Jack's ugly Porsche on the street and step out onto clean wet pavement under the full orange moon rising late in a velvet sky. The pulsing neon outside the bar beckons me, so I pick up a pack of Royals at the kiosk next door and then go on in.

Tonight feels like death. Amazing how death makes you horny. I learned that when my mother died and, in shock, I grabbed Jack and lost it. He'd been pushing me for months, said he was embarrassed dating a twenty-year-old virgin. It feels like that tonight, like somebody just died. More than revenge, more than anything else, that's what brings me here to this bar to turn thirty with a stranger.

When I get inside I know it's the right bar. I smell it. It smells old: lots of history here. Smoky, brick dust; old, high dark ceilings; old ghosts. The walls shine with polished mahogany wainscoting; there are high-backed booths, circular, with generous, honey-colored leather interiors like an old Jag or a Packard. You could take a nice ride with a stranger here. Amber liquids line the glass shelves, Glenlivet, Chivas Regal, Galliano; golden lights repeating themselves over and over in the mirror, stretching out the length of the bar.

I wait to catch the rhythm—and by the time I strut my stuff, walking the line, I've got them all looking. The guys, and it's mostly guys here tonight, feel it and swivel to watch me walk. I'm carrying a lot of atmosphere with me—stormy weather, small craft warning. Let's all watch the waves, boys.

They melt away to let me through, can't help themselves: boys. I take the last post, shiny chrome, leather dome under my thighs. The empty seat next to me remains a naked invitation.

I cross sheer black magic Christian Dior thighs, smooth slick slide of toned nylon. Elastic recross. Beat beat. I dig in my daughter's tiny heart-shaped purse, it's just big enough for cigarettes. At seven, Paige uses it for playing dress-up. This is the first time I've dressed for seduction. Until now, Jack's been the only one.

I take out the cigarettes, first cigarettes since Jack—ten years of Jack and no nicotine. I tap tap the pack on the slick surface of the bar and draw one out slowly. Royals: French, long and menthol. A double whammy. I stick the end in my mouth, crimson velvet, like my skirt. I make the letter O with my lips and kind of roll it around to get it moist.

"What can I get you?" It's Dracula behind the bar, thick black widow's peak, slicked-back ponytail, black silk shirt tucked loosely into small waist, waiting in motion, quick bounce from one foot to the other, yes, light on his feet.

"So what is it, lady?"

"Something potent, I don't want to remember any of this."

"Can you get a little more specific?" His eyes say *get on with it,* he's seen too many ladies on the hunt to humor me now.

"Maybe...tequila. Potent and specific, wouldn't you say?"

"Cuervo?"

"I don't know, sure. Say, do you have a light?"

"Look, lady, I can come back when you're ready."

"Okay, Cuervo, a double—please?" But he's gone for the drink, attitude bristling from his shoulders and his tight mouth. What did I do to him?

"Can I give you a light?" This from the eager boy on my left. Fresh-faced, college-sweatered.

All right, here we go. "Please. I was beginning to think no one smoked anymore, but then I smelled this bar from the street."

"Good ventilation though, I come here a lot. Here you go." He flicks a square silver lighter with a strong flame.

"Thanks." I steady his hand with mine, dead white with crimson nails against his tan. I lean into him and suck it in long and deep, following his eyes up from my short skirt to the heart-shaped cutout where my breasts press each other. He reads my eyes and smiles.

"You really suck that down," he says.

"Nervy, I guess—it's been a long time."

"Oh yeah?"

"Since I've smoked, I mean."

"It doesn't look like it."

"I could get to like it again." I look at the lit cylinder in my hand. He straddles the leather seat next to me and lights a Marlboro for himself.

"I haven't seen you here before. I would have remembered." Again with the slow smile.

"Like I said," I take another drag, "it's been a long time."

"So what's with the outfit, you a dancer or something?"

"I didn't have anything else to wear."

"Don't get me wrong, I like it. I just thought...you might get cold."

"I may just have to cozy up to some warm stranger."

"Now that sounds..." He moves in close, but Drac, the bartender, is back.

"Drinks, shooter, double Cuervo for the lady. And you, Joe College, what'd you have down there—Red Hook? Draft?"

"I'll get the lady's, too."

"No, that's okay," I say. "I'll pay for it." I give the bartender a fifty. "This should cover it, and a Red Hook for my friend." He makes a face. "Just take that and run a tab," I tell him. I add a "please," real sweet, but no smile from Drac. He's off for the beer on the turn of a heel. Nice ass, but I'm back to the bird in the hand.

"I'll get the next round," he says.

"Sounds great. So, where were we?"

"We were talking about keeping you warm."

"Right, and you're the man with the fire!" I say, taking out another cigarette; he's just as quick with his lighter. This time he leans in a little closer and I take a little longer with my hand on his and we are fast coming to an understanding, I think. I cross my legs again and shift on the slippery leather, and this time my knee just happens to end up against his.

Keeping cozy, he stubs his cigarette into the glass ashtray, and pops a mint into his mouth. "I've gotta start tapering off," he says. "I have to quit this fall."

"Why this fall?"

He kind of clears his throat and I can see he knows I'll be impressed, so I get my face ready with the proper level of interest.

"I start medical school this fall, and quitting smoking, well, it's practically a requirement."

"Medical school?" My face freezes, my mouth can barely form the words. Medical school. Just like fucking Jack. Can't I get away from him tonight? I slam down my shooter, and choke on the hot fire going down my throat.

"Are you okay?" He can see that I'm not.

I see the bartender again through the water in my eyes. "Another double," I tell him. It comes out a choke, and Mr. Future Doctor starts hitting me on the back.

"That won't help," Drac tells him, and hands me a glass of water. "Drink this," he says, and watches me, his eyes a little softer now. "You sure you want another double?"

I get my voice back. "I know what I want." I slide off the stool, bumping into Mr. Future Doctor, Future God, Future Jack—it makes me queasy, or maybe that's the cigarettes. Forget him. I'm picking my stranger by how much he doesn't have in common with my husband. "Excuse me." I get up, leaving my coat. I have to get away from this guy, suddenly he looks too smug, too sure of himself, too Jack. I point vaguely toward the ladies' room and take off, still coughing.

I walk down the line. This may be harder than I thought. He's too old, he's too young, ugh, too tall—opposite of Jack, there we go, short and dark, kind of stocky, over there, farther down the line. I pause in front of gray flannel, briefcase at his feet, straight edges, maybe too straight. Wait. He's loosening the knot on the burgundy tie with the tiny sperm-shaped paisleys. His eyes say *give me a chance,* and I think I will. Hello, short and dark, Jack's antithesis in gray flannel. Nothing to do with Jack. I've been so stupid.

"Excuse me, are you waiting for someone?" He's quick, looks like a lawyer.

"Absolutely," I say, jumping right in there. "Someone like you."

"Sit down, then." He pats the leather seat next to him, "Let's talk about it."

I turn into the leather round as he moves the seat closer to him and I collide with his Manhattan. "Oh, sorry, look, I got you all wet."

"No problem," he says, mopping it up. "Really."

"Let me replace that drink, please—it's the least I can do. Here, have some more napkins."

"Really, it's no problem." He's being a good sport about it.

"I am sorry...all that pretty gray flannel. Soda water would help. Here, let me help you." Now we're both mopping. "Oh, your pants, too. Oh, *sorry,* I...you'd better do that.... What we need is soda water. Where is that bartender?"

"There he is."

"Can you get him? I don't think he likes me."

"He's seen us, he's coming."

"You think he looks like Dracula?" I ask.

"What are you talking about?"

"The guy, the bartender, see it? That widow's peak, the slicked-back hair, those eyes."

He considers it, but then he shakes his head. "Nope," he says, "he's not pale enough. Dracula's been dead for centuries—his skin's like chalk—kind of like yours."

"You like white ladies?"

"Among others."

"Excuse me, um, Cesar," I'm reading the bartender's name tag, "is that how you say it—Seh-zar? I like that. Nice."

"It's my name."

"And—what's in a name, right?" Nice eyes, too, I'm thinking.

"Did you have something in mind?" he asks.

"Absolutely," I reply.

"To drink."

"Yes, to drink. Another double shot of Cuervo, for me. And this gentleman in the wet gray suit needs some soda water for his pants and something to wet his whistle. Was that a Manhattan, mister, ah, maybe I should know your name now that I've soaked you to the skin?"

"It's Robins, Bob Robins." He sticks out his hand.

"Dina Jarvis. It's a pleasure."

"The pleasure's mutual, believe me."

Drac, no, *Cesar* leans across the bar. "I hate to break this up, but I need your order." He looks at me. "That guy you left at the end of the bar still thinks he's guarding your coat. Maybe you want a drink for him, too?"

"Good idea, Cesar, get the little med student a drink, bring ours, and buy yourself one at the same time—maybe chill out while you're at it."

He doesn't stop looking into my eyes, but he says, "Not

now, thanks." This time I take my time getting back to the little lawyer. *Okay,* I think, *let's move this thing,* and then he says, "What he doesn't like about you is you're too obvious."

"Obvious? Me, in my slashed Lycra?"

"It's more where the Lycra *isn't.*"

"That's the point."

"Obviously. Forget him—let's talk terms here."

"Terms?"

"Terms of endearment, getting logistic, you and me—how much for this evening?"

"This eve... Oh. Oh no, you've got the wrong idea, Bob Robins."

"I thought you wanted to party."

"I do." I exhale a stream of smoke. "But I hadn't planned on charging admission."

His eyes flick over me. "Could have fooled me."

Now I don't like his eyes, I see something there in a new light. "So you pay for sex," I say.

"I pay for everything."

"I don't think so, Bob, not this time."

"C'mon," he says, "what's the difference, you want it."

I put out my cigarette, he grabs my hand and forces it down to his wet crotch. "You did this," he says. "I think you'd better take care of it." Under the wet folds of flannel there's a lot of hot and hard.

"Impressive," I say, "but you'd better stick to the pros. What you lack in charm you can make up for in cash."

I twist my hand out of his grasp and stand up, rubbing my wrist.

The bartender walks into our antagonism. "Soda water, no lime, double Cuervo and a Manhattan." He looks from Bob to me. "Everything okay here?"

"I'm moving over to that booth." I lock on his eyes. "Alone."

"Yeah, for how long?" the little lawyer wants to know.

Neither of us look at him. I pick up the Cuervo Gold and down it in one swallow. This time the molten heat is just what I need. "How about one more, Cesar." I like the way his name feels between my teeth and I slide it out again, "Ssseh-Zar. In the booth, Cesar."

"In the booth," he says.

I like the way the booth feels around me now, a nest of honey leather, cool comfort against my hot skin. I stretch out both arms and sink into it, c'mon boys, it's getting late. The brass-rimmed face of time hangs like a moon at the end of the bar. Forty-five minutes until tomorrow, less than an hour left of my twenties. And I have no idea where my thirties will take me. *Shattered dreams, worthless years,* an old Stevie Wonder song curls around in my head, a sad song. And then he's here, Cesar, with two small cups and my coat over his arm like a towel.

Much laughter suddenly down at the end of the bar where most of the crowd is. I want to be laughing, too. I look up at him and I've got to tell him. "I'm turning thirty tonight. At midnight."

"So you're kind of like Cinderella?"

"Only I didn't even get to the ball."

"Where's the guy?"

"How do you know about the guy?"

"There's always a guy when a woman looks the way you do."

"Oh, I forgot, the bartender's seen it all." He sets the cups of espresso on the table and unwinds his apron. "Are you off now?"

"I'm a free man," he says. "And you offered me a drink." He indicates the espresso. "On the house."

"Never had anything on the house." I slide over, my skirt sticking to the leather and corkscrewing up around my thighs. He tosses my coat over the side of the booth and slides in next to me. I feel the heat from his thigh.

"First time for everything," he says, and we drink the espresso. It's sweet and thick. Just as I'm thinking that this guy's too pretty to be straight, his gaze drops to the heart-shaped window in my leotard; when it meets mine again I know he likes women.

"You wanted to go dancing on your birthday?" he asks.

"That's one way of putting it."

"I like to dance," he says. "It's one of the things I like. Hot salsa," he says, with a big, fine smile, his lips pulled back, his white canines gleaming.

So Dracula dances, and why not. He looks like he dances, has nice moves. "How about slow jazz?" I ask.

"Slow jazz. Sure, we could warm up with a little slow jazz. I know the best place in Seattle."

I wait.

"Upstairs."

"Upstairs."

"I have a studio upstairs. I live there."

Behind his face the brass ring of the clock is a halo, a golden nimbus, reminding me of the time. "Yes," I say, "all right." I pull my coat off the back of the booth. He gets out and I slide into him. He holds me for a couple of heartbeats; I fall into the deep black pull of his eyes. When he lets go my skin burns where his hands touched me.

"Ready?" he asks.

"Slow jazz," I say. "Just a minute." I turn back to the coffee, tiny cups of thick and dark and sweet, and I finish mine in a long swallow. "Let's go." I slip Paige's purse over my bare shoulder.

Walking upstairs our hips touch and bump and waffle back, and then we push together into the apartment behind the gray door. Heavy door, steel riveted, warehouse wide, it clangs heavily into the dim room. Tequila magic fills my head, moonlight streams through the windows. Behind my neck I feel his hand stretch out, groping against the wall, reaching for lights.

"Wait." I lean against him and stop his hand.

"You like dancing in the dark?" He twists close to my face; I can feel his breath. He watches my eyes; I like it when he does that.

"It won't be dark," I say. "Look at the moon."

"You're right," he says, glancing up. "It's coming up late tonight—almost midnight."

Almost thirty, I think, and I say, "So what was that claim about the best jazz in Seattle?"

"That was slow jazz you wanted?"

"Real slow," I say.

He walks toward bookcases of sound, CDs and tapes just to the left of the hallway, cases on cases on cases, a wall of music. I follow him, brush past him. The bathroom must be down this hall. *Who is this man,* I think. *What is this place?* Wide hallway of painted white brick leads to the bathroom. Black and white octagons on the floor remind me of old movies. Twelve-foot ceilings. A two-person shower. Lots of air and space around this man, he surrounds himself with space. Buffer zone, safety zone, that's right, condoms, here, in my purse. I check my hair in the mirror. My god, what am I doing here? Jack, Jack in the fucking bed with that woman is what I'm doing here.

Click click of my heels, changing from ceramic to hardwood. I walk into the sound of piano music. Slow piano; I know this song. My heels against hardwood. Well polished. A dancer's dream, suspended wood floor, my feet feel the give. He's ready for me, standing in the center of the room, lit only by the rising summer moon, swaying to Sarah Vaughn singing "Embraceable You." Who is this man?

"Who are you?" I ask him, walking into his steady arms. We are already moving. Real slow. We touch, we hold, but light and kind of formal. Easy to follow, clean moves and, he whirls me out and pulls me in. Neat.

"Who am I?" He smiles. "I'm the guy who takes you dancing on your birthday, Dina."

Out again, then in, out one more time, and then he lets me go to slow dance with the shadows as he reaches into his back pocket and pulls out scissors. Small and orange handled—a child's pair with rounded tips for cutting out snowflakes and paper dolls. What's he doing? His eyes show mischief and daring; they dance with his smile and reassure me. We're on the same side in this adventure.

"I like the way you cut up your clothes, Dina."

My body is moving liquid, to slow jazz. My naked shoulders pulse heat into the air around them and my breasts press against Lycra. He comes forward with the little scissors. His hips move to mine moving to his. We dance together, then back. He slides the scissors down around his thumb and forefinger and snaps them together a few times to the music. I squeeze my fingers against each other to recall the rub of my scissors back there in the closet, cutting life into old dancing clothes. Now I feel the jagged edge of my rehearsal skirt scraping against the tops of my thighs. It swishes across and over and back again. It saws against the Christian Dior sheers, keeping time. He closes the distance between us, barely moving, just swaying to the beat, and holds the toy scissors against his cheek.

"Want me to warm them up for you?" he asks.

"Are you trying to scare me?"

"Not tonight, Dina, nothing scares you tonight. Maybe tomorrow, but tonight nothing bad can happen. This I promise you. Only good things tonight." He flashes teeth again. Then he runs his finger around the little heart window I cut between my breasts. The hard ridge of his fingernail pushes against my breastbone, over the inside curve of my breasts. He traces the heart again. "I think we'll cut through this little heart," he whispers against my ear, and while the tip of his tongue travels the coiled channels of my ear the little scissors cut the Lycra, snip by slow snip. I get it now: he's easing me out of my chrysalis. My breasts push at the opening he's made. "Other side now," he says, and snips once, twice, and then three snips and my breasts push all the way through the lycra. We are so close my nipples can feel the heat from his chest. We don't touch but we move, fused, and then he pulls his heat back with his body. My breasts, freed of Lycra, burn under his eyes. His fingers snip the scissors to the beat of the music. *Snip snip,* like pure percussion.

"So nice," he says. Every smile reaches his eyes. I could die in those smiles. His canines flash again, white and sharp. He runs his tongue over his sharp, shiny teeth. Then he sticks four fingers into the waistband of my shredded wraparound skirt, pulls it away from my waist, and with his little scissors cuts it off me. It slithers down my thighs and quivers at my feet, a crimson pool.

"You know you're going to have to give me something to wear home," I tell him.

216

"Don't worry, Conchita, I'll take care of you."

"Will you Cesar, will you...now?" I step out over the skirt into his arms and we dance slow jazz pressed up against each other, feet planted, our bodies making their own rhythms; we're leading the music and we can't slow down.

"You know it, Conchita," he says, and pushes harder, more urgently.

"Why do you call me that, Conchita? What does it mean?"

"It means I like your ears." He takes the lobe of my left ear between his teeth and gently bites.

"Just my ears?"

His lips, full and soft, leave my ear and travel down my neck.

"I like this neck and this throat." He kisses the hollow and flicks his tongue over the pulse. He moves his lips down my throat, slowly kissing as he goes. "And I like these breasts," he murmurs, "these wonderful breasts." His lips and tongue make circles around my nipples—circling closer but never touching them. "But then you knew that already, when I had to see them." He snips the scissors.

I am melting, wet from wanting him. I can barely whisper, "What else do you like?"

"Come with me. I'll show you everything I like."

He leads me past the shelves of books, folios, and albums, over to a wooden ladder, bolted against the brick wall.

"You first," he says, running his hand up and down the side of the ladder.

"Where does it go?"

"'Up to my bed. It's kind of an upper bunk—go on." He pats a rung. "You'll like it."

My feet get halfway up the ladder and I'm face to face with a platform covered by a down featherbed. I bury my face in the down and smell laundry soap and his musk. I turn and look down at him as he's starting up the ladder, and he stops me with his hand around my bottom foot. He comes up under me and pulls my leotard and tights where the seams join and gathers them into his fist. He works fast with the scissors. He climbs up behind me then, his strong foot pushing hard against mine on the wood. The scissors clatter to the floor and he explores my nakedness with one hand, and shows me the silver face of his Timex on the other. Just minutes until midnight; through my rising pulse I hear the clink of buckle and feel his pants sliding down his legs.

"Are we going for that deadline?" he asks low in my ear, rubbing against me.

"No…Yes…I don't know." I'm having trouble concentrating. I want all of this man—right now. "In my purse…I brought some…protection."

"I already did that," he says, and he pushes into me.

I moan at the force of him, all that strong immediate presence, and I pull with both hands on the mattress, my cheek pressed deep into the down. We are both way too ready; all that foreplay on the dance floor. It doesn't take much; he rolls the puckered flesh of my nipples, now hard knobs, under his fingers; passion-crazed I thrust and moan and rub against the hard wood of the ladder. He moves to my moans, synchronized in time, and then he whispers, "Four, three, two, one." I blast into a new decade. Fireworks and Happy Birthday, Dina.

Spent, I hold the ladder and he holds me until my breathing and my heart slow down. I'm pressed against the ladder and he's pressed against me, but I feel, for the first time in a long time, unencumbered and free.

MAIL-ORDER BRIDE

Saira Ramasastry

My name is Hubert W. Humphrey. Hube Boob. Hube Tube. Humpty Hubert. Hubris. I've been called every name on every possible occasion and it's all very funny.

I'm not what you'd call a ladies' man. Though I am tempted to blame this on my name, it really has nothing to do with that. My name actually suits me well. I'm big-boned—obese, my doctor calls it. I'm short. I don't exercise. My favorite things to eat are donuts and fast foods. I'm just a regular guy.

But I have never been able to get a date. My lowest point was when I asked Harriet, the checkout clerk, to go with me to the office Christmas party. Harriet is a member of the fat pack, a group of mall chicks who hang out together during coffee breaks. She has the least presentable face in the fat pack—oily skin, pockmarks, and buckteeth to boot. But she has enormous breasts. I figured if we were in the back of a car, in the darkness of night, I could bury my head in her tits and get laid. So I asked Harriet to go with me.

"No way," she responded, "am I going to be a Hairy Hump!" She walked away, taking her heavenly 40DDD tits with her.

Let's face it: if I couldn't get a fuck out of Harriet, there wasn't much hope for me. I didn't go to college, where women get naked just for the intellectual experience. I couldn't afford a decent whore on my paycheck as manager of the local Kmart—a prestigious job where I come from, but the salary caps at fifteen bucks an hour. Maybe I could find myself a cheap hooker—but with the threat of AIDS and other diseases, I didn't want to risk it.

So I turned to the Internet. Free porn, free live streaming video, free tits—whatever I wanted, whenever I wanted it. No dates, no hassles, no fear of disease. I discovered a site that would change my life: www.XoticMailOrderBrides.com.

It was 3:00 A.M. I had just finished jerking off to some soft porn, but was still unsatisfied. I went to the mail-order brides site and began browsing.

Online, I was the pickiest son of a bitch in the world. I passed over pretty Thai women because I decided they were too scrawny. I clicked past the Russian ones for being fake blondes. Most of these women were stunningly beautiful: a guy like me had no business overlooking them.

I spent hours that night trying to find The One. The One what? The one ultimate fuck of my life is how I thought of it. I like curvy women with thick black hair and easy bedroom eyes.

My random clicking patterns weren't bringing her to me, so I consulted the advanced search engine.

South Asian brides came up. Indian chicks? Why not?

I followed the link and there she was: Siliidi. I clicked to see her profile and instantly got hard.

She was practically naked. Her stats were listed on the sidebar: 5'9", 38D-26-38. Her skin was the color of coffee ice cream and looked every bit as tasty. She had great tits—definitely real—with round, suckable brown nipples. Her hips flared out from her tiny waist and flat stomach. Her legs were long and lean, but had that fleshy female roundness that I love.

With a package like that, I wouldn't have cared if she had Harriet's face. But of course she didn't: she was absolutely gorgeous. Her hip-length black hair was spread across a white pillow, and her huge, liquid brown eyes stared at me as if she wanted to devour me. As if she wanted to fuck me.

I connected to the site and sent Siliidi a private message.

<HUBACCA> Hello Siliidi.

<SILIIDI> Hello there. Who are you? ;)

<HUBACCA> My name is William. I saw your page and wanted to say hello.

<SILIIDI> Well hello, William. You obviously already know my name....

<HUBACCA> Are you in India?

<SILIIDI> No....

<HUBACCA> Where are you?

<SILIIDI> I'm from Sri Lanka. It's very hot here tonight, so I'm not wearing any clothes.

<HUBACCA> Do you look like your picture?

<SILIIDI> Yes, except for one thing.

<HUBACCA> What's that?

<SILIIDI> I'm wet. I want you, William.

She was getting right down to business. I didn't have to do a thing. She proceeded to send a series of dirty messages while I jerked off again and again. Before I knew it, the sun was rising and I had to get ready for work.

Over the next two weeks we continued our virtual meetings nightly. Eventually I sent her a naked picture of myself and told her my real name was Hubert. I didn't want to be caught in a lie if I got to meet her in person. To my surprise, she said my photo turned her on. That night I typed out the things I wanted to do to her while she touched herself. Then I sent her a hot 69 and was completely spent.

Later that night, I wrote her a short email asking if she wanted to marry me.

She was still online. Yes, she said, she would marry me and yes, she would fuck me.

I waited outside International Arrivals for Sri Lankan Airlines Flight 24824. I had given up fast food for a few weeks, so my stomach wasn't rolling over my belt quite as much as usual. I had also bought a new pair of pants; this was as good as I was going to look.

I couldn't wait to meet Siliidi. It wasn't only that I wanted to get regular sex—I certainly did—but this was the first time in my life that a woman had learned almost everything about me and still wanted me. I felt incredible. She was the hottest thing I'd ever seen—at least, there weren't any women I'd jerked off to who were better than Siliidi.

We didn't love each other, but neither of us minded. We were adults, and each of us would be getting something we needed. She wanted a green card; I wanted to get fucked and have my house cleaned. Besides, I genuinely liked Siliidi—and to be honest, I'd never really liked a woman before.

I'd agreed to our getting married in the airport chapel. She had said that if I didn't marry her right then and there, she would get on the next plane back to Sri Lanka. Those were her terms; if it meant getting sex right after I took her home, I was more than willing to oblige.

I saw Siliidi on the security camera as she walked out of customs and shivered—in person she was even better looking than her Internet photo. She wore a sundress tight across her tits. Her hair hung sexily down her back. Gorgeous.

Siliidi pushed her luggage cart toward me, showing off, swaying her hips. I shoved a bouquet of airport flowers in her face and waited for her to speak. I was sweating profusely. I couldn't wait to finally hear her voice. She turned out to have the voice of a phone sex operator. I got hard instantly.

"Hubert, have you been dieting? You are so handsome," she intoned in her lilting Sri Lankan accent. She took the flowers and inhaled them as if she wanted to eat them. Even that got me hot.

All I managed to say was a charming, "Hello, Siliidi. You look very nice."

She grabbed me by the collar and kissed me as if she had been missing me intensely. She wrapped her luscious arms around me and squeezed. "Marry me now, Hubert," she whispered.

She had traveled halfway around the world to be with me, and I wanted to be with her more than anything. We parked the luggage cart at the chapel, went inside, and tied the knot.

Strangely, Siliidi didn't say a word on the way home from the airport—she just massaged my cock. If I had just come to a new country to marry some stranger, I think I would have felt something, had lots to say, questions to ask. Not Siliidi. She smiled calmly and stared out the window, crossing and uncrossing her legs. She asked a few questions about the town. I pointed out the supermarket, local bar, dry cleaners, and coffee hangouts. She nodded and smiled, and touched me some more.

We arrived home. Siliidi was impressed by my suburban house, and I guess it did seem pretty big compared to the trailers down the street. It has white vinyl siding that I clean on a semiannual basis, and a moderately mowed lawn. As far as the interior, I was hoping that Siliidi would redecorate and make it nicer.

I carried Siliidi's suitcases inside and let her look around for a while. I could hear her slow, sexy footsteps clicking through the rooms. She made it from the bathroom to the bedroom, and then there was silence.

"Siliidi?" I called. No answer. I walked toward the bedroom.

"Siliidi? Where are you?" I was too nervous to have a hard-on. I crept into the bedroom.

She was standing naked on the bed in a pair of high heels, admiring herself in the mirror. She looked like someone straight out of a live streaming video. My cock banged against my boxers. I'm sure I was drooling out of the corner of my mouth. There on my bed with the *Star Wars* comforter and matching pillows was the sexiest woman alive—who also just happened to be my wife.

The spiked heels caught me off guard. "Where...in Sri Lanka...did you get...*those?*"

Siliidi jumped off the bed and slapped me across the face. "You dirty boy," she said, unfastening my belt and unzipping my fly. "Pull those down. Now."

Though I can get hot about being dominated once in awhile, this was not the way I had planned our first fuck. But I decided to pull down my pants, because it would bring me closer to actually getting laid.

She circled me, but didn't touch me. My eyes lowered to her nipples; they looked like the chocolate icing on mocha cupcakes. I wanted to press my lips to her smooth skin and suck, but I was interrupted by a painful blow across my buttocks.

"Take off your shirt and your boxers," she growled. "Get completely naked."

"Ouch, you bitch!" I whimpered, rubbing my butt. I wanted to tell her to fuck off, but if I upset her I might miss the fuck of my life.

I stood naked in the middle of the room. Though I had shed a few pounds across my midsection, I was still fat and pasty white. My man breasts wobbled over three rolls of stomach flesh. My cock, though above average in size by most standards, was dwarfed by my fat. I was sure Siliidi would make fun of me.

But she didn't. She got down on her knees and her face turned soft and gentle. She touched my cock as if it was a precious thing to protect and cherish. She took it in her mouth and worked it between her luscious red lips, moaning softly, like a woman eating her favorite dessert.

I grabbed a cluster of her raven tendrils and moved her head up and down my cock. She sucked harder; moaned louder; applied more pressure to the tip. My ass tightened and I felt an orgasm starting. She stopped abruptly.

She dragged her nails up my chest and looked at me with narrowed eyes. "You have displeased me. Now lie down!"

"What?" I covered my red raging cock with both hands and

took a few steps back. "What kind of crazy bitch are you?" What had happened? Things had been going so well.

Siliidi pushed me down on the bed with a surprisingly strong movement of her arms. She raised her leg over me, enough to give me a shot of her wet lips, and kneed me in my doughboy stomach.

When I saw that she was dripping, I calmed down a little. Maybe this was part of her game. I reminded myself that I had an actual, real live female in my bedroom who was wet and ready.

"Apologize to me," Siliidi said.

"For...?"

Siliidi grabbed my belt and whipped the pillow next to me. "Just do it. Do it or never get fucked." She straddled me so her wet cunt was near the tip of my cock. She softened again, turning from bitch to loving wife, and stroked her wetness to remind me she wanted it.

I was so weak—and so close to satisfaction. When I felt her juices on the head of my cock and saw her fondling her breasts, her confusing games didn't matter. I meekly told her I was sorry, though I did not know for what.

She took three minutes to sit down on my cock, making me beg every thirty seconds to go further inside her. I had never seen such developed thigh muscles on a woman. She was able to freeze her toned body just to torture me. Finally, I figured out what she really wanted.

"Mistress," I said, "I will be a good boy. Please, please sit down on me."

I had guessed correctly: she loved my obedience. Now she turned sweet and tumbled down onto my cock. Pressing her hands on my chest, she worked her body over me vigorously, providing maximum pleasure. She brought my head close to her breasts so I could fondle and suck while she moved up and down on me. Using every muscle in her strong and sculpted legs, she pushed me in and out of her.

I had intended to keep it going for a long time, but since this was my first real fuck, it lasted only five minutes—still a record over my hand jobs.

Siliidi looked no more than twenty, so I was stunned to learn that she was actually thirty-five. She had been married once before, to a man with a turban, but she divorced him once she realized he had no intentions of moving her to New York City. Ironically, after they were divorced her ex-husband had wed, in an arranged marriage, a much younger American-born Indian. After that Siliidi became even more determined to get to the United States.

Her parents couldn't arrange another marriage for her, since divorce branded her "damaged goods." So she took matters into her own hands and put herself on the exotic mail-order brides site. She told me she had gotten over a hundred hits a night.

Most of her clients were Germans with brown-girl fetishes. She didn't get much American traffic through her page; American men seemed to want the petite East Asian types. I had been the first American man over eighteen to enter her site.

Was she as desperate as I was? Apparently.

When I realized this, I really fell in love with Siliidi.

In our home, Siliidi ruled. Outside, though, she played the role of the subservient woman, turning me into a living legend in our small town. For instance, every Wednesday she would come to the Kmart with a basket of homemade curries and breads as if she were delivering my lunch. I hated Sri Lankan cooking, but these lunches served an important purpose: every man in Kmart noticed her. She wore a tight spandex miniskirt with no panties, and the curves of her ass showed through the shiny black material. Her tank top, in some loud color like turquoise or yellow, revealed plenty of cleavage, not to mention the outline of her nipples. The men at Kmart couldn't believe that I had married this exotic beauty with "a tight ass and a nice rack"—and that I had her wrapped around my little finger.

"Hubert!" she would call, running through the store, sending her breasts flying up to her chin.

"Hello, Siliidi," I'd repy in an aloof manner. To the guys around me, it looked like I had everything under control. She wanted me; I could care less about her. (Inside my pants, of course, my erection was almost ready to pop.)

Siliidi embraced and kissed me; I just stood still. "I made you some special treats because I was thinking about you, Hubert!"

Her voice was syrupy sweet. I wanted to melt, but I remained cool—and all the staff could see it. I pointed to my office with the plastic furniture, and blinds on the windows. "In there," I told my wife.

Siliidi bowed with a sexy flick of her waist. She ran her hands hungrily over my blue polyester uniform and tugged at my name tag. She left the food on the customer service counter and we went into my office. I closed the blinds and moaned loudly for a good five to ten minutes while she gave me head—which anyone in the vicinity could not help but hear. I would munch on a cafeteria hot dog I'd bought earlier so I wouldn't have to eat Siliidi's curry. I loved eating lunch while having my cock sucked. Later I'd throw the Sri Lankan food out in the dumpster, carefully wrapping it so nobody would see that I hadn't eaten it.

This thing that I had going with Siliidi couldn't last, and I knew it. She was eventually going to get her citizenship, and then she wouldn't need me anymore.

After two years in the United States, she was losing her accent. Now, when she told me to strip, she could have been any woman in a porn video. She was losing her uniqueness. I still got instantly hard at the sight of her, but I was less than satisfied with our sex. At first Siliidi had been so exciting, I had to have her, I needed so badly to be inside her. Now, while we were fucking I would think about the stale Twinkies on top of the refrigerator.

One night Siliidi was sitting on her side of the bed smoking a cigarette. She extinguished it only halfway through. "I get my citizenship next week," she said.

Siliidi wasn't desperate anymore. She moved out a few months after she got her papers from the government. I didn't try to stop her.

Sexually, Siliidi had spoiled me. I hadn't jerked off for the entire two years we were married, and I didn't want to jerk off again. Sex with a hot kinky woman with humongous tits had turned out to be everything I'd always wanted, at least in the beginning. Now, I want it again.

But I am faced with the dilemma of being Hubert W. Humphrey—a middle-aged, obese, pasty white, fast-food junkie with a middle management job at Kmart. I may not be the most pathetic man in the world, but I'm never going to be an ace on the singles scene. And I still can't afford a classy whore.

On the Internet, though, I'm a king. I choose who to get off with and when. On the Internet, there are women who need me—women even more desperate than I am.

So, I'm back to XoticMailOrderBrides.com. I've even lowered my standards. Now, I chat with them all—scrawny Thais, fake blondes from Russia. After all, you never know when you might find a woman who's desperate for a green card.

INFIDELITIES

G. L. Morrison

HOW DID I KNOW HE WAS UNFAITHFUL? I KNEW
it because I was his second wife. He'd been
unfaithful to his first wife—with me. I remember the excuses he gave her: working late,
"business trips" we took together, absurdly
frequent engine trouble or flat tires.

"She didn't fall for that?" I asked him. He
assured me that she believed every word.

I now know that she didn't. I don't. I am
just too amazed at his audacity to argue. Now
I also know what I didn't know when he and
I were making love for hours, pretzeling into
impossible, playful, passionate positions and
then sleeping, twisted into each other's arms
in a borrowed apartment of a friend who was
out of town for the weekend while Stephen was
supposedly on one of those "business trips." I

know that Stephen had sex with his wife, though he told me he
didn't. I know it because he is still having sex with me. Tender,
guilty, exhausted sex.

Now, six years after our illicit affair has been legalized, sani-
tized into a state of respectability, I am twice wounded. My
husband is cheating on me with another woman. And all those
years ago my lover, the same man, was cheating on me with his
wife. I don't know which betrayal I resent more. I should be
angry. I should resist the seductions and cut flowers, as short-
lived as his excuses. But I don't, because Stephen's a really great
lover. I don't know where he finds the energy. Does it excite
him to crawl into my bed with the scent of another woman still
clinging to him? To kiss me hungrily…?

Yes, Jennifer. He does still kiss me hungrily.

The other woman's name is Jennifer. Stephen crawls into
my bed as little as fifteen minutes after leaving hers. She lives
only a few miles away from us. I've never met her. But I know
where she lives. Does it excite him to rush in to me after making love to her? To twine his tongue around mine so that I
can almost taste her? So that the smell of her cunt, still wet
on his chin, overwhelms me. It excites me. It doesn't lessen
my jealousy, but it excites me. When his kisses have inflamed
me enough, I push his head down. His rough tongue patiently
tickles the inside of my thighs.

"Quickly," I hurry him. I want some of her juice still on his
tongue while he's licking me. Is it me he's thinking of while his
tongue wriggles into the muscled cave of my cunt? Is her cunt
lightly downed as mine, the hair thinned with age, or is she
young and rebelliously shaved smooth? I read his diary but he
leaves out details like these. "Jennifer," I heard him say into
the phone as he hung up very quickly. (*J* in his diary.) There

were only two Jennifers in his address book. One of them I recognized as an eighty-year-old great-aunt. I wrote down the other's address and phone number. *Sloppy, Stephen. Very sloppy.* Which is how his first wife caught us. I wasn't surprised his habits hadn't much changed.

I didn't call her. What would I have said? I've driven by her house, hoping to catch sight of her. My jealous curiosity drew me there. One day when I knew him to be on a real business trip, I stopped. *(Let this be a warning to you, Husbands of the World. It is not that difficult to check.)* I got out of the car. I rang her doorbell. She could just as easily have been on the trip with him. She wasn't.

Twenty-something with red braided hair answered the door.

"Hello," I said, cold and defiant.

"Hello," she said sweetly.

"Do you know who I am?" I demanded.

She looked puzzled. She shook her head apologetically. "I haven't lived here very long."

I didn't know what to say. This interview wasn't going at all as I had imagined it.

"I'm Karyn," I said. "Karyn Feinberg."

Her red braid bobbed amiably.

"Stephen Feinberg's wife."

She didn't bat an eyelash. Not a flicker of recognition.

"Are you Jennifer?" Maybe I was at the wrong address.

"Jennifer Reidenbach." She shook my hand politely.

I felt a little foolish. I kept waiting for Rod Serling to step out from behind a well-manicured bush. Should I ask her, "Are you having an affair with my husband?" Should I demand to smell her pubic hair? Would it be the same salty-sweet I licked off his cheek some nights?

Jennifer Reidenbach was looking at me kindly. "Can I help you?" she asked.

"I've lost my..." (Mind. I've definitely lost my mind.) "...My puppy. Have you seen him?"

"What does he look like?"

Like every other imaginary pet. "Brown, furry. About this high. Comes to the name of Romeo."

"That's a funny name for a dog."

"Isn't it?"

Jennifer Reidenbach shook her red braid. "No. I haven't seen him."

"Maybe your husband has seen him."

"I'm not married."

"Can I use your phone?" I asked.

"Sure," the fly said to the spider.

She led me to a kitchen phone. I stared at her pointedly. She left to give me privacy. I hit each of the auto-dial numbers programmed into her phone. One of them was certain to be Stephen's office number or my home. I hung up whenever anyone answered. I didn't hear a voice or message machine that I recognized. *That doesn't prove anything,* I told myself.

The walls of the kitchen and hallways were covered with snapshots. I looked for pictures of him, of them together. They were all of people I didn't know. I took in as much as I could of her apartment. "Are you a photographer?"

"I wish," she said wistfully. "I mean, yes, I am. I'm trying to be."

In spite of myself, I liked her. I went from room to room, looking at the photographs; looking around for some evidence, some telltale sign of Stephen.

"Maybe Romeo will come home on his own," Jennifer suggested.

"What?"

"Your dog. I hope you find him."

"Oh, him. He's the wandering type, seems like he forgets where home is."

"You should have him neutered," Jennifer said.

"That's a good idea," I agreed. Then I saw it—a picture of Stephen, a Polaroid of the two of them at the County Fair. *Last year's* fair!

"Who is this?" I tapped the photo.

"That's my boyfriend, Mark."

"Mark?"

"Uh-huh."

"He looks familiar," I told her. My teeth felt sharper for saying it.

"Does he? He lives in Philadelphia."

"Philadelphia?" I choked.

"Yes, he calls me when he comes to town. He comes here a lot on business. But not often enough. You know how long-distance relationships are."

"No...why don't you tell me?" So she did. Every word she said made my eyes a little wider. She was a very young, very beautiful, very gullible girl. He'd told her his name was Mark Smith.

"Smith?" I said. "You must be kidding."

She laughed, a completely guileless laugh. "That's what I said when he first told me. But somebody has to be named Smith, right?"

"Right."

She made me coffee and told me how they met, the last time

she'd seen him, every implausible word he'd ever said, how fervently she believed them all, and of course, what a wonderful lover he was. I ground my teeth silently.

"How do you know he's not married?" I asked her.

"Oh," she shrugged the idea off. "I'd know. I want to show you something." She took me by the hand and led me to her bedroom. The bed was covered in tie-dyed silk. The walls were crowded with pictures. Here was Stephen. There was Stephen. Stephen everywhere. It was a temple. The walls were altars and Stephen's face blazed like a candle in every corner.

In one he held his hand out in protest. *No more pictures.* Another was clearly taken in the garden of his mother's house. (What had they been doing there? Where had his mother been? Whose house had "Mark" said it was?) Every piece of the puzzle fragmented into more questions. I was more confused than ever. More pictures were of him sprawled on her bed, this very bed. I looked at the rumpled sheets, smoothed them with my hand. In some he was naked. In some, sleeping. In some he was looking out at her with undisguised lust. It was odd, since he seemed to be looking right out of the picture at me. He seemed to be saying *I want you. Now.* Although I knew it was not me he had been wanting, my clit leaped like a candlewick under the familiar attention of a match.

Jennifer grinned like a child sharing a secret treasure with a friend, which is in fact what she was. I ruffled her hair.

As I was leaving, Jennifer hugged me earnestly. "I hope you get Romeo back. I know how terrible it is to lose something you love."

"Thank you," I said.

"Please come back again."

I grinned wickedly. "I will."

After that, I did what any vigilant dog-owner would do. I kept my husband on a tight leash. I made plans to do things in the evening, couple things, command-performance things like dinner at his mother's. I became good friends with the boss's wife. We had dinner with them once a week. I'd have finagled more if I could but it was difficult to wrench the boss away from *his* mistress—a girl who worked in the office and looked no more than sixteen. I dropped in at Stephen's office unexpectedly "to have lunch together." I was suspiciously romantic and spontaneous. Stephen retaliated by varying his lunch hour erratically and saying, "If I'd only known you were coming," hoping to force me to call and announce my surprise inspections. It was a statistical certainty that one day I would be arriving as he was leaving. That day came. He didn't see me, so what choice did I have but to follow him? What would I do if he led me to her house? Would I burst in on them, catch them in bed, wipe the lust and bliss off their amazed faces, while the lustful, blissful photos stared down from the bedroom walls at us—a jury of our peers? Would I sit frozen in the car while they made love inside? What if I rang the bell and no one answered? Who would untangle her limbs from her lover to answer the door? Leave him for Jehovah's witnesses, Girl Scout cookies, or pseudoneighbors' lost dogs? And when they didn't answer the door, what would I do? Crawl in a window? Break down the door? Call 911? *Help. My husband is making love to a beautiful woman.*

I shouldn't have worried. He didn't go to her house. He went to a restaurant. For lunch. Not a terribly suspicious way to spend one's lunch hour. And oh, how fortunate for me...to be able to "surprise" him here. "Honey, what a nice surprise!" I'd exclaim brightly. I could feel the leash tighten. I hid my face behind a menu and sauntered toward his table. But the chair across from him wasn't empty. Jennifer's hair fell around her shoulders in tight, red curls. They framed her face like a halo. I sat where I could watch them. I ordered something. I ate it without tasting it. I watched "Mark" and "his girl." Jennifer fed him cheesecake with her fork. I noticed she saved him the last bite. Neither of them saw me. Neither of them looked in my direction even once. They left separately. On a whim, I decided to follow *her*.

We ended up at the mall. I followed her from the parking lot, through the stores, unseen. I felt like that character in a Woody Allen movie who turns invisible after drinking a strange Chinese tea. Could anyone see me? Had I eaten something at lunch that might make me invisible? Was I really this stealthy or was I dreaming? I'd felt a little dreamy ever since I'd rung Jennifer's doorbell that day, or maybe even before that, when I first saw her name in Stephen's address book. I had that disconnected, floaty feeling. It wasn't dreaming. It was waking up from the dream, a lie that had been my life. So this was being awake? This half-angry, half-horny, half-grieving, curious, bewildered, excited, half-mad, more-than-a-hundred-percent feeling?

Three teenagers, walking astride, scowled at me. In my reverie I hadn't noticed that I was supposed to have stepped aside for them. At least that's what I interpreted from their scowls. It could also have meant "I hate the world, not just you." I stepped aside. An elderly mall-walker who had stopped to tie her shoe shook her head regretfully. Whether she felt sorry for me or the teens, who knows? But it was confirmed: I was not invisible. I walked a little faster. I caught up with Jennifer. I put my hand on her shoulder.

"It's you!" she said.

The delight in her voice startled me. It also warmed me. She was glad to see me. I was surprised how much I liked that. I felt a twinge of guilt for deceiving her. I hooked my arm in hers and we walked through the shops together like old friends. She must be lonely, I thought, to have taken to me so quickly. Is that why she let herself fall in love with Stephen, believe every word he said? Is that why I had? Loneliness and passion—a dangerous elixir.

I pointed to Victoria's Secret. "Come help me pick out a bra."

Giggling, she followed me into the store. Jennifer was out of her element there. She looked as dumbstruck and embarrassed as if she'd been caught going through her mother's underwear drawer. What gives? I thought mistresses were born with the Kama Sutra in one hand and a suitcase of elegant lingerie in the other. Clearly someone had forgotten to tell Jennifer this.

I pulled her into the dressing room. "Help me with this strap."

She buckled the red velvet bra. We both admired my reflection in the mirror.

"What do you think?"

"You're beautiful," she said innocently.

I jiggled in it for effect, watching my velvet-clad breasts bounce in the mirror.

"But is it sexy?"

She bit her lip. "Oh, yes."

I smiled. She was so easy. *Like shooting fish in a barrel, Stephen. Where's the sport in that?* Emotions played over her face in shades of pink. I brushed a strand of red hair out of her eyes, tenderly. She swallowed hard.

"If you think it looks good, I'll buy it," I said.

"Shall I wrap it for you?" the teenage sales clerk asked,

sounding as if she assumed I was buying it for someone younger, infinitely hipper, than myself.

"No, I'll wear it." I tore off the tag, handing it and my credit
card to the clerk. I whispered in Jennifer's ear, "I love the way
it feels. The way I feel knowing I have something so sexy on
under my clothes." Jennifer squirmed. I moved away from her
as abruptly as I had moved near her. I scrutinized the racks.

"What do you think of this?" I held up a daring bit of lace.

"Oh, well…" Jennifer stuttered. "It's very, um. There's not
much to it, is there?"

"Do you think what's-his-name would like this?"

"Who?"

"Your friend," I smiled patiently.

"Mark?" she choked, a cough that ended in giggling. "What
man *wouldn't* like it?"

"What man indeed?" I asked.

The sales clerk snickered. She had clearly gotten the wrong
idea about us.

"We'll take it. Charge it to my card." I threw it on the counter.

"Oh, no!" Jennifer groaned. "I could never wear something
like that. I'd be too shy. I couldn't…it's just not…it's just not
me!" She blushed just looking at it on the hanger.

"Exactly why it would be such a lovely surprise." *Just not
the surprise you're expecting,* I thought.

Jennifer continued to protest halfheartedly as the salesgirl
rang it up.

"Thank you." Jennifer kissed me on the cheek, shyly, as she
took the unwanted package.

The sales clerk snickered her signature snicker. Lesbians were
the height of comedy in her small world. As I was signing the

receipt, I leaned close to the clerk and purred, "Try it. You might like it."

"What?" Jennifer hadn't quite heard me, but thought I was speaking to her.

"Nothing," I said. I slipped my arm around her waist in a friendly gesture.

Since we were "neighbors" and my car was in the shop, I caught a ride "home" with her. Actually my car was parked in the row behind hers. It surprised me how easily lies fell off my lips now. How quickly they came to me, how confidently I spouted them. *I see the appeal, Stephen.* It's not just sex. It's the ability to be anyone, anyone at all. To make up a life on the spur of the moment and then to wear it like an expensive suit. Chic, well fitted, and in whatever color you want. What no longer surprised me was Jennifer's unconditional belief in everything I said. She was well trained. She was the perfect accomplice to my lies: so willing to believe anything. Who could resist lying to her?

In the car we talked about music and food and our childhoods. I wondered how much of what I told her was true. The truth sounded tinny to me: small and unbelievable. I retold stories I had told a million times before, but now I heard them with a new ear. Is that the truth, I wondered? Is the way I remember it true? Lying had made the truth enigmatic, a sort of unachievable ideal. What is true? I even doubted my likes and dislikes. Was artichoke chicken with corkscrew pasta really my favorite dish? Or had I simply believed it the first time I told myself it was? Believed it, stopped asking questions, and from then on reported it as the truth.

Every story Jennifer told me about Mark was the truth—the

truth as she knew it. She asked me if I had found my dog. I admitted to keeping him on a chain now but that he still managed to wriggle out of his collar and run free. That was the truth, wasn't it?

At her house, I didn't need a lie to get inside. She welcomed me in. She made me feel at home.

"I'd like a drink."

"Herbal tea or Coke?" Jennifer asked. "Or I think I have some orange juice."

"Something stronger."

She brought out a bottle of wine. I took it into the bedroom. I sat in a chair and she sat on the bed. We drank and talked and laughed. All around us, pictures of Stephen/Mark smiled.

Halfway through the bottle I suggested she model her lingerie. There was much blushing and a little protesting. Not as much protesting as I'd expected.

Just enough "Oh, I couldn't" to oil the machine of my "It'll be fun." I was sure that was true.

She unzipped her jeans. Wriggled out of her silk blouse, her red curls bouncing riotously over her bare shoulders. I watched her. I was fascinated—and hungry. Had Stephen watched her like this, shucking off the day's clothing and burdens to reveal this blinding skin? Had he sat in this very chair and seen what I was seeing? The chair's hard back kept me alert, aware of a slight discomfort. Jennifer watched me. It wasn't Stephen she was seeing in the chair; it was me. She undressed slowly. She pulled her shirt over her head like a burlesque stripper removing a glove. Slowly. Her back was lightly muscled, yet classic as a Greek statue. This Aphrodite looked over her shoulder and smiled at me.

I picked up Jennifer's camera from her dresser and checked

for film. I snapped her picture. Whirr. Click. She quickly turned toward me, surprised and embarrassed. She laughed and hurried to put her clothes back on. I kept taking pictures. Whirr. Click. She was as beautiful re-dressing. Hopping, half in and half out of her pants, she raised her hand in impatient surrender. It was the same gesture I'd seen in Stephen's picture.

No more pictures.

"Stop," she laughed.

I didn't.

Pants on, but unzipped. Blouse in hand. "Stop, really."

I really didn't. Whirr. Click. I snapped another picture of her crossing the room. I got another, a close-up of her jostling breasts, before she reached the chair.

"Give it to me." She held out her hand for the camera.

"Are you shy?" I snapped another picture. Her red-brown nipple. Her frowning lips.

"C'mon. Give it to me."

"What will you give me if I do?"

Jennifer licked her hesitant lips. "What do you want?"

"I want to take pictures of you."

She took the camera from me and turned it over in her hand. "I'm not comfortable on that side of the camera. I like to see, not to be seen."

"Jennifer, there's so much you don't see."

"Huh?"

"Let me show you how other people see you. How I see you."

I held my hand out for the camera. She looked dubious. I refilled our wineglasses.

"You take my picture," I said, "and then I'll take yours. Fair?"

"Fair," she agreed.

On the dresser where I'd found the camera there was a clock radio. I turned it on. I unbuttoned my shirt, seductively swaying to the music. Whirr. Click. Whirr. Click. I danced for her to the metronome of the camera, the strobe of the flash. I told myself brilliant, exciting lies. I was Cleopatra. My hips could bring a nation to its knees. I stepped out of my clothes. Dancing, whirling for her. I was Salome, only even John the Baptist couldn't resist me. The taste of me was sweeter than heaven. I was a stripper in a filthy nightclub. Jennifer was hordes of men hungry to stick dollar bills—hundred-dollar bills!—into my G-string. I used the chair as a pole, bumping and grinding. I swung my leg over the chair. I was a housewife seducing my husband's mistress. I laughed. No, that fantasy was too farfetched. I was every model seducing every photographer through the raw art of her body.

Walking toward her so that she had to back up to keep me in the frame, I steered Jennifer toward the bed. She backed up until she could back up no further. Whirr. Click. I leaned over her, pressing my navel to the camera lens; blinding the camera. She was mine now. I didn't know if this was how Stephen had her and by now I didn't care. I tugged her jeans off and tossed them on the floor beside her shirt. She was wearing Batman undies. I threw my own clothes on the growing pile. I gently parted the lips that Batman had recently guarded and kissed her cunt. I reveled in the smell of her, not the faraway hinted-at scent mixed with soap that I smelled on Stephen's half-washed face. This was the real smell of woman. An alive, musk-breaded smell. I wanted to swallow her whole.

I'd never touched any cunt but my own. I'd never seen one so close. It was fascinating, elaborate, more stunning than I'd fantasized. The pictures I'd seen barely hinted at the color and intricacy of the flesh that lay open before me. In every way imaginable I was swimming in forbidden, unfamiliar waters. Tongue-first, I dived in. I began licking her gingerly, but encouraged by the noises she was making, I threw myself into her cave with all the enthusiasm of a more experienced spelunker. Though I tired quickly—unprepared for the vigorous exercise this sport required of my jaw—I didn't let up for a minute. I wanted to feel her, to taste her coming into my eager mouth. She didn't disappoint me. There was a sharp taste like metal amid the musk and she came, writhing wildly, so that I could barely keep my mouth on her. Then she turned me over and gave me (or had) a taste of my own medicine.

Curious and tireless as only virgins can be, I licked every inch of her and she nibbled most of me, including territory I never remember having had nibbled before. After hours and orgasms—neither of us bothered to count—I parted her cunt lips and kissed them more fondly than passionately.

"I wish you could see what I see."

Jennifer handed me the camera. She held her lips open so that I could photograph the velvet inside. I tried to coax her clit into the picture but, overworked and camera shy, it hid stubbornly beneath its hood. Still she was beautiful, different in every frame. Click. I held the camera in my right hand and took a picture of my finger on her clit, deep inside her. My finger here. There. Two fingers. Click. Click. Jennifer softly moaned until I ran out of film. She reloaded the camera. I held it out to get pictures of us together. She did the same. We agreed they'd be terrible pictures, off-centered, oddly angled, random and beautiful...like our love.

She used the word *love*. It surprised me. *Oh, Stephen. She's so easy. So innocent. So inexperienced that she thinks sex is love.* But maybe it is. How could a liar like me know the truth about love? I remembered what she'd said in the lingerie store: "I couldn't wear that. It's not me!" How would Jennifer know that what we'd done tonight was anything but the real "me"? It made sense that she would interpret my actions as love. She wasn't the sort of girl who jumped into bed with strange women. She wasn't the sort of girl who had affairs. That wasn't her.

I didn't ask the obvious: what about Mark? I was sure she'd break it to him gently. If she chose to break it to him at all. Perhaps she intended to cheat on me with him. As she'd cheated on him with me. Which was it? Perhaps she didn't know what would happen next. I certainly didn't. If the new "me" she'd discovered was capable of this, wasn't it capable of anything?

That picture of Stephen leered down at us. The one with the look, the smug look, the I-want-you-and-you're-mine look. I'd wipe that look right off his face.

"Promise me one thing," I said.

"Anything."

"Promise you'll put up a picture of me, a picture of us, right here." I took the leering picture down and put it under the bed. "So I can watch you sleep."

"Whatever you want," she whispered into the small of my neck.

That answered all the questions I might have about Mark. If he ever came into this bedroom again, he'd see what I wanted him to see. That I'd been here. That he didn't know her or me at all. That women are not numbers that lie flat in your address book just waiting for you to call. And what could he say to that? To her? To my triumphant picture?

Love is a fickle religion. The next time I came to her house—

if I ever came again—I might find my own face and skin and hers, wet with my kisses, lit like a candle in every corner. Or she might promise me anything and then do as she liked. My picture might come out of the closet like some aunt's tacky, unwelcome gift that you put on display whenever you expect her visit. Anything was possible. Hadn't I just proven that? Her devotion was so believable. But believable is not the same as truthful, is it? What if Jennifer wasn't so simple, so easy? What if she'd played us both, Stephen and me? What if she believed my lies (and his!) the way that Stephen thought I believed his lies? Yes, I laughed, and what if I really *was* Cleopatra?

Liars believe that everyone's lying. After a really big lie, no truth seems possible. Was I lying when I said I loved her? I whispered it again into her soft neck. If a good lie sounds like the truth, then what does the truth sound like?

I let myself out while she was sleeping. The lingerie sat untouched in the Victoria's Secret bag. I pulled out the leering picture of Mark from under the bed and put it into the bag. I took it with me. I called a taxi from the corner. The taxi took me to the mall, where I'd left my car. From there, I drove to "Philadelphia." *You remember Philadelphia, that's where Mark lives.* Fortunately it was only ten minutes away.

Mark...no, Stephen...was waiting up for me.

"Where have you been?"

Oh, what a tightrope is jealousy! Why had I never thought to make him follow me, watch me, wonder where I was when he wasn't around?

"Where have you been?" he demanded, louder.

"Shopping," I said, although the mall had been closed for hours. I hefted the Victoria's Secret bag for effect. Then

I showed him that bit of lace Jennifer had thought was too daring. That little bit of covering that was more naked than being naked. And I dared and dared. I turned on the radio. I tuned it to the same station Jennifer listened to. I danced for him. I didn't show the same energy and enthusiasm as I had a few hours before. I was tired. And he was my husband, not a conquered general or a biblical prophet or an intoxicating, nubile, redheaded, new woman-lover. He was just my husband. He was a sure thing. My sure thing. And I was his sure thing. (Though not, perhaps, as sure as he'd thought.) It isn't so bad being or having a sure thing. I knew which wiggle and oomph would get a sigh or a smile. I could predict his expressions before they found their way from his brain to his face. And that was a good thing. I liked his expressions. I especially liked the one he wore now, a heat burning in his eyes as he pulled the lace off me—a little too roughly. It was the same hunger and satisfaction, the same look as in the picture.

We made love. It was Stephen's turn to taste the other woman on me. Did he know what he was tasting? As I was coming, I thought about calling out "Mark," but why spoil a nice moment? The idea was so funny to me that what came out of my mouth was *oh*-laugh-*oh*-laugh-*ohmygod*.

While he was brushing his teeth—what a familiar sound—I put the lacy thing in my underwear drawer. I put that damn picture in there as well. What should I do with it? Hang it over our bed? Or in his office, replacing that irritating cowboy print?

Stephen looked up at me from the underwear drawer, grinning lewdly. I buried him in bras and panties. For now, he was fine where he was until I thought of someplace better.

DANKE SCHOEN

Helena Settimana

VEGAS. ONE HUNDRED AND FIVE DEGREES. THE
ice-maker sweated, so did the Coke machine. I
had gotten on a Greyhound in Buffalo, aiming
for Hollywood, but was persuaded by chance
to stop short. During most of the journey
I had been poked and prodded by a randy
shoe salesman from Tonawanda; I wasn't that
desperate. He was going on to L.A.; I quickly
decided I wasn't, *thank god*. I stepped off the
bus, stiff and worn and relieved, into the hazy
glare. One suitcase, a one-way ticket and two
hundred bucks left to my name.

Found a motel with a stuttering neon sign,
_otel Vac_nc_, blue, white, and faded red,
like an old billboard painted on the side of
a factory. Called, apropos of nothing, the
Ocean View. A used car dealership on one side,

with its vinyl pennant flags fluttering in the dusty breeze like harlequin sharks' teeth. Strip club two doors down on the other side. Weedy, empty lot across the street.

The charms of the Ocean View: crumbling stucco, rust stains in the sink, air-conditioning that didn't work 'cause the wires were all pulled out. Twenty-year-old TV with rabbit ears. Mildew in the bath. A musty, creaking bed that sagged in the middle. Twenty bucks a night. One hundred and five degrees at two in the afternoon, in the shade of the overhanging roof. Sat outside on a white plastic lawn chair and fanned myself with the bus schedule. Felt the trickle run down my back, wriggle between my buttcheeks. It felt like an ant crawling on my skin.

Wandered for a week. Got chucked from most of the casinos for loitering. "No vagrants," they said. Christ, it's a hundred and five out, and a girl can't cut a break. Went to auditions, grueling nightmares of tap in heels, flashing crotches flagging the director. *Woo hoo, look at me! I've got the widest gap between my legs! See how high I can kick!* Walking, aching, falling through doors into the wall of heat, seas of tourists— *yentas* in Tyrolean hats, obese polyester-clad Midwesterners, chattering Japanese in cotton sun-hats clutching their cameras. Swam through the mobs with *Call you in the morning / I don't have a phone* echoing in my ears. Used the pay phone to check back. *Sorry, not what we're looking for...Tits are too small, doll...Legs are too heavy...Not enough experience...Looking for someone younger.*

Turned ten tricks within the week. Four businessmen, a bus driver, a cop, three guys on leave from their wives' love affairs with the slots, and the Arab barber from down the street. Ten hermetically sealed cocks of vastly different proportion made my acquaintance and left. Never once heard a complaint about my legs or my tits. I flushed their passing down the drain; I'm noncommittal. It paid for the room, food, and the movies, where it was cool. I'd climb, holding my popcorn and mega-cup, all the way to the balcony, where I'd fish the ice out of my Diet Coke and hold it to my scorched skin. Escape.

Took a job at the strip club. Work seven to three—seven shows a night. In bed by four, if I'm alone, which is usually.

Voices in the blue morning told me I had neighbors moving in. Women. A woman. I didn't know; I heard voices. Doors slamming. I checked the view. No one there, just a big beat-up Dodge Ram parked in front of my room. I padded back to bed and closed my eyes.

The moaning started after about five minutes. Thumping against the wall, sighs coming through. I pulled the pillow over my head. Squeezed the dawning light out of my eyes. The moans got louder and my hand trailed between my legs in spite of my fatigue. I worked it hard. Swelled and gushed and pulled until I flooded with the final trailing cry and fell into a fitful sleep. The roar of an engine woke me at noon. The Ram peeled out of the lot.

Had to work at three. Took a shower. Fished in my cooler for a beer; found none, so I padded to the Coke machine in my flip-flops and cutoffs, T-shirt, whatever was lying around. The Ram roared back. I found myself saying hello to the driver, surprised when I realized it was a woman. I mean, I'd heard the voices all right—but the person at the wheel didn't strike me as female.

This was the funny thing: she looked like Wayne Newton. Okay, okay, like Wayne Newton when he was a kid, before he became smarmy Mr. Vegas and grew the moustache and all. Same swept-back mound of dark hair, cupid's-bow mouth, deep dimples, crinkled eyes, bolo tie. Not that I have a thing for Newton, it was just...unusual. When she spoke, I had the same reaction: *Wayne Newton.* That voice—like a lady hockey player. Like Jodie Foster. Jock-ish. A friend calls it *Lesbanian,* as if there's a country that produces this particular accent—Lesbania—which has a province where all the womyn look and sound like Vegas lounge-singers and wear western-style tuxes. *Thank you, you've been a wonderful...I love you. Good night.*

I opened the door to my room, then turned around. "Hey. Are you staying here?" I asked. That's me—Einstein.

She nodded, looking me over. "Yeah. Till Sunday. Who's asking?"

"Trish," I said, holding out my hand.

"Casey," said she, offering hers.

"Where's your friend?" I asked, thinking of the morning. The moaning.

"Friend?" A pause. "Oh!" She laughed. "Just company." Blushing. "I'm here on my own."

"Why?" I asked, nosy and direct. She told me that she was in town for a celebrity look-alike contest. I told her I bet I could tell who she was appearing as. She laughed again.

"I sing a mean 'Danke Schoen,'" she said, and burst into song. Fingers snapping, she stood in the parking space beside her truck and treated me to the whole thing.

I applauded.

The contest was on Saturday. It was now just Thursday afternoon. I told her I had to go to work and hooked a thumb in the direction of the club. She nodded and said, "Okay, see ya."

Around midnight I was sliding down the pole for the fifth time when I glanced down and spotted her. She had her rhinestone shirt on, with a big turquoise arrowhead clip on her tie. Cowboy boots. Man, was she playing it up. I finished my set and went to sit with her. Had a drink.

"I want a dance," she said in my ear. "A dance—just you an' me."

I looked around, confused. "A dance, where?" I asked.

"Aw, fercrissakes! *Here,*" she said. "Twenty bucks, right? Take me back there and show me what you can do."

I looked around again. Place was deader than usual for a Thursday night. "Sure," I said. "But no touching—unless I say so."

She sat on the banquette, legs spread—no different a posture from the countless men who strained in that room—cigarette in one hand, glass of Scotch beside her. Hooked a finger in my direction and said, "Dance." Actually, it came out as, "Dansh"—*Lesbanian,* you know.

I danced, wanting suddenly to prove myself braver and wilder than any other, moving closer to her with every step, hovered over her quavering thigh and watched her chest heave. Pushed my crotch close to her face and danced away again. Bent from the waist, looking at her from between my legs. Pulled the string aside, gave her a peek. Tease. I came back and settled on her thigh, moved a knee into her crotch, messed her pomaded hair, let my tits graze her hungry mouth and rocked until she joined me.

I took my twenty and kissed her cheek. Walked to the bar, lit a smoke. Left her on the sofa, sprawled and sweaty. A minute later she followed, trailed her palm across my ass on her way to the door, and left.

I left through the back door of the club at three-thirty and found her waiting in the truck. It was only a couple of doors to the motel, but there she was, staring out the rolled-down window. She leaned over and opened the passenger door.

"Give you a ride?" she offered.

"Where to?"

"Wherever. Outta here. Get in."

I slid into the seat beside her. She leaned over and kissed me hard on the mouth. Her teeth on mine, tongue probing, hot. I thought I'd explode.

"I felt bad about the club," she said, coming up for air.

"Why? It's my job." I lit one and blew smoke out the window, heart hammering between my legs.

"I felt bad about it because I could feel you wet on my thigh and I couldn't touch." *Busted.* Her hand fished a breast out of my blouse, thumbed the nipple. She watched me intently; my lips parted, and by now I was trembling. She turned the key in the ignition. "Let's get out of here."

"Okay," I said weakly. "Go back to the motel?"

"Nah...have a place in mind."

She pointed the Ram toward the desert and thirty minutes later pulled into the ruins of an old service station, drove to the back and killed the lights.

I was breathing hard; her hand was on my mound, her tongue in my mouth. Shooting stars raced across the sky.

"Get out of the truck," she said, and, shivering, I did as I was told. "Get on the hood." I did. It sagged and buckled a bit under my weight, but it was warm and I didn't much mind the cold air, with that much heat rising beneath me. My breath escaped, vaporous in the dark.

"Lie down." She ran her hands up my legs, yanked my thong off and tossed it into the dust. Licked a nipple, flicked it with her tongue. It contracted in the cold; got stiff. Hands like hard little animals spidered down my sides, burrowed in the folds between my legs. Her tongue stiff, pushy, burning. Two fingers neatly hooked into me, pulling me toward oblivion. Satellites raced overhead, and I rose up and screamed into the empty desert night.

On the ride back to the motel, I fell into a deep sleep. I called in sick the next day. We ran off to the movies, sat in the balcony necking. I showed her my trick with the ice. She held a chip in her mouth and another to my nipple, secretively, silent in the dark. Cooled my neck, my earlobe with her tongue. I unzipped her pants, felt the damp curl of hair through her briefs. A rush of heat. She pushed her hips forward and, stunned, I found her clit. It was enormous. Hell, I'd had tricks with smaller dicks than that. I looked at her. Into my ear, through my hair, she whispered, "Stroke it...I like it when it's stroked."

I jerked her off between my fingers, almost like I would a man, while she bit my neck and stifled her voice. I'd lost mine.

Back at the motel, I asked her to fuck me with it. She was happy to oblige. It wasn't so much the penetration that was satisfying—it was just barely possible—it was just the *idea* of it. It stuck out through the cotton of her briefs: a freak thing she said she'd had all her life, enhanced somewhat by a treatment she was taking. She was sopping wet and hard as a date pit and my insides knotted up as soon as it tickled the mouth of my cunt. We came crashing together, our legs tense, toes cocked, trails of ooze shining on our thighs, our bellies. Her perfect backswept coif hung in her eyes; her small, dark tits pointed. She was a study in points. When she lay back, nipples and clit strained at the ceiling, then faded into the planes of her body as her arousal ebbed.

Saturday, I went to see her show. She sang "Danke Schoen" and winked at me when she came to the line *"Picture shows,*

second balcony…" She placed second and won a shitpile
of money. Got beaten by some guy from San Fran who
impersonated Siegfried, Roy, *and* the tigers. He got even more
dough.

Back at the motel she announced that she was going to go on
to Oakland where there awaited the matter of a little surgery
she wanted to have done. The winnings, added to what she'd
already saved, would get her there.

She packed the Ram on Sunday. Rolled out into the morning
sun, tossed her last bag next to her seat in the cab. I stayed
behind, still believing I'd make the chorus line, get a little
apartment; even in winter it's warmer than Buffalo.

She promised she'd be back. I watched her drive off in the
truck with a wink and a wave. Watched her drive off to become
a man. Maybe then she could actually pass, maybe grow that
mustache, maybe *win* next time. I thought she was fine just as
she was, but it wasn't my life. No, sir, not at all.

SHADOW CHILD

Cheyenne Blue

SHE HAS ALWAYS FOLLOWED PEOPLE, SLIPPING through the shadows in their wake, pattering on soft-shod feet in and out of darkness and pools of light, daring them to turn and see her.

When she was small, she would follow her mother around the house, peering out of closet doors and spying under the shower curtain at her mother's dimpled and voluptuous figure shaving her legs in the shower.

"Adrienne?" Her mother's tired voice, separating each syllable of her name, rising up at the end in warning, would result in cascading giggles through chubby fingers and inevitably the wide-eyed horror of the chase, the capture, and the punishment.

But even the humiliation of a red, stinging bottom would not stop her stalking. She would watch her mother, plump thighs spread on the toilet bowl, belly quivering, the wipe of the brown furred gash with the pink paper. She would watch her brother, fingering his pee-pee, playing with the pinched tip and the hairless empty sacs of skin that hung below.

Daringly, she followed her third-grade teacher out of school, into the parking lot. She slunk into the backseat of her car when the teacher placed books and papers on the passenger seat and fumbled for the dropped keys at her feet. Huddled on the floor, feeling the thrum of the driveshaft under her cheek on the puppy-pee–smelling carpet, Adrienne rode home with her teacher, creeping out of the unlocked car in the darkened garage long after dinnertime.

As a teenager the thrill of the hunt fully enraptured her. Brett the bastard, Brett the unfaithful, Brett the pubescent hero who captured her imagination and taught her what the space between her legs was really for. Hurried encounters on the cracked vinyl seats of his Chevy, the faded floral upholstery of his parents' couch, and once, daringly, in their bed.

"Hurry," she would whisper in mock terror in his ear as he heaved and grunted above her. "We'll get caught."

Brett the bastard, who used the constant fear of discovery as an excuse to evade her satisfaction. "It takes too long, Addy," he would say, shaking his head in pretend sympathy when she guided his hand to her aching center. "They'll catch us."

Brett the unfaithful, who had time aplenty to pleasure her best friend, with his hands and with his mouth. Those same twisted thin lips that he would never place on her, Addy, not where she wanted it most.

She suspected him of infidelity, and in the hot haze of teenage jealousy followed him one night, in black jeans and black sweatshirt, her bright hair caught under a dark cap: the spy, the wronged one, sick and heartsore.

She remembers well how the thump of her heart drowned out her soft footfalls on rain-soaked streets. She followed him, flitting in and out of doorways, a vampire child in black merging with the shadows, dodging the shimmering pools of streetlights. It was too easy. Brett the arrogant never looked back, just walked with purposeful stride to his assignation. The dark dead-end alley, that cliché of spy stories, the garbage bins, the metal fire escape, even, she saw, the flick of a rat's tail.

She waited, hidden in the shadow of a fire escape, and watched in clenching horror as her friend approached. Brett the betrayer grabbed her friend around the waist, his mouth descending to claim, his hands moving to her breasts.

It was fast and it was urgent. It was heated. It was everything she'd never had. She watched as his mouth moved on soft, white breasts, biting and sucking with fevered urgency, his hands popping buttons, curling down into lace panties. She watched her friend rip open his fly, free his cock, wrap her small hand around the shaft, and stroke it rhythmically. She saw the thrust of that cock repeatedly into the hand, the clench of the buttocks, the guttural cries of completion, and the spill of the seed over the hand, over the cloth, and onto the ground. Brett the selfish dropped to his knees, flaccid cock drooping out of his pants, and put his mouth to her friend. She saw the blonde head roll back in ecstasy as he slurped and suckled her, howls of release echoing in the empty alley.

Adrienne's hand was down her own pants, snaking into her sodden panties, parting her curls with a delicate finger to probe up, into the heat and moisture of her arousal. She watched, panting, as Brett the philanderer drove his renewed hardness into her friend, thrusting and grinding, pressing her back against the wet stone of the alleyway, pumping into her with the short, hard spurts she knew so well.

She came when he did, her flickering finger and the sight of his urgent thrusts driving her over the edge into the silent spasms of release.

They passed her as they left, hand in hand. She turned her face from them so that its pale oval wouldn't give her presence away. She didn't want them to find her here, jeans undone, panties twisted and soaked with her juices.

She followed them at other times too. Compulsively into their secret hideaways in bleachers and alleys, in drive-ins and park bushes. It was too easy. And it was better than Brett the uncaring ever was.

She has always followed people, slipping through the shadows in their wake, pattering on soft-shod feet in and out of darkness and pools of light, daring them to turn and see her.

Now she follows strangers. It is an altogether different proposition, fraught with risk and the dangers of discovery. She has a sixth sense that tells her when someone is just sliding off to be alone and when they are off to meet a lover or husband. She cannot define it; maybe it's the release of musk and pheromones into the air, maybe it's that yeasty smell of arousal; maybe she has become so attuned to the gestures of secrecy that she knows them without conscious thought. Whatever it is, she is rarely wrong.

Adrienne waits outside the glass monolith. An office building like many others, nondescript in its conformity of sleek and soulless design. Her latest vicarious lover works here, and he will be leaving soon, leaving to meet his lover. She wonders what he tells his wife, what apologetic story of work and dead-lines he will weave to cover his deception.

She watches him leave, striding into the windblown street, head lowered, dark trousers flapping around his legs. The colors of fall surround him: russet leaves, pumpkin-orange candy wrappers—and Adrienne's fox-red head as she slipstreams in his wake.

He enters a church. It is unlocked at this hour, although later it will be barred against the homeless who sleep under its lintels. She slips in behind him, creeping into a pew in the middle, falling to her knees on the hassock and peering through laced fingers at her prey as he hesitates, looking around before he slips into the vestibule at one side of the altar.

Apart from herself, Adrienne the irreverent, the church is now empty. She waits, head bowed in mock penitence until she hears the swift tapping of purposeful heels hurrying down the aisle. It's Wednesday. It's five o'clock, time for an illicit quickie. Hail Mary, mother of grace.

The heels fade into silence, entering the vestibule. Adrienne imagines the soft kiss of greeting, the rustle of hands moving over crisp business linens, the sigh against the exposed neck. She waits, counting her heartbeats. Too soon and she risks discovery. Too late and she misses the heated foreplay, the bites and the panting.

On silent feet she approaches the wooden door. Her gut clenches as she slowly pushes the door open. She offers a prayer of gratitude to whoever has kept the door so silent on its oiled hinges. A dart, a duck, a flurry of skirts, and she's in, holed up like a ferret, tucked behind the stacked music stands and trestle tables. One hand burrows under her skirt and into her panties in hot anticipation of what is to come.

She spreads her legs, and dips between them. Through the stalks of table legs and dusty surfaces she can see them. His mouth is already moving on bared breasts, the dark business suit hanging open as the infidel gropes with pale hands. A pinch of the rosy nipple, puckered and erect, quivering in anticipation. The open mouth on her breast.

"No marks," whispers the woman, then stifles a scream as he bites. A rosy bloom on the soft skin. The hot, sweet smell of arousal coils lazily into the room.

Adrienne's fingers circle her own sex, around and around, slowly, touching the tender lips with careful fingers. She mustn't come too soon. She watches through drooping lids as the man lifts the dark skirt, bunching it in his large hand. Slender legs come into view. Higher, he drags the skirt higher, sliding it over quivering thighs, the rasp of linen on nylon sending sparks of static leaping into the charged air. Adrienne fancies that they could ignite in the heated tension of the room.

The skirt is around the woman's waist now as she leans back, arched over the stacked chairs. Her lover drops to his knees and pulls stockings and panties down and off in one swift movement. His mouth drops and latches on to her, sucking on her open flushed sex. Adrienne sees the golden hands spreading the creamy thighs, sees the shining moisture as he plants his face deep into the pungent crevice, slurping loudly, swallowing, and sucking.

Her own finger dips deep into the cream of her sex, and she brings it to her mouth, tasting the salt and sour. She fixes her eyes on the man, and mimics his pistoning tongue with her finger.

The woman's orgasm is sudden. Her upper body jolts, jolts again. The little death. Her mouth forms an O, rosebud pale, funeral rose pink.

The man rises, undoes his trousers, freeing his shaft, shiny and taut with tension. Adrienne can almost feel the silky smoothness of it. She can imagine the slippery moisture oozing from the slotted tip. She is circling with two fingers now, slipping easily in and out of her own sodden sex, wet to the wrist, the tops of her thighs sticky and sweat-filmed.

He positions himself and plunges in, a smooth, sliding thrust, all the way to the hilt. The woman's hands delve down the back of his trousers, grasping his undulating buttocks, dragging him deeper and closer. She wraps a slender leg possessively around the back of his thighs, rubbing catlike over the expensive suit.

Adrienne plunges in and out with matching rhythm. Her breathing seems loud and erratic in the sepulchral room, but she knows from experience that they will not hear her. Their inner worlds are building, tension deep in the pits of their bellies consumes them, the heavy breathing of the watcher in the shadows will go unnoticed in the sweet release of climax.

Adrienne comes, shuddering through her orgasm, mouth trembling open, eyes wide, struggling to control the timbre of her breathing, struggling to fill her lungs quietly enough to avoid discovery. She spirals down from her peak, still fingering the damp curls, touching her swollen lips with a gentle finger. She likes it when she comes first, so that she can watch their conclusion unhampered.

They are nearly there. She watches as the thrusts get shorter, shuddering, straddle-legged thrusts, and then the fractured moment of climax as his thrusts become short, deep spurts. His head falls onto the woman's neck and he lies there panting for a moment.

They never indulge in the tender afterplay of lovers who truly care. The man raises his head, kisses his partner once on the lips. Then he lifts himself off, his penis damp and flaccid, and tucks it away in his pants. His partner stems the gush of semen down her thighs with her fingers, catching the viscous fluid and bringing it to her mouth.

Adrienne closes her eyes momentarily, vicariously enjoying the grassy, sour taste of freshly spilled seed. She wonders if they shower before returning to their homes, or do they tell their partners they're sweaty from the gym or the office? She wonders if they will make love to their own partners this evening after their irreverent encounter. There is nothing sacred about this sex.

He kisses the woman again briefly, then dresses and strides away without a backward glance. From her hiding place, Adrienne the shadow child holds her breath as he passes, then resumes watching the woman, who gazes after her lover, momentarily wistful. Then she wipes herself with her nylons and pulls on her panties. She takes a new pair of nylons from her bag and smoothes the creases out of the once crisp executive suit. A slash of funeral rose to the kiss-crushed lips, then she leaves, striding past the stalker in the shadows.

She has always followed people, slipping through the shadows in their wake, pattering on soft-shod feet in and out of darkness and pools of light, daring them to turn and see her.

CONTENTED CLIENTS

Kate Dominic

ANDRE WAS MORE THAN A LITTLE MIFFED. I'D
been quite specific in letting him know that the
matronly outfit he'd designed for me was about
as sexy as a burlap sack.

"I want to show boobs, dear," I snapped,
dumping the custom-made '50s-style house-
dress on the neck of the naked, headless man-
nequin. "Mother's naughty 'little boys and
girls' need to be squirming in anticipation of a
nice, comforting nipple to suck on, even before
I turn them over across my knees."

"As Madame wishes," Andre sniffed, his
beautiful green eyes flashing with righteous
indignation as he tossed his short blond curls.
In a flash of dramatic pique that only a former
runway model could master, he turned and
swept up the yards of atrocious yellow floral

print. He froze in mid-pirouette when my hand snaked out and gripped his slender, denim-covered buttcheek. Hard. I wasn't sure what Andre's problem was today. His costumes were usually exquisite. But I was in no mood for an artistic temper tantrum when I had clients scheduled for that scene in less than a week.

"Madame damn well wishes," I said quietly. "And if Andre has a problem with that, perhaps Madame should call Andre's sweet, smiling lover over to give dear little Andre an attitude adjustment."

Andre looked nervously over his shoulder, his eyes locking on the large bearded man hunched intently over the computer screen on the other side of the room. The only time I'd ever seen Bedford's lips so much as curve upward was when he was paddling the bejeezus out of Andre's ass.

Andre shivered as Bedford clicked onto a new screen, leaned back, and carefully stroked his chin. The latest design appeared on the web page he was updating, and Bedford nodded once, so slowly that the long brown hair tied back at his neck barely moved over the flannel shirt covering his thickly muscled shoulders.

"That won't be necessary," Andre said primly, almost hiding his shiver as he carefully set the discarded material onto a side table. He glanced once more in the direction of his bearish lover. "Shall Madame and I sit down at the other workstation and discuss alternative design options?"

"The operative word being *sit*," I snapped, releasing his asscheek. I managed to control my smile as Andre politely escorted me over to the computer, offering me a chair before he called up my profile with even more efficiency than usual. From the way his ass was twitching, I gathered that sweet, pouty little Andre's entire snit had been staged purely to let Bedford know that he was hungry for a good, old-fashioned ass-warming. Despite Bedford's apparent lack of attention, I had no doubt that he'd heard every word—and that a very sore and well-fucked Andre would be working standing up for the next couple of days.

It wasn't the first time I'd been an unwitting prop in one of my friends' private little scenes. I doubted it would be the last. I shook my head and bit back a grin as my voluptuous cyber-model filled the screen and a nervous, eager-to-please Andre and I got back to designing the perfect costume for my stable of submissive little boys and girls. Overall, I'd been quite pleased with Personal Fetish Attire, Inc. PFA had provided me with my first dominatrix outfits with almost off-the-rack speed—no mean feat, given my well-endowed size-2X proportions. As my clientele grew, Andre and I worked together to design some very chic leather teddies and harnesses that emphasized my Rubenesque curves for my hard-core "mistress" clients, as well as the flowing drapes of satin and lace that highlighted the ample padding so comforting to my naughty adult children. When I'd branched out into less traditional fetishes, PFA had quietly made some introductions to other clients, for whom they then also supplied costumes. Several of my fantasy scenes had even been Bedford's idea.

"We've got this guy who's really into horror flicks," Bedford had said one fall afternoon. He was lacing me into my new black corset as Andre put the finishing touches on my Halloween vampire costume. "Cleavage" didn't begin to describe the size of the valley developing between my boobs as Bedford cinched me into place. Andre had somehow managed to build in a truly comfortable support bra without losing the sleek lines of the corset. "This dude would think he'd died and gone to heaven if you had your way with him in this costume, Ms. Amanda, especially if you bit his neck a couple of times. Hell, if you let him nurse on these mamas, he'd pay whatever you wanted. And honey," Bedford winked at me as he tucked the lacing ends under the intricately tied knots, "he can afford to pay whatever you want."

In short order, I'd found out that Timmy could indeed afford my services. Frequently. From there, it was a short step to a half-dozen men who wanted to be spanked and diapered and fed a cup of warm milk, then held on Mama's large, comforting lap to nurse contentedly on her huge ol' boobs while they went to sleep. That costume was easy, too. I set the scene to be one of "baby" waking up at night, so the seductive peignoirs that, along with leatherwear, were the mainstay of PFA needed only a complementary pair of feathered satin mules to have baby's hard, horny dick drooling into the neatly pinned cloth-cotton diapers Andre had custom-made for them. At the end of the scene, I'd sit in the oversized rocker Bedford had built and unhook my specially made "nursing bra," one cup at a time, and let baby suckle my huge, dark red nipples until the heavenly stimulation—and the ben wa balls in my pussy—made me explode in orgasm. The sucking, along with my usual expert wrist action, usually had baby creaming into his diaper as soon as he'd sucked me through my climax.

My submissive and infantilist clients were an excellent match for me, as my breasts were about the most sensitive part of my body. After a good session of nipple stimulation and roasting naked backsides, all it took was a few quick flicks to my clit or a well-placed toy to make my cunt gush.

Although my clients paid well enough that I needed to have only a few regulars, I was interested in branching out again.

For the first time, I also had a couple of women clients. One of
the girls, Cherise, was into enemas. Because of her prior problems with bulimia, I'd had a long talk with her doctor before I
accepted her as a client. With his permission, I'd written her a
"prescription" for one enema each month, of no more than one
quart, administered by the stern, uniform-clad Nurse Harriet,
so long as Cherise kept her weight up and stayed completely
away from laxatives in the interim.

Cherise had been following her program like a champ since
we started, cuddling contentedly into my lap to nuzzle after
a long medical session with prim, no-nonsense Nurse Harriet.
Andre's costume had combined an extremely short, starched,
white hospital skirt with a matching low-cut top that unbuttoned to show a soft, white-lace bustier. Cherise had been so
tired after her session and her overwhelming climax that she'd
spent the last half hour of our time together dozing in my lap,
my nipple resting on her thin red lips as I stroked her hair.

Cherise was not into infantilism, though. Spanking, yes. But
at twenty-six, she saw herself more as a naughty high-schooler
who needed someone to take her firmly in hand and to teach
her to be good and do right—and to help her gain a healthy
dose of the self-esteem she was fighting so hard to achieve. After
her last visit, I'd told her that next week her mother wanted to
discuss her report card with her—most specifically, her citizenship grades. And to be sure to wear her best school clothes and
saddle shoes. Cherise had shivered, her face positively glowing
as she kissed my hand and whispered, "Yes, Ma'am. I'll be
here right after school." Which meant 6:30 P.M. sharp, after
she'd finished work and eaten exactly as the doctor's regimen
directed.

Part of the success of our session, however, hinged on whether Andre got off his butt and got me a sexy enough loving-but-stern 1950s-middle-class Mom costume for Cherise. Andre hadn't shown me the real design but he told me I'd be pleased. He also assured me that my costume would most definitely be ready by Thursday evening. I assured him that it had better be, or I'd be lending Bedford one wicked fucking Lucite paddle.

As I suspected, Bedford had heard the whole exchange. As I walked toward the door I heard him growl, "Drop yer pants and get over my knees, boy!" followed by the sound of a chair being pushed back, the clink of a belt being unbuckled, and Andre's plaintive, "I'm sorreeeee, Bedford!" I smiled and turned the window sign to *closed* on my way out, locking the door behind me.

Whether it was the hiding Bedford gave him for sassing the customers (for which Andre tearfully apologized into my answering machine) or just his usual desire to create gorgeously sexy attire, Andre outdid himself with the new and improved version of my happy-housewife ensemble. The soft, full, autumn-colored skirt brushed just below my knees, a wide leather belt cinching Mother's ample waist just enough to show her well-rounded hips. A simple beige silk button-down blouse tucked into the waist, veiling but definitely not hiding the cream-colored peekaboo satin-and-lace front-hook bra that was, again, wonderfully supportive and comfortable.

Since it was a warm fall day when Cherise was scheduled to visit, Mother wasn't wearing underwear per se, just a butterfly vibrator in a thin-strapped thong-type harness, a lacy garter belt that matched her brassiere and held the tiny control box for the vibrator, and thigh-high seamed nylons. Whether or not my errant daughter was going to discover what was beneath my skirt remained to be seen. A pristine starched white-cotton apron tied at the waist rounded out my attire, along with low brown-leather heels and a pearl necklace and earrings. By the time I took the hot rollers out of my hair and sprayed my period do into place, I had just enough time to spritz on some White Shoulders before the front door quietly opened.

I walked to the stove and lifted the lid of the hearty vegetable soup that was simmering, picked up a long-handled wooden spoon, and started to stir as I heard Cherise come into the kitchen. I looked up at her and smiled.

"Hello, dear. How was school?"

Andre had outdone himself again. Cherise wore a poodle skirt and a fluffy pink angora sweater that softened the angular planes that were slowly filling out as she grew healthier. When I nodded appreciatively, Cherise blushed and slowly turned around, the careful draping of the thick skirt flowing with her as she moved to show off how her pretty bottom was finally rounding out. Her legs were bare except for ankle socks and saddle shoes, and her fragile, usually pale face was suffused with a happy blush. The three textbooks she carried under her arm added more to her teenage look than her blonde ponytail held in place by a charming pink satin bow.

"School was fine, Mother." Cherise smiled, a truly happy smile, even as she quickly lowered her gaze. I was surprised to realize how much I'd come to anticipate that quiet, shy look. "I got all my homework done, and I had lunch with my friends."

But Cherise was studiously concentrating on the pattern in the linoleum. Her deliberately averted eyes told my mother's intuition that something was up. I cleared my throat and set the spoon down on the counter.

"Cherise, are you wearing lipstick?" I asked sharply, clucking in feigned disapproval. "Young lady, someone as naturally beautiful as you does not need artificial enhancements!"

The creamy red ribbon of color would have been impossible to miss. Andre had no doubt spent hours ensuring that it would compliment the natural blush that slowly suffused Cherise's face. She obediently looked up at me, her blue eyes sparkling.

"I wanted to look pretty today, Mother," she said shyly.

"Cherise," I said, shaking my head in mock exasperation. "You are always pretty. This," I pointed sternly at her lips, "is like adding lipstick to a rose. I am sorely tempted to turn you over my knee!"

"Oh, no, Mother. I'm much too old to be spanked."

She moved to the table and set down her books. A bright yellow folded sheet of paper fell out: *REPORT CARD.* Quickly she tucked it under her algebra book. I bit my lip and very deliberately wiped my hands on my apron.

"Nonsense, sweetheart. A pretty young lady like you is definitely still of an age for a good, sound dose of Mother's hairbrush when she deserves it. I hope you're hiding that report card because you want to surprise me with your wonderful grades, and not because of bad citizenship marks again." I carefully unfolded the card. One *B*, three *C*s, and a *D* were marked in heavy black letters in the academics columns—right across from five bright red *F*s in citizenship.

"Cherise!" I said sternly. "What is the meaning of this?"

"Um, I don't know, Mother," she said nervously, shifting her weight from one foot to the other as she peered over my shoulder. "Maybe the teacher made a mistake?"

"Have you been doing your homework?" I demanded, giving her bottom a quick, sharp swat.

"Yes." She quickly stepped back out of the line of fire, lowered her eyes again, and stirred her foot in a nervous circle.

"Well, most of the time. Sometimes I forgot."

"I see," I said icily, tapping the card on my fingers. "And the tardiness, talking in class, and lack of participation were also caused by forgetfulness?"

"Um, sometimes." Cherise licked her lips nervously, calling attention to her bright red lipstick.

"Yet you could still remember to put on your makeup."

Cherise clamped her hand over her mouth and stammered, "Just today!"

"Give me the lipstick." I held out my hand. "It had better be almost unused."

Andre knew me well. Cherise reached into her purse, and as she drew out the well-worn tube and twisted up the color, I could see that the contents had been carefully honed down so that only half a stick was left.

"So, now you've started lying as well, young lady?"

Cherise hung her head in shame. Her pert little nipples were hard under her sweater. My labia started to tingle.

"I'm sorry, Mother," she whispered. "I won't do it again."

"You certainly won't," I snapped, tossing the report card on the table and turning the soup down to simmer. "You've earned a good, sound bottom-roasting, young lady."

"Mother!" Cherise wailed. She backed up against the cupboard. I shook my head sternly at her.

"Not in here, Cherise." I took off my apron and carefully folded it over the back of the kitchen chair. "I'm going to be taking down your panties. If your crying draws the neighbors, we can't have them looking through the window and seeing your bare, red bottom wiggling all over my lap. We're going to your room."

Ignoring the increasingly loud protestations of innocence

and the promises to do better in the future, I took my errant daughter's hand and marched her resolutely down the hall, hurrying her with a few well-placed swats when she dawdled. We entered her room, and I locked the door behind us.

For a moment, Cherise just stared at what was behind the door; it had been labeled *Doctor's Laboratory* the last time she'd been here. I'd changed the room that usually doubled as Mama's bedroom for the infantilists into a teenaged girl's dream, with delicately flowered chenille bedspread, turntable with rock-n-roll records, vintage movie posters, and a neat study desk, complete with dictionary, sharpened pencils, and a new, lined notebook. As Cherise looked around the room, I purposefully strode to the window and lowered the blinds.

"It's too hot to close the windows, Cherise. So don't even think to complain that the whole neighborhood is going to hear your spanking. You should have thought of that beforehand. Neighbors or not, I'm going to spank you until you're crying at the top of your lungs. Maybe it will do you some good to realize that everyone knows your mother loves you much too much to let a good girl like you get away with such nonsense."

"Mother!" Cherise seemed shocked, but she could hear the air-conditioning running and knew this room was as soundproof as the rest of the house. However, Cherise's low self-esteem in public was a big source of her problems, and the instinctive shiver that ran up her spine told me how much she was enjoying the idea of "public" proof of her value to me.

I walked over to the nightstand and moved the thick maple hairbrush to the front edge, within easy reach. Then I sat down on the bed and pointed in front of me.

"Come here, Cherise, and lift up your skirt and your slip."

"Motherrrrrr," she wailed, stomping her foot. I'd learned on our first visit how much Cherise enjoyed losing the battle to avoid her spankings. "I'm too old to be spanked bare!"

"Right now, young lady," I snapped my fingers. "And for your insolence, you will now take your skirt and slip *off!*"

With a loud sniffle she shuffled over to me and slowly unbuttoned and lowered her skirt. The delicate white satin slip that hugged her hips was a work of art. When she removed that as well, I needed a moment of reprieve while she carefully folded her clothing and placed it on the nightstand. Andre had outdone himself: pristine white satin tap pants, bordered with Irish lace and decorated with dainty pink butterflies, framed the softly swelling mound between Cherise's legs and clung to the new fullness of her bottom. I slipped my shaking fingers into the waistband and slowly lowered the exquisite panties, exposing the neatly trimmed soft blonde tufts covering her vulva.

"I'm too big to be spanked bare," she sniffed, reluctantly lifting first one leg, then the other.

"Nonsense." I smoothed my skirt and patted my thigh. "Mother's lap is quite big enough to hold you." Cherise slowly lowered herself across my legs, reaching forward to grab a thick handful of the plush chenille bedspread as I pulled her into position. She jumped and twitched as I situated her so that her angular bones were cushioned comfortably over my full thighs. I wanted all of Cherise's attention to be focused on her bottom.

"This is going to be a very serious spanking, Cherise." She whimpered as I slowly slid my hand over the smooth, creamy curve of her bare behind. "I'm going to paddle your bottom until it's so red and sore you won't be able to sit down for the rest of the week." I wanted every inch of her backside awakened and hungry to be touched. I caressed her until she was squirming.

"You will give your best effort, Cherise, in everything you do." I brought my hand down sharply across her right cheek. She yelped, jerking, and I brought my hand down hard on the other side.

"Ow!" Cherise arched her bottom up to meet each slap. "Mother! That hurts! Ow! Ow! *Owwww!!*"

A dozen sound hand-spanks later, her bottom was pinkening nicely. After another dozen, she was sniffling loudly, though she didn't try to move out of the way. I knew that would change the moment I picked up the brush.

"By not doing your best, you're only hurting yourself, dear." I quietly lifted the cool-handled maple brush and, with no warning, smacked it loudly over her right bottom cheek. Cherise howled, and her hand came up to cover her behind. I firmly held her wrist against her waist and spanked her again.

"We'll have none of that, young lady."

"It hurts!" she wailed, her legs flailing on the bed as I began to paddle her in earnest. She twisted and bucked, yelling at the top of her lungs as I covered her entire bottom with sharp, hard swats, up one side and down the other, with the steady rhythm I knew she so enjoyed.

"Of course it hurts," I snapped, stopping just long enough to pull her tightly to me. "Mother is punishing you, dear. I want your bottom good and sore."

Cherise's ensuing howls told me she was really feeling each swat. She kicked her way through another half-dozen sound, hard cracks. Then I paused and set the brush down, cupping her heated bottom and sliding my fingers between her legs and over her labia. Cherise's whole cunt was drenched. She arched into my hand, crying out as my fingertip slid forward to caress her swollen clit. Cherise spread her legs, sniffling loudly.

The smell of her arousal filled my nostrils. My own pussy clenched in response.

"Good girls are always doing their best." I gently pinched her swollen nub, my nipples hardening as she cried out and pressed back into my hand. "They take care of themselves so they are strong and confident." I slid my hand back and squeezed her hot, red flesh, first one side, then the other. "You will remember always to do your best—for yourself, dear, but also because you know that Mother will spank you if you don't." I picked up the brush again. "Do you hear me, Cherise? You... will...always...do...your...best!" I punctuated each word with another blazing wallop.

"I will, Mommy! Ow! I will! I will!" After another ten scorching smacks, Cherise's screeches suddenly dissolved in great, heaving sobs. Her body shook as the cleansing tears finally started flowing into the soft, fluffy threads of the bedspread.

I set the brush down and gently pulled Cherise into my arms. "There, there, dear," I murmured, holding her tenderly to my breast. She clung to me, sobbing, as I unbuttoned my blouse. I'd barely finished when Cherise pulled the fabric aside and immediately began rubbing her tear-stained face against the soft, creamy lace. Without a word, I unhooked the front latch. My breasts fell forward and Cherise nuzzled her face against my nipple, taking deep, gulping breaths as she shook and licked. Sensations shuddered through me as her cat-rough tongue dragged over first one side, then the other, outlining and laving the areolas. My pussy throbbed. I lifted a shaking hand and gently stroked her cheek.

"My bottom hurts, Mommy," she whispered, her tongue never missing a beat.

"It's supposed to hurt, sweetie." She tickled her tongue over the sensitive tip of my nipple. "That's how you learn. Suckle Mommy's breast if it will make you feel better."

Cherise opened her tear-filled blue eyes to meet mine. Then she smiled, and with a long low sigh, wrapped her lips around my areola and sucked the entire nipple into her mouth like a lonely, frightened child. She inhaled deeply and started to nurse.

I held her close, panting hard with pleasure. Each tug brought exquisite sensations. For a while we just sat there, the only sounds the hum of the air conditioner and Cherise's contented suckling, and my occasional moan. When Cherise's fingers slid down to her vulva, I moved my hand to her thigh.

"Would you like an orgasm, dear?"

When Cherise nodded, I eased her legs apart. She slid further down, spreading wider for me, wincing, sucking hard. Her full weight rested on her well-spanked bottom cheeks and my hand slid into her slick folds.

"Don't fight the pain, sweetheart." I stroked my fingers up and down her slit. She whimpered, her legs stiffening as she leaned more heavily on her tender behind. "The soreness will remind you to listen to me, dear one."

Cherise wiggled uncomfortably a few more times, then looked at me and smiled tearfully. She kissed my nipple slowly. Carefully I slipped my middle finger into her quivering hole and caressed her clit with the pad of my thumb.

"You are truly beautiful, Cherise, from the inside out." Her eyes filled again as I pressed my finger deep, curving up toward her belly. She trembled against me as I found the sensitive spot deep inside her vagina.

"Only a healthy body can feel this intensely." With my finger still inside her, I started massaging her juice-slicked clit with a slow, rolling motion. She cried out, sucking ferociously.

"Take care of your body, sweetie, so it can enjoy the pleasure of a healthy, happy climax." I kept up a steady rhythm, pressing deeply.

Cherise's skin started to flush. "That's it, beautiful. Let your wonderful, young body come like the strong, lusty animal you are."

Cherise sucked so hard that my whole body quivered. Then with a loud cry she arched into my hand, bucking and thrashing as her body convulsed with an orgasm that shook her from her toes to her lips, still latched tightly onto me. She clutched me fiercely to her, sucking her way through a long, rolling climax.

She left me shaking with need.

Cherise slowly caught her breath, her lips falling free of my swollen breast. My nipple was a deep, bruised burgundy against her cheek as she lifted a shaking hand to my face. Her fingers traced the outline of my chin.

"Thank you, Ms. Amanda." Her face glowed. "I feel so good all over." She stared at me, slowly brushing her hand over my cheek while another flush burned deeper and darker over her face. "Um, Ma'am, I was just curious, but..." She took a deep breath but this time didn't look away as she blurted out, "Do you get turned on by my, um..." Even the skin beneath her ponytail seemed to be blushing. I laughed and hugged her tightly.

"Yes, love," I kissed her hand. "Pleasuring you is intensely arousing to me."

"But you didn't...?" Her eyes stayed intently on me as she stammered out her question.

"No, dear," I smiled. "I'll take care of it later."

Cherise nodded and snuggled back into my arms. Her breath was cool over my wet nipple as she sighed contentedly and whispered, "In two weeks, I get my report card from my Greek and Latin tutor. Do you want to see that, too, Ma'am?"

The possibilities for those costumes were mind-boggling.

I kissed the top of her head and settled in for a final bit of cuddling. Andre was going to be very busy.

DOING THE DISHES

Rachel Kramer Bussel

THE FIRST TIME I DID IT, I DID IT FOR LOVE.

The second time I did it, I did it to seduce.

The third time, I was ordered to do it.

And I loved every minute of it.

No, it's not something filthy at all. In fact, it's the opposite of filthy. I'm talking about doing dishes. I know, you're thinking, *How crazy is that?* but please understand. I get off on doing dishes. I cannot pass by a sink filled to the brim, or anything but empty, and just keep going. I'm lured to it by some force that draws my hands under the water, into the depths of suds and spoons and discards. Sometimes I even do it with my eyes closed.

Just as with people, all dishes and sinks are not created equal. While I'm an equal opportunity dishwasher, only certain people's dishes can affect me in *that special way*.

It all started with Alan. Before him, I was never much of a housekeeper and the furthest thing from a housewife that you could get. I reveled in my slovenly ways, thinking I was exerting some backwards feminist statement by being just as messy as the guys.

But in Alan's apartment, something changed. When I saw that huge pile of dishes soaking in his sink, something stirred inside of me, and I was drawn to them, almost magically, like Alice—only instead of a mushroom, my intoxicant was dishes. They weren't really soaking, most of them; they were piled so high that some spilled over onto the counter and stove. I could tell they'd been there for ages, and I just wanted to get started on them. I stared at them, entranced, ready for my first fix. But when I asked, he told me not to do them. "I couldn't have you do all those dishes, there are three weeks' worth there! Don't go to all that trouble, I'll just put them in the dishwasher."

I didn't bother to point out that if it was that easy, he'd have done it already, or that so many dishes wouldn't even come close to fitting in his dishwasher. I didn't say anything, just nodded, fingers crossed behind my back.

Now, if it were up to me, all the dishwashing companies would go out of business and start making microwaves or something. We could give everyone with a dishwasher a free microwave and be done with it. Who'd want a cold, impersonal machine doing this special, seductive job? Not me. In fact, anyone dissatisfied with the policy could come to me for a very personal dishwashing. And whoever invented the dishwasher should just be banished to some island and forced to eat only with his hands.

So even though Alan asked me to leave them, I ignored him.

It wasn't easy, let me tell you, to wait two whole days for him to leave the house. I didn't want to seem too eager about him leaving—but when he was finally gone, and I'd made sure I heard him head down the stairs and slam the door, I did a little dance of glee before racing over to the obscenely piled sink.

First I turned the hot water on, holding my hands under the heated spray. I let it wash over my fingers for a few minutes, getting them used to the heat. I don't use those icky yellow gloves either; they make my hands smell like rubber, and if I were going to do that, I might as well delegate the dishes to an evil dishwasher. No, I like doing my dishes naked.

I then went to fetch my shoes; I wanted to wear high heels so I could reach everything more easily. Also, something about this job just calls for high heels—especially for someone of my rather short height; it looks much nicer than balancing on the tips of my toes. I felt almost like I was being filmed, and I wanted to look the part. Some of the plates and utensils needed soaking, so I drained the old water, filled the sink up with new, hot water and poured the liquid green soap into the mix. I lifted one plate, relatively clean, and lightly ran his purple sponge over it.

I smiled when I noticed the days-old coffee in a mug next to the sink; he'd probably been in too much of a hurry to finish it. I ran the tip of my index finger around the edge of the mug, thinking of him sipping the steaming brew with his soft lips, then slamming the mug down on the counter before rushing off to work. I lifted it to my lips and gently licked the rim, wanting to stay connected to him for just a little bit longer. I'd been making progress with the dishes, and only about half a sink full were left.

In another mug, I found fresh remains of hot chocolate, and smiled indulgently. How adorable. I dipped my index finger into the sweet sludge, then slowly ran it across my tongue. A shiver passed through my cunt at the taste. *Mmm...* I took many more dips before plunging the mug underwater, erasing all remaining traces of chocolate.

By the time I reached the bottom, where there were mostly pots, I was really into it. For these, I'd have to work. I opened the cabinet under the sink, looking for a thicker sponge. I found a heavy-duty one, unopened, and ripped the plastic with my teeth. I attacked the first pot with as much vigor as I could. I had the water on full blast and was scrubbing away, so I didn't hear the door open.

All of a sudden, Alan was in the kitchen doorway, a scowl on his face. "*What* are you doing?" he screamed.

"I know you said not to do them, but I just couldn't help it. Please, please don't be mad. Actually, well, I didn't want to tell you this, but it turns me on. I've been doing your dishes for half an hour and now I'm covered in water and turned on. Don't you want to come over here?"

He stared at me for a good minute, taking in the way my nightie clung to my chest in the many areas where water had splashed onto it. I still held the purple sponge in my hand. He came toward me and pressed my back up against the sink. The sponge fell to the floor but I didn't care. He lifted me up so I was sitting on the edge of the wet counter. "So this gets you turned on now, does it?" he asked, stroking me through my panties.

"Yes, it does," I said, leaning back with my arms on either side of the sink. I knew I'd be able to get him to see dishes in a whole new way, and I was right.

The next time, dishes helped me get the girl—at least that's what I told myself.

We'd been having a pleasant enough date, but one that looked like it was going to end with a sweet kiss on the lips and an "I'll call you soon." She was going to drive me home, but said she needed to take a shower first. Well, that was a weird sign, but short of asking to join her, I couldn't figure out how to spin that into her bed.

So while she turned on the blast of the shower spray, I turned on the tap. I rolled up my lacy long sleeves, knowing they'd still get a bit wet. I didn't mind. I let the hot water run, no gloves, feeling its heat course through my body. I plunged my hands in, soaking them as I scrubbed. I thought of all the commercials I'd seen as a child, talking about "dishpan hands," the dreaded disease of mothers everywhere. But I liked the way my hands felt after a good scrubbing—all wrinkly and used.

I worked slowly, savoring each dish. I rinsed the bowl we'd used for the salad, removing traces of oil-covered lettuce leaves. I found the knife I recognized as hers and slipped it into my mouth, savoring the tangy metal against my tongue. Finally I slid it out and washed it properly, wondering how it would feel inside me.

I was nearing the end when she stepped out of the shower, wrapped in a robe, a towel atop her head. I sensed her pause on her way to her room and just watch me, but I didn't turn around. With the next knife I found, I again opened my mouth and slid it in, pushing it back and forth in a fucking motion that she'd have to be completely dense to miss.

She came closer, dropping the towel to the floor. She walked right up behind me and pressed herself against me. She reached for the knife and slid it into her own mouth, then pushed my head forward and trailed it over the back of my neck. I gave a startled jump, and she pressed it in tighter. She led the knife down the ridges of my back, slowly, while I tried to stand perfectly still. When she reached my ass, I couldn't help but move, and I spread my legs a little wider. She was now standing a few inches away, her attention focused on her kitchen knife. She tapped it lightly against my ass and I moaned, and she did it again, harder. I lifted my ass to give her better access, but she was beyond that. The knife was about to enter the place I'd fantasized about earlier. She'd turned it around, but the heavy end slowly entered my slick pussy. I moaned and tightly gripped the edge of the sink.

She slid a finger in alongside the knife handle and I felt like I would explode. She didn't move the knife too much, just slowly back and forth, but the whole experience pushed me over the edge. My body shook; I had to hold on to the sink harder and press my feet firmly to the floor to keep from collapsing in bliss.

She handed me the knife and steadied me against the counter. "Keep washing, we're not done yet."

I took a deep breath and turned the water back on. I held "our" knife under the hot spray for a moment, ignoring the ecological implications of wasted water in favor of watching it splash off the silver metal. She reached around and fondled my nipples. "Keep washing, remember?" she reminded me, twisting my nipple with her fingers. I kept the water going, moving slowly, determined to take as long as possible. She kept on twisting my nipples, occasionally rubbing my clit while I did my best not to drop the dishes. Occasionally she'd grab a utensil and fuck me with it, making a never-ending cycle of dishes that I was more than happy to play my part in washing, and getting dirty.

I smiled happily. Maybe tomorrow I'd start on mopping the floor.

Within a year, my dishwashing fetish gained me quite a repu-
tation. I was frequently asked over to friends' houses after
dinner parties, and they'd covertly imply that they wanted me
to do their dishes, or they'd ask me outright.

But this time, I was caught off guard. I'd spent the night at a
kinky party flirting shamelessly with Alex, a dyke top who until
now had seemed totally aloof and unapproachable. But tonight,
while she whipped several other girls into nicely streaked
creatures, their marks proudly displayed for any interested
bystander to admire, she kept sneaking looks at me; I could
feel them from across the room. I couldn't even look at anyone
else, just kept crossing and uncrossing my legs, wondering how
my ass looked in my black leather mini skirt. I drank so much
soda that I started to get jittery, and had to keep going to the
bathroom—which meant passing Alex. Finally, near the end
of the night, she grabbed me on one of my return trips. "Are
you coming home with me tonight or what, you little tease?" I
don't know what came over me, but I kissed her, pushing my
nervously-bitten lips up against hers and rubbing the rest of me
against her as well.

"I guess that's a yes. Go wait for me by the door." In a fog,
I gathered my things and waited at the appointed spot. We
drove silently to her place, her hand on my thigh for most of
the trip. If we didn't get there soon, I was going to have to move
her hand up a bit higher for some relief. After the longest ten
minutes I could remember ever experiencing, we pulled into
a driveway. I didn't take in the scenery, just followed her up
some stairs and into a large living room filled with thick white
carpeting and a plush leather couch. I went to sit down on the
couch, but she grabbed the waistband of my skirt and steered
me in another direction, to the kitchen. What I saw took my

breath away. It was like the backup at Alan's—but much, much worse. This woman owned more dishes than I'd ever seen in one place, ever. And they were scattered all over the room, on every possible surface. It was like some surreal art exhibit, with honey and chocolate sauce and spaghetti sticking to each plate, cup and spoon. It looked like a food fight had erupted amongst the edibles in her refrigerator, each one battling for the title of "able to do the most damage to a single kitchen."

"I've heard about you, Missy, so I had some friends make a little treat for Miss Dishes." She reached her hand under my skirt and pressed her fist against my cunt, the hard edges of her knuckles making me even wetter. "Now I know you're just dying to have me beat the shit out of you; I thought you were going to pass out watching me at the club. But as much as that hot little body of yours deserves it, you're going to have to make this kitchen sparkle before you get any of my treats. Do you understand? Now, I'm going upstairs to rest for a while. Don't bother me unless it's an emergency. When I get back I want this kitchen perfectly clean, okay?"

I sucked in my breath and nodded; while she'd been talking she'd been kneading my pussy in a way that brought me close to orgasm—but then she took that fist right with her up the stairs. I stared longingly after her for a minute, before trying to figure out how to tackle this mess.

The first thing to do was strip. I threw my clothes into the only clean corner of the room I could find, and set to work. I brought all the dishes over, close to the sink and stove, placing them in like order.

I started with the silverware, even though conventional wisdom says that with any major project you're supposed to tackle the larger items first. But that's never worked with me.

For me, the silverware is foreplay. I can go quickly, stacking the shiny spoons and sharp forks, and listen to them jingle together. I like to build up the anticipation before I get to a really huge pot, one I can linger over and fondle.

But before I got anywhere near the pots, Alex came back. She stared at me from across the room, barking orders, telling me to work faster or to go back and redo a certain plate; how she could tell the state of its cleanliness from ten feet away I don't know, but apparently she could.

As soon as she'd come downstairs, I'd started getting wet (again), and was nervous that some of my juices might dribble down my thigh. But her voice would brook no argument, and, truth be told, that's exactly why I got so wet. She marched over, closer to me. I noticed her holding a miniature alarm clock—it made me feel like we were at boot camp. She set it for five minutes. The sink still held an overabundance of dishes, and the kitchen itself looked like a war zone. There was seriously no way I could get it all done.

"Bend over, right here," she instructed, pointing to yet another pile of dishes. "Since you don't seem to be doing too well the traditional way, I'm going to have you lick these plates clean. Go ahead, I want your tongue on that top one there." No sooner had my tongue reached out than she lifted up my skirt and started spanking me, first with a light hand and then much harder. She meant business. My tongue lapped and lapped, wishing it was her pussy, working frantically to get through even one dish. I did, somehow getting it to look relatively clean—though who she'd get to eat on a licked-clean plate I didn't know.

"Good girl, now, let's move along." She placed the clean plate in its own new pile and presented me with more. Some had chocolate sauce, but even that was hardening into an unappetizing mess. She took pity on me, opening the fridge to take out some whipped cream, then covering the entire plate with it.

"Knock yourself out."

I plunged my face into the cream, not caring about making a mess (what difference did that really make in this environment?), eager for more strokes. This time, I went at it with gusto, and the more I licked, the harder she spanked me. Then she slipped her fingers into me, not starting with a delicate single digit but pushing three fat fingers inside. I could barely keep up with my whipped cream but I knew I had to if I wanted to keep getting fucked. Just as I was about to come, the alarm went off. Had five minutes already passed?

"Okay, darlin', you're off the hook for now." She blew a whistle that had been hidden in her pocket and two sexy women in French maid outfits appeared out of nowhere. (I guess I'm not the only one with a cleaning fetish.) Alex led me upstairs and fucked me for the rest of the night, whispering dirty words about suds and sponges and silverware in my ear the whole time.

KALI

Maryanne Mohanraj

So you're walking up and down Telegraph
Avenue, up and down, trying not to look like
the new dyke in town, trying not to broadcast
that you're fresh off the boat, innocent new
meat just in from Indiana, come to the big city.
Actually, the small city—to Berkeley in fact,
because San Francisco is a little intimidating to
start off with if you're a twenty-two-year-old
dyke who came all the way to California to get
laid because you've been dumped by the only
other lesbian in Franklin, Indiana, and you just
can't take it any more.

The women certainly are pretty, in Berkeley,
in the springtime. Campus chicks in blue jeans
and T-shirts and bandannas; skin in shades
you've never seen on a TV set. Lots of skin—
they don't seem to feel the cold that's prickling

your skin. You are determined not to pull the sweatshirt out of your backpack, not to shiver in this dark-green tank top with the scoop neck that shows your ample cleavage for the benefit of any cute chick who might happen to like tall redheads who probably still look like farm girls.

You've been cruising Berkeley for weeks now. Days working over on Shattuck, over at the games store whose owners seemed surprised to have a woman actually want the job. Boys and their toys! Evenings on the street, up and down, occasionally smiling at a woman with short dark hair and long legs, the kind of legs that could reach back and wrap all the way around your neck as you bump and grind, oh yes. Smiling at her and she smiles back and your heart does the thump-thing and then she keeps going down the street, or asks you if you have the time and then keeps going and you're back to walking the street again wondering where the hell women go to get laid in this town.

Up past the hippie chicks, up past the man who tries to sell you beads for your hair at three times what it would cost in Franklin, all the way up to the campus, turn and start walking down again. Maybe it's time to get up the nerve to go into San Francisco, find one of those girl-gyms, those dyke-diners you keep hearing about, uh-huh. You walk down past Cody's Bookstore, hover in the window of the poster shop, scope out the new new age books at Shambhala.

It sure would be a lot easier to walk into one of those diners with a beautiful woman on your arm, a pretty little thing like that dark-skinned girl behind the counter, the one with the long black hair braided down her back, with the tight white shirt that outlines breasts the size of softballs, the one walking over to take something out of a window, the one smiling at you through the glass. Right. And now she's going to turn away or come to the door and ask if you wanted to actually buy anything or were just planning to hang out there and scare away the customers. You brace yourself, and then she stares at you real serious, and then she winks. Long and slow, and you can't believe what you're seeing, and you check to make sure you've got your pink triangle earring in where she can see it and oh yes, it's there, and then she's coming to the door and it's "I get off in fifteen minutes. Want to buy me coffee?" and you are stumbling over yourself to say yes.

Fifteen minutes and the coffee shop and her name all slide by in a blur—you've forgotten her name but you can't admit it, so you just keep smiling and hope and pray that she doesn't think you're a total twit, a ditz, a baby dyke without a clue. After coffee you're walking down the street and you tell her all about your last relationship and how bad it went, doing your damnedest to convince her of your dyke credentials until she grins and says, "Hush—now is not the time," and then she pulls you into a doorway and starts kissing you. She is at least a foot shorter than you, but she's up on her toes and pulling you down with no hesitation and the kissing is easy, so easy and hot you're melting into it, and then the door you're leaning on starts to open and you realize that her hand is on the doorknob and her key is in the door and this is, of course, the door to her apartment and she's taking you upstairs, woohoo!

She kisses you all the way up three flights of stairs, and her hands are all over you, over the T-shirt, under the T-shirt, under your bra to cup your breasts, squeeze your nipples, pull you up the last steps with her fingers tight on your nipples and her mouth latched to yours, and you are tumbling into her apartment and closing the door with your bodies 'cause your hands are too damn busy to spare. She breaks long enough to turn on the light and fire up some candles and incense and turn off the light again and then you are falling to the futon in the living room, lit by candles, the room is full of candles and statues and flowers and incense. You're a little dizzy, but when she pulls off your shirt and bra and starts licking a nipple you have to know, you say, "Hang on," and "I hate to ask this," and "What's your name again?" and wait for her to throw you out.

She laughs instead, and says, "Kali; my name is Kali," and then she gets this wide grin and lies back on the futon and says, "Kali is a goddess, you know? Worship me."

You've never touched a goddess before, but your mama didn't raise no fools, and so you get her and you out of clothes as fast as you can, before she has a chance to take a proper breath or change her mind, and then you're kissing her. Sucking on her toes and calves and knees and thighs, up around her clit, up her curving stomach and softball breasts, down to fingers and up again, kissing and sucking and licking until your mouth is dry and her skin is wet and shaking in the wavering light of what seem a hundred candles.

You worship her with mouth and hands, you slide a finger in her cunt and then another until they are slick and salty, and you bring them up to your mouth and taste them, lick them with Kali's eyes on you, glittering, and she breathes "More," and you go down, you breathe on, lick, and suck her clit, slide two fingers in again, thrust back and forth and she is writhing beneath you, she is silent but her body speaks. It whispers and moans and whimpers and screams and she is almost there and you can't quite do it, you can't get her there, you can feel the crest waiting there, the last lap, the last mile, and you're not going to make it, you're not good enough and you are ready to lay your head down on her stomach and cry if she will permit it.

You stop, removing the once-thrusting, now-sore fingers. She whimpers, and your stomach churns, and you take a deep, gasping breath. Kali opens her eyes then and sees you and she is not angry. She is twisted in on herself, she is bathed in sweat, dripping in the candlelight, and she says, "It's okay," and takes a deep breath and you can see that she is going to try to come down, to relax, to let it go and, dammit, that is not good enough, you know you can do better than this—and then inspiration hits. You slide back down, your mouth is on her again, on that sweet-salty mound, on that wet nubbin, and while you lick and she convulses silently again, starting the climb again, your hand reaches out and grabs a candle.

Your eyes are closed against her skin but you can feel the slim, cool shape of it, bubbled with old dripped wax, long and hard and untiring. You wave it in the air to put it out, you wait for it to cool as your tongue tickles and touches, twisting to penetrate every crevice, every inch it can reach, and when it is exhausted, when it feels that it is about to break in two, to shatter into a thousand pieces, that is when you reverse the shape in your hand and slide it into her, into her dripping cavity, sliding it smooth and hard into her, and Kali gasps beneath you and her hands come down to your shoulders, her fingers dig into your skin, and you know that you guessed right. You push and pull, thrusting hard and fast until finally, finally her back arches, her hips convulse, and she freezes still and silent for an endless, aching time, and even if your fingers and tongue fall off you are not going to move one inch in the wrong direction. And then she relaxes.

She pulls you up, after a time, and you make love in all the

clever ways that two young dykes in the prime of their strength
and stamina can, and she discovers how easily you come, how
even nipple-sucking can do it, and she says that she might forgive you for that someday. Hours pass, and the candles are long
burned out, and you are settling down to sleep but can't quite
get comfortable, there's a lump, a bump in the sheets under
your hip, and you realize that you've left the candle there and
are surprised it's still in one piece and you reach down and pull
it out and in the thin moonlight you realize that it isn't a candle
after all.

A statue of a goddess, a naked goddess, and the bumps you
took for dripping candle wax are breasts and curved hands,
many hands, and you catch your breath, wondering if you have
committed some form of sacrilege, if Kali will recoil in shock,
horror, dismay, and she must see it in your eyes because she
laughs and laughs and eventually, gently, explains that she is
not religious, definitely not Hindu, that her family was in fact
Catholic.

She herself had turned atheist long ago, she says, and got the
statues from the new age bookstore free. She tells you that she
only keeps them around 'cause they're pretty and they seem to
turn on the chicks, and you blush and are grateful for the thin-
ness of the light. She also says that even if she did believe in the
goddess, she doesn't think She would mind being deep inside
a woman's wet cunt. Then she confesses a secret—that Kali is
only her work name, after all, that it impresses the bookstore
clients. Her true name is something she takes seriously, and
she never tells it to lovers unless they stay around long enough
for breakfast. And when you get over being embarrassed and
amused and slightly shocked, you tell her that you think you
could probably arrange that.

JEALOUSY. THE PERSON WHO HASN'T FELT IT cannot know how much it hurts, or imagine the madness committed in its name. In my thirty years I have suffered it only once, but I was burned so brutally that I have scars that still haven't healed, and I hope never will, as a reminder to avoid that feeling in the future. Diego wasn't mine—no person can belong to another—and the fact that I was his wife gave me no right over him or his feelings; love is a free contract that begins with a spark and can end the same way. A thousand dangers threaten love, but if the couple defends it, it can be saved; it can grow like a tree and give shade and fruit, but that happens only when both partners participate. Diego never did; our relationship was damned from the start. I realize that today, but then I was blind, at first with pure rage and later with grief.

Spying on him, watch in hand, I began to be aware that my husband's absences did not coincide with his explanations. When supposedly he had gone out hunting with Eduardo, he would come back hours earlier or later than his brother; when the other men in the family were at the sawmill or at the roundup branding cattle, he would suddenly show up in the patio, and later, if I raised the subject at the table, I would find that he hadn't been with them at any time during the day. When he went to town for supplies he would come back without anything presumably because he hadn't found what he was looking for, although it might be something as common as an ax or a saw. In the countless hours the family spent together, he avoided conversation at all cost; he was always the one who organized the card games or asked Susana to sing. If she came down with one of her headaches, he was quickly bored and would go off on his horse with his shotgun over his shoulder. I couldn't follow him on horseback without his seeing me or raising suspicion in the family, but I could keep an eye on him when he was around the house. That was how I noticed that sometimes he got up in the middle of the night, and that he didn't go to the kitchen to get something to eat, as I had always thought, but dressed, went out to the patio, disappeared for an hour or two, then quietly slipped back to bed. Following him in the darkness was easier than during the day, when a dozen eyes were watching us; it was all a matter of staying awake and avoiding wine at dinner and the bedtime opium drops.

One night in mid-May I noticed when he slipped out of bed, and in the pale light of the oil lamp we always kept lit before the cross, I watched him put on his pants and boots, pick up his shirt and jacket, and leave the room. I waited a few instants, then quickly got out of bed and followed him, with my heart about to burst out of my breast. I couldn't see him very well in the shadows of the house, but when he went out on the patio his silhouette stood out sharply in the light of the full moon, which for moments at a time shone bright in the heavens. The sky was streaked with clouds that cloaked everything in darkness when they hid the moon. I heard the dogs bark and was afraid they would come to me and betray my presence, but they didn't; then I understood that Diego had tied them up earlier.

My husband made a complete circle of the house and then walked rapidly toward one of the stables where the family's personal mounts were kept, the ones not used in the fields; he swung the crossbar that fastened the door and went inside. I stood waiting, protected by the blackness of an elm a few yards from the barn, barefoot and wearing nothing but a thin nightgown, not daring to take another step, convinced that Diego would come out on horseback, and I wouldn't be able to follow him. I waited for a period that seemed very long, but nothing happened.

Suddenly I glimpsed a light through the slit of the open door, maybe a candle or small lantern. My teeth were chattering, and I was shivering from cold and fright. I was about to give up and go back to bed when I saw another figure approaching from the east—obviously not from the big house—and also go into the stable, closing the door behind. I let almost fifteen minutes go by before I made a decision, then forced myself to take a few steps. I was stiff from the cold and barely able to move. I crept toward the door, terrified, unable to imagine how Diego would react if he found me spying on him, but incapable of retreating.

Softly I pushed the door, which opened without resistance because the bar was on the outside and it couldn't be secured from the inside, and slipped like a thief through the narrow opening. It was dark in the stable, but a pale light flickered far at the back, and I tiptoed in that direction, almost not breathing—unnecessary precautions since the straw deadened my footsteps and several of the horses were awake; I could hear them shifting and snuffling in their stalls.

In the faint light of a lantern hanging from a beam and swayed by the wind filtering between the wooden timbers, I saw them. They had spread blankets out in a clump of hay, like a nest, where she was lying on her back, dressed in a heavy, unbuttoned overcoat under which she was naked. Her arms and her legs were spread open, her head tilted toward her shoulder, her black hair covering her face, and her skin shining like blond wood in the delicate, orangeish glow of the lantern.

Diego, wearing nothing but his shirt, was kneeling before her, licking her sex. There was such absolute abandon in Susana's position and such contained passion in Diego's actions that I understood in an instant how irrelevant I was to all that. In truth, I didn't exist, nor did Eduardo or the three children, no one else, only the two of them and the inevitability of their lovemaking. My husband had never caressed me in that way. It was easy to see that they had been like this a thousand times before, that they had loved each other for years; I understood finally that Diego had married me because he needed a screen to hide his love affair with Susana. In one instant the pieces of that painful jigsaw puzzle fell into place; I could explain his indifference to me, the absences that coincided with Susana's headaches, Diego's tense relationship with his brother Eduardo, the deceit in his behavior toward the rest of the family, and how he arranged always to be near her, touching her, his foot against hers, his hand on her elbow or her shoulder, and sometimes, as if coincidentally, at her waist or her neck, unmistakable signs the photographs had revealed to me. I remembered how much Diego loved her children, and I speculated that maybe they weren't his nephews but his sons, all three with blue eyes, the mark of the Domînguezes. I stood motionless, gradually turning to ice as voluptuously they made love, savoring every stroke, every moan, unhurried, as if they had all the rest of their lives. They did not seem like a couple of lovers in a hasty clandestine meeting but like a pair of newlyweds in the second week of their honeymoon, when passion is still intact, but with added confidence and the mutual knowledge of each other's flesh. I, nevertheless, had never experienced intimacy of that kind with my husband, nor would I have been able to invent it in my most audacious fantasies. Diego's tongue was running over Susana's inner thighs, from her ankles upward, pausing between her legs and then back down again, while his hands moved from her waist to her round, opulent breasts, playing with her nipples, hard and lustrous as grapes. Susana's soft, smooth body shivered and undulated; she was a fish in the river, her head turning from side to side in the desperation of her pleasure, her hair spread across her face, her lips open in a long moan, her hands seeking Diego to guide him over the beautiful topography of her body, until his tongue made her explode in pleasure. Susana arched backward from the ecstasy that shot through her like lightning, and she uttered a hoarse cry that he choked off with his mouth upon hers. Then Diego took her in his arms, rocking her, petting her like a cat, whispering a rosary of secret words into her ear with a delicacy and tenderness I never thought possible in him. At some moment she sat up in the straw, took off her coat, and began to kiss him, first his forehead, then his eyelids, his temples, lingering on his mouth; her tongue mischievously explored Diego's ears, swerved to his Adam's apple, brushed across his throat, her teeth nibbling his nipples, her fingers combing the hair on his chest. Then it was his turn to abandon himself completely to her caresses; he lay face down on the blanket and she sat astride him, biting the nape of his neck, covering his shoulders with brief playful kisses, moving down to his buttocks, exploring, smelling, savoring him, and leaving a trail of saliva as she went. Diego turned over, and her mouth enveloped his erect, pulsing penis in an interminable labor of pleasure, of give and take in the most profound intimacy conceivable, until he could not wait any longer and threw himself on her, penetrated her, and they rolled like enemies in a tangle of arms and legs and kisses and panting and sighs and expressions of love that I had never heard before. Then they dozed in a warm embrace, covered with blankets and Susana's overcoat like a pair of innocent children. Silently I retreated and went back to the house, while the icy cold of the night poured inexorably through my soul.

A chasm opened before me; I felt vertigo pulling me downward, a temptation to leap and annihilate myself in the depths of suffering and fear. Diego's betrayal and my dread of the future left me floating with nothing to cling to, lost, disconsolate. The fury that had shaken me at first lasted only briefly, then I was crushed by a sensation of death, of absolute agony. I had entrusted my life to Diego, he had promised me his protection as a husband; I believed literally the ritual words of marriage: that we were joined until death us did part. There was no way out. The scene in the stable had confronted me with a reality that I had perceived for a long time but had refused to face.

My first impulse was to run to the big house, to stand in the middle of the patio and howl like a madwoman, to wake the family, the servants, the dogs, and make them witnesses to adultery and incest. My timidity, however, was stronger than my desperation. Silently, feeling my way in the dark, I dragged myself back to the room I shared with Diego and sat in my bed shivering and sobbing, my tears soaking into the neck of my nightgown. In the following minutes or hours I had time to think about what I had seen and to accept my powerlessness. It wasn't a sexual affair that joined Diego and Susana, it was a proven love; they were prepared to run every risk and sweep aside any obstacle that stood in their way, rolling onward like an uncontainable river of molten lava. Neither Eduardo nor I counted; we were disposable, barely insects in the enormity of their passion.

I should tell my brother-in-law before anyone else, I decided, but when I pictured the blow such a confession would be to that good man, I knew I wouldn't have the courage to do it. Eduardo would discover it himself some day, or with luck, he might never know. Perhaps he suspected, as I did, but didn't want to confirm it in order to maintain the fragile equilibrium of his illusions; he had the three children, his love for Susana, and the monolithic cohesion of his clan.

Diego came back some time during the night, shortly before dawn. By the light of the oil lamp he saw me sitting on my bed, my face puffy from crying, unable to speak, and he thought I had woken with another of my nightmares. He sat beside me and tried to draw me to his chest, as he had on similar occasions, but instinctively I pulled away from him, and I must have worn an expression of terrible anger, because immediately he moved back to his own bed. We sat looking at each other, he surprised and I despising him, until the truth took form between the two of us, as undeniable and conclusive as a dragon.

"What are we going to do now?" were the only words I could utter.

He didn't try to deny anything or justify himself; he defied me with a steely stare, ready to defend his love in any way necessary, even if he had to kill me. Then the dam of pride, good breeding, and politeness that had held me back during months of frustration collapsed, and silent reproaches were converted into a flood of recriminations that I couldn't contain, that he listened to quietly and without emotion, attentive to every word. I accused him of everything that had gone through my mind and then begged him to reconsider; I told him that I was willing to forgive and forget, that we could go far away somewhere no one knew us, and start over.

By the time my words and tears were exhausted, it was broad daylight. Diego crossed the distance that separated our beds, sat beside me, took my hands, and calmly and seriously explained that he had loved Susana for many years, and that their love was the most important thing in his life, more compelling than honor, than the other members of his family, than the salvation of his very soul. To make me feel better, he said, he could promise that he would give her up, but it would be an empty promise. He added that he had tried to do that when he went to Europe, leaving her behind for six months, but it hadn't worked. Then he had gone so far as to marry me, to see whether in that way he might break that terrible tie to his sister-in-law, but far from helping him in the decision to leave her, marriage had made it easier because it diluted the suspicions of Eduardo and the rest of the family. He was, however, happy that finally I had discovered the truth because it was painful to him to deceive me. He had nothing to say against me, he assured me. I was a good wife, and he deeply regretted that he couldn't give me the love I deserved. He felt miserable every time he slipped away from me to be with Susana; it would be a relief not to lie to me anymore. Everything was in the open now.

"And Eduardo doesn't count?" I asked.

"What happens between him and Susana is up to them. It's the relation between you and me that we must decide now."

"You have already decided, Diego. I don't have anything to do here, I will go back home," I told him.

"This is your house now, we are husband and wife, Aurora. What God has joined together you cannot put asunder."

"You are the one who has violated holy commandments," I pointed out.

"We can live together like brother and sister. You won't want for anything. I will always respect you, you will be protected and free to devote yourself to your photographs, or whatever you want. The only thing I ask is, please do not create a scandal."

"You can't ask anything of me, Diego."

"I'm not asking for myself. I have thick skin, and I can face it like a man. I'm asking for my mother's sake. She couldn't bear it."

So for Doña Elvira's sake, I stayed...

I was willing to stay at Caleufu, hiding my humiliation as a rejected wife, because if I left and she discovered the truth she would die of grief and shame. Her life turned around that family, around the needs of each of the persons who lived within the walls of their compound: that was her entire universe. My agreement with Diego was that I would play my part as long as Doña Elvira lived, and after that I would be free; he would let me leave and would never contact me again. I would have to live with the stigma—calamitous for many—of being "separated," and would not be able to marry again, but at least I wouldn't have to live with a man who didn't love me.

Translated by Margaret Sayers Peden

WHAT YOU'RE IN FOR

Zonna

DEN FELT ALL THE HAIRS STAND UP ON THE back of her neck, the way it is when you get a chill or when you know somebody's watching you. Seeing as it was the middle of July, she figured someone was checking her out. She didn't turn around right away, though. Had to be cool, make it seem casual, like she was bored. She waited a few minutes, working a rock loose with the toe of her sneaker and kicking it aimlessly along the fence.

This was one of the few institutions she'd been in where they still had dirt. Most seemed to cover it up with concrete as soon as they could, denying you even that small amount of nature. It was like they didn't want you to come in contact with any living thing in these places, like that might give you hope or something. Hope was a dangerous thing in a prison. Hope makes a woman careless. Makes her forget. She might not take what they give so easy, thinking maybe she could change things. There'd be an end to look toward, instead of just doing what you have to, trying to make it through each day like it's all you're gonna get. Hope is words like *more,* or *better.* There ain't no room in lockup for words like that. Sometimes, though, when no one was looking, Den would pretend to bend down to tie her shoe, and instead she'd run her fingers through that dirt and maybe put a little in her shirt pocket. That night in her cell, she'd lie there in the dark and smell it. It smelled like *tomorrow;* like *could be.* It smelled like hope.

When she did finally turn around, it was slow and easy like she didn't care, running a hand through her short blonde hair and squinting into the sun hanging over the prison wall. She took in the whole yard with one glance. Sure enough, that crazy bitch, Cole, was staring at her. Some girls called her Ice Cole 'cause her eyes were ice blue and she never showed no emotion on that stone-cold face of hers.

Den continued her stroll along the fence, away from Cole's scrutinizing gaze, ignoring the sweat that had started to trickle down her back. Cole was a menace. If Cole wanted to make things bad for Den, then they'd be bad.

Den was trying to do good time. She'd had more than enough hard time, in and out of institutions for one thing or another since she was fourteen. Twenty-seven was too old to have to be proving herself all over again. She didn't want any trouble. But if Cole started sniffing around, Den wasn't about to just roll over, belly-up. She'd have to be on alert; use those eyes she'd grown in the back of her head.

The whistle blew and they lined up. Den was careful to

put a healthy number of bodies between Cole's and her own, but the other woman pushed through the line until she stood directly behind Den.

A finger traced a bead of sweat as it traveled from Den's hairline down her spine.

"You're mine." Cole's breath blew in Den's ear, making her shudder.

"Keep your fuckin' hands off me."

"We'll see," Cole chuckled under her breath.

"No talking." The guard tapped them both on the shoulders as she passed.

Cole took advantage of the moment to sneak her hand around and quickly pinch Den's nipple. She knew Den wouldn't protest with the guard so near.

Without thinking, Den stepped back, putting her heel down hard on Cole's foot. Immediately, the intruder's hand was gone.

"You're gonna be real sorry you did that," Cole hissed between clenched teeth.

Den stood up straighter as the line started moving forward.

"Real sorry," Cole promised.

"Someone's been aksin' 'bout you."

Den waited to hear if Beth was going to finish that thought or leave it dangling in the air. She'd learned not to appear too curious.

"Don't ya wanna know who?"

"Not particularly." Den figured she already knew.

"I bet if you knew who it was, you'd wanna know."

Den didn't even laugh anymore when her dumb-ass cell mate said stupid shit like that. She watched a hairy little spider finish spinning a web by the foot of her bed. Waited till it was almost finished, then destroyed the whole thing with one sweep of her hand. Almost immediately, the spider started over.

"It's Cole."

Den pretended she didn't care.

"She's sure been aksin' a lotta questions." Beth was dying to tell.

"Like?"

"Like, how long you in for, what you done to get here, where you was before, and like that."

"Who she been asking?"

"Just everyone," Beth rolled her eyes.

"Like you?"

"Maybe me."

Den rolled over onto her back and stared at the ceiling. She busied herself with a loose thread on the pocket of her shirt. She'd made a promise to herself that when she got out she'd never wear nothing blue again. Why'd they pick the color of sky, the color of freedom, to remind you that you weren't free? Some sick joke.

"I'll tell you what-all for a smoke," Beth said.

"Got none."

Den knew Beth would give it up sooner or later; she wasn't about to buy information she could get for free. Cigarettes were money; but time in a prison wasn't worth a damn. She could wait.

By lights out, Beth had told everything she knew, which wasn't really much.

Den lay awake for hours, her mind racing. Cole was definitely looking for trouble. And a woman like Cole usually found what she was looking for. In all the years she'd been behind bars, Den had never been nobody's property. Not like some hadn't tried to own her, big as she was. Seemed sometimes the bigger ones had more to worry about on the inside—so many wanted to cut you down. Bigger size, bigger prize. She'd managed to talk her way out of a lot of bad situations, but she'd learned way back in juvie that a quick right cross was just as valuable as a quick mind on this side of the wall. Her rep was pretty solid, just like she was. Even so, Den made a mental note to up her workout, just in case. A few more ounces of muscle behind her wouldn't hurt none.

"Go, girl... One more... That's it."

Den grunted as she lifted the barbell up and over, Tracy's hands guiding but not touching, till the weight clicked back into place.

"Yeah! That was good." Tracy smiled in admiration. "You working toward something, or just working?"

Den sat up and rubbed the sweat into her muscles, kneading her sore arms, secretly enjoying the pain. Pain was a marker. If you could feel something, that meant you were still alive.

Tracy let her hands down easy onto Den's shoulders and started a slow massage, careful to keep it all business, even though she wished it was more. Den was hot—pumped, her muscles tight like she was carved out of solid rock. Tracy liked to be around her; to watch her lift, or run, or shoot hoops. Den was smooth, like water running down a hill. She had that certain grace you find in tall things, like giraffes or palm trees. When she moved, it was almost in slow motion. Tracy wished she could get closer to Den somehow. Wished she could move with her, feel Den's body rise and fall; wrap herself up in those strong arms.

WHAT YOU'RE IN FOR

"Den?"

"Mmm?"

"Why you working so hard today?"

"No reason," Den lied easily.

"Okay, if you say so. Seems to me you don't need to work so hard, though."

"No reason to get lazy."

Tracy tried to swallow the words in her throat before they fell out, but her mouth was too dry. "Den, I got something to say."

"So, say it."

"I'm scared you might get pissed off."

Den turned around to face Tracy, whose hands had dropped uselessly to her sides.

"I'll try not to get pissed. What is it?"

"I...I was wondering...I got feelings—"

"No fucking on the benches."

Cole's voice cut Tracy's sentence right in half.

Den stood up slowly, flexing her muscles, ready for trouble. Tracy all but disappeared in her shadow.

"You're looking real good, Denny." Cole flashed a greasy smile and reached out a hand to stroke Den's biceps.

Den shook her off.

"I told you before, don't be touching me, Cole."

"Why not?" Cole peered around Den's shoulder. Her frosty eyes zeroed in on Tracy. "Is this what you're turning me down for?"

Den ignored the question and started to walk away, bumping Cole's shoulder as she passed. A dangerous move, but a necessary one, Den decided.

Three steps later, a sound like "woof" made Den spin

around. Tracy was doubled up on the ground. Two of Cole's girls stood nearby. Cole herself sat on the bench, shrugging her shoulders and shaking her head.

"Prison yard's a dangerous place. Never know what might happen. Best not to get too close to anybody." Cole checked the weights and started to lift where Den had left off.

Den hurried over to her friend. "You all right?" She helped Tracy to her feet.

"Yeah. I think so." Tracy brushed the dirt off her clothes.

"I'm sorry. That was about me, not you."

They started walking back toward the cells.

"You Cole's girl?" Tracy asked right out.

"Hell, no."

"But she wants you, right?"

"Yeah, well, I don't care much what she wants."

Tracy's knees got a little weak; she felt Den's arms holding her up.

"You sure you're all right?"

"I'm scared, Den."

"Don't be scared. I'll watch out for you. I promise. From now on, you just stick by me."

Tracy weighed the pain in her stomach against the words in her ear. She considered the scales even enough.

Den closed her eyes and turned her face up to the nozzle, felt the cool water splash over her, washing away the prison smell, if only for a few hours. It always returned, though: a strange mix of perspiration, desperation, and resignation. It got in your hair and under your skin. You could smell it on your own breath, and everyone else's. It was a part of the place, issued on the first day, along with your toothbrush and uniform. It was woven into the light blue fabric, tucked under the corner of every worn bed sheet. It was in the gravy, in the soap, pumped in through the air vents. There was no escaping it.

Suddenly, she felt rough hands pinning her arms behind her back and a bar of soap being shoved into her mouth. Her legs were pulled open by more hands. Her eyes snapped open.

"You sure are one hot-looking bitch."

Cole stood directly in front of her, wearing only her tattoos. She reached out a hand and ran it over Den's stomach.

"What's the matter? Nothing to say this time? Don't want me to stop?"

Den tried not to swallow and choke on the bitter soapsuds. She stood perfectly still. She knew she couldn't move and didn't want Cole to see her struggle.

"I see you're a natural blonde, Denny." Cole tangled her fingers in Den's pubic hair and gave it a yank. The four girls restraining her tightened their grip.

"Tell you what. We'll make it a fair game. Since you don't seem able to voice your opinions at the moment, I'll read your body language instead. If your nipples don't get hard, then I won't fuck you. Sounds fair, don't it?"

Cole moved in closer and began licking the water from Den's breasts. Her tongue circled each nipple again and again; they rose like mountains from the sea.

"Well, well—looks like you been lying. Seems you want me to fuck you after all." Cole reached down between her captive's legs and—

Den woke up so hard she sat straight up. Her heart was pounding loud and fast, like the way the cops bang on your door in the middle of the night. She could still hear the shower running, still see the tiles all around her; still feel Cole's hands on her. She couldn't catch her breath. Sweat ran in her eyes and burned. She put her head between her knees and tried not to panic. Slowly, things started to wind back down to normal.

"What you doin'?" Beth's sleepy voice called from the lower bunk.

"Nothing."

"You sick or somethin'?"

"No. Go back to sleep."

"Don't puke in here. I hate that smell."

"I won't. Go to sleep."

Beth drifted off again, snoring softly.

Den stood up and tried to walk the dream off like a leg cramp. What was this about? A premonition? Some kind of warning? She didn't believe much in omens and such; didn't believe much in anything. Didn't make no sense to her that any kind of higher power would be bothering with someone in here. She knew Cole was after her ass. She didn't need a stupid dream to remind her.

So, what then? If it wasn't something she was supposed to watch out for, then what was it? Some people thought dreams were about things you wanted but couldn't say out loud, even to yourself. Well, she was damn sure she didn't want Cole raping her in no shower. *Damn* sure of that.

Maybe it was just about sex. Been years since she'd had any. Couldn't be healthy. Certainly not if it was giving her nightmares like this. Maybe it was time to get herself someone. Plenty to choose from—Tracy, for one. Den could see herself with Tracy. And she knew Tracy was interested. She wouldn't suggest nothing serious or long-term; just for here and now. Maybe they could soften the time a little by sharing it. No harm in that.

Den chased her food around the plate but didn't swallow much. She was convinced most of it wasn't really made for swallowing. The bread was all right, if you liked stale bread. The vegetables were usually overcooked, though; boiled till the flavor evaporated along with any nutritional value they might have once had. And the meat seemed to be boiled, as well. You couldn't tell if it was supposed to be turkey, or beef, or ham. It was always sliced into the same thin, tasteless, pale gray strips. You could try to eat it like that, or you could hide it under a spoonful of lukewarm brown gravy. The choice was yours. The only time you knew for sure what you were eating was when they served hot dogs. Den thought that was pretty ironic.

She felt Tracy's leg rub against hers. It reminded her of what she'd decided.

"Sorry." Tracy shifted in her seat.

"You about finished?" Den stood up.

Tracy pushed her tray away. "Yeah. I can't eat any more of this."

"Come with me, then."

Tracy followed, thinking they were headed for the yard, until they walked right past the exit and kept on walking.

"Where we going, Den?"

"Someplace quiet."

"Library?" Tracy had seen Den read a book once. She couldn't remember what it was about, but the cover had been a pretty shade of green.

Den continued down the corridor and turned the corner to the laundry room.

Tracy's feet stopped moving when she realized where they were going.

Den turned and took her hand. "Do you wanna go with me?"

"For real?" Tracy couldn't believe her wish was about to come true.

"Only if you want to." Den seemed almost shy, asking like that. Tracy stood up on her toes and kissed Den on the mouth.

Den had traded another inmate her next two days off to sneak them into the linen room for two hours. It was common practice, and most of the guards were usually willing to look the other way. The way they figured, if their charges were busy fucking, they wouldn't be fighting. And that suited them just fine.

As soon as the door closed behind them, Den set some sheets out on the linoleum floor. The only problem was the heat. The long, narrow room had no ventilation and the steam from the laundry slid in under the door. In the dim glow of a night-light you could almost see the droplets of water in the air.

Den sat down on the damp sheets and motioned for Tracy to join her. They had barely started to kiss when it became apparent they weren't alone. Whispers drifted over from the far corner, then silence; then a low moan. In the shadows, they could make out two bodies moving together. Tracy and Den smiled at one another and shrugged. Who ever heard of a private room in a prison anyway?

Tracy ran her hands up and down Den's arms, drawing her partner's attention back to their own corner.

"I've wanted to be with you for a long time, Denny."

"Oh, yeah?"

"I just didn't know if you wanted me, too."

"Sure I do."

Den began unbuttoning Tracy's shirt.

"Let me show you how much I want you. Sit back and watch me."

Den watched as Tracy stood and began to slowly strip away her uniform, swaying her hips real sexy-like, running her hands over her breasts the way she'd wanted Denny to do for months.

Maybe it was the close quarters or the heat, but Den started feeling kind of woozy. She was getting slick between her legs just watching Tracy's show and could hardly wait to get her hands on the girl. This was definitely something she needed. She was glad she'd had that crazy dream after all.

Just then she sensed a sudden movement from across the room. The shadow women were sitting up, watching Tracy's striptease with great interest. The taller one caught Den's eye and raised a finger to her lips as if to say, "Shhh. Don't do nothing to ruin the spell now."

Den, mesmerized by the dance and the steam and the want growing inside her, found herself even more turned on by the thought of an audience. She rose to her knees and pulled Tracy's naked form to her, running her lips across the girl's stomach, till she felt Tracy's legs start to tremble. She stood then, scooped the girl up in her powerful arms and lowered her to the floor. Den kissed Tracy's mouth, their tongues tangling together like slippery snakes. She blazed a trail of kisses down Tracy's neck, across her shoulders, and took each nipple into her mouth, first one, then the other.

Tracy responded with soft sighs and shivers, reaching up to pull at Denny's shirt.

Den sat back and tugged it off over her head. As she did, she got a clear look at her spectators. The shorter one she'd seen around, but didn't know her name. The tall one, though, was Cole. As soon as she realized who it was, Den felt her passion flare as if someone had poured gasoline on a barbecue. She stared into Cole's eyes and saw a sly smile creep across her face.

Cole motioned to Den with her hand, "Bring it on," like some kind of a challenge. Then she lay back against the wall, spread her legs wide, and pulled her partner's head toward her crotch. She stared right at Den and mouthed the words, "Fuck me."

Den lowered her body on top of Tracy's, their breasts rubbing together as they kissed. Her muscles rippled as she raised herself up and began grinding her thigh into Tracy's cunt, her eyes locked on Cole's.

"Oh, Denny," Tracy moaned, pulling Den's attention away from Cole, making her feel a slight pang of guilt.

"Yeah, baby. Feels good?" She gazed down at Tracy.

"Yessss."

Den couldn't keep her focus, though, and as soon as Tracy's eyes closed again, she found herself studying Cole; waiting for signs, as if Cole was the one she was doing. She kept up a steady pace, driving Tracy wild, determined to get to Cole through her. Sweat coated their bodies as Den brought Tracy closer and closer to the edge.

Tracy cried out and clawed at Den's back just as Cole's hips started to buck. The two women came together, filling the room with the sounds and smells of sex.

Den held Tracy close and rocked her back to earth, at the same time keeping one eye on Cole. She knew they weren't through yet. She knew what Cole wanted from her now.

Cole licked her lips and repositioned her partner, blocking

herself from Den's view for a few moments while she did so.

Den let Tracy slip her shorts down; felt the cool of the sheets against her skin, which was just about on fire. She leaned back against the wall so she would have a clear view across the room. She felt Tracy's lips on her breasts, then Tracy's fingers teasing her clit, sliding deliciously up and down and around. She still couldn't see what Cole was up to, though, and it made her wary.

"You're so wet." Tracy's voice drew Den's attention.

"Feels real good, baby, don't stop." Den held Tracy's head to her chest, urging her forward.

Cole had one of the only dildos in the whole lockup, which made her quite a popular girl. When she rose to her knees, Den could see the strap around her waist, and the heavy latex cock hanging down between her legs. She watched Cole stroke the length of it before sinking it into her girlfriend's pussy from behind with one hard shove. Cole grinned at Den as she slammed into her partner's cunt, each thrust a little deeper than the one before.

Den knew it was meant for her. Cole was fucking her, like she would have in the dream if Den hadn't woken up.

She whispered to Tracy, "Do me harder, baby—like that, yeah."

Tracy took the direction and her hand fucked Den harder, unconsciously matching Cole's strokes.

Den felt her cunt trying to swallow Tracy's hand; heard the *slurp slurp slurp* of her own juices. She fought the urge to close her eyes and give in to the feeling, concentrating instead on Cole's hips; imagining Cole pounding into her, tearing her apart, forcing her to face a desire so overwhelming she had no control over it. She knew she shouldn't want Cole to fuck her; she knew it was wrong, even as she lay there. Yet even if she'd wanted to stop, she couldn't. She was like a deep well with a bucket on a too-short string. She couldn't get enough. Sweat ran freely from every pore. She felt the climax coming, and for a minute she couldn't breathe. When she came, she let go with a groan that grew from the back of her throat like a growl. Her body spasmed as she watched a satisfied smile split Cole's face in two.

Tracy looked up at Den, damn proud of herself—until she saw the truth in Denny's eyes. Busted. Then she just got real quiet, put her clothes on without a word, and went back to her cell.

That night, Den lay in her bed, reliving it all. Like a scene from a movie she didn't understand, she played it over and over in her mind, trying to figure out where she'd lost the thread. She didn't want Cole, did she? She'd wanted to be with Tracy. So why had she been so turned on by Cole's game? Why hadn't she been able to stop it, to get up and leave? It was as if she was chained and shackled by the lust Cole had drawn to the surface. Had it always been there? Den closed her eyes and drifted off to a troubled sleep, doubting everything she'd ever known.

It doesn't matter what you're in for. It doesn't matter how guilty or innocent you think you are. There're prisons on either side of the wall.

RATATOUILLE

Susannah Indigo

"Miles, did you know that zucchinis make the best cocks?" Isabelle asked me on our first date. She twirled her angel-hair pasta and looked fondly at the veggie stabbed on the end of her fork.

She had my attention. I tried to guess at a good response. Isabelle had long, wavy red hair and dancer's legs, and there wasn't much I wouldn't consider for her.

"Better than cucumbers?" I asked rather dumbly but with great gusto, as though we were discussing favorite recipes over the back fence.

She laughed. "Hell, yes. Better than men, sometimes. Better than vibrators, always. No batteries, and much more organic."

I was speechless. I had watched Isabelle pass

by my office for weeks on the way to the dance studio before I found the nerve to ask her out. I was developing a serious navy-blue leg-warmer fetish by the time I just stepped into the hall and blurted out my name and invited her to dinner.

"Sure, Miles," she had said, quite casually. "But it has to be vegetarian for me, okay?"

She had looked pure and angelic with that pale white skin and the sprinkling of freckles across her nose. I researched every health food restaurant in town.

"Organic is good," I finally answered her at dinner, feeling like a sixteen-year-old kid on his first date instead of the lawyer that I was. "Do you peel the zucchini?" I had to know.

"Sometimes, Miles," she answered. "But sometimes rougher is better, you know?"

I thought then that maybe it was possible to fall in love with a girl who said "you know?" all the time and who wore heavy silver rings and bracelets that weighed her down, bracelets that looked like handcuffs on her delicate wrists.

I took her home to her tiny walk-up apartment at the top of an old building not far from Coors Field. "This neighborhood is not safe," I told her.

She just laughed at me. "Life is not safe, darling."

She was right, of course. There's hardly any safety in hating what you do every day for a living. When I chose law school over art so long ago, I didn't know the difference between financial security and being safe.

She invited me in and lit six black candles all around the room. "Six," she informed me, "is the sacred number of Aphrodite, the goddess of love." She served me hot tea on an elegant silver tray and then looked straight into my eyes and told me how it was going to be.

"A girl has to have rules, you know," she said. "I never have full sex with a man until the third date." She smiled. "By then I can always tell if they're fuckable or not."

I was thirty-seven years old and a man of the world when she said this, and I swear I couldn't remember ever having sex before in my life, or if I even knew how.

"That sounds fair," I mumbled, smoothing my hair.

She excused herself and went to the bathroom. I confess I sneaked a look in her fridge while she was gone. Never before had a crisper looked so sexy. I counted the zucchinis—there were six. All in a row.

She came back, and her hair was tied up and she pressed one of her strong legs next to mine on the futon. Without a word she picked up a jar of honey from the tea tray, stuck her finger into it, and smeared honey all over her lips. Honey over lipstick, honey around her mouth, honey on her tongue, never taking her eyes off mine.

She stopped. "Kiss me, Miles. Kiss me until all my honey is gone."

Dear god. I started with a lick and then I was devouring her, and nothing else existed but Isabelle and her mouth. Long, soulful kisses that went on forever, or maybe it was just one kiss that kept inventing itself over and over and over until I thought her rules were only a tease and my hand was high on her thigh and my cock was raving wild. She paused and whispered, "You kiss like a man who is hungry. This is a good thing." And then she kicked me out the door.

I bought her things. I showed up for the second date with flowers and candy and a gift of tiny, delicate crystal ballet slippers that reminded me of her. She laughed and thanked me, but later she told me that the things she wanted in life couldn't be bought.

She was wearing a shiny white leotard, the kind with long sleeves that looked as if it would fall off her shoulders any minute, the kind you can see nipples through in the right light, and a long, swirling, deep-blue skirt that made me want to lift it and bend her over and fuck her hard and fast. But it was only the second date, and rules are rules.

"Are you a natural redhead?" I asked, admiring her hair.

"You'll never know, darling. Don't you know that dancers wax everywhere but their heads?" She laughed and lifted her skirt, slid the leotard aside, and twirled and flashed me the loveliest bare pussy I will ever see in my life.

And then she led me out the door to the theater.

We saw *Cats*. She made me. She kept my hand high on her thigh under her skirt the whole time. I was wrong: *Cats* is a wonderful show.

Back at her place, she asked if I was hungry. I believe the exact words were "What are you hungry for?"

The possibilities raced through my head. "Oh, something vegetarian," I said casually, still trying to impress.

Her eyes lit up. "I have lots of fresh veggies in my crisper. Let's marinate some of them before we cook."

She took me into the kitchen. We peeled. Two zucchinis, three carrots, a handful of mushrooms, and a large purple onion. "The living room is better for this," she whispered when we were finished with our plate.

Lavender-scented candles, incense, the aroma of fresh zucchini—these smells will stay with me all of my life. She turned on the music, stretched out on the tiny rug on the hardwood floor, took off her leotard, and lifted that blue skirt around her waist and asked me if I wanted to watch or to help. I could barely move; I said I would love to watch her. I touched the pale skin high between her thighs and petted her gently as if she were a kitten; she closed her eyes and threw her head back and showed me possibilities I didn't know existed. She loved that vegetable as if it were a cock, stroking herself with it, rubbing it slowly around her clit, entering her pussy slowly, so slowly, in and out, teasing me, teasing herself, and then finally fucking herself hard—my cock beat right to her rhythm. I came when she came; I came in my pants as if I was fifteen again. She was lying back on the floor and I kissed her pussy, I kissed that cock, and I kissed her legs from thigh to ankle over and over again.

And then we cooked.

Stir-fry veggies over tomato-basil pasta; peppermint tea; fortune cookies. It was an extraordinary meal—I suspect it was the special sauce. "You will attend a royal banquet and meet your first lover," my fortune cookie said, and I knew I just had.

She changed into a little-girl flannel nightgown and took me into her bed. We slept. No sex. The trust implicit in this act was overwhelming. I never touched her except to hold her tight.

In the morning we laughed together. "Carrots just don't quite work, you know?" she said. "Too thin. But they have some uses. Eggplants and tomatoes and onions and peppers all have uses sometimes too." She told me that her practice was as old as the Kama Sutra: "How else do you think all those women in the harems got satisfied? Hell, that book even goes into using the root of the sweet potato! Sometimes," she confessed, almost blushing, "I go out with something inside me, when I'm going someplace quiet like the museum. It makes you think about sex all day. Melon balls are my favorite—kind of an organic set of ben wa balls."

If this was foreplay, I wasn't sure I was ready for full sex. I went to see her dance on the third date. She was beautiful. We went back to her place, and I lit the candles and the incense. "I'm yours tonight," she whispered. "You've passed. What would you like?"

I was ready. What else could a man want? "I want you to love me, to worship me just like you did that zucchini."

She undressed me while I stood there, and then she knelt in front of me and began. It all came back to me in that moment, why sex is the most important damned thing in the world. She kissed my feet and then she worked her way up, taking forever, kissing and licking my balls and holding them gently in her mouth. Talking to me, saying things, telling me how good I tasted; telling me how much she wanted me inside her, how much she needed to ride me hard. She took my cock deep into her throat all at once, and then there were no rules or they were only my rules and she was mine and I was lying back and holding her small hips and lifting her up onto my cock and driving up into her hard and fast. The world stopped; that was all I knew—that she could make the outside world stop and take me back to where I belonged. She came for me over and over, before I stopped and took her long hair in my fist and held her still for a minute.

"Do you want to please me?" I whispered, knowing that she did, knowing that this girl lived for sex and that I could give her what she needed.

"God, yes," she whispered, nodding.

"Turn over."

I owned her. I fucked every part of her body, and she begged for more. I couldn't quite imagine matching her sexual imagination, but I discovered I could more than match her energy and desire. When my cock was finally deep in her ass and my own vision of heaven was high on the horizon, I suddenly knew: I knew this was it and this girl was going to change my life. I didn't tell her this; I thought there would be time later.

I don't believe we slept that night. But I do know that I never let her near the kitchen.

I started drawing again. I sketched her constantly. I still have some of the drawings—*Isabelle in Iceberg* is my favorite one, framed on my wall. Even though she swore the lettuce just didn't do a thing for her.

I stopped eating meat. Isabelle—her name in my mouth was better than any sirloin in town.

I went dancing with her. I don't dance. Little clubs that nobody my age has ever heard of; dark entrances, pounding music, Isabelle twirling and twirling and always coming back to my arms.

She let me go to the beauty parlor with her and watch her get waxed all over. I only went because she told me she loved it, loved the pain, loved the discipline of it all. "Discipline is everything in dance," she told me.

I would ask her to show me her pussy and she would. Any time. She danced for me whenever I wanted. I wouldn't call it stripping, but I guess that's what it was. And the world would stop one more time.

But when I wasn't with her, she would rarely answer the phone, and I just *knew* she was in bed with a zucchini, and I couldn't stand it. She'd see me once a week—that was all—and I knew the girl was getting fucked every day.

I got stupid like men do. I followed her—saw her at the produce stand, watched her dancing through the studio window, saw her go out with friends and then go home alone. I knew there was no other man. When I asked her, she told me she'd been in love once and that was enough.

She liked me; I knew she did. And then I realized the problem. It still pains me to admit it. She preferred her vegetables over me, just as she had told me on that first date. How on earth can a man compete with an edible cock?

I couldn't get past once a week, and summer was running down and I wanted Isabelle in my bed every night. She wasn't a tease. There was no game. God, how she could fuck. Some nights she would just lift her skirt and wiggle her ass onto my lap, pressing down hard on my cock before we'd even go out. She'd tell me how much she needed my cock. "It's my real kink," she confessed, "just being penetrated. Everywhere."

I tried to force the issue. I asked her outright what the story was, why we couldn't spend more time together. "Trust all joy," she'd say mysteriously, and then she'd wrap her hair around my cock and take me in her throat until I forgot even what the question was. "You taste wonderful since you stopped eating meat," she'd whisper after she'd swallowed and licked me clean. She was very into taste. "You taste like cinnamon, you taste like a perfect cup of hot chocolate on a cold winter night," and somehow I knew this was true and nobody had ever noticed it before.

Saturday nights were heaven. By Tuesday I'd be going crazy. I moaned, I fretted. I knew I was driving her nuts with my demands but I couldn't stop. I studied myself in the mirror and contemplated my fuckability factor. When you're in competition with a vegetable, every little bit helps.

Other women called me and I simply had no interest. "Isabelle"—her name in my mouth was more appealing than an onion.

What could I do? Move her to the country and give her a farm? Buy out a local produce stand? I couldn't imagine. I studied her apartment. All she owned was cheap furniture and beautiful candles and scarves and one shelf each of music and books. "I used to own a lot more," she told me when I asked, "but then I learned that possessions mean nothing. So now I read a book and then just pass it on to a friend for their pleasure. The same with music, unless it feeds my soul. I pass it on." There were no clues about how to get to her. So I got stupider. I bribed her grocer to tell me every single thing she bought each trip. Six-inch zukes, bunches of carrots, scallions...scallions? I had to do something.

One Saturday night, late in August, I tried joining forces with the produce. I used them to fuck her every which way, and it was hot and satisfying, but I was still relegated to Saturday night while they got the other six. I got jealous. I hoped they would wilt under the pressure.

I decided to try an intervention. There are no support groups for this kind of thing. She canceled our date one Saturday night, and I knew I'd never make it another week without her. I laid the plan for Tuesday night: I would simply show up, lock the door, and clean out her fridge. I knew if I could spend enough time with her I could somehow make her replace her veggie vice with me. I certainly knew I could measure up: I'd spent one night with a ruler and tape measure back near the beginning of stupid.

I knocked on her door that Tuesday night and there was

no answer; it pushed open easily. She was gone. No books, no candles, no music, no Isabelle. I could picture her in front of me twirling and laughing in that blue skirt; but when I reached out to touch her, there was nothing but ordinary space. I believe I stood there for close to forever; the world may have even stopped for me one last time.

Then I checked the fridge. It was empty except for one zucchini with a note wrapped around it: "I've gone on tour, darling," it said. "Pass it on."

ABOUT THE AUTHORS

KIM ADDONIZIO is the author of several collections of poetry, including *Tell Me* and *What Is This Thing Called Love*. Her first novel, *Little Beauties,* is due from Simon & Schuster in August 2005. She lives in Oakland, California. Visit her at http://addonizio.home. mindspring.com.

ISABEL ALLENDE was born in Peru and raised in Chile. She is the author of the novels *Portrait in Sepia, Daughter of Fortune, The Infinite Plan, Eva Luna, Of Love and Shadows,* and *The House of the Spirits*; the short story collection *The Stories of Eva Luna*; the memoir *Paula*; and *Aphrodite: A Memoir of the Senses.* She lives in California.

CHEYENNE BLUE combines her two passions in life and writes travel guides and erotica. Her erotica has appeared in various anthologies, including *Best Women's Erotica, The Mammoth Best New Erotica, Best Lesbian Erotica, Best Lesbian Love Stories, Foreign Affairs: Erotic Travel Tales,* and on several websites. Her travel guides have been jammed into many glove boxes underneath the chocolate wrappers. You can see more of her work on her website, www.cheyenneblue.com.

MICHELLE BOUCHÉ is a writer, teacher, consultant, and rabble-rouser. Her erotica has been published in *Best Women's Erotica 2001, Myths Fantastic, Moist,* and the forthcoming *Blowing Kisses.* Special thanks to Liz, who taught me that writing good erotica first and foremost means writing a good story.

KATHLEEN BRADEAN's stories have been featured in *Best Women's Erotica 2004, Desdemona.com, Blood Surrender,* Logical Lust's e-anthology *Eternally Erotic,* and the Erotica Readers and Writers Association website. She can be contacted at KathleenBradean@KathleenBradean.com.

CARA BRUCE is the editor of *Best Fetish Erotica, Best Bisexual Women's Erotica,* and *Viscera.* She is coauthor of *The First Year—Hepatitis C.* Her fiction has been published in tons of anthologies, including *Best Women's Erotica, Best American Erotica, Best Lesbian Erotica,* and *The Mammoth Book of Best New Erotica.* Her fiction and nonfiction have appeared in magazines, newspapers, and websites, including Salon.com, *San Francisco Bay Guardian,* and *While You Were Sleeping.* She is the founder of www.venusorvixen.com and Venus or Vixen Press.

RACHEL KRAMER BUSSEL (www.rachelkramerbussel.com and lustylady.blogspot.com) serves as senior editor at *Penthouse Variations*. Her books include *The Lesbian Sex Book* (second edition), *Up All Night: Adventures in Lesbian Sex, Naughty Spanking Stories from A to Z,* and the forthcoming *Cheeky: Essays on Spanking and Being Spanked* and *Glamour Girls: Femme/Femme Erotica.* Her writing has been published in over 40 anthologies, including *Best American Erotica 2004* and *Best Women's Erotica 2003* and *2004,* as well as in *AVN, Bust, Curve, New York Blade, Playgirl, The San Francisco Chronicle,* and *The Village Voice.*

ISABELLE CARRUTHERS lives and writes in New Orleans. Her fiction has been published in *Prometheus, Slow Trains Literary Journal, The Mainline, From Porn to Poetry,* and *Mammoth's Best Erotica,* and has appeared in various Internet magazines, including *Zoetrope All-Story Extra, Suspect Thoughts, Clean Sheets, Mind Caviar,* and others.

MARIANNA CHERRY has been published in *The 2001 Pushcart Prize XXV, Chelsea Magazine* (Chelsea Award for Fiction 1998), *Fourteen Hills,* and *Libido.* She received a BA from Columbia University and an MFA from San Francisco State University, and is currently working on her first novel.

KATE DOMINIC is the author of *Any 2 People, Kissing,* which was a finalist for the 2004 Foreword Magazine Book of the Year Award in the Category of Fiction: Short Stories. Kate has published over 300 erotic short stories, writing under a variety of pen names in both female and male voices, and sliding up and down the Kinsey scale in a variety of orientations. Her

most recent work is available in *The Many Joys of Sex Toys,
Naughty Spanking Stories from A-Z, Dyke the Halls,* and at
www.katedominic.com.

ANN DULANEY lives and writes in Copenhagen. Her work has
been published in *Clean Sheets, Mind Caviar, Erotic Travel
Tales,* and *Best Lesbian Erotica 2002.* Feel free to contact her
at anndulaney@yahoo.com.

SACCHI GREEN writes in western Massachusetts and the
mountains of New Hampshire. Her work has appeared in
five volumes of *Best Lesbian Erotica,* four volumes of *Best
Women's Erotica, The Mammoth Book of Best New Erotica
3, Penthouse, Best S/M Erotica, Best Transgender Erotica,*
and a knee-high stack of other anthologies with inspirational
covers. Her first coeditorial venture, *Rode Hard, Put Away
Wet: Lesbian Cowboy Erotica,* is scheduled for release in June
2005.

SUSIE HARA lives and writes in the San Francisco Bay Area. Her
stories were previously published under the name Lisa Wolfe
in *Clean Sheets* magazine and in several anthologies, including *Best American Erotica 2003* and *The Big Book of Hot
Women's Erotica 2004.* Writing erotica is the most fun she's
ever had with a laptop.

DEBRA HYDE considers "Tic Sex" her signature piece, and she's
delighted to see it merits inclusion in this "best of the best"
collection. Elsewhere, her erotic fiction appears in *Naughty
Spanking Stories from A to Z, The Mammoth Book of Best
New Erotica, Best S/M Erotica 2, Foreign Affairs: Erotic*

Travel Tales, and many other anthologies. She's also the brains behind Pursed Lips, one of the Web's first sex blogs. Google that, won't you?

SUSANNAH INDIGO (www.susannahindigo.com) is the editor-in-chief of *Clean Sheets* (www.cleansheets.com), and is also the editor and founder of *Slow Trains Literary Journal* (www.slowtrains.com). Her books include *Oysters Among Us*; *Many Kisses: Stories of Dominant Love, Sex & Laughter*; and the *From Porn to Poetry* series.

MARYANNE MOHANRAJ is a visiting professor at Vermont College and a PhD candidate at the University of Utah, specializing in post-colonial literature and creative writing. She is the author of several books, including her forthcoming dissertation novel, *Bodies In Motion,* an exploration of sexuality, marriage, and Sri Lankan/American immigrant concerns. www.mamohanraj.com.

G. L. MORRISON is a righteous, leftist, white, working-poor, omnivorous, vitamin-deficient professional poet, amateur mother, publisher of the zine *Poetic Licentious,* editor, writing teacher, reluctant journalist, and sometime scrawler of fiction, essays, and bathroom graffiti. Her work appears in *Early Embraces 2, Pillow Talk 2, Burning Ambitions*, and other print and online anthologies.

LISA PROSIMO's stories, articles, and essays have appeared in anthologies, journals, and online forums. She lives in Northern California with her husband and several thousand grapevines. When she isn't writing, you'll find her traipsing the Sonoma hills sans shoes, her feet stained a curious purple.

ELSPETH POTTER lives in Philadelphia. Her erotica has appeared in the 2001-2004 editions of *Best Lesbian Erotica, Best Women's Erotica 2002* and *2005,* and *Tough Girls.* She is a member of the Science Fiction and Fantasy Writers of America and of Broad Universe (www.broaduniverse.org).

CAROL QUEEN got a doctorate in sexology so she could impart more realistic detail to her smut. She's the founding director of The Center for Sex & Culture in San Francisco (www.sexandculture.org) and has worked at Good Vibrations since 1990. Her work has been published in dozens of anthologies and she's the author or editor of several books, including *Five-Minute Erotica, Exhibitionism for the Shy,* and *The Leather Daddy and the Femme.* For more see www.carolqueen.com.

SAIRA RAMASASTRY was an English-speaking Union Scholar to Cambridge University, where she received her MPhil; she received her MS and BA from Stanford. Her stories have appeared in *Scifidimensions, Rosebud,* and *ZYZZYVA.*

MARÍA ELENA DE LA SELVA was born in Panama and grew up in a temporary clearing now being reclaimed by the jungle. She lives in Seattle, where she cofounded the School Alliance Program at the Richard Hugo House, an urban writing center. She is a winner of the Mendocino Coast Writer's Conference Poetry Contest.

HELENA SETTIMANA lives in Toronto, Canada. Her fiction, poetry, and essays have appeared online at *Scarlet Letters, Clean Sheets,* and *Dare.* Her work has been featured in many anthologies, including *Best Women's Erotica 2001* and *2002,*

Erotic Travel Tales, Best Bisexual Women's Erotica, and *From Porn to Poetry: Clean Sheets Celebrates the Erotic Mind.* She moonlights as features editor at the Erotica Readers and Writers Association (www.erotica-readers.com).

SUSAN ST. AUBIN is a mild-mannered administrative coordinator by day and a racy pornographer at night. Her work has appeared in diverse journals and anthologies, including *The Reed, Short Story Review, Yellow Silk, Libido,* the *Herotica* series, *Best American Erotica, Best Lesbian Erotica, Seduce Me: Twelve Erotic Tales,* and *Dyke The Halls: Lesbian Erotic Christmas Tales,* as well as online in *Clean Sheets.*

CECILIA TAN's erotic writings have appeared almost everywhere: *Ms., Penthouse, Best American Erotica, Asimov's,* and many, many best-of anthologies. She is the author of *The Velderet, Black Feathers,* and *Telepaths Don't Need Safewords,* and the founder/editor of Circlet Press, Inc., publishers of erotic science fiction. She writes about her many passions, which include food, sex, and baseball, from her home in the Boston area. Visit www.ceciliatan.com to find out more.

ANNE TOURNEY started writing erotica in the early '90s. Since then, she has published erotic fiction and dark fantasy in numerous magazines and anthologies. Her stories have been included in the *Best Women's Erotica, Best American Erotica,* and the *Mammoth Book of Best New Erotica* series. Anne lives in Denver, Colorado.

ALISON TYLER's stories have appeared in anthologies including *Sweet Life, Taboo, Wicked Words, Best S/M Erotica,* and *Best Fetish Erotica.* She is the editor of *Best Bondage Erotica, Heat Wave,* and the *Naughty Stories from A to Z* series. She lives with Sam, her partner of nine years.

ZONNA died December 1, 2003, from heart failure due to complications from diabetes and colon cancer. A prolific song-writer, author, and seven-time *Billboard Magazine* songwriting contest winner, Zonna's published output includes over a half-dozen recordings as well as stories in anthologies from Cleis Press, Alyson, Seal Press, and Arsenal Pulp Press. It has been requested that those who wish to do so make a contribution in Zonna's memory "to the left-wing charity of their choice."

ABOUT THE EDITOR

MARCY SHEINER has edited six editions of the annual *Best Women's Erotica* series. She is also the editor of *Herotica 4, 5,* and *6,* and *The Oy of Sex: Jewish Women Write Erotica.* She is the author of *Sex for the Clueless* and *Perfectly Normal: A Mother's Memoir.* Her fiction and essays have been published in numerous anthologies, the most recent being *The Essential Hip Mama: Writing from the Cutting Edge of Parenting,* edited by Ariel Gore; *My Body of Knowledge: Stories of Illness, Disability, Healing and Life*; and Carol Queen's *Five-Minute Erotica.* Her stories have also appeared on the websites *Pulse* and *Slow Trains.*